D0571571

BY TAYLOR JENKINS REID

CARRIE
SOTO
IS BACK

CARRIE SOTO IS BACK

a novel

TAYLOR JENKINS REID

BALLANTINE BOOKS
NEW YORK

Published in the United States by Ballantine Books, an imprint of Random House, a division of Penguin Random House LLC, New York.

BALLANTINE is a registered trademark and the colophon is a trademark of Penguin Random House LLC.

Library of Congress Cataloging-in-Publication Data
Names: Reid, Taylor Jenkins, author.
Title: Carrie Soto is back : a novel / Taylor Jenkins Reid.
Description: First Edition. | New York : Ballantine Books, [2022]
Identifiers: LCCN 2022004245 (print) | LCCN 2022004246 (ebook) |
ISBN 9780593158685 (hardcover) | ISBN 9780593158692 (ebook)
Subjects: LCGFT: Novels.
Classification: LCC PS3618.E5478 C37 2022 (print) |
LCC PS3618.E5478 (ebook) | DDC 813/.6—dc23
LC record available at https://lccn.loc.gov/2022004245
LC ebook record available at https://lccn.loc.gov/2022004246

International edition ISBN 978-0-593-50095-8

Printed in the United States of America on acid-free paper

randomhousebooks.com

2 4 6 8 9 7 5 3 1

First Edition

Book design by Susan Turner

To Brad Mendelsohn, the closest thing I've ever had to a coach

CARRIE
SOTO
IS BACK

CHAN VS. CORTEZ

US Open

September 1994

MY ENTIRE LIFE'S WORK RESTS ON THE OUTCOME OF THIS MATCH.

My father, Javier, and I sit front row center at Flushing Meadows, the sidelines just out of reach. The linesmen stand with their arms behind their backs on either side of the court. Straight in front of us, the umpire presides over the crowd high in his chair. The ball girls crouch low, ready to sprint at a moment's notice.

This is the third set. Nicki Chan took the first, and Ingrid Cortez squeaked out the second. This last one will determine the winner.

My father and I watch—along with the twenty thousand others in the stadium—as Nicki Chan approaches the baseline. She bends her knees and steadies herself. Then she rises onto her toes, tosses the ball in the air, and with a snap of her wrist sends a blistering serve at 126 miles per hour toward Ingrid Cortez's backhand.

Cortez returns it with startling power. It falls just inside the line. Nicki isn't able to get to it. Point Cortez.

I let my eyes close and exhale.

"*Cuidado*. The cameras are watching our reactions," my father says through gritted teeth. He's wearing one of his many panama hats, his curly silver hair creeping out the back.

"Dad, *everyone's* watching our reactions."

Nicki Chan has won two Slam titles this year already—the Australian Open and the French Open. If she wins this match, she'll tie my lifetime record of twenty Grand Slam singles titles. I set that record back in 1987, when I won Wimbledon for the ninth time and established myself as the greatest tennis player of all time.

Nicki's particular style of play—brash and loud, played almost exclusively from the baseline, with incredible violence to her serves and groundstrokes—has enabled her to dominate women's tennis over the past five years. But when she was starting out on the WTA tour back in the late eighties, I found her to be an unremarkable opponent. Good on clay, perhaps, but I could beat her handily on her home turf of London.

Things changed after I retired in 1989. Nicki began racking up Slams at an alarming rate. Now she's at my heels.

My jaw tenses as I watch her.

My father looks at me, his face placid. "I'm saying that the photographers are trying to get a shot of you looking angry, or rooting against her."

I am wearing a black sleeveless shirt and jeans. A pair of tortoise-shell Oliver Peoples sunglasses. My hair is down. At almost thirty-seven, I look as good as I've ever looked, in my opinion. So let them take as many pictures as they want.

"What did I always tell you in junior championships?"

"Don't let it show on your face."

"*Exacto, hija.*"

Ingrid Cortez is a seventeen-year-old Spanish player who has surprised almost everyone with her quick ascent up the rankings. Her style is a bit like Nicki's—powerful, loud—but she plays her angles more. She's surprisingly emotional on the court. She hits a scorcher of an ace past Nicki and hollers with glee.

"You know, maybe it's Cortez who's going to stop her," I say.

My father shakes his head. "*Lo dudo.*" He barely moves his lips when he talks, his eye consciously avoiding the camera. I have no doubt that tomorrow morning, my father will open the paper and scan the sports pages looking for his photo. He will smile to himself when he sees that he looks nothing short of handsome. Although he lost weight earlier this year from the rounds of chemo he endured, he is cancer-free now. His body has bounced back. His color looks good.

As the sun beats down on his face, I hand him a tube of sunscreen. He squints and shakes his head, as if it is an insult to us both.

"Cortez got one good one in," my father says. "But Nicki saves her power for the third set."

My pulse quickens. Nicki hits three winners in a row, takes the game. It's now 3–3 in the third set.

My father looks at me, lowering his glasses so I can see his eyes. "*Entonces,* what are you going to do?" he asks.

I look away. "I don't know."

He puts his glasses back on and looks at the court, giving me a small nod. "Well, if you do nothing, that is what you are doing. Nothing."

"*Sí, papá,* I got it."

Nicki serves wide. Cortez runs and scrambles to catch it on the rise, but it flies into the net.

I look at my father. He wears a slight frown.

In the players' box, Cortez's coach is hunched over in his seat, his hands cupping his face.

Nicki doesn't have a coach. She left her last one almost three years ago and has taken six Slams since then without anyone's guidance.

My dad makes a lot of cracks about players who don't have coaches. But with Nicki, he seems to withhold judgment.

Cortez is bent over, holding her hand down on her hips and trying to catch her breath. Nicki doesn't let up. She fires off another serve across the court. Cortez takes off running but misses it.

Nicki smiles.

I know that smile. I've been here before.

On the next point, Nicki takes the game.

"Dammit," I say at the changeover.

My father raises his eyebrows. "Cortez crumbles as soon as she doesn't control the court. And Nicki knows it."

"Nicki's powerful," I say. "But she's also hugely adaptable. When you play her, you're playing somebody who is adjusting on the fly, tailoring their game to your specific weakness."

My father nods.

"Every player has a weak spot," I say. "And Nicki is great at finding it."

"Right."

"So what's hers?"

My father is now holding back a smile. He lifts his drink and takes a sip.

"What?" I ask.

"Nothing," my father says.

"I haven't made a decision."

"All right."

Both players head back out onto the court.

"Nicki is just a tiny bit slow," I say, watching her walk to the baseline. "She has a lot of power, but she's not fast—not in her footwork or her shot selection. She's not quite as quick as Cortez, even today. But especially not as quick as Moretti, Antonovich, even Perez."

"Or you," my father says. "There's nobody on the tour right now who is as fast as you were. Not just with your feet, but with your head, *también*."

I nod.

He continues. "I'm talking about getting into position, taking the ball out of the air early, taking the pace off so Nicki can't hit it back with that power. Nobody on the tour is doing that. Not like you did."

"I'd have to meet her power, though," I tell him. "And somehow still maintain speed."

"Which will not be easy."

"Not at my age and not with my knee," I say. "I don't have the jumps I used to have."

"*Es verdad*," my father says. "It will take everything you have to give."

"*If* I did it," I say.

My father rolls his eyes but then swiftly paints another false smile on his face.

I laugh. "Honestly, who cares if they get a picture of you frowning?"

"I'm staying off your back," my father says. "You stay off mine. *¿Lo entendés, hija?*"

I laugh again. "*Sí, lo entiendo, papá.*"

Nicki takes the next game too. One more and it's over. She'll tie my record.

My temples begin to pound as I envision it all unfolding. Cortez is not going to stave off Nicki Chan, not today. And I'm stuck up here in the seats. I have to sit here and watch Nicki take away everything I've worked for.

"Who's going to coach me?" I say. "You?"

My father does not look at me, but I can see his shoulders stiffen. He takes a breath, chooses his words.

"That's for you to answer," he finally says. "It's not my choice to make."

"So, what? I'm gonna call up Lars?"

"You are going to do whatever you want to do, *pichona*," my father says. "That is how adulthood works."

He is going to make me beg. And I deserve it.

Cortez is busting her ass to make the shots. But she's tired. You can see it in the way her legs shake when she's standing still. She nets a return. It's now 30–love.

Motherfucker.

I look around at the crowd. People are leaning forward; some are tapping their fingers. Every one of them seems to be breathing a little faster. I can only imagine what the sportscasters are saying.

The spectators sitting around us are looking at my father and me out of the corner of their eyes, watching my reaction. I'm starting to feel caged.

"If I do it . . ." I say softly. "I want you to coach me. That's what I'm saying, Dad."

He looks at me as Cortez scores a point off Nicki. The crowd holds their breath, eager to see history being made. I might be too if it weren't *my* history on the line.

"Are you sure, *hija?* I am not the man I once was. I don't have the . . . stamina I once did."

"That makes two of us," I say. "You'll be coaching a has-been."

Now it's 40–15. Nicki is at championship point.

"I'd be coaching the greatest tennis player of all time," my father says. He turns to me and grabs my hand. I am staring down forty, but still, somehow, his hands dwarf mine. And just like when I was a child, they are warm and rough and strong. When he squeezes my palm, I feel so small—as if I am forever a child and he is this giant I will have to gaze up at to meet his eye.

Nicki serves the ball. I inhale sharply.

"So you'll do it?" I ask.

Cortez sends it back.

"We might lose . . . badly," I say. "Prove to everyone the Battle Axe can't hack it now. They'd love that. I'd tarnish not only my record but my legacy. It might . . . ruin everything."

Nicki hits a groundstroke.

My father shakes his head. "We cannot ruin everything. Because tennis is not everything, *pichona.*"

I am not sure I agree.

Cortez returns the shot.

"Still," I say. "We'd have to work harder together than we ever have. Are you up for that?"

"It would be the honor of my lifetime," my father says. I can tell there are tears forming in his eyes, and I stop myself from looking away. He holds my hand tighter. "To coach you again, *pichona,* I'd die happy."

I try to move past the tender ache taking hold in my chest. "So I guess that decides it, then," I say.

A smile takes over my father's face.

Nicki lobs the ball. It arcs through the air, slowly. The stadium watches as it flies high, then starts its descent.

"I guess I'm coming out of retirement," I say.

The ball looks like it is going to be out. If so, Cortez will delay defeat for the moment.

My father puts his arm around me, hugging me tight. I can barely breathe. He whispers in my ear, "*Nunca estuve más orgulloso, cielo.*" He lets go.

The ball falls, landing just inside the baseline. The crowd is silent as it bounces, high and fast. Cortez has already backed off, thinking it would be long, and it is too late now. It's impossible to return. She lunges forward and misses.

There is no sound for a split second, and then the roar erupts.

Nicki Chan just won the US Open.

Cortez falls to the ground. Nicki throws her fists into the air.

My father and I smile. Ready.

THE
FIRST TIME
AROUND

1955–1965

MY FATHER MOVED TO THE UNITED STATES FROM BUENOS AIRES AT AGE twenty-seven. He had been an excellent tennis player back in Argentina, winning thirteen championships over his eleven-year career. They called him "Javier el Jaguar." He was graceful but deadly.

But, as he would tell it, he went too hard on his knees. His jumps were too high, and he didn't always land properly. As he approached thirty, he knew that they wouldn't hold up for much longer. He retired in 1953—something he never talked to me about without tensing up and eventually leaving the room. Soon after that, he started making plans to come to the United States.

In Miami, he got a job at a fancy tennis club as a hitter, available all day to play with any member who wanted a game. It was a job normally reserved for college students home for the summer—but he did it with the same focus with which he competed. As he told many of the members at that first club, "I do not know how to play tennis without my full heart."

It wasn't long until people started asking him for private lessons. He was known for his commitment to proper form, his high expectations, and the fact that if you listened to *el Jaguar,* you'd probably start winning your matches.

By 1956, he had offers to work as a tennis instructor all over the country. That's how he landed at the Palm Tennis Club in Los Angeles, where he met my mother, Alicia. She was a dancer, teaching the waltz and foxtrot to club members.

My mother was tall and stood taller, wearing four-inch heels wherever she went. She walked slowly, purposefully, and always looked people in the eye. And it was hard to make her laugh, but when she finally did, it was so loud you could hear it through the walls.

On their first date, she told my father that she thought he had tunnel vision when it came to tennis. "It is something you have to grow out of soon, Javier. Or else, how will you learn to be whole?".

My father told her she was out of her mind. Tennis was what *made* him whole.

She responded by saying, "Ah, so you're stubborn too."

Still, he showed up the next day at the end of one of her classes with a dozen red roses. She took them and said thank you, but he noticed she didn't smell them before she set them down. My father got the sense that while he had given flowers to only a few women in his life, my mother had received flowers from dozens of hopeful men.

"Will you teach me the tango?" he said.

She looked at him sideways, not buying for one minute that this Argentine didn't have at least a passing knowledge of the tango. But then she put one hand on his shoulder and another in the air, and said, "Come on, then." He took her hand, and she taught him how to lead her across the dance floor.

My father says he couldn't take his eyes off her; he says he marveled at how easy it was to glide with her across the room.

When they got to the end, my father dipped her and she smiled at him and then said, rather impatiently, "Javier, this is when you kiss me."

Within a few months, he'd convinced her to elope. He told her that he had big dreams for them. And my mother told him his dreams were his own. She didn't need much at all besides him.

The night my mother told him she was pregnant, she sat in his lap in their Santa Monica apartment and asked if he could feel that he held the weight of two people. He teared up as he smiled at her. And then he told her he could feel in his gut that I was a boy, and that I was going to be twice the tennis player he'd ever been.

When I was a baby, my father would bring a high chair to the courts so I could watch him play. He says I would dart my head back and forth, tracking the ball. According to him, my mother would sometimes come and try to take me out of the high chair to sit in the shade or have a snack, but I'd cry until she brought me back to the court.

My father loved to tell the story of the time when I was just barely a toddler and he first put a racket in my hand. He softly tossed the ball to me, and he swears that on that fateful day, I swung and made contact.

He ran back to the house, carrying me on his shoulders, to tell my mother. She smiled at him and continued making dinner.

"Do you understand what I'm telling you?" he said.

My mother laughed. "That our daughter likes tennis? Of course she likes tennis—it's the only thing you've shown her."

"That's like saying Achilles was a great warrior simply because he lived during wartime. Achilles was a great warrior because it was his *destiny* to be one."

"I see. So Carolina is Achilles?" my mother asked, smiling. "And what does that make you, a god?"

My father waved her away. "She's destined," he said. "It is plain as day. With your grace and my strength, she can be the greatest tennis player the world has ever seen. They will tell stories about her one day."

My mother rolled her eyes at him as she began to put dinner on the table. "I would rather she was kind and happy."

"Alicia," my father said as he stood behind my mother and wrapped his arms around her. "No one ever tells stories about that."

I do not remember being told my mother had died. Nor do I remember her funeral, though my father says I was there. As he tells it, my mother was making soup and realized we were out of tomato paste, so she put her shoes on and left me with him in the garage while he was changing the oil in the car.

When she didn't come home, he knocked on our neighbors' door and asked them to watch me while he searched through the streets.

He saw the ambulance a few blocks away and his stomach sank. My mother had been hit by a car when she was crossing the street on her way home.

After my mother's body was buried, my father refused to go into their bedroom. He started sleeping in the living room; he kept his clothes in a hamper by the TV. It went on for months. Whenever I had a bad dream, I'd leave my own bed and walk right to the couch. He was always there, with the TV on, static hissing as he slept.

And then, one day, light flooded into the hallway. Their bedroom door was open, the dust that had long accumulated was off the handle, and everything of my mother's was packed into cardboard boxes. Her dresses, her high heels, her necklaces, her rings. Even her bobby pins. Somebody came to the house and took them all out. And that was it.

There wasn't much left of her. Barely any proof she'd ever lived. Just a few pictures I'd found in my father's top drawer. I took my favorite one and stashed it under my pillow. I was afraid that if I didn't, it would soon be gone too.

For a while after that, my dad would tell me stories about my mother. He'd talk about how she wanted me to be *happy*. That she was *good* and *fair.* But he cried when he told them, and pretty soon, he stopped telling them altogether.

To this day, the only significant memory I have of my mother is hazy. I can't tell what is real and what are the gaps that I've filled in over time.

In my head, I can see her standing in the kitchen over the stove. She is in a maroon dress with a pattern on it, something like polka dots or tiny flowers. I know that her hair is curly and full. My father calls from across the house to me, using the name he had for me then, "*Guerrerita.*" But then my mother shakes her head and says, "Don't let him call you a warrior—you are a queen."

Most of the time, I'm absolutely positive that all of this actually happened. But sometimes, it feels so obvious that the entire thing must have been a dream.

What I actually remember most about her is the emptiness she left behind. There was this sense, within the house, that there used to be someone else here.

But now it was just my father and me.

In my first concrete memories, I am young but already annoyed. I am annoyed at all of the other girls' questions: "Where is your mom?" "Why isn't your hair ever brushed?" Annoyed at the teacher's insistence that I speak English without any traces of my father's accent. Annoyed at being told to play nicer during recess, when all I wanted to do was race the other kids across the field or see who could swing highest on the swing set.

I suspected the problem was that I was always the winner. But I could not for the life of me understand why that made people want to play with me *less* instead of more.

Those early memories of trying to make friends are all accompanied by the same twinge of confusion: *I'm doing something wrong, and I don't know what it is.*

When school let out, I used to watch all the other students greet their mothers at pickup. My classmates told their moms about their days, bristled at the squeezes their moms gave them by the car, wiped their mothers' kisses off their cheeks.

I could have watched them for hours. What else did they do with their moms after school? Did they go out for ice cream? Did they go shopping together for those pretty pencil cases some of them had? Where were they all getting those hair bows?

As they drove away, I would dutifully begin my walk two blocks over, to meet my father on the public tennis courts.

I grew up on the court. The public courts after school, the country club courts during the summers and on weekends. I grew up in tennis skirts and ponytails. I grew up sitting in the shade by the sidelines, waiting while my father finished a lesson.

He loomed over the net. His serves were always fluid, his groundstrokes smooth. His opponent, or whomever he was teaching, always looked so chaotic in comparison. My father was unfailingly in control of the court.

In hindsight, I can see that he must have been tense and lonely most days of my young life. He was a widowed single father in a country that was not his home, with no one else to rely on. It seems obvious to me now that my dad was likely stretched so tight he could nearly have snapped.

But if his days were hard, his nights restless, he grew very good at hiding it from me. The time I got to spend with him felt like a gift that other kids didn't get. Unlike them, my time had *purpose*; my father and I were working toward something of *meaning*. *I* was going to be the best.

Every day after school, when my father was finally done with his paid lessons, he would turn and look at me. "*Vamos*," he would say. "*Los fundamentos*." At which point, I would pick up my racket and join him at the baseline.

"Game, set, match: Why do we say this?" my father would ask me.

"Because each time you play, it is a game. You must win the most games to win the set. And then you must win the most sets to win the match," I'd recite.

"In a game, the first point is . . ."

"Fifteen. Then 30. Then 40. Then you win. But you have to win by two."

"When the score is 40–all, what do we call that?"

"Deuce. And if you're at deuce and win a point, that brings you to either advantage-in or advantage-out, depending on whether you're serving or not."

"So how do you win?"

"If you are serving at ad-in, you have to win the next point to win the game. You have to win six games to win the set, but, again, you have to win by two. You can't just win a set 6–5."

"And a match?"

"Women play three sets, men often play five."

"And love? What does it mean?"

"It means nothing."

"Well, it means zero."

"Right, you have no points. Love means nothing."

Having gotten all the answers right, I would get a pat on the shoulder. And then we would practice.

There are many coaches out there who innovate, but that was never my father's style. He believed in the beauty and simplicity of doing something the way it has always been done but better than anyone else has ever done it. "If I had been as committed to proper form as you will be, *hijita*," he would say, "I would still be playing professional tennis." That was one of the only times he told me something that I suspected wasn't true. I knew even then that not many people ever played tennis professionally past age thirty.

"*Bueno, papá*," I would say as we began our drills.

My entire childhood was drills. Drill after drill after drill. Serves, groundstrokes, footwork, volleys. Serves, groundstrokes, footwork, volleys. Again and again. All summer long, after school, every weekend. My dad and I. Always together. Our little team of two. Proud coach and star student.

I loved that each element of the game had a *wrong* way and a *right* way to execute it. There was always something concrete to strive for.

"*De nuevo,*" my dad would say, as I tried for the fiftieth time that day to perfect my flat serve. "I want both arms coming up at the same speed at the same time."

"*De nuevo,*" he'd say, a grown man crouching down low to get eye-to-eye with me when I was no taller than his hip. "In a pinpoint stance, you must bring your back foot in before you connect."

"*De nuevo,*" he'd say, smiling. "Save that spin for a second serve, *hijita. ¿Entendido?*"

And each time, at the ages of five, six, seven, eight, he'd be met with the same response. "*Sí, papá.*" *Sí, papá. Sí, papá. Sí, papá.*

Over time, my father started peppering his "*De nuevo*" with "*Excelente.*"

I reached every day for those "*excelentes.*" I dreamed about them. I lay in bed at night on my Linus and Lucy sheets, staring at the framed Rod Laver press photo I'd begged my father for, going over my form in my head.

Soon enough, my groundstrokes were strong, my volleys were sharp, my serves were deadly. I was an eight-year-old able to serve from the baseline and hit the small target of a milk carton one hundred times in a row.

People walking by the courts would think they were clever when they called me "Little Billie Jean King," as if I didn't hear it ten times a day.

Soon, my father introduced the idea of strategy.

"A lot of players can win the games they serve," my father would say. "*Decime por qué.*"

"Because a serve is the only time a player can control the ball."

"*¿Y qué más?*"

"If you serve it right, you control the serve and then the return. And even the rally."

"*Exacto.* Holding your game when you serve is the basis of your strategy."

"*Bueno, entiendo.*"

"But most people, they focus all their energy on their serve. They perfect their serve so much, and they forget the most important part."

"The return."

"*Exacto.* Your serve is your defense, but you can *win* games with a good return. If you hold all the games you serve, and your opponent holds all their games, who is going to win the set?"

"The first person to break the other one's service game."

"*Exacto.* If you break their serve in just one game—just one—and you hold all of your own, you will win the set."

"So I have to be a good server and a good returner."

"You have to be what we call an 'all-court player,'" he said. "Great at serving, volleying, groundstrokes, and your return. Okay, let's play."

He always won, day after day. But I kept trying. Match after match, every evening after school, sometimes twice on weekends.

Until one cloudy January afternoon, when the air was just a bit too crisp. All day it had been threatening to do the very thing the Southern California sky had promised to almost never do.

We were tied in the first set when I returned two serves in a row with cross-court forehands that were so fast, my father couldn't get to them.

And for the first time in my young life, I broke his serve.

"*¡Excelente!*" he said with his arms in the air, running over to my side of the court. He spun me in the air.

"I did it!" I said. "I broke your serve!"

"Yes, you did," he told me. "Yes, you did."

About two minutes after I won the set, the sky cracked open and the rain started pouring down. My father put his jacket over my head as we raced to the car.

After we got in and shut the doors, I looked over at him. His face was all lit up even as he shivered from the cold. "*Excelente, pichoncita,*" he said as he grabbed my hand and squeezed. "*Muy pero muy bien.*" He was still smiling as he turned the key in the ignition and backed out of the parking lot.

From that moment on, though I still couldn't beat him in a match, I set my mind to breaking his serve at least once every day. And I did it.

At the end of every session, my father and I would drive home with two doggie bags of food from the dining room at the club staying warm in my lap. I'd watch the big houses go by as we made our way back to our apartment.

My father would park, and then, before we got out, he'd say, "We did well today. But what are we going to do better tomorrow?"

I'd give him the list I'd been working on the entire way home.

"Get my feet up faster," I'd say. "And keep my wrist down." Or "Make sure I don't pull back too far before I hit the drop volley."

Each night, he would add one more thing I didn't think of. "And keep your eye on the ball, not on your racket." "Follow through on the forehand groundstroke."

Each night, I would nod. *Of course. How could I forget?*

Then we would go inside and eat dinner together in front of the TV. Most of the time it was just the evening news, but I always loved those rare nights when he'd let us watch *The Lucy Show.* Him in his recliner, me on the couch, a pair of TV trays. He would laugh so hard. And so I laughed too.

Later, after I brushed my teeth and put on my pajamas, my father would give me a kiss on the forehead and say, "Good night, my Achilles, the greatest warrior tennis has ever seen."

When the light was off, I would put my hand under my pillow, searching for the photo of my mother that I had taken from my father's dresser.

In it, my mother is lying in a hammock in our backyard, holding me and smiling at the camera. There is an orange tree above us. I am asleep in her arms, her chin is resting on my head, her hand is on my back. Her hair is long and her curls soft. I used to run my finger over the photo, the length of her dress, from her shoulders to her feet.

I would hold the photo to my chest and then tuck it back under my pillow and go to sleep.

One night when I was about eight years old, I went to find the photo and it was gone.

I threw my pillow onto the ground. I jumped off my bed and lifted the mattress onto its side. How could I have lost it, something so important? I started screaming, tears falling down my cheeks.

My father came in and saw me sitting there, red-faced, my eyes wet, my room torn apart. He calmly put my mattress back on the frame and took me in his arms.

"*Pichoncita,*" he said. "*No te preocupés.* The photo is fine. I put it back in my dresser. It's time to stop looking at it every night."

"*Pero* I want to look at it every night."

He shook his head and held me tight. "*Cariño,* put it out of your mind. It is too heavy of a weight for you to bear."

1966

BY MY NINTH BIRTHDAY, I'D BEATEN EVERY KID MY AGE AT THE CLUB. SO my father recruited the son of one of the adults he taught to play me, a thirteen-year-old boy named Chris.

"I don't understand why you're allowed to play here," Chris said to me. "You're not a member." We were standing by the net, waiting to start. Our fathers were talking, laughing.

"Neither are you," I said.

"My dad is. Your dad *works* here. Your dad works for *us.*"

Our fathers headed in our direction, and Chris groaned. "Can we just get this over with? I don't feel like playing a seven-year-old girl."

I stared at him for a moment, feeling my shoulders tighten. "I'm nine, you moron."

Chris looked at me with his eyes wide, but he didn't say anything else. Something I learned early is that most assholes don't have comebacks.

"All right, kids, best out of three," my dad said.

Chris served first and I crouched, ready. He tossed the ball up and hit it in a slow curve. I smacked it back, cross-court. My point. *Love–15.*

Chris served again. I returned it with a passing shot. *Love–30.*

The next time, I feigned yawning. *Love–40.*

"Game for Carrie," my father said.

Chris's face grew slightly red. I couldn't tell if he was angry or embarrassed. I smiled at him.

The rest of the match was over quick.

On the last serve, I tapped the ball over, unwilling to bother with any topspin or speed. But he still hit it wide.

"You are terrible at tennis," I said to him when I shook his hand.

"Carolina!" my father called out.

"Sorry, but he is," I said. I looked over at Chris. "You are."

I watched Chris glance at his father on the side of the court. His father shook his head and put out the cigarette he'd been smoking, rolling his eyes.

I remember thinking, *That's why you should practice, Chris.*

When we walked off the court, my father put his hand on my shoulder and said, "That was something."

"I didn't even have to try," I said as we headed toward the locker rooms.

"Oh, you made that clear. And you were mean."

"Why should I be nice to him? He called me a seven-year-old."

"People are going to call you a lot of things in your life," he said. "People always call people like us all kinds of things."

"Because we aren't members here?" I asked as I put my things down.

My father stopped in place. "Because we are winners. Do not grow a chip on your shoulder, Carolina," he said. "Do not let what anyone says about you determine how you feel about yourself."

I looked at him.

"If I say your hair is purple, does that mean it's purple?" he asked.

"No, it's brown."

"Does it mean you have to prove to me it's brown?"

I shook my head. "No, you can see it is."

"You are going to be one of the greatest tennis players in the world someday, *cariño*. That is as true as your brown hair. You don't need to show them. You just need to be."

I considered.

"Next time you play a kid like Chris, I expect you to still play a beautiful game of tennis," he said. "Do you understand?"

I nodded. "*Está bien.*"

"And we don't cry when we lose, but we also don't gloat when we win."

"*Bueno, entiendo.*"

"You're not playing your opponent, you understand that, yes?"

I stared at him, unsure. But I needed him to believe that I understood everything I was supposed to be—it seemed like an unbearable betrayal of our mission for me to be confused about any of it.

"Every time you get out on that court, you must play a better tennis game than you played the time before. Did you play your best game of tennis today?"

"No," I said.

"Next time, I want you to beat yourself. Every day you must beat the day before."

I sat down on the bench next to me and considered. What my father was proposing was a much, much harder endeavor. But once the thought had been put in my head, I had to rise to it. I could not expel it.

"*Entiendo,*" I said.

"Now go get your things. We are driving to the beach."

"No, Dad," I said. "Please, no. Can't we just go home? Or what if we went out for ice cream? This girl in my class said there is a place that has great ice cream sandwiches. I thought we could go."

He laughed. "We are not going to condition your legs sitting around eating ice cream sandwiches. We can only do that by . . ."

I frowned. "Running in the sand."

"*Sí,* running in the sand, *entonces vámonos.*"

1968

AFTER ABOUT TWO MORE YEARS OF BEATING EVERY KID IN TOWN, WE got a call from Lars Van de Berg, one of the biggest junior tennis coaches in the country.

He was coaching a fourteen-year-old named Mary-Louise Bryant down in Laguna Beach. Mary-Louise had already started winning junior championships. She'd gotten to the semifinals at Junior Wimbledon that year.

"Lars called because everyone in L.A. is talking about you," my father said as we drove south on the freeway toward Laguna Beach. I was in a white tennis skirt and polo shirt, a cream-colored cardigan on top. I wore new socks and a brand-new blindingly white pair of tennis shoes on my feet.

My father had gone out and bought the whole outfit the week before. He'd washed it all and laid it out for me that morning. When I saw the ruffles on the butt of the tennis underpants for the skirt, I looked at him for a moment, hoping he was not serious. But from the look on his face, it was clear he was. So I put it on.

"He's pretending it's just a friendly match," my father continued. "But he wants to see if you're a threat to Mary-Louise."

There were already whispers about my future. Competing was something I knew I would do soon, the way some kids know they will go to college. And just like college, I got the impression my father was silently working out how to pay for it.

I wriggled in my seat, trying to stop the sweater from chafing my neck. "*Am* I a threat to Mary-Louise?" I asked.

"Yes," my father said.

I rolled down my window and watched the Pacific Ocean fly by.

"I want you thinking of your game plan," my father said. "Mary-Louise is three years older, so you have to assume she's taller, stronger, maybe more confident. How will that affect your strategy? You have five minutes."

"Okay," I said.

My father turned the radio up and focused on the road. Soon enough, traffic slowed considerably and we came to a full stop. I looked out the window, watching kids on the beach, playing in the sand. I saw two girls around my age building a sandcastle.

The gap between myself and girls like that—girls like the ones I went to school with—had always felt significant, but it seemed nearly insurmountable now.

A half second later, we started moving again and I wondered why anyone would want to build anything out of sand, when tomorrow it will be gone, and you'd have nothing to show for your day.

"*Bueno, contame,*" my dad said. "What's your plan?"

"If she's stronger than me, I need to get her up to the net as much as I can, use my angles. And she's probably feeling pretty confident, so I need to shake her, right at the beginning. If I can get her worrying about whether an eleven-year-old is gonna beat her, then an eleven-year-old is gonna beat her."

"*Muy bien,*" he said as he lifted his hand, to give me a high five. "My Achilles. Greatest of the Greeks."

I held back a smile as we sped down the freeway.

Mary-Louise won the toss and elected to serve first.

I stood at the baseline and bounced the taut strings of my racket against my palm. I held the grip and turned it over in my hand.

I looked down at my brand-new shoes. I noticed there was a scuff on the toe. So I bent down and rubbed it off.

My father and Lars were on the bench. Lars was over six feet tall, with sandy hair and a smile that never made it to his eyes. He had introduced my father as "the Jaguar" to Mary-Louise in a tone that bothered me.

Mary-Louise was standing across the court, in a white tennis skirt and sweater with a matching headband in her hair. As she stood up, I could see just how tall and lanky she was, her face angular and delicate. Maybe it was the perfect creases in her skirt or the casual way she held her wooden Dunlop Maxply Fort racket, but I could tell that while she and I might both be at home on this court, we would not recognize the rest of each other's worlds.

She smiled at me, and I wondered if she might be the prettiest girl I'd ever seen in my life.

I fostered no illusions that I was beautiful. I was stocky and broad-shouldered, my calves and forearms thicker than those of the other girls in my class. Some of the more popular girls—the ones who wore bows in their hair and cardigans over their dresses, the ones the boys chased at recess—had started calling me names when the teacher wasn't listening.

As I'd walked into class one morning, Christina Williams whispered loudly to Diane Richards, "There she goes. *Boom, boom, boom,*" as if the weight of my steps was shaking the room when I walked to my desk.

The whole class laughed.

"At least I didn't get a D on the math quiz, you loser," I said as I sat down.

The class laughed at that too. But then Christina started crying. My teacher noticed and called us both to the front of the room.

When pressed, Christina cried even harder and denied she'd ever teased me. I kept my head up and admitted what I'd said.

And somehow, the coward went free, and I got sent to the principal's office, who then called my father. He came and picked me up and took me home.

After hearing my side of the story, my father reprimanded me and then made me look in the mirror. He told me I was beautiful. *"Pichona, sos hermosa."*

I scanned my face for a glimpse of what he was talking about. I had my mother's olive skin and green eyes. I had my father's hair color. But my body, my features . . . I could not tell where they came from. I wanted curls like my mother and father both had, I wanted my mother's length, her thin wrists, her perfect nose. I had none of it.

"I look nothing like Mom," I said finally. She had been so undeniably beautiful, her worth written right across her face.

"Yes, you do," he said. "And you are strong like her."

My eyes took in my broad shoulders, my powerful arms. Luckily, I did not need to be pretty. My body was built to wage war.

And thank God, because I was about to use it to crush pretty Mary-Louise Bryant.

Love serving love.

Mary-Louise tossed the ball up in the air and then cut across it with her racket. As I ran for the ball, I thought that my best bet was to take it out of the air quick. But as I got in position, I saw Mary-Louise approach the net. She was assuming I didn't have the power to hit a passing shot. And so, at the last minute, I hit a deep groundstroke. She had to rush her return and hit it into the net.

The first point was mine. *Love serving 15.*

I looked at my father as I made my way back to the baseline. Both he and Lars were watching me, and Lars's eyes were wide. My father was fighting off a smile.

I crouched and waited for her next serve. Mary-Louise's face was tight now. Suddenly, the ball came across the net, fast as a whip. I couldn't return it.

15–all.

Serve after serve stunned me.

30–15.

40–15.

And just like that, she'd won the first game.

I glanced over at my father and saw his brow furrowed. I couldn't tell what he was thinking.

Now it was my serve. I landed each one exactly where I wanted it to go. I was setting up my shots a few strokes ahead. I kept her running all over the court. But every time, she returned it. Our long rallies would inevitably end in her favor.

I stayed alert. I met the ball each time. But regardless of how good my shots were, it just didn't matter.

She took the first set 7–5.

I was exhausted already. My father handed me a towel, not saying a single word. I breathed in deeply. I could not lose; it was not an option.

I thought that by getting that first point off her, I would have thrown her off. But I'd awakened her. I'd given her a reason to play her best.

I had to take away her opportunities to hit winners. I was going to try for aces, each and every serve. It was risky; I could double-fault. But it felt like my only shot.

My first serve was hard and bounced high. She dove for it and hit it out. *15–love.*

I did it again. *30–love.*

I glanced over at my father as I went to pick up the ball, and I saw a smile creep over his face.

I hit another flat serve, but this time I kept it close to the T. It whizzed past her. *40–love.*

I had her. I could feel the tingle in the top of my head and down my back. I could feel the space in between my joints, the fluidity of my muscles. I felt a hum in my bones.

I served the ball low and fast. She returned it with spin that I *understood* innately. I knew where it would go, how it would bounce. I hit it back with the full force of my shoulder. Her return went long.

I went on to win the set. The score was now 1–1, and it would come down to who won the third.

Mary-Louise's first serve on the next game had us rallying back and forth for the point but ended in her hitting a low groundstroke that whizzed past me. I wanted to scream as I saw the ball bounce past my racket. But I knew my father wouldn't stand for that.

Here's the thing about that hum: It can leave just as quickly as it comes.

Mary-Louise took control of the court. She broke my serve, and she held her own. I showed up to the ball. I ran like hell. But it wasn't enough.

When she scored the last point, I fell to my knees. I felt like the world was splitting into pieces. I held on to the ground for a moment and closed my eyes.

When I opened them, Mary-Louise and Lars were by the bench talking calmly and my father was standing over me, offering me his hand.

My father had a warm face with curly dark hair. His eyelashes were long, his eyebrows were full, and his eyes were a soft brown. I had trouble meeting them.

"*Vámonos,*" he said. "We are ready to go."

I stood up and focused my gaze on Mary-Louise. I knew what I had to do. I just had to find the will to do it.

I walked over to her. "You played a beautiful game," I said. I could hear, as I was saying it, that I didn't sound like myself. My voice remained hard and cold, its various melodies not available to me at that moment. I put my hand out for her to shake, and she smiled and took it immediately.

"Carrie," she said. "That was the hardest match I've played in a long time."

"Thank you for saying that," I said. "But you won."

"Still," she said. "I would not have beaten you when I was eleven."

"Thanks," I said. But surely she knew that all that mattered was that I had lost.

My father and I packed up our stuff and walked back to the car. I zipped my racket in its cover and threw it into the back, then sank myself into the front seat.

When my dad got in, I stared at the glove box, trying to hold back the tears that were forming in my eyes.

"*Hablemos,*" he said.

"You shouldn't have made me play her," I said, my voice catching and breaking.

My father shook his head. "*Ni lo intentes,*" he said. "That was not the lesson you should take from this. Try again."

"I hate tennis," I said, and then I kicked the glove box.

"Get your foot off my car," he said. "You know better."

I closed my eyes and tried to breathe. When I opened them, I couldn't look at my father. I looked out the window and watched as, across the street, a woman came out of her house and got her mail. I wondered if she was having a terrible day too. Or maybe her life looked nothing like mine. Maybe she lived free from all this pressure, this sense that she lived or died by how good she was at something. Was she burdened by the need to win everything she did? Or did she live for nothing?

I looked up at my father, but he didn't turn back at first. And that was when I suspected that I had finally failed him, that I had proven myself unworthy of all the faith he had in me.

"Are you done?" he said as he turned to look at me. "With the hysterics?"

"Do you still . . . want to coach me?" I asked.

My father's face contorted in ways I could not read. He shook his head and put his hand on my cheek, wiping away my tears with his thumb. "*Cariño,* how could you ever ask that?" He lowered his gaze until he caught mine. "I am prouder to be your father and your coach today than I have ever been in my life."

"How is that possible?"

"I know you're upset because you lost," he said.

"I *lost,*" I said. "Which makes me a *loser.*"

Dad shook his head with the smile still on his face. "You are so much like me, *hija.* But listen now, please," he said. "I have been so focused on teaching you how to win that I have not taught you that everybody loses matches."

"I'm not everybody. I'm supposed to be the greatest."

My father nodded. "And you will be. Today you proved that. You played the best you've ever played in your life today."

I looked up at him.

"Have you ever hit that many groundstrokes that bounced *just* in front of the baseline?" he asked.

"No," I said.

"Have you ever served three aces in a row like you did today?"

I started tapping my foot as I listened to him. "No," I said. "My first serve was great today."

"You were on fire, *cariño,*" he said. "You ran down the ball almost every shot."

"Yeah, but then I hit it into the net half the time."

"Because you are not yet who you will one day be."

I looked up at him, my guarded heart opening ever so slightly.

"Every match you play, you are one match closer to becoming the greatest tennis player the world has ever seen. You were not born that person. You were born to *become* that person. And that is why you must best yourself every time you get on the court. Not so that you beat the other person—"

"But so that I become more myself," I finished.

"Now you're getting it," my father said. "You played the best tennis you've ever played in your life."

"And you're happy," I said. "With me. Because I played great."

"Because you played *the best* you ever have."

"And every day I will play better and better," I said. "Until one day, I am the greatest."

"Until you've reached the fullest of your potential. That's the most important thing. We don't stop for one second until you are the best you can be," he said. "We don't rest. Until it's finally true. *Algún día.*"

"Because then I will be who I was born to be."

"*Exacto.*"

My father turned back to the steering wheel and put the car in drive. But before he pulled out onto the road, he looked at me one more time. "Do not wonder again, *hija,* if I would stop coaching you," he said. "Do not ever wonder that. *Nunca.*"

I nodded, smiling. I thought I understood perfectly what he was trying to tell me.

"Since today went okay," I said a few moments later, on the drive home, "I was thinking, about what I did. You know, that worked."

My father nodded. "*Contame.*"

I gave him a list of the strategies I'd used, a few of my split-second decisions. And then the last one, "*También,* just before the match, I cleaned the tops of my shoes."

My father raised his eyebrows.

"I think maybe it's a good-luck thing," I said. "You know? Like some of the pros do."

My father smiled. "*Me encanta.*"

"Yeah," I said. "And I think that will help me, you know? I'll just keep getting better and better. Until one day, when I'm good enough to go pro."

1971–1975

AT AGE THIRTEEN, I ENTERED THE JUNIOR CHAMPIONSHIPS. I SHOCKED everyone except my father and myself when I won the SoCal Junior Championships that year and catapulted myself up the rankings.

My first time at Junior Wimbledon, I made it all the way to the quarterfinals. The next year, I made it to the final. Quickly, my father and I came to understand that while I was great on a hard surface and could hold my own on clay, I dominated on grass. Winning Junior Wimbledon went from a dream to a goal.

My father took my already aggressive training schedule and kicked it into its highest gear. We went to every tournament we could, regardless of my school schedule. We flew all over the country.

Also, I noticed that my father took on twice as many clients when we were home. Occasionally, he would return to the house late at night with a bounce in his step that I found puzzling.

At first, I thought that maybe he had a girlfriend. But one night,

I dragged the truth out of him: He'd been hustling blue bloods at the club. He was making hundreds of dollars in a night.

When I asked him why, he said it kept his mind sharp. But I knew the prices for renting out grass courts, and flights to New York and London, and the entry fees for tournaments.

The next time I saw him leave to go play a match, I walked out onto our tiny stoop and called to him just as his hand grabbed the car door handle.

"Are you sure about all of this?" I asked.

He looked up at me. "Never been more sure of anything in my life," he said.

I took a deep breath. "I want to drop out of school and dedicate my full days to tennis."

The Virginia Slims tour was proving to be a significant money-maker for women who went pro. I was already good enough to compete in some of the main draws. He wouldn't need to hustle dupes much longer.

"Not yet," he said. But I could see the corners of his lips turning up. And I could feel the rest of the sentence, though it remained unsaid. *Not yet, but soon.*

Unless I was competing, I was out on the court from eight A.M. every morning until early afternoon.

From about three to five P.M., I took a break to study with a tutor my father had hired from the yellow pages. And then my dad and I went over strategy for about an hour, which would sometimes bleed into dinner.

After that, if I didn't have homework, I could do my own thing for an hour or so, and then I went to bed by ten so that I could be up by five-thirty to run, eat breakfast, and study strategy before getting back to the court at eight.

In the spring of '73, when I was fifteen, my father and I set up shop at Saddlebrook in Florida so that we could play on their grass courts day after day, sharpening every single shot I had in my arsenal, preparing for my third Junior Wimbledon in July.

It was at Saddlebrook that I met Marco.

My father had hired me a hitter named Elena to help me work on my returns. Elena was almost twenty and had an incredible serve. I often wondered, as we played together, why she didn't hone the rest of her game to try to play professionally. But she seemed entirely uninterested. A fact that I was exceedingly unnerved by.

Instead, every day Elena would show up, hit these incredible serves that made me think faster than I'd ever had to before, and then go on her way.

One day a few weeks in, her younger brother, Marco, came by the courts.

Marco was sixteen and over six feet tall, so he was impossible to miss as he stood outside the green chain-link fence, waiting for Elena to be done. Toward the end of our session, I found myself staring at him for the briefest of seconds. He caught my eye, and I quickly turned away.

But after that, he kept coming back to watch.

I did not know what it meant to have a crush—to feel that inexplicable pull toward another person—but by the third day that Marco showed up, I started to feel a lightness in me that was entirely new.

For weeks, Marco would come earlier and earlier to wait for Elena. Sometimes I could feel him watching me, and I would strain to stay focused on my game.

I would will myself not to look at the perfect square of Marco's shoulders, his deep brown hair, the slight pout to his lips, the way he leaned so casually against the fence. I tried not to imagine what his hands would feel like across my back.

"Keep your eye on the ball, Carrie!" my father said to me one afternoon. "C'mon now!" He shook his head. And my heart sank, but I straightened up and finished strong.

After we were done, my father went to go book our next court time. As Elena packed up her things, Marco came onto the court and approached me.

"Hi," he said.

"Hi."

"I'm Marco," he said.

"Carrie."

"I know," he said, smiling. "Everybody here seems to know who you are."

Elena put her kit over her shoulder and gestured that she wanted to go. Marco told her he'd meet her at the car and turned back to me.

"I've wanted to talk to you for a while, but your dad is always around."

"Oh." For a moment, I envisioned him asking me out, and my pulse quickened so intensely that I thought I might pass out.

If he asked me out, what would I even say?

My father had told me earlier in the week to expect double sessions on my backhand and my inside-out forehand. And I'd failed—actually failed—the practice GED my tutor had given me the week before. I'd promised my father I'd study all weekend. Answering yes was entirely impossible. And yet the wish that he would ask grew stronger and stronger in my belly by the second.

"Yeah, so . . ." he said, but then never finished his sentence. I watched his face, desperate to know what he was thinking. I felt a heaviness, a leaded feeling in my hips. I did not even know what it was that I needed so badly from him, but I could feel how much I needed it.

Instead of saying anything further, Marco put one hand against the fence and closed the gap between us. I watched his lips as he leaned his mouth toward mine. When he finally kissed me, I did not hesitate. I kissed him back with my entire body, pressing myself against him, wanting every inch of me to touch every inch of him.

His lips were so soft and his hands felt warm as they traveled from my shoulders down my torso.

I tilted my head back as his mouth went to my neck, and I moaned quietly, forgetting everything except this boy and his hands and how they felt.

And then suddenly, we could hear the crunch of the gravel that was my father walking back up the path. Marco pulled his hands away.

It was over almost as quickly as it had begun. Marco whispered, "I'll see you around," and then took off just as my father came back. My father picked up his racket and stood across the court from me and started calling out the shots he wanted to do.

I hit the ball the same as I always did, but inside, I felt flushed and in possession of my first real secret. It was like opening the front door and letting fresh air into the house.

For the next month, every day after training, Marco would be there. Whenever my father and Elena weren't around, he would kiss me in the corner of the court. I felt embarrassed by how much I looked forward to it, by how desperate I was to feel more of him, how often I thought of him when he was gone.

I felt such an insatiable need for him to touch me, a hunger for his body. It felt exactly like the hunger I felt to win. The sense that at the center of my being there was an unfillable void. There would never be enough matches to win. There would never be enough of Marco.

And it wasn't one-sided. He seemed to need me too. I could tell in the hurried way he grabbed me, in the look on his face when I had to leave. I felt bright and shiny for maybe the first time in my life, glowing with the knowledge that I was wanted.

I'm stunned at what Marco and I got away with in those small pockets of time that spring in Florida, just how far things went. Eventually, we found our way to the back of his parents' old sedan, parked in the far corner of the parking lot.

Marco opened up a whole slice of the world for me, a whole new thing my body could do. And I felt consumed by it. I could torture my body all day—making my muscles so tired that my whole body felt heavy. And then in just a few minutes, Marco could lighten every limb, loosen my chest.

"Are you my boyfriend?" I asked him one afternoon in June,

pulling my shirt down and fixing my hair. The start of Junior Wimbledon was only two short weeks away.

"I don't think so," Marco said. "We don't hang out or anything."

"Well, maybe we could," I said. "After the tournament. It's in a couple weeks, and when it's over, I could convince my dad we should come back here."

"I don't want you to come back here just for me," Marco said as he kissed me on the lips. When he pulled away, he was smiling. I loved his smile—the way his dimples were barely there but I was close enough to see them.

"But if we like each other . . ."

"Sure," he said. "But it's good, how it works now. Where we both do our own thing but then do . . . this." He kissed my neck, and all over again I found myself closing my eyes, on the verge of surrendering.

What little I knew of Marco outside of our time together mystified me. He got Cs in school and didn't play a single sport. His mother and father never kept track of where he was. All he did was play guitar and try to get his band together in his garage to practice. I could barely imagine his world, and yet I could not stop trying.

I liked the way he talked a lot but never said much. That he never took anything seriously. That nothing ever felt like a big deal. Sometimes, I pictured being with him outside that car. I pictured me sitting across the table from him at a restaurant and having him reach his hand out for mine. For other people to see that *he chose me*. "I'm just saying, if we wanted to, we could figure it out," I said.

"It's not like you even have time to go to a party with me or do anything I want to do. You're obsessed with tennis."

"I'm not *obsessed* with anything," I said. "I'm dedicated to winning. And I work hard at that."

"Right," Marco said. "And so let's just keep doing what we're doing."

I did not like his answer, but the next afternoon, I met him right back in that car with a smile on my face.

Maybe Marco and I would never go out to dinner. Maybe I was

not the sort of girl who became a girlfriend at all. Maybe I was the type of girl you kissed when no one was looking and that was it. If that was the case, then fine. I would not demean myself enough to want more. But that did not mean I could not have the rest, that my body did not deserve what he could give it.

When we left Saddlebrook for London, I knew I would probably never see Marco again. But I did not cry. As I watched the plane lift up above the clouds, it seemed obvious to me that there would be other Marcos—that Marcos were easy to find now that I knew to look for them.

But then as the plane leveled out, I glanced back at my father, who was talking to the flight attendant. I couldn't quite make sense of him. I kept staring at his face, trying to understand why he looked so foreign to me now.

There was a space between us that had not ever been there before, a gulf for which there would be no bridge.

Weeks later, I won Junior Wimbledon. I went on to win the next three juniors events. All the coverage started touting me as "the Next Tennis Phenom."

My father cut out the headlines from the sports papers. They said things like UPSTART CARRIE SOTO PROVES UNSTOPPABLE. He put them in frames and hung them up in my bedroom. When they ran an article with the headline IS JAVIER SOTO'S STYLE THE FUTURE OF WOMEN'S TENNIS? he hung that one on the fridge.

Our phone started ringing so often we had to get an answering machine. Journalists wanted interviews; a racket company was offering me an endorsement deal.

And there was also a representative from the Virginia Slims tour. In her message, she suggested that it was time for me to enter the main women's draw.

My father and I looked at each other.

My moment was here.

1975–1976

THE MORNING OF MY FIRST MATCH ON THE VIRGINIA SLIMS TOUR, MY
father gave me a pep talk before I went into the locker rooms. "You
can talk and joke around with the other players if you have to," he
said, "but remember they are not your friends, they are your . . ."

"Enemies."

"Opponents," he said.

"Same thing," I said.

"And like we talked about, everyone will be looking at you, looking to see if you're as good as they've heard. Ignore all that. Just *be*
good—don't try to prove it."

"Bueno, entiendo."

As I turned to go into the locker room, the door swung open and
hit me hard in the shoulder. Out walked Paulina Stepanova.

Eighteen years old, six feet tall, white-blond hair and arms like
cannons—she had come out of nowhere. A baseliner from just outside Moscow, she was the kind of competitor I was not expecting.

She had just joined the tour two months prior and had already gotten to the final in the Australian Open.

As Paulina walked by, she barely looked at me. "*Izvinite menya,* I did not see you there. You are so short."

I gave a tight smile and then turned to my father. "I want to beat her to the ground."

My first year on the tour, I clinched some big titles and quickly turned pro, bringing in tens of thousands of dollars. I was up against some of the biggest names in tennis, women I had looked up to for years, like Amparo Pereira, and players who had long eluded me, like Mary-Louise Bryant. But it was Stepanova the newspapers were talking about.

PAULINA THE POWERFUL DOMINATES THE REST. STEPANOVA STEPS OUT TO DEAFENING APPLAUSE.

Publicly, I kept my face neutral. But afterward, in the hotels and on the long flights, I raged.

"She is in *my way,*" I told my father.

"It is your first year on the tour," he said. "Not everything comes the second you want it. Keep your head down and keep working. You will get there."

I did what he told me. I did *everything* he told me. Extra training sessions, no Sundays off, studying tapes of other opponents' matches. I watched Mary-Louise Bryant up against Tanya McLeod, Olga Zeman vs. Amparo Pereira. I watched tape of Stepanova up against everybody. Even me.

And my father and I adjusted. I learned to take it out of the air earlier with Stepanova, slow the game down against Mary-Louise, come out of the gate strong against Tanya McLeod, try to piss off Pereira.

Throughout '75, I climbed my way up the rankings.

61st

59th

30th
18th
16th
12th
11th

During the fall of '75, I finally got the chance to go head-to-head with Stepanova for a title when the two of us made the final of the Thunderbird Classic. I'd never beaten her in a meaningful tournament before. But as we got to the third set, I felt a groundedness, an energy, and started to sense that familiar hum in my bones.

When the score was 6–6, we went to a tiebreaker. I kept on her. The tiebreaker went to 12–12, but I could see her slowing. She double-faulted, and then I served an ace.

And it was over. I'd won.

Afterward, during my press conference, it was confirmed that my win had officially broken me into the top ten. I was seventeen years old and the number ten player in the world. I smiled when I heard the news. One of the reporters commented, "We are not used to seeing you smile. You should smile more." I immediately pulled my lips tight.

In her post-match, someone asked Stepanova, "You and Carrie Soto have proven to be well-matched competitors. Do you agree?"

She said nothing for a moment and then leaned into the microphone. "My shoulder started aching earlier this morning. I played through the pain, but it took a toll. Carrie would not have won otherwise. She does not have the ability to beat me when I am playing my best."

"Is this a joke?" I said to my father as I watched it on TV. "She was fine! She wasn't injured! What a crock!"

My father insisted I ignore her, and so I tried.

By the end of the year, I was ranked number four. Stepanova was three.

In an interview with *SportsPages*, Paulina was asked how she felt about "Soto vs. Stepanova" becoming a rivalry for the ages. We had gone up against each other in the final of two Slams that year, as well as a number of tournaments around the world. Sportswriters were calling it "the Cold War."

"Carrie Soto, people talk about her a lot now, yes," Stepanova said. "But she needs to lose about ten pounds or so if she wants to win against me when I am not injured. That is not a rivalry."

When I read that quote, I put the magazine down and then kicked a trash can in my hotel suite, sending it across the room and making a dent in the wall.

My father shook his head. "Control yourself, *hija*. You are not competing with her. You are competing with yourself."

"I *am* competing with her," I said. "And I'm losing."

"This is a long game," my father said to me as we were flying back from the Australian Open in 1976, where I'd lost to Stepanova in the semifinals and she'd gone on to win the damn thing.

"I'm done with the long game," I said. The flight attendants had just served us a full breakfast, and my father had devoured his. Mine was untouched. "I need to win every single time I go up against her," I said.

"She is playing better than you right now," he said. "But you are capable of more. That is your secret, that you have even more potential. We will figure it out."

I slammed my window shade up. "I don't want potential. I want wins now."

Despite the fact that I was eighteen, my father put his hand gently on my shoulder and said, "We are Sotos. We do not yell, and we do not throw temper tantrums if we're not good enough. What do we do?"

"We get good enough," I said as I turned my head away from him and settled my gaze out the window. For a moment, I couldn't remember which country we'd left and which we were going to. I looked down, and that was when I remembered we were over the Pacific.

"*Bien,*" he said.

A few moments later, I turned back to him. "I'm holding my serve pretty well against her. She's having to win in tiebreakers half the time."

"*Es cierto,*" my dad said, not looking up from his magazine.

"But she has more power than me," I said. "I have trouble taking her pace off the ball sometimes. I'm picking the wrong shots."

He was silent.

"You said I'm supposed to be the greatest tennis player of a generation. You said I had to grow into who I would become. What are we going to do? I need you . . ." I said. "I need you to figure it out."

He closed his magazine and looked at me. "*Dame un minuto.* I'm thinking."

He stood up, stretched out his back, and started pacing along the aisle of the plane. Then suddenly he was back. "Your slice."

"My slice?"

"Let's refine it, make it sharper, make it bulletproof. It will take away all of her momentum. We make it deadly and then . . ." He nodded. "That will kill her."

My father and I practiced my slice for months. We made it my very best shot. We perfected it over hours and hours of drills. My angle was brutal. And I knew how and when to implement it.

Amparo Pereira capsized when I used it. Tanya McLeod didn't stand a chance against me anymore. Olga Zeman fell to her knees that summer and cried when I beat her in straight sets. After that match, a reporter asked me on camera what advice I had for the opponents struggling to keep up with me.

I said, "Honestly? Get better at tennis."

That sound bite was played on every single sports show in the country. My father would shake his head every time. "That was unnecessary, Carolina."

"But that's what *I* did," I'd remind him. "Why is everyone so sensitive about the truth?"

"They are calling you 'Cold-Hearted Carrie' now," my dad lamented once.

Nobody liked my style. But who could argue with the results? It wasn't just McLeod and Pereira and Zeman I was taking down.

Stepanova was crumbling. I'd annihilated her with that slice in the semis at Wimbledon. And then two days later, I won my first Grand Slam when I defeated Mary-Louise Bryant in the final.

My first Wimbledon trophy.

The next day after winning, I slept in until eight for the first time in what felt like years. When I woke up, I could hear the television in the living room of the suite, my father delighting in the moment we both had worked so hard for.

"We may just be seeing the beginning of a stunning Wimbledon career," I heard the announcer say as I got out of bed. "Carrie Soto's slice has proven to be a dangerous weapon indeed, as it helped her take down fellow American Mary-Louise Bryant yesterday. And, maybe more notable, it slayed her fiercest rival, Paulina Stepanova, in the semis."

"Although, Brent," the commenter said, "Paulina has gone on record as saying her ankle was giving her trouble."

I marched into the living room and shut the TV off.

US Open 1976.

Stepanova and I were in the semifinals.

I took the first set easily. We were 5–4 in the second. All I had to do was hold the next game and I'd take Stepanova in straight sets, passing through to the final.

I served an ace right on the line. Stepanova stomped her foot. She walked over to the umpire and appealed, but it held. My point.

Stepanova walked back to the baseline, shaking her head. When fans booed on her behalf, she put her hand to her chest and pouted, as if she were the victim of a bad call.

I ignored her and served again, watching it land on the line and then bounce far and high.

Stepanova ran for it, lunging as far as she could. She returned it but landed on the edge of her foot, which buckled under her weight, rolling her ankle.

By the time I hit the ball back over, she was folded over on the ground. A medic came rushing onto the court. Soon he was holding Stepanova up as she started hobbling off. They called a medical time-out.

I sat down and wiped my forehead. I ate a banana. I drank some water. Shortly after, an official came up to me.

"Ms. Stepanova is asking if you would consider a delay."

"What?" I said.

"Her team is requesting more time for her to have her ankle wrapped and assess the injury."

"A delay?" I said, taking another sip of water. "No, absolutely not. If the roles were reversed, she would not grant me a delay in a million years. No."

The man went to tell Stepanova. I looked over at my father in the box. I could tell he understood exactly what had been asked. He nodded at me.

As we made our way back onto the court, Stepanova stared at me with a scowl. I truly could not believe it. What right did she have to be angry?

"If you really are hurt, you should retire," I said. "As you always tell the press, I only beat you when you're injured."

"Never," she spat.

"It just kills you to think I might be better than you, doesn't it?" I said.

She laughed. "You cannot be better than me if I'm always above you in the rankings, *druzhok.*"

The crowd was cheering for her. She waved to them as she limped to the baseline.

She was brilliant. She knew she was going to lose this match, but at least now she had the sympathy of the world. She'd somehow seized the moral high ground by implying that I was exploiting her injuries for the win.

She had trapped me.

Fuck it, I thought. If she was insisting on playing, then she had to be willing to play on that ankle. And I was going to go after it.

I sent a thunderous serve right to the far corner of the box, making her run to meet it. When she managed a return, I sent it to the opposite side of the court. I watched her scramble to it, limping. The grimace on her face made it clear she was in agony. I took the point.

I could imagine it—could almost *feel* it—myself. The tenderness of her ankle, the twinging agony that ran through her as she had to turn on it, the awareness that it might buckle again at any moment.

Still, this was match point.

Before Stepanova hobbled back to the baseline, she took a step toward the net and said, "This is the only way you'll win against me. So I hope you enjoy it."

"You understand I'm going to run you into the ground, right?" I said, not bothering to keep my voice low. The cameras were on us; the umpire was watching. "I'm gonna make you run so hard on that ankle you're going to break it in half."

My heart started to bang against my chest. I walked to the baseline. I took a deep breath. And then I served the ball, as fast as a bullet, right to her fucking feet.

She jumped out of the way—falling onto the ground. She was in tears.

"Game, set, and match. Soto."

Half the crowd was cheering, and the other half was booing louder than I'd ever heard before.

In the post-match interview, one of the reporters asked me if I felt bad, going after Stepanova's ankle. I leaned into the microphone and said, "No."

The room went so silent I could hear my own heartbeat.

The next morning, under a headline dubbing the match "The Coldest War," one of the journalists called me "the Battle Axe." Within days, it had become my name.

JANUARY 23, 1979

BY THE TIME I WAS TWENTY, I HAD FOUR SLAM TITLES. TWO WERE AT Wimbledon, one was at the US Open, and I'd beaten Stepanova in the final of the Australian Open in a nearly three-hour battle, one of the longest and most-watched matches in tennis history.

Our rivalry dominated the sports pages. THE COLD WAR CONTINUES ON THE COURT. SOTO WINS SLAMS, BUT STEPANOVA TAKES MORE TITLES. STEPANOVA VS. SOTO GETS UGLY IN LONDON. And yet, in the end-of-the-year rankings, she still took the top spot.

The rivalry had become so popular—and made such good television—that it made my father famous too. The camera loved the handsome Javier Soto. The papers all printed photos of "the Jaguar" sitting proudly in the players' box. One of them was captioned *The man who taught Carrie Soto everything she knows.*

In 1978, he released a book, *Beautiful Fundamentals,* that hit the bestseller lists and quickly became a mainstay of tennis instruction.

There was even a moment when he became a recurring guest on *Johnny Carson*.

People loved him. And he took to it. He seemed satisfied with what we had done together, what we'd accomplished. His dreams had been fulfilled.

Mine had not.

"I should be number one," I said to him as we ate lunch at a tennis club in Florida. I'd just beaten Stepanova in the final at Houston at an Avon Championships event. "At this point, I've earned it."

"Let's enjoy our food, please," my father said.

"I want to hold the record for the most Grand Slams for any player ever," I said, my voice rising. "And I can't do that until I destroy her *every time* we play."

"Hija . . ." my father said, a gentle warning. He maintained his insistence that I never make a scene on or off the court. And I did my best, but it required a great effort. And as a result, sportscasters started referring to me as "stiff" and "robotic."

I'd seen more than a few op-eds in sports magazines about how *Carrie Soto acts more like a machine than a woman* and *The Battle Axe never seems to enjoy her wins.* Other players on the tour would mention in interviews that I wasn't very friendly. As if I was supposed to befriend the very same women I was defeating week after week.

I would read tabloids in airports, and whenever my name was mentioned, there was always some crack about how I didn't smile enough.

I can't tell you how many times I flipped through a magazine only to come across someone trashing me in print. I'd hand it to my father so that I wouldn't look at it. But five minutes later, I'd take it back and continue torturing myself.

No matter how good I was on the court, I was never good enough for the public.

It wasn't enough to play nearly perfect tennis. I had to do that and *also* be charming. And that charm had to appear effortless.

I couldn't seem to be *trying* to get them to like me. I could not let anyone ever suspect that I might *want* their approval. I saw the way they wrote about a player like Tanya McLeod, the way they had contempt for her for trying so hard to be cute. I had contempt for it too.

But c'mon. That's an awfully small needle to thread.

And the eye of that needle just got smaller and smaller the more successful I became.

It was okay to win as long as I acted *surprised* when I did and attributed it to luck. I should never let on how much I *wanted* to win or, worse, that I believed I *deserved* to win. And I should never, under any circumstances, admit that I did not believe all of my opponents were just as worthy as I was.

The bulk of the commentators . . . they wanted a woman whose eyes would tear up with gratitude, as if she owed them her victory, as if she owed them everything she had.

I don't know if it had ever been within me to act like that, but by the age of twenty, it was long gone.

And it cost me.

By the time I was a Grand Slam champion, ranked number two in the world, I had fewer endorsement deals than any of the other players in the top ten. I had no real friendships on the tour or elsewhere.

And while I'd slept around a lot, the longest relationship I'd ever had was with an actor I'd been with a few times at the Chateau Marmont when he was filming in L.A.

He was a huge tennis fan. He'd been there when I won Wimbledon the year before. Maybe it was because of that that I had thought he might actually *like* me. But after a few weeks, without warning, he stopped calling.

I convinced myself that he'd lost my number. So I tracked down his agent and tried to leave him a message. Upon hearing his agent's cringing pause, I realized he hadn't lost my number at all.

So I fucking better be ranked number one. What else did I have?

"Stepanova's not as good as I am, Dad," I said. "But she's still squeaking out way more titles than she should, and that's how she's beating me in the end-of-the-year rankings."

"You go weeks at a time where you're ranked number one," he said. "The end-of-the-year ranking is not the best metric."

"I'm supposed to be the greatest *by all metrics*," I said.

My father put his fork down and looked at me as I continued.

"If I am not number one at the end of the year, it is because I did not win enough of the right matches, and thus I am not yet the greatest."

My father frowned. "*Como quieras*, Carolina."

"We need to work *harder*," I said. "Both of us. We need to be out on the court twice as much. You need to look inside your little bag of tricks and come up with another angle I'm not seeing. Stepanova has gotten quicker now, to keep up with me. Have you noticed that?"

"*Hija*, you are everything we wanted you to be. And time will show that you are the better player," he said. "Stepanova's going to be out in just a few years. She's already ruining her shoulder. And then your reign will be longer."

"If I am number one only after she's done, I'm not the greatest. She is."

"But you will go down in history as the more decorated player."

"I want the record to show that *now*. We need a plan."

My father pushed his plate away. "*Hija*, I don't know how much better you can get."

"What are you talking about?"

"I think I have done you a disservice," my father finally said, looking me in the eye. "I told you from such a young age that you could be the very best. But I never explained to you that it's about aiming for excellence, not about stats."

"What?"

"I am just saying that when you were a child, I spoke in . . . grandiosities. But, Carrie, there is no actual unequivocal greatest in the world. Tennis doesn't work like that. The world doesn't work like that."

"I'm not going to sit here and be insulted."

"How am I insulting you? I am telling you there is no one way to define the greatest of all time. You're focusing right now on rankings. But what about the person who gets the most titles over the span of their career? Are they the greatest? How about the person with the fastest recorded serve? Or the highest paid? I'm asking you to take a minute and recalibrate your expectations."

"Excuse me?" I said, standing up. "Recalibrate my expectations?"

"Carrie," my father said. "Please listen to me."

"No," I said, putting my hands up. "Don't use your calm voice and act like you're being nice. Because you're not. Having someone on this planet who is as good as me—or better—means I have not achieved my goal. If you would like to coach someone who is fine being second, go coach someone else."

I threw my napkin down and walked out of the restaurant. I made my way through the lobby to the parking lot. I was still furious by the time my father caught up to me by my car.

"Carolina, stop, you're making a scene," he said.

"Do you have any idea how hard it is?" I shouted. It felt shocking to me, to hear my own voice that loud. "To give everything you have to something and still not be able to grasp it! To fail to reach the top day after day and be expected to do it with a smile on your face? Maybe I'm not allowed to make a scene on the court, but I will make a scene here, Dad. It is the very least you can give me. Just for once in my life, let me scream about something!"

There were people gathering in the parking lot, and each one of them, I could tell, knew my name. Knew my father's name. Knew exactly what they were witnessing.

"WHAT ARE YOU ALL LOOKING AT? GO ON ABOUT YOUR SAD LITTLE DAYS!"

I got in my convertible and drove away.

· · ·

The second I got back to my hotel suite, I sat down on the sofa and grabbed the phone off the side table. I put it in front of me and stared at it for a brief moment before picking up the receiver and dialing.

"Hello?"

"Hi, it's Carrie." My heart rate was rising; I could feel my face flushing. I kept looking at the door, knowing my father could walk through it at any moment.

"The Battle Axe! Finally!" Lars Van de Berg said. "I have left you countless messages."

He'd been calling more and more as Mary-Louise's career began to plateau.

"Yes, well," I said. "It has been a complicated call to return."

"Yes, I'd imagine it is."

"I'm the number two player in the world," I said. I cradled the phone between my ear and my shoulder. I hunched over, my elbows on my knees. "I should be number one."

"I agree," Lars said.

"Javier thinks that being second is a great achievement and I should be proud," I said.

"Well, he is your father. I have three children, and I want, very much, for them to be happy," Lars said. "But sometimes I think being the very best is antithetical to being happy."

"Yes," I said. "*Exactly.*" I stood up and carried the phone with me to my balcony. I watched the palm trees sway in the wind. There was a breeze coming through, and I was thankful for it, despite the January chill in Florida.

"Carrie, listen to me. I am one of the best coaches in women's tennis, you know this. Everyone has known this since I coached Chrissy Salvos to take eight titles in '62. What Mary-Louise and I have done together is truly spectacular, given her ability. But she is not performing at the level I need."

"This would hasten the end of her career," I say. "If you were to leave her now."

"It might. But you cannot worry about that."

"She'd be worried about it, if the situation were reversed. She'd be considering my feelings."

"Yes," he said, then sighed. "She would. And she wonders why she never reached her full potential. Look, I have never coached a player with as much natural talent as you. And as coaches, we can't do our best work without the *perfect* player. I will never know what I am truly capable of until I have the chance to coach someone as good as you. I need you to do my greatest work. I am a sculptor. And you are the finest piece of clay I could ever work with. I saw that back in '68 when you first played Mary-Louise. And I will tell you now what I told your father then: He has done a fine job honing your talent. And I can take it from here."

I looked back at the door of the suite. "What are you going to do that my father has not done?"

"Are you ready to have this conversation now?" he asked.

I stared at the people walking on the streets below me. The cars pulling away from the curb into traffic. The family chatting on the corner while they waited for a walk signal.

"It is the only reason I called," I said.

"Well," he said. "The gap between the player you are today and the player you want to be—"

"I want to be the greatest tennis player in the world," I said.

"That gap is not big. We are talking about that vital half-percent improvement. And that's not found in changing your strategy. It's in shortening the nanosecond of time between getting to the ball and slicing it across the court. It is going to be found in the minute change you make to the angle of your serve. The details are fine, and they are going to get finer. It is going to be nearly imperceptible, the ways we need to change your game. No one will be able to see it from the outside, but Stepanova is going to feel it. Every time she loses to you for the next ten years."

I could feel my pulse in my ears; my face felt hot. "Okay," I said. "How do we do that?"

"Are you cross-training?" he asked.

"I run and do drills."

Lars laughed. "That's not enough. Stepanova is right about one thing—you need to lose at least a couple pounds. We need you doing sprints, lunges, weight training. You can jump higher to hit overheads. You rarely do—it's a weakness in your game, in my opinion. I want to see what happens when you blast off the court into the air. Take out some of Stepanova's lobs before they hit the ground. We start there and see where we get."

"No," I said, shaking my head. "If we are doing this, I need to know right now that you believe I can bury her. That I can be number one."

"If I am your coach and you do not become the number-one-ranked player for the year," he said, "I will be disgusted."

A shield was forming over me, a hard edge. "Okay," I said. "I will call you soon to discuss this more. Don't say a word. To anyone."

When I turned back into my suite, my father was standing by the coffee table.

He was staring at me, his eyes wide and tearing up. I had never seen this version of him before.

"What have you done?" he said softly. His voice was barely a whisper. It cracked as it escaped his mouth. "Carolina."

"I cannot have a coach who is less ambitious for me than I am for myself," I said. My voice was strong and clear despite the fact that I could not look at him.

"You're misunderstanding me if you think that's the case," my father said. "*Y lo sabés.*"

"I *don't* know that," I said.

"*Cariño,* since the time you could hold a racket, I have told you that you have the potential to be extraordinary," Dad said. "I do not know what more ambition a person can have for their child."

"You said you believed I was born to be *the greatest,*" I said. "And now, suddenly, I'm supposed to settle for what I have. For second best."

"That's not what I said. I said that you are already great. That you have achieved everything I dreamed for you."

"Why? Because you've sold enough books now?"

My father's jaw dropped. "How could you say that?"

I didn't respond. He already knew. If a coach needs clay, my father had made me his.

"When I see you play, I see perfection," he said. "I see the player I always believed you could be. So be happy, right here and now. Because of what you have done, who you've become. And not on some condition of being number one."

"But why stop striving *now*, Dad? You've raised me to be *the very best*. That means number one. And I'm not yet. Why are you changing the rules?"

My father sat down in the chair next to him. But I could not sit down.

"At least be honest," I said, shaking my head. "*Decime la verdad, papá.*" My eyes were burning and starting to tear. "Do you not believe I can do it?" I asked him. "Do you not think I can knock her out of first place?"

He closed his eyes and sighed. I stared at him, wiping away the tear that fell out of my eye. "After all this time," I said, "have you given up on me?"

He did not open his eyes. He did not respond.

"*Respondeme*," I said. "*¿Creés que puedo hacerlo?*"

He threw his hands into the air. "Why won't you listen to what I'm trying to tell you, Carolina?"

I stepped closer to him. My breath slowed; my mouth turned down. "Do you think I can beat her, Dad?" I asked him. "Yes or no."

He finally looked up at me, and I swear my heart started breaking before he even said it. "I do not know."

I closed my eyes and tried to stay upright, but my legs nearly gave out. I sat down, but then just as quickly, I was back on my feet.

"*Te podés ir,*" I said.

I ran to my hotel room door and opened it. "*¡ANDATE DE ACÁ!*" I said to him.

"Carolina," my father said.

"Get out of my room," I said. "We're done."

"Carolina, you cannot be done with your father."

"I'm talking to you as my coach," I said. "Get out."

My father stood, his shoulders low. His eyelids half closed, suddenly heavy. He hung his head.

"*Te amo, hija,*" he said as he walked into the hallway.

I shut the door behind him.

In the morning, I got up and went to the court alone. My father flew home to L.A. later that day.

1979–1982

SOON AFTER, I BEGAN TRAINING WITH LARS SIX DAYS A WEEK, EVEN ON match days. Within a few months, I'd lost three pounds of fat and gained a pound of muscle, almost entirely in my arms and shoulders.

My serve got bigger. I could run half a second faster. My ground-strokes got harder.

But it was my jump that improved the most. Lars had me getting higher than I'd ever gone. Suddenly, I had better angles on my serves, I was taking balls out of the air faster, and I was returning shots that were nearly *unreturnable*. I hadn't seen that big a difference in my performance since the work on my slice. It was now almost impossible to get a ball past me.

By September, I'd beaten Stepanova at the Italian and French Opens, advanced further than her at Wimbledon.

The morning of the first round of the US Open, I went into the locker room seeded second. I knew that if I played Stepanova, it would not be until the final. There were players all around the lockers chatting with one another. I didn't make eye contact.

Suze Carter, a seventeen-year-old player new to the tour, came up to me. "I hope you win," she said. "Everyone's saying that if you take the trophy, there's no way Stepanova can hold on to number one."

Ines Dell'oro, a volleyer who had been around a few years, put her hand on Suze's shoulder. "Don't waste your breath. The Battle Axe doesn't talk to us," she said. "We are beneath her."

I looked at Suze. "Thank you," I said.

And then I looked at Ines. "I am ranked number two. And you are ranked—what? Maybe thirty? So in this case, yes, you are beneath me."

As predicted, Stepanova and I met in the final.

And while the end-of-the-year rankings were still months away, she and I both knew the stakes of the match. It would determine who ended the year number one.

And over the course of two hours and ten minutes, I took the match and championship.

After the cheering and the award ceremony, as I made my way back to the locker room, I saw Lars in the tunnel standing there, grinning. "*Prachtig*, Soto! Great air, just like I taught you," he said. "And now, you will end this year best in the world." He smacked me on my back, and then suddenly he was gone. He'd left to talk to the reporters.

I didn't take a step toward the lockers. I stood there, unmoving. I was waiting for it to feel the way I'd always imagined it would. For someone to hug me and tell me I had vanquished the enemy like the Greeks against Troy . . .

But, of course, there was none of that.

• • •

That fall, I beat Stepanova at the US Indoor, the Thunderbird Classic, and the Porsche Grand Prix. With her shoulder out of commission at the Emeron Lion Cup, I took her down in straight sets.

In December—having been ranked number one for thirty straight weeks—I flew to Melbourne. The Australian Open started on Christmas Eve. In a little less than a week, the end-of-the-year rankings would come out.

That night, as I sat in my hotel room, hearing Christmas music from the streets below, I finally picked up the phone to call my father. It had been almost eleven months since we had spoken.

"Hello?"

His voice, once such an everyday presence that it was as if it were my own, had been gone from my life. I expected it to sound foreign or strange to me now. But instead, it felt utterly familiar, as if nothing had changed.

"*Hola, papá. Feliz Navidad.*"

The line was quiet for a moment, and I wondered, briefly, if he'd hung up.

"*Feliz Navidad, cariño.* I am so incredibly proud of you."

My chest began to heave, and I could not stop the tears from falling down my face. He was quiet as I caught my breath.

"*Pichona,* you have to know that whatever happens between us, I am always proud of you. Always watching you."

"I miss you," I said.

My dad laughed. "You think I've been having such a grand old time?"

I dried my eyes.

"But you are doing beautifully," he said. "So you keep going. You fight for what you want. Like you always have. And I'll be here for you."

I ended the year as the number-one-ranked player on the women's tour. When it became official, I popped open a bottle of champagne by myself in my hotel room. But then I couldn't bring myself to pour a glass for only one person.

After the Australian Open, I flew to my father's house. When he opened the door, he was holding two glasses of Dom Pérignon. I hugged him and drank the whole glass right there at his door.

Later, I unpacked my bags in his guest room. My father seared steaks on the grill. And we tried to find a new way of speaking.

Should I ask my father why there was a women's razor and an extra toothbrush in his bathroom? Was he going to ask about the tabloid photos that had recently started appearing of me being spotted outside hotels with a few different men?

Instead, our conversations only went as deep as "It feels wetter this winter than in the past, yes?" and "Oh, so you've been drinking Fresca now instead of ginger ale?"

But my second day home, he came into the living room and asked me if I wanted to go out for ice cream sandwiches.

"Ice cream sandwiches?" I said. "What are you talking about?"

"You don't remember when you were a kid and you always wanted an ice cream sandwich or a sundae?"

"That . . . doesn't sound like me."

My father sighed and picked up his car keys. "Come with me, *por favor, hija.*"

I looked at my watch. "I mean, I should get to the courts soon to practice."

"It will take a half hour," he said. "You can spare a half hour."

That afternoon, I sat in the front seat of my father's new Mercedes and ate an ice cream sandwich beside him as we people-watched. "These are good," I said.

He nodded. "I'm sorry I never let you have one."

"No," I said. "I'm better for it."

I could tell from the look on his face that he wasn't sure that was true. And I thought, *See, Dad, this is why you're not my coach anymore.*

But after that, something broke open between us. We went to the movies together. We went out to eat. I bought him a new panama hat. He gave me his old chessboard, "because you must always keep thinking four moves ahead."

On my last day before heading back out on the tour, I was packing when my father came and found me. "I wanted to talk to you about something," he said as I gathered pair after pair of Adidas. They were my biggest endorsement deal after Wilson rackets, and I had been designing a shoe line with them, the Carrie Soto Break Points. While I was not as popular as Stepanova or McLeod, I did have my fans. You couldn't deny that when I was playing, you were going to see a show. And the number of spectators—and thus endorsement deals—were starting to reflect that.

"Okay," I said.

"You're getting higher and higher out there on the court, reaching for Stepanova's lobs."

"Yes, I know," I said. I stopped packing and looked at him. "And it's working. I'm beating her every time now."

"But you're landing hard," he said. "Maybe during clay season it won't be too much of a problem, but on the hard courts coming up . . ."

"I'm landing fine."

"Trust me, I know what I'm talking about. You need to bend your leg more when you land. I'm worried your knee—"

"Lars says it's fine. Without adding in that height, I'd never—"

"I don't want to talk about Lars with you," my dad said.

"And I don't want to talk about my *tennis game* with *you*."

"*Está bien,*" my father said. And he left the room.

We talked on the phone every day I was on tour in the early eighties. And we started opening up about things we'd never discussed before.

He finally started talking about my mother, telling me how much he missed her. I told him I thought about her when things around me got too quiet. He told me about the things she had wanted for me.

"She never thought tennis was terribly important," he told me once, when I was in Rome for the Italian Open. "She thought joy was more important."

I laughed. "Winning is joy," I said.

"Exactly, *pichona*, I tried to tell her that. But she was less competitive than you and me. More happy in the moment. And she was so open-minded and accepting about things. She probably would have been fine with all your dating. But, *cariño,* I don't know if I want to see many more of these photos in the magazines of you and your . . . suitors."

I sighed. "I'm having fun. That's all."

I didn't know how to tell my father that these men weren't suitors, that they rarely even called me twice. But I let him assume that it was me who chose not to see them again, instead of the other way around.

I was "the Battle Axe." I was cold. I was a machine. Sure, a lot of them were intrigued by the idea of the sheer power of my body. But I was not the woman that men were looking to bring home to their mothers.

I reminded myself not to fall for the bullshit they peddled. How much they admired me, how I was unlike anyone else they had ever met before. So often there was talk of going on vacation together, ideas of renting a yacht in the south of France, conversations about some imaginary future. I knew I had to ignore the promises they made so casually, the promises I wanted so badly for at least one of them to keep.

"Maybe you can find someone good for you," my father said. "Someone for more than one date."

"It's not that simple, Dad. It's not . . ." I wanted to get off the phone. But at the same time, I did want to tell someone, anyone, the growing fear that had started feeling as if it could corrode the lining of my stomach. *No one wants me.*

"You are picking the wrong men, like that Bowe Huntley. What are you doing being photographed coming out of a hotel with that walking tantrum? He's the number two player in the ATP and he's screaming at the umpire? That's not the guy you pick."

"So then who is the guy I pick?"

"That Brandon Randall is a good one."

Brandon Randall was the number one player in the ATP. They called him "the Nice Guy of Tennis."

"*Sí, claro, papá*," I said. "I would love to go out on a date with Brandon Randall. But he's married. To Nina Riva, a swimsuit model."

"Mick Riva's kid?" my dad said. "I cannot stand that guy. Oh. Well, someone *like* Brandon, then. A nice guy. Go for a nice guy. Please."

1983

BRANDON RANDALL *WAS* MARRIED. AND HE WAS *NOT* AS NICE A GUY AS my father thought he was.

I know because I went back to his hotel room with him in Paris after the final of the French Open in 1983.

I'd never won the French Open before. It's a clay court, which is the hardest kind for a fast-moving serve-and-volley player like me. Plenty of greats have gone their entire careers without winning it.

But then I defeated Renee Levy in the final that year, and in that moment, I felt the breathtaking joy of knowing I had the rare distinction of claiming each and every Slam.

Brandon and I ran into each other in the elevator the weekend we each took our singles titles. When we stopped on Brandon's floor, he took a step out but then put his arm out to stop the elevator door from closing. He looked me in the eye and said, "Do you want to grab a cocktail in my room? A toast, maybe? To our success."

I searched his face for some clue as to what he wanted—what he was really asking. I wasn't quite sure. But I still said yes.

As he made me a drink, he told me his marriage to Nina was on the rocks. "She doesn't understand me," he said. "Though I get the distinct impression you do."

I am embarrassed by how unoriginal it all was.

In the morning, as we lay underneath the bright white sheets, Brandon told me he thought that I might be the only person in the world who made him feel less alone.

"I try to tell the people around me the pressure I feel, just how low the lows are sometimes. But they can't relate. And I'm kicking myself because it seems so obvious now: Who else but you, my equal, could ever truly understand?"

It was presumptuous of him to call us equals. I had significantly more Slams than he did. Still, I let him compare us.

Lying in his bed, with the sun shining through the big windows, I felt like maybe I wasn't destined to be alone after all. Maybe I was the sort of woman who was so singular, so exceptional, that I could only form a connection with someone like Brandon, someone as driven as me.

I feared it might still end up a one-night thing. But Brandon kept calling. He kept calling! This closeness between us, it continued growing, like a balloon filling with air.

There was a moment, there in the middle of it all—when he and I were together in secret and winning titles and taking Wimbledon side by side—that it felt like fate. I could look back at my own history with men and see that every single one of them had been a domino that had to fall in order to trigger this one.

For the months we were together, I finally belonged to somebody. And it was just as good as I'd made it out to be.

During the summer of 1983, I demolished Paulina Stepanova every time we played each other. Her shoulder, once just an excuse, was now deteriorating rapidly. She'd fallen thirty spots in the rankings.

Just before the US Open, she announced she was retiring. I was shocked that the woman who had once been my greatest adversary would become a footnote.

Upon retirement, Stepanova had only nine Slams to her name. I had twelve. And now she was done.

The morning after the announcement, Brandon called down to room service and had them bring up breakfast. When it arrived, he congratulated me on burying Stepanova once and for all.

"It's over," he said. "There's no more rivalry. There's no question who came out the victor."

I put my hands over my face, my smile so wide I had to contain it.

He kissed me, and I thought, *I have everything.*

Like a complete fucking dope.

We got caught in late July. He left Nina shortly after, and the tabloids reported it all that August—which was when the cruelty of what I was doing became obvious.

It was on the cover of every magazine in the checkout aisle. LOVE–LOVE: BRANDON AND CARRIE SET UP LOVE NEST AT BEVERLY HILLS HOTEL, LEAVING NINA RIVA BROKENHEARTED and BRANDON AND CARRIE TAKE A BATTLE AXE TO NINA RIVA'S HEART.

And yet I didn't end it.

Not when the paparazzi started following us or when *NowThis* showed a photo of Nina crying outside a grocery store in Malibu. Not even when he tried to go back to her and she rejected him. He came crawling back to me, and I stuck with him then too. I was too far gone, too desperate to believe I'd found the real thing.

And after all that, he was the one who ended it when he left me for another woman in December.

It took a while for me to dust myself off. But even then, I couldn't ignore the power of the hatred of the fans in the stands. The tabloid headlines only got worse. Things like CARRIE SOTO: LONELY AT THE TOP. And then, perhaps worst of all, WHO COULD LOVE A BATTLE AXE?

I was used to being disliked, but nothing prepared me for being mobbed by paparazzi as I was coming out of a restaurant, having them casually ask things like "How do you feel about the fact that people think you're a whore?"

I wore sunglasses and baseball caps outside. I ran from anybody with a camera. I hid in hotel rooms. I barely looked up into the crowds at my matches. Sportsade dropped me from their commercials; ticket sales for tournaments were down, and people were reporting that it was my fault.

I felt a million things.

But I felt one thing the strongest: Whatever soft parts of my heart I had tentatively exposed to Brandon, it had been a mistake. I would never again be that type of fool.

1984–1989

A LOT OF PEOPLE HATED ME IN 1984. BUT I KEPT MY HEAD DOWN, AND I took three Grand Slams. I set a record for most weeks at number one. And winning, I've found, does sway a lot of people. I seemed to have won some of their affection back.

In 1985, I took Wimbledon for the third year in a row. In 1986, I won it and the US Open.

Going into Wimbledon in '87, I was twenty-nine years old. Everyone was watching to see if I could win my twentieth Slam and set the record for most singles Slam titles. The papers were all saying that surely I was nearing the end of my career.

I won the final match in straight sets. And there it was. My world record.

Just shy of thirty and I was not just great. But *the greatest.* Of all time.

As I stood there on the court, watching the officials walk toward me with the plate, my entire career flashed in front of me.

Doing drills with my father as a kid. Playing Mary-Louise Bryant. Winning juniors, entering the main draws. Climbing up the rankings, improving my slice, learning that jump, defeating Stepanova once and for all. Domination.

I was now the most decorated tennis player by nearly every measure. Most Grand Slam singles titles ever. Most weeks at number one for any player in the history of the tour. Most singles titles, most aces over the course of a career. Most years ending number one. Highest-paid female athlete of all time.

I was the Carrie Soto I had always believed I could be.

I accepted the trophy that day as I had accepted all the others—my face stoic, my speech short. But this time, as I waved and turned to leave, I had to hobble off the court.

My left knee was killing me. It was often aching and tender all day. I'd get sharp pains when I bent it too far or put too much weight on it. I was getting cortisone shots, but they weren't doing enough. It was beginning to slow me down on the court. And while I'd been able to withstand the pain through sheer force of will up until now, I knew I couldn't do so much longer.

"*Hija*," my father said over the phone. "You need surgery."

"Stop," I said, my voice clipped.

But I knew he was right. Before the US Open, my knee was so bad that I had to have painkillers injected directly into it, and I still lost in the semis to Suze Carter. Early the next year, I had to pull out of the Australian Open.

I took some time off, and when I came back, I could not get a foothold. In all of '88, I did not win a single title.

Just before the start of Wimbledon in 1989, Lars sat me down at a hotel gym in London.

"It's over, Carrie," he said. "I have done all I can do. You have achieved what you will achieve."

"No, it's not over. I just . . ." I looked down at the floor and then back up at him, ready to admit what I had long been denying. "I need to get the surgery. Then I can come back."

"Come back so you can lose more? Let everyone see the queen is dead?"

I flinched. "The queen is not dead," I said.

Lars nodded his head. "Carrie, your body, your skills, they always had an expiration date. And it is now. You are thirty-one. It is time."

"I don't know about that. Maybe it is. But maybe it's not."

"It is."

I looked him in the eye, starting to sense what was happening. "You already have another player lined up," I said. "You've already decided."

"It does not matter. Your body is done, Carrie," he said. "I do not want to stick around to see what less-than-perfect version of yourself awaits us on the other end of your surgeries. I'm not interested in it."

"I could bounce back. I could have the best parts of my career ahead of me."

"Not in your thirties," he said. "Don't make me humor you about that. If you continue after Wimbledon, it will be without me as your coach."

Lars stood up and left. And I sat there in the stale, cold gym, staring at a stationary bike. My knee ached just thinking about riding it.

Still, I ignored him and entered the main draw at Wimbledon. For the first time in almost ten years, I did not make it to the round of sixteen.

I fell so far in the rankings that I would have been unseeded at the US Open.

"Get surgery and see where you are," my father said on the phone. I was in New York, preparing to enter the Open as a wild card. He was back in L.A., getting settled into the compound I had bought for the two of us. A main house for me, a guest house for him, a pool, and a tennis court. "You won't know if your knee can be rehabilitated unless you try."

"And take the chance I'll lose again? In front of all of them?" I said. "Do you see how much they are loving this? My failure? No. I won't give it to them. No."

"So what are you going to do?" he said.

"I am not discussing this with you," I said. "Ever. It's not for you to say."

"Okay," he said. *"Está bien."*

Two days later, in August 1989, I pulled out of the US Open and announced my retirement. "I have had a momentous run during a truly outstanding time in the world of tennis," I said as I read my prepared statement at the lectern. "I have achieved everything I set out to achieve. I believe my accomplishments will be remembered in the decades to come. And now, I am done. Thank you."

I did not play a professional match again.

Until now.

THE
COMEBACK

OCTOBER 1994

Three and a half months before Melbourne

I WAKE UP AT SEVEN-FIFTEEN. I DRINK A BLUEBERRY SMOOTHIE AND eat raw unsalted almonds for breakfast. I put on my track pants and a T-shirt. I slip a sweatband across my forehead.

And at eight A.M. on the dot, half a decade after my retirement—and fifteen years since my father last coached me—I step onto my tennis court, prepared to train.

The sun is shining bright against the mountains, and the sky is clear except for the fifty-foot palm trees lining my yard. It is quiet here, even though the frenzy of L.A. traffic is just beyond my gates.

I do not care about the rest of the city. I am focused on *this* court, *this* ground underneath my feet. I will defend my record. I will take down Nicki Chan.

"We begin," my father says. He is in a polo shirt and chinos. Looking at him, I can see he's so much grayer since the last time we were on the court together, skinnier too. But he stands just as tall as he did when I was a child.

"I'm ready," I say. He cannot hold back his smile.

"Three things I want to get a good sense of today," he says.

I bend down and reach for my toes, stretching my legs. "My serve, first," I say as I bounce, grabbing my right foot with both hands, then my left.

My father shakes his head. "No, I'm *telling you* what I want to see—you're not guessing. It's not a quiz."

I stand up and blink at his tone. "Okay."

He sits down on the bench on the side of the court, and I put one foot up beside him and stretch again.

My father starts counting off. "*Uno,*" he says, "your serve. By which I mean, I want to know what kind of firepower you still have, I want to see your control."

"*Está bien.*"

"Second is footwork. I want to know: How fast are you getting from one end of the court to the other? How agile can you be?"

"*Perfecto. ¿Qué más?* Endurance?"

He ignores me. "Third, endurance."

I nod.

"Your endurance greatly improved with Lars," my father says. I flinch at the mention of Lars's name. "What did he add to your training to get you there?"

I am not sure how to respond, unsure how to have this conversation with him. "You mean other than the jump?" I finally say.

"We're not putting your knee through too much jumping. You had surgery to fix your ACL and you're not gonna tear it up again—"

"*Bueno, papá. Basta, ya lo entendi.*"

"So what else did he add to your game?" He meets my gaze and holds it. "*Contame.*"

"Cross-training," I say. "You and I always ran, but he added aerobics, calisthenics, weight lifting."

He nods and rolls his eyes. "You train for tennis doing things other than tennis. What a genius."

"You asked. And it worked."

My father nods. "*Bien, bien, bien.*"

We are both quiet for a moment. I can hear the gardener starting a lawn mower at the estate behind mine. "So . . . do you want to do that or . . . ?"

My father nods. "*Sí, estoy pensando.*"

I wait for him to finish his thought. I start rolling my neck.

My father says, "Nicki's going to assume her best bet is to wear you out."

"Anyone playing me is going to assume that. I'm thirty-seven years old. All you have to do is wear out the old lady."

My dad laughs. "You have no idea what it feels like to be old."

"In the grand scheme of things, Dad, sure," I tell him. "But in tennis . . ."

He nods. "So the most important thing we can do for you right now is work on your stamina."

"Yes, agreed."

"So, let's start with—every day—you run ten miles."

I haven't run ten miles in a few years. But fine. "And then we start hitting balls?"

He shakes his head. "And then squats and sprints, plus jump rope for the footwork. I'm assuming that's what you'd do the most with Lars? Then you'll swim, to further condition your muscles but keep it low impact. Then you can have lunch, and then in the afternoon, you hit."

"I'm gonna die," I say.

"Don't whine."

"I am not going to perform a triathlon every day and *not* whine about it," I say.

My father starts to open his mouth, and I stop him. "I'm not a child anymore. Sometimes I'm going to have an opinion. Sometimes, when I'm ten miles and fifty laps in, I'm going to complain. But I'll do what you say, and you deal with my attitude, and maybe one day soon, we'll win another Slam title, *¿Está bien?*"

He looks at me, emotionless for a moment. And then he smiles and holds out his hand. "*Perfecto.*"

• • •

Every day for seven days, I put on my running shoes and take off.

I run as fast as I can as my father rides in a golf cart next to me, yelling, "*¡Más rápido! ¡Más rápido!*"

My feet hit the pavement, over and over and over again. He yells, "If you are not ahead, you are behind!"

"*Sí,*" I say each time. "*Lo sé.*"

"*¡Vamos, más rápido!*" he yells the second he can tell I'm slowing down. "We are not out for a nice jog! We are running to win a title!"

I try to yell back to him from time to time, in whatever language comes to me first. But by the end of ten miles, I stop wasting any extra breath.

The runs are manageable. It is after that, when I'm jumping rope as he stands there barking out things like "*¡Más rápido!*" and "*¡No pares!*" that make me want to scream.

Instead, I focus on the burning of my calves, the ache of my arms.

And then there is the swimming. Lap after lap. As my legs and shoulders start to slow from wear, my father stands on the edge of the pool chanting, "*Usá esos brazos,*" like some sort of military command.

Every day when I come out of the pool, my arms are limp, my legs wobbly. I am a newborn calf, unable to find my footing.

On the seventh day, after my last lap, I can barely get myself up the ladder. Everything hurts—my hamstrings and quads are sore, my shoulders and biceps ache. I wasn't able to stay on my lap pace.

I lie down on the deck, and my father comes over and hands me a towel. He sits beside me.

I look up at him. I can feel his frown before it makes its way to his face.

"How bad is it?" I ask.

My father tilts his head from side to side. "You're half a mile per hour too slow on the runs. Your form needs work. Your swimming is . . ." He inhales deeply. "*Mirá,* considering your age and how long you've been off the court, it's impressive. But you are not where you need to be to win a Slam, *cariño.*"

"*Sí, lo sé.*" I dry my face. I sit up. I shake my head and look up at the sky. It is clear and bright, not a single cloud, not a single impediment.

This whole thing is a fucking joke. A player coming out of retirement after this many years? And I think I'm going to win a Slam? Am I insane?

"I do think you are on the path," he says.

I look up at him.

"You are the hardest-working person I know," he says. "If you decide to dedicate yourself to this, you will do it."

I nod, already resenting that we are starting with the old "effort" chestnut and not the "sheer talent" one. "Thanks."

He bumps me on the shoulder and smiles. "What I'm telling you is even though there is a lot of ground to cover, I believe you can be the greatest in the world again. I have that faith."

I start fiddling with the nails on my left hand. "Yeah?" I ask. "Are you sure?"

"I'm positive. But listen, *hija,*" my father says, putting his arm around my shoulders and squeezing me. "It does not matter if I have faith."

"It does, actually," I say. There is an edge to my voice that startles us both.

My father nods but leaves it at that. Like me, he has no interest in excavating what is long buried.

"Your faith in yourself drove you to the top once. And it can drive you there again," my father says finally.

I know that he is right. For decades, my talent and drive were utterly devastating to those who stood in my wake. If each person is blessed with an individual gift, determination is mine.

"Do *you* think you can beat her?" my father says.

I respond quicker than I intend. "Yes."

"And will you be able to bear it if you don't?"

That one takes me far longer to answer. "No."

He closes his eyes and then nods. "All right," he says, sighing. "Then there is no time to waste."

I SIT DOWN IN A CHAIR IN MY AGENT'S OFFICE, NEXT TO HER FLOOR-TO-ceiling windows. I've been with Gwen for about seven years now.

I signed with her after being at two different agencies run by men who kept telling me to "be reasonable" about things I was already being reasonable about. I took meetings with every agency in town, and then at one, in walked Gwen Davis. She is a Black woman born and raised in L.A. who had been a talent agent at a massive agency, and then pivoted to sports stars and struck out on her own.

"If you need to, I expect you to tell me to fuck off," she said in that first meeting. "And if I need to, I'm going to throw it right back at you. We have to have a relationship that is brutally honest. I'm not interested in being your yes man. It's not worth your time or mine."

I signed with her right then and there.

Today, in her office, I look out over Beverly Hills—the palm trees and wide streets and large lots. From here, I can see the golden crown that sits atop city hall.

I turn toward Gwen as she sits down on the sofa next to me. She's in her late fifties, dressed in a red pantsuit and mules. Sometimes I wonder if she's in the wrong field; she's too striking, too glamorous to be the one behind the scenes.

Ali, her assistant, comes in. Her long black hair is pulled into a bun with a pen, and it is already falling apart. She's in a flannel shirt and black jeans with a pair of boots. Something about the fact that Gwen doesn't care what her assistant wears in the office while she, herself, looks like a runway model makes me like them both even more.

"An herbal tea for you," Ali says as she hands me a mug. "With a muffin I know you won't eat."

I laugh. "I have to be back on the court this afternoon, and I don't even like muffins," I say.

"Next time, I'll get you raw unsalted almonds," Ali says. And I know she's making fun of me, but honestly, I *would* rather have the almonds.

Ali hands Gwen a coffee and then leaves.

Gwen takes a sip from her mug and then looks at me. She raises her eyebrow as she gently sets her mug on the glass table, next to a coffee table book with my face on it. It was released in 1990 and features shots of me at Wimbledon spanning about fifteen years. *Soto on Grass.*

Gwen meets my eye as she leans back on the sofa. "Are you sure about returning?"

"I would not be here if I wasn't sure."

"It's not something to be taken lightly," she adds.

"Do I look like I'm taking it lightly?"

"Well, your sponsorships . . ."

"I know."

"You're supposed to shoot the new Elite Gold campaign this spring."

"I know."

"And Gatorade is running the 'Champions' commercial soon too, with you front and center."

I nod.

"Your Break Points are outselling all other tennis shoes for Adidas right now."

One of the most surprising things about my retirement was that it turned out to be very lucrative. Apparently, when I wasn't around anymore, people forgot how much they disliked me—and remembered how much they liked my shoes.

"I know that too," I say.

"These endorsements are all based on the premise that you are now a legend. That you were one of the *very best* athletes in the world."

"Right, and I'm going to prove that I *still* am."

"But if . . ."

I look her dead in the eye, daring her to say it.

She pivots. "If it's a matter of earning, I think, for you, there is more money to be made as a commentator or a WTA official than as a player. We position you as an elder stateswoman of tennis. That's how we keep you relevant and active."

"First of all, nobody wants to hear what I have to say," I tell her.

Gwen raises her eyebrows, considering, and then nods, conceding the point.

"But second of all, it's not a matter of money. It's a matter of honor."

Gwen reaches out and puts her hand on my arm. "I need you to really think about this, Carrie. *Honor* is . . . sometimes just a nice word for *ego*. And I will always choose money over ego. Personally."

I look at her. "I appreciate your advice, but it's not up for debate."

"I'm just trying to look out for your future," Gwen says, pulling back. She picks up the muffin, tears a piece off, and eats it.

"Gwen, all I've ever had is this game," I say.

She nods. "I know that."

"And now it's about to be ripped from my hands. Leaving me with nothing."

"That's not tr—"

"Yes," I say, cutting her off. "It is true. I cannot let Nicki overtake the record. And I need you on board."

Gwen takes a sip of her coffee, then puts the mug back down. "And you are confident this is the right move?"

"It is the only move. I cannot conceive of any other future."

"Okay," she says. "Then I'm on board. I'm all in."

I can tell from the timid look on her face that she is worried I'm about to lose us both a lot of money. And while I feel a spark of rage at her lack of confidence, I'm smart enough to take the win.

"Thank you," I say. "And get ready to be proven wrong."

"There's nothing to prove me wrong about," she says. "I believe in you. So what's the plan?"

"I'm going to play in all four Slams this year, and I am going to win at least one to reclaim my record."

"So your first year out of retirement, you're confident you can win a Slam?" Gwen says.

"Yes," I say. "I am."

"And what if Nicki wins another one first?"

My shoulders tense, and I try to unclench my teeth. "Let me worry about that."

"Okay," she says. "Understood. And you're not rejoining the full WTA tour?"

I shake my head. "No, I just want to play select tournaments. But I don't know my standing with the ITF or the WTA."

Gwen gets up and hits the intercom on her desk phone. "Ali, can you get someone from ITF or WTA on the line and find out—as coyly as possible, please—whether a player like Carrie would get wild cards at all four Slams if she entered?"

"On it."

Gwen lets go of the intercom. "Okay, what's next? What else do you need?"

"Well, I could use a good hitter, if you have any ideas. Not just someone to rally with. I need someone really high-level. So I can gauge whether I'm ready for the best players."

Gwen nods. "You need someone at the top of the game, somebody who can help you get to where Nicki is."

I wince at the implication that we are that far apart. "Well, Nicki's . . . yeah, someone at top level."

"We can make some calls," Gwen says. "And see who wants to practice with you."

"Okay," I say. "Fine. But not Suze Carter—I can't stand her. Or Brenda Johns. But anyone else is fine. The two of them are just so . . . perky. What about Ingrid Cortez? She keeps giving Nicki a run for her money in the final. Maybe she and I can work together a little."

"Anything else?"

"I need Wilson to send me new rackets. I'll need Adidas to send outfits and new Break Points in this season's colors. Should I hire an assistant again? To book my travel and coordinate hotels?"

"If it's just four tournaments, Ali can do it."

"Okay, thank you."

"But you're packing your own luggage. I'm not your mother."

The joke sits there, heavy in the air for a moment. When your mother is dead, it follows you everywhere—popping up in offhand remarks. I notice them all the time, even if the person speaking doesn't. I can tell that Gwen realizes what she said was insensitive, and I appreciate that she decides to breeze past it. There is nothing worse than having to make someone else feel better that your mom died.

"What's next?" Gwen asks.

But for the briefest of moments, I wonder what my mother would think of me today. If she would be proud of what I'm attempting to do. I don't know the answer. And I realize just how long it's been since I asked myself that question.

Ali knocks on the door and comes in. "Okay! This is exciting. I have our answers."

"Tell me," I say.

"Because you are a former WTA number one and have won all

four Slams previously, you are guaranteed a wild card at any WTA or ITF event you choose."

"Yeah!" I say. "Now we're talkin'."

"You can pick and choose what tournaments you want to enter. We have to file some paperwork, but it will be no problem to get you in as a wild card draw for the Australian Open in three months."

"Will I be seeded?"

"No," Ali says. "All your past points are irrelevant now. You don't have any current ranking to seed from. Until you start winning," she adds, grinning.

I see a flash of myself, three months from now, standing on that green hard court in Melbourne, looking across the net at my opponent, whoever she is going to be. I can almost hear the crowd, can practically feel the sweltering tense air.

It has been such a long time since I've played a tournament. And it's been almost three times as long as that since I've played one unseeded.

It sends a tiny thrill through me, like I'm a teenager again, staring up at a mountain I have yet to scale, each match a step toward the top. It has been so long since I have felt the perfect ache of climbing.

The following statement was released today by Carrie Soto through her agent, Gwen Davis.

For Immediate Release 10/11/1994

CARRIE SOTO IS BACK

I am coming out of retirement for the 1995 season to play all four Grand Slam events—the Australian Open in January, the French Open in May, Wimbledon in June, and the US Open in August—in order to reclaim the world record for most Grand Slam singles titles.

I congratulate Nicki Chan on her accomplishments in women's tennis. But her domination is over.

I'm back.

Soto to Come Out of Retirement to Take On Chan

Los Angeles Daily
October 12, 1994

Women's tennis great Carrie Soto, 37, once known as "the Battle Axe," has announced her intention to come out of retirement in order to defend her Grand Slam singles title record. Force of nature Nicki Chan, 30, has been the leading figure in women's tennis since 1989 when Soto retired, holding a record of twenty Slam titles. Chan, often called "the Beast" by tennis fans, tied that record last month.

Soto has long been a polarizing figure in women's tennis, known for her sharp tongue and her ruthless strategies toward other players on the court. If the former champion were to win a Slam, she would be the oldest woman to do so in the history of the game.

"I welcome her return," Nicki Chan said in a press conference yesterday, after being informed of Soto's decision. "I've looked up to Carrie Soto my entire career. It would be an honor to play her once more."

When asked if she thought Carrie Soto could beat her, Chan appeared amused. "Well," she said. "We are going to see, aren't we?"

Transcript

SportsNews Network
Wild Sports with Bill Evans
October 12, 1994

Bill Evans: So, we have some drama coming out of the women's tennis world. Jimmy, what is your take here? Carrie "the Battle Axe" Soto is back? What do we make of this?

Jimmy Wallace, editor of *SportsSunday*: It's certainly unexpected.

Evans: "Unexpected" seems like an understatement. Carrie Soto ended her career after a pretty sharp drop in the rankings back in the late eighties.

Wallace: Yes, she did. Though I think she would argue that's on account of her knee. Which has since healed.

Evans: But she's been gone—what—five years now? It's been a big five years in women's tennis.

Wallace: Certainly. And over that period of time we have seen the rise of Nicki Chan.

Evans: And a new type of tennis.

Wallace: Yes, I think that's true. Women's tennis has shifted away from serve and volley. We are seeing more baseliners, more power players. Soto was always a dancer—agile, graceful on the court. Chan is a brute—she's a boxer. She's tough.

Evans: Can the Battle Axe still compete in today's game?

Wallace: We will see. There's something else here that I think it's important to note.

Evans: And what is that?

Wallace: Soto isn't just playing an old style—she herself is old. No woman has won a Slam in her late thirties.

Evans: And here is another question: Do we even want her back? She's not the most . . . well-liked, is she?

Wallace: Well, they don't call her the Battle Axe for nothing.

Evans: So maybe she shows up in Melbourne and gets sent home quickly. And then she does the elegant thing and bows out again.

Wallace: I think that's very possible, Bill. Time will tell. Otherwise, Chan will have to put her down.

MY FATHER HAS BEEN READING TOO MANY SPORTS PAGES AND WATCHING too much news.

"Absurd," my father says, sitting at my breakfast table. "The way they are implying you cannot win."

I sip my smoothie. The coverage bothers me, but I know there's nothing I can do about it. When I decided to play professional tennis, I apparently signed a contract to let people talk shit about me for the rest of my life.

My father continues to read the paper. "I just think they should remember who they are talking about," he says.

"My sentiments exactly," I say.

He turns toward the TV, which is on mute. "Wait," he says, getting up and turning the volume up. "They are talking about you on *Morning in America.*"

I look over at the kitchen TV.

News anchor Greg Phillips speaks directly into the camera with an image of me at Wimbledon over his shoulder. I cannot stand him. He's interviewed me at least a dozen times over the years and constantly asks about my skirt lengths. We once got into a spat, back in the eighties, when he said I held the record for most Grand Slam trophies in women's tennis. I corrected him on air, pointing out that I held the most trophies out of *anyone* in tennis.

"You thought she was gone!" Greg says. "But American tennis champion Carrie Soto is returning to women's tennis in order to defend her Grand Slam record. Soto has been retired for over five years and, at the age of thirty-seven, will be the *oldest* tennis player on the circuit. Still, she has made the bold claim that she will win at least one tournament this year, a feat that, should she do it, would make her the first woman in the Open Era to win a Slam title in her late thirties. Regardless of how things go for her, it should prove for a wild year in women's tennis now that the Battle Axe is back!"

I move to turn off the TV as Greg announces a commercial break and the show's logo appears. Then, just as my hand touches the dial, we can hear Greg's voice, plain as day, saying to someone, "C'mon, 'The Battle Axe is back'? We should just say, 'The bitch is back.' That's what she is."

Then comes the sound of a woman gasping, jarring feedback, and dead air as the station cuts away from the hot mic. A second later, the screen changes to a commercial of a teenage boy riffling through the refrigerator, pushing away the "purple stuff" because he wants Sunny D.

I turn off the TV and look at my dad. He looks right back at me, his eyes wide.

Finally, I speak. "Did Greg Phillips just call me a bitch on national television?"

My father's face is flushed; his neck is growing redder by the second.

"He did, didn't he?" I say, frozen in place. "He just called me a bitch."

My father gets up from the table and throws away the newspaper.

"I mean . . ." I say. "I knew they thought it. I just . . . I didn't think they said it out loud."

My father puts one of his hands on each of my shoulders. "*Pichona,*" he says, his voice pleading. "Listen to me carefully."

"It shouldn't surprise me. But . . . it does. Why does it feel different than anything else they've called me?"

"Because it's disrespectful," he says. "And you have earned the right of their respect. But listen closely, *hija.* I am serious."

"*Bueno,*" I say, looking him in the eye.

"Fuck 'em," he says. "You go win every goddamn match and you show them that you don't care what they think, you are not going anywhere."

EARLY NOVEMBER

Two and a half months until Melbourne

MY FATHER AND I ARE ON MY HOME COURT, WORKING ON MY FIRST serve.

"*De nuevo,*" he calls out, standing there in his tracksuit on the other side of the net. "*Necesitás ser mucho más rápida, hija.*"

He has put a shopping cart full of tennis balls to my right. I pull one out, ready to serve again. We will be here all day, just like when I was a child. I will aim for that milk carton until my father is satisfied.

Over the month that I have been training, my game has come back to me. I can feel my muscles coming to attention. My speed is picking up; my power is increasing by the day. My serve is fast—sometimes clocking in at over 120 miles per hour. My control and accuracy are excellent. My dad is having a harder and harder time calling out where my serves will land.

But still.

I am not in the same body I was in at age twenty-nine. I am not running as fast. I am tiring more quickly. I am slower to pivot. I can feel the cartilage of my knee sometimes as I bounce. When I'm hitting against a ball machine, I'm not always getting my racket back fast enough. And even when I succeed—it is harder. It is taking more effort to do all of it.

By the second hour of the afternoon these days, I can feel myself begin to tire. My swings are wider and less controlled. My follow-throughs are sloppier. My hits are just a tad softer.

And when that happens, I am quicker to lose my cool. I start missing more shots, growing frustrated, overthinking. It is maddening, working just as hard for a less impressive result. Playing with this body is like trying to cut a steak with a dull blade.

As I stand at the baseline and hit yet another serve over the net, I think about Björn Borg. He was the best male player on the tour in the seventies, but when he came out of retirement three years ago, he couldn't even win a single set. A world champion, the gold standard. Now look at him.

What the fuck was I thinking?

There is a reason that I will be setting a world record if I win a Slam at my age: because no one has ever been able to do it before.

I hit the carton again. I now have not missed in ten serves.

"*¡Excelente!*" my father says as he grabs the carton and moves it to a new spot, farther back. "I want to see four or five, smoked right past me into the corner. *¡Vamos!*"

"*Sí, papá.*"

I toss the ball up in the air and send it flying across the net, right to the top of the carton. It falls once more. I look to my father, but his attention has shifted. Gwen is parking her Benz in my driveway.

I put my racket down, grab a towel, and drink a sip of water as Gwen walks toward us.

"Gwen!" my dad says, his voice booming as he walks toward her, pulling her in for a hug. What is it with hugging? Why would anyone want to press themself up against someone's body to say hello? A wave will do; a handshake is more than enough.

"Javi!" Gwen says, hugging him back.

"You look radiant, as always," my father says.

"Oh, stop it, Javier," Gwen says. And then she turns to me. "I come bearing news."

"Which must be bad, otherwise you would have called," I say.

"Carrie, you don't know that," my dad says.

"No, she's right. I'm here to hand-hold."

I sit down on the bench. "What is it?"

"We are having trouble finding you someone to practice with."

"Seriously?"

Gwen sits next to me. "We called . . . almost everyone on the WTA."

"Surely one of the young players wants to learn a thing or two from me," I say. "Did you point out that the benefits go both ways? What about Ingrid Cortez?"

Gwen's eyes dance around. "Ingrid feels that because she is the number four player in the world, she does not have anything to gain by hitting with you."

My father guffaws. "Her backhand is terrible, and she's giving her opponents opportunities to break serve because of it. She's a child."

"And the rest of the tour?" I ask.

"I think, you know, the women who haven't played you yet are probably a little scared. And the women who have . . ."

"Hate me," I say.

"I think some have held on to some hurt feelings, yes."

"Because I whipped their asses and I'll do it again?" I ask.

"You know you have a way of . . . grinding your opponents down. You know people have not always liked your way of winning."

"Next time I mop the court with someone, I'll remind myself to pretend I'm 'shocked that it went my way' and that it 'could have been anyone's game,'" I say.

Gwen laughs. "Right, but in the meantime, it does not leave us with many options."

I look at my dad. "This is kind of funny, right?" I ask him. "I'm thirty-seven years old, and still no one wants to play with me."

"So we get you a regular hitter," he says. "It's not like we've needed to practice against other professionals before."

"But I want to know how I stack up before I go out there," I tell him. "This isn't like before. This is . . . I need to play against my peers. To see if I still can. I need to do that here on a private court. Before I go out there in front of the world."

Gwen nods.

"Did you ask Nicki?" I say.

"You want me to ask Nicki Chan to hit with you?" Gwen says.

"No," I say.

"Okay, well," Gwen says, "Ali did have one idea."

I look at her and realize she has not driven all the way here to *hold my hand*. She's here to *pitch me* on something. "What is it?"

"I have an old client who is in a similar boat to you," Gwen says.

"Who on earth is in a similar boat to *me*?"

Gwen laughs. "A tennis player I used to work with, who is on the older side of things, trying to give it one last go around the block. And you two might be able to help each other out."

"Who are you talking about? Ilona Heady? She's barely thirty."

"No," Gwen says. "Not Ilona."

"Will Ilona play me?"

"You beat Ilona at Monte Carlo in '88 and then told reporters it was 'embarrassingly easy,' so no, Ilona does not want to play you."

"It *was* embarrassingly easy. I was embarrassed for her. That's *empathy*."

"So who is it?" my dad says.

"Just . . . please get yourself in the right mind space to hear me out."

"Spit it out."

"Bowe Huntley."

I haven't spoken to Bowe Huntley since we slept together in Madrid and he never called me again. "You've got to be kidding me," I say.

"That man is an embarrassment to tennis," my father says. "Yelling at linesmen? Throwing his racket?"

"Bowe has stopped drinking. He got divorced last year. He's in a period of . . . reflection. And, despite what you may think of his tantrums . . . he's a very talented tennis player. Even still. But this is going to be his last year on the ATP."

"He's older than me," I say.

"He's thirty-nine."

"He hasn't won a Slam in almost a decade," I remind her.

"Yes, that's true. Though he does still win a title here and there. And he is a good guy. Truly. He left the agency to go over to YRTA about ten years ago, but we stay in touch. He's not what he seems."

"Yes," my dad says. "I believe Carrie knows him . . . well."

I glare at my father. "All right, keep it to yourself."

Gwen looks at me. "The bottom line is, if it's uncomfortable for you, don't do it. But if you do want a player you can test yourself against . . . Bowe is in."

"You already asked him?"

"I wasn't going to get you on board without knowing if he would do it."

I look at my dad.

"You can just get a hitter," he says. "We can even do two-on-ones, to keep you running around the court."

I consider it. I imagine myself growing more and more confident heading into Melbourne, hitting against amateurs. Only to be clobbered once I'm up against anybody on the circuit. The thought of it knocks the wind out of me.

But I also really don't want to see Bowe Huntley. That knocks the wind out of me too.

"I don't know," I say. "I have to think about it."

• • •

Later that evening, I am in my sweatpants with a seltzer water in my hand, sitting down to watch *ER*, when the phone rings. I mute the television just as the theme song begins.

I put my drink down and pick up the receiver, expecting it to be my father telling me he ran out of toilet paper or shampoo and asking me if I have any.

But it's Bowe.

"Oh, hi," I say.

"Long time," he says.

"Yeah," I say. "I guess it has been."

"Well," he says, "sorry to call so late, but Gwen said you might want to hit together, and I realized if we're doing this, we need to make a plan ASAP."

"You are interrupting my new favorite show, but fine, we can talk."

Bowe laughs. "Are you watching *ER*? What's happening?"

"I don't know, I'm talking to you instead of watching because you think it's all right to call people at ten at night."

"Well, I'll wait," he says.

"You want me to tell you what's happening on *ER*? You can't just turn it on?"

"I'm staying at the home of a nice lady friend I just met who doesn't believe in owning a television."

"Oh, jeez," I say. "I don't know who is worse, you or her." I turn to the TV. "Dr. Lewis is talking to Carter." I pause. "Do you really want me to give you the play-by-play on this entire episode?"

"Sort of," he says. "The rerun won't be until summer."

I sit down on my sofa, crossing my legs. "Okay, fine. Now they have rushed a teenager into an OR. Oh, here we go! Here's George Clooney!"

"Love Dr. Ross."

"I like the one who doesn't put up with the bullshit. What's his name?"

"Benton."

"Yeah, he's my favorite."

"Of course he is," Bowe says.

"Is this really why you called?" I ask. "To have *ER* narrated to you?"

"No," he says. "I want to know if we're doing this thing. Gwen said you weren't fully on board with the idea."

"I just said I wanted to think about it."

"Well, what is there to think about?"

"I don't know, Bowe. That's why I need time."

"You have to *think about* what to *think about*?"

"I'm trying to be thoughtful about everything I'm doing over the next few months."

"Look," he says. "This is a good idea. We can both help each other a lot. You need somebody who can help you get back in fighting shape. I need someone to help me . . ."

"Remember how to win a match?" I ask.

Bowe is silent for a moment, and then he says, "You are not as charming as you think you are."

"If I remember correctly, you're the one people are supposed to find charming."

"A lot of people *do* find me charming."

"How nice for them."

"I remember this about you—every sentence that comes out of your mouth is like a razor blade."

"Yeah, maybe that's why you slept with me and never called me again."

He laughs. "Bullshit."

"It's what happened."

"It is not. I might have spent a big portion of the eighties drunk and confused about what tournament I was at, but let me make one thing perfectly clear, Soto. Before you left my hotel in Madrid, I said, 'I'll call you.' And you said, 'This can just be what it is.' And I remember that because I thought, *Wow, she's so cool,* and I also thought, *She doesn't want to see me again.*"

"Am I supposed to believe that I left you heartbroken?"

"Not at all. I just don't want you pretending I'm a womanizer, because I'm not."

"You are a womanizer. Everyone knows that."

Bowe is the most fined tennis player in history. But he was once also one of the best. He has eleven Grand Slam titles—mostly from the Australian Open and the US Open in the early eighties. He was one of the best returners I'd ever seen. He was also loud and handsome and intoxicating. And almost all of the women on the WTA tour knew they should stay away from him—which was why none of us did.

"Well, I wasn't just trying to get in your pants is my point."

"Yeah, sure. Regardless, everyone on both tours thinks you're a dick."

"And they call you a bitch, apparently."

I laugh. *The Dick and the Bitch,* coming this fall to NBC."

Bowe laughs, uproariously loud. And I can't help but smile.

"So what do you say, then? Do you want to play together or not?" he asks me. "My ankle is shot. My wrist never really fully recovered from my surgery two years ago. My back is killing me. I'm the oldest guy on the tour. But I still have some fire. And I know you do too. Plus, I know your game, Soto. I know you're the best goddamn player tennis has. I don't care how long you've been off the court. If I can hit a few balls off you—if I can learn from you—I want to."

I look around the room, thinking, trying to come up with a reason to say no. But the truth is, he is my best shot at refining my game in time. And that has to be the most important thing. That has to outweigh everything else. "Fine," I say. "Yes. When are you back in town?"

"I play Frankfurt on Monday; I fly straight home to L.A. after. How about the Sunday I'm back, first thing, we can get started. I'll come to you."

"Sounds like a plan," I say. "Javier will join. And what about you? Who's coaching you now? Still Gardner?"

"Uh, no," he says. "Pete's gone on to Washington Lomal, of all people. It's just me now. No coach."

I let the silence last too long. Bowe chimes in after a few seconds. "It's fine. He stuck by me as long as he could. I know what I am, Soto. I'll see you next week."

After I hang up the phone, I sit there holding on to the receiver, not yet letting it go.

MID-NOVEMBER

Two months until Melbourne

I AM SITTING OUTSIDE ON THE COURT, STRETCHING, AT EIGHT-THIRTY IN the morning.

The air is dewy and brisk. The sun has begun to warm up the day. I keep looking over my shoulder at the driveway, wondering when Bowe will arrive.

My father paces by the sideline. "He's already two minutes late."

"Maybe this whole thing was a mistake," I say.

My father whips his head in my direction. "I thought Bowe was a mistake the second Gwen suggested it."

Another few minutes go by as I stand up and stretch out my shoulders and my arms, glancing at the driveway one more time. My father looks at me. "You're nervous," he says. "But you shouldn't be. You're serving at a speed that the midtier players can't hit. Chan, sure. Cortez or Antonovich, I think so. But that's it. You're quicker than you were even last week. You're disguising your shots beautifully. And that's just off a month and a half of training. You are playing at an elite level already."

I look at him.

"And each day you're getting better," he adds. "Have you noticed that?"

I let go of my shoulder and stand up straighter. He's right. At some point in my career, I'd stopped thinking that way. I let myself focus entirely on stats and records. But that had never been the real goal. I shake my head, recalibrating, stunned for a moment at just how easy it had been for me to forget the most basic ideals I grew up with.

People act like you can never forget your own name, but if you're not paying attention, you can veer so incredibly far away from everything you know about yourself to the point where you stop recognizing what they call you.

"Every day," I say, "I'm playing better than the day before."

My father nods. "So do not live in the future, cariño. Don't play the first match in Melbourne months before you've gotten there. We don't know what kind of player you'll be that day."

"I will be two months better of a player than I am today," I say.

A Jeep pulls into the driveway and Bowe gets out. He looks older and grayer than the last time I saw him, weathered—like a leather wallet that has lightened and wrinkled at the folds. He sees us and waves as he heads toward the court.

My father pats me on the back. "Let's see what this thug over here has got left in him. He's already ten minutes late."

"Be nice, Dad."

"I will be perfectly nice to his face, you know that," he says. "But it is my God-given right to complain about him behind his back."

One of the great injustices of this rigged world we live in is that women are considered to be depleting with age and men are somehow deepening.

But Bowe swiftly puts any of my resentments about that to rest. He looks like shit and I take him in straight sets.

When the match is over, he sits on the ground, staring at the racket in his hand. "You demolished me," he says.

"My daughter is one of the very best in the world," my father reminds him.

"Yes, I know," Bowe says. "But still."

My father rolls his eyes and goes inside to get more water. I sit down next to Bowe.

"Today went well for me," I say. "I'm not going to lie."

Bowe looks up. His brown eyes are so big and wide, and his hair is cut close to his head, gray creeping across his temples. His skin is sun-beaten. It has been a big ten years.

"You played well," he says. "You're not all that far from the Carrie I knew."

I am surprised by his magnanimity. I would not possess it in his position.

"Thank you," I say. "There is still a long way to go. Still seems like I'm running through mud out there."

Bowe nods. "I know what you mean."

"And it is not enough to be *good*," I say. "It's not even enough to be great. I have to be . . ."

"You have to be better than you've ever been," Bowe says, "to go up against this crop of women. I've seen some of them. Chan's a killer, but Cortez is deadly too."

"I know," I say, feeling myself tense up.

"Look, I've been in this part of my career for years now. Competing against people half my age, practically. Some of these women you're going to face are twenty years younger than us. They have brand-new knees—fresh from the factory. Brand-new everything, not a stress fracture on them."

"That is not helping—"

"Brand-new hearts too. They haven't been shattered yet, haven't taken a beating over and over. New hearts bounce back faster."

"You're not—"

"You know what my heart is—no, my soul? It's like an old

mattress that's been bounced on so many times that now, if you put your hand on it, it leaves a permanent imprint. That's what my soul is now. Just a big old mattress showing every dent."

"Were you always so good at self-pity?"

Bowe laughs. "Why do you think I drank so much?"

I turn from him and let a tennis ball roll away from me, just watching it drift farther and farther into the court.

I say, "Listen, I can't get better unless you get better. I need to play somebody good, and I need it *now*. So quit it with the crying and try to play the game."

Bowe looks away. "I don't know. It might be better to get someone else. Somebody on the WTA."

I sigh. "It's not that simple." I look at the net, rattling in the breeze, and then back at him. "Nobody on the WTA will play me."

Bowe's eyes go wide. "Are you serious?"

"Bowe, I've heard it enough times; I don't need it from you too. Nobody likes me—I get it."

Bowe catches my gaze. "I always liked you."

I roll my eyes. "Being attracted to me and liking me are two different things."

Bowe looks at me a moment longer. "Huh," he says. "Wow."

"What?"

"I . . . you're right."

"You didn't already know that?" I shake my head. "You're almost forty. How emotionally stunted can you be?"

Bowe looks at me and frowns. But he has the grace to refrain from pointing out that I am throwing stones from my glass house.

"Why are you coming back?" Bowe says. "Why put yourself through this?"

I shrug. "I just can't . . ." I tell him. "I just can't let her have it."

Bowe nods.

"Why are you doing it?" I ask. "Why not quit?"

"I don't know," Bowe says, sighing. "Maybe I should."

"But you haven't. So it must be for some reason."

"I suppose it must," he says. He stands up and wipes the dirt off himself. He reaches his hand out to pull me up, but I stand up on my own.

"Let's go again," he says. "Two out of three. I'm not gonna win any tournaments playing how I played this morning. And quite frankly, neither are you."

"You sure you're ready to play me again?" I ask him as I walk toward the baseline. "Can you suffer the indignity of losing to a woman twice in one day?"

"I told you, Carrie," Bowe says. "You're not as charming as you think you are."

"Okay," I say, shrugging. "But I don't think I'm very charming at all."

Just Because Soto Can Doesn't Mean She Should

By John Fowler

Op-Ed, Sports Section
California Post

Much has been made of Carrie Soto's comeback. In her interview with *SportsPages* last week, Carrie seems to think she has a great chance of winning in Melbourne at the top of next year. "A lot of people think I'm crazy. But I've done exceptional things in my career. Remember that." As if she would ever let us forget.

Soto is just one more in a string of desperate celebrities who cannot live without a spotlight. One would hope by now she would have moved on to starting a family or running her foundation. But no. She's back on the court.

Over the course of my lifetime, I have watched many of the sports I love become commodified into celebrity-industrial-complex machines, churning out champions who turn out to be no role models at all. Tonya Harding and Pete Rose come to mind. And I write this as the nation waits with bated breath to find out what kind of man O. J. Simpson truly is.

It seems the best we can hope for from our legends is that they merely become self-obsessed image-conscious shills for soft drinks, sneakers, and watches.

And who is surprised? This is but the natural conse-
quence of putting athletes on the front of a Wheaties box
all those years ago. When they retire, they cannot stand
to be like the rest of us, seeing our own faces only in
family photos and mirrors. They yearn for yet another
billboard.

Soon, Carrie Soto is sure to show us just exactly what
five years of retirement does to a tennis player's body.
But I'm more interested in what those five years have
done to her brain.

It appears she is today even worse than she was back
then: even more self-absorbed and wickedly ambitious.

If it makes for a good show, then who am I to stand in
the way of the spectacle? But I can tell you this: When
the players set this kind of example in a gentleman's
sport, no one wins.

Why I'm Thankful for Carrie Soto

Letter from the Editor

Helene Johannes
Vivant Magazine

When I was eleven years old, my mother sat me down at the table and explained to me that I was now too old to wrestle in the backyard with my younger brothers.

"It's not appropriate anymore," she said. She had softened the reprimand by making me a warm apple cider. "I need you inside with me from now on, helping with dinner."

That evening, I sat at the kitchen table watching my three little brothers wrestle as I peeled the potatoes.

My mother has long passed away and my brothers and I are all adults now. But I would be lying if I said that the memory of losing my favorite pastime with my brothers—running around in the crisp fall weather, hearing the crunching of leaves as I tackled one of them—didn't ache.

Some men's childhoods are permitted to last forever, but women are so often reminded that there is work to be done.

And yet here is Carrie Soto, daring to play.

I felt a sense of thrill at her announcement last month. And it's not just me; so many of my friends seem to agree. Carrie Soto is living the dream for all of us, coming back for one last go around the block.

As we look ahead to what 1995 may have in store for us, our writers this month have focused on *what's new:* the ingénues, the rookies, and the Young Turks. We have our cover story with breakout star Cameron Diaz, an upcoming look at what's next for Aaliyah, and a conversation with Ethan Hawke and Julie Delpy, the cast of Richard Linklater's upcoming *Before Sunrise.*

But I would like to take the time to also celebrate those of us from the previous generation who are staying in the fight.

We know that Carrie Soto is likely not going to win a single title next year. And it would, perhaps, behoove her to admit it now and spare us all the embarrassment of having to pretend otherwise. One cannot deny the toll age takes on an athlete's body, no matter how unjust. She will be a shadow of the dominant Battle Axe we knew in the eighties. But that is far from the point.

It is her right to have fun, to keep playing. To not help with dinner.

And I, for one, am glad she's exercising it.

DECEMBER 1994

A month and a half before Melbourne

I STOP READING THE SPORTS PAGES FOR NOW. INSTEAD, IN THE MORNINGS as I drink my smoothie and eat my almonds, I read the tabloids. Cindy Crawford and Richard Gere are getting divorced, which sort of shocks me, though I don't know why.

I love gossip magazines. I cannot get enough of the delicious buzz of who is sleeping with who and what they are naming their babies. It is one of the many benefits to my dating life no longer making the covers of the magazines. I can read them at breakfast without fear. One tiny moment of peace in an otherwise grueling day.

After breakfast, every morning, I work out. Then, in the afternoon, I do drills. And then every evening, a little after five P.M., the lights kick on, and Bowe shows up and we play in the cool evening air.

At first, I win almost every time. But he improves quickly, too quickly. Soon, I am only winning when we play two out of three. Bowe starts winning when we play three out of five. An acute reminder that I need to work on my stamina.

Now, today, Bowe is playing the best he's ever played. His serve is sharper, his focus is there. His shots are surprising me. He's broken my serve multiple times today.

"This!" my father shouts to him across the court. "This is the player I wanted to see!"

"What?" Bowe calls out.

"I said this is the player I wanted to see!"

Bowe nods and then serves the ball. I suspect he heard my father the first time and simply hadn't known how to respond.

Bowe and I play until about eight, when he squeezes out a win. I started tripping up in the last set, sending my forehands wide, my backhands into the net.

My father does not need to say anything. I can tell what he's thinking when he catches my eye. If I play this way in the Open, I'm done for.

Bowe packs up his kit.

"So, tomorrow?" he says. We had agreed to one more session before he heads out for the ATP tour. We'll play in Melbourne a bit too, before the tournament starts—acclimate to the weather and the courts. My father has already planned out which days I'll be doing drills and practice matches and resting. He can tell you in December what I'll be doing down to the minute at the end of January.

"Tomorrow it is," I say.

"I'd be open to just hitting drills back and forth, instead of a match," Bowe says. "We both could use some work on our serves. I'm breaking your serve more. I can feel that my backhand is getting more precise. But my own serve . . . I still need . . ."

"You need to work on your first serve for a solid week," my father interjects. "Your form right now is pathetic compared to what you are capable of."

"Dad . . ."

"No, it's fine," Bowe says.

"Of course it's fine!" Javier says. "Because you know I'm right. You should not be using a pinpoint stance. You do not need power. You need precision, you need to—"

"I've used a pinpoint stance my whole life. That's why I can smoke 'em past fuckers like Randall."

"Randall quit tennis seven years ago. And you aren't smoking them past anybody anymore."

"So what's your point?" Bowe says, his voice rising.

"My point is, practice a platform stance. You still have power, somehow. But you have lost your accuracy. You're relying on your second serve way too much. Get your first serve past the net and you will win more."

Bowe looks at my father. And then at me.

"He's right," I say.

"Yeah," Bowe says, grabbing his things and walking off. "I fucking know he's right. I'll see you both tomorrow morning."

As Bowe drives away, I look at my father.

"Why did you do that?" I say. "You're not his coach—you don't even like him."

My father shakes his head from side to side. "He's . . . he's improving significantly just playing against you. And you . . . you're hitting about three to four miles per hour faster on some strokes than just last week. He's throwing shots at you just like ones we can expect from Nicki and Cortez and maybe Antonovich. And you're . . . you're hitting them better than you have all fall, *hija*. Do you see that?"

"So this is . . . it's working," I say.

"Yes," my dad says. "It's working."

The next morning when Bowe shows up, he will barely look at my father.

But on his first serve, he's using a platform stance.

My father stands on the sidelines and clocks it. I can see him hold back a smile.

JANUARY 1995

Melbourne

Less than a week before the beginning of the Australian Open

MY FATHER AND I HAVE BEEN IN MELBOURNE FOR TWO WEEKS NOW.
Bowe has been in and out of town, playing in the Hard Court Championships in Adelaide and the Sydney Outdoor.

I feel a sense of missing out as he goes off to the ATP tour. The 1995 tennis season has begun, and it feels wrong not to be a part of it. But I am not the player I was fifteen years ago. My best shot at winning any of these is to stay focused on the Slams.

Every morning, my father and I cross-train until lunch. And then, on the days when Bowe is in town, he and I play a match in the afternoon.

A fan or two have found us some days, watching us rally back and forth. But today the crowd has grown significantly. There must be twenty people hanging around, trying to get a glimpse.

I can't stop glancing at them. I can't keep my eye on the court like it should be. I miss a few shots.

"Can we tell them to leave?" I ask my father during a changeover. Bowe is up a set.

"I've already asked them to," my dad says. "I'm not sure what else we can do. Especially because Bowe's pandering to them."

I look at Bowe as he waves and then walks over to the crowd. I watch him sign an autograph and take a picture. His smile is big and wide, nearly brilliant under his baseball cap.

These past weeks he's played a couple great matches in his tournaments. He's lifted himself a few spots in the rankings. It is obvious to me now that there is an element of Bowe's game that I haven't accounted for. When the energy of the crowd is there for him, when eyes are on him, he rises to it.

"C'mon, Soto!" Bowe yells as he makes his way back to the baseline, ready to begin again.

I get in position, and he serves it to me—fast, deadly. An ace.

I look to my father and see that his face is completely blank. I feel my shoulders tense.

So much of my game is coming back, as if my muscles have a long and generous memory. But sometimes I lose control of my swing, or I choose the wrong shots. And that is not a sign of a player who is ready for a Slam.

Bowe hits two more aces past me over the course of three games. When he sends a groundstroke down the center and I mis-hit, I nearly throw my racket. I glance at my father, whose face has grown tighter.

Bowe takes the next game, making it 4–1 in the second set. I want to stop the match. I do not want all these spectators watching me—it's their first sight of me after five years and I am *tanking*. I want to jump out of my skin. On my next serve, I double-fault twice in a row. *Fuck. Fuck. FUCK.*

My father pulls me aside. "What's going on?"

"I don't know."

"You do know."

"I don't want to embarrass myself in front of these people."

"When you get out there, in the first round next week, everyone is going to be watching you."

"Thanks, Dad."

"Get. It. Together," he says. "You did not work this hard for the past four months to choke now."

"I know that!" I say.

"*Hija,* you can either beat the other players out there or you can't. This is when you will find out. But I have never known you to be afraid of the truth."

I take a deep breath. The truth was always in my favor before.

"Let's go!" Bowe yells. "No coaching during a match."

"It's not a real match, Huntley!"

"It is if I'm winning it, Soto!"

Three hours later, Bowe and I are sitting at a bar a few blocks from the arena. Bowe's drinking a seltzer water with lemon. I've ordered an iced tea.

"You didn't have to do that," he says as I pick up my glass. "You can have alcohol in front of me."

"You're not tempted?"

"I'm tempted every day. I just . . . It's not your problem."

"Why did you quit?" I ask.

"Is this therapy?" he says, and then sighs. "I quit because I don't want the life I had when I was drinking. I'm ready for something quieter, less stressful, less dramatic. Less getting arrested for public intoxication, more staying in on Saturday nights."

"It was only once, right?" I say. "You getting arrested?"

"Once was enough for me, thank you," he says.

I am sitting with the sun in my face. The glare is making me squint.

"Do you want to switch spots?" Bowe asks. I shake my head; I have always liked the sun.

I look out into the bright afternoon. I can't stop tapping my foot on the ground. I look back at Bowe. I beat him so easily on my home court just six weeks ago. But now, in Melbourne, when I should be playing even better, he's just destroyed me.

"Are we friends?" I ask him.

Bowe sips his seltzer and raises his eyebrows. He puts his drink down. "I don't know. Maybe we're friends. Maybe we're more colleagues?"

"We spend a lot of time together," I say.

"Working."

"Helping each other out," I offer.

"Because it's good for both of us."

I nod and drink my iced tea.

"You act like you've never had a friend before," Bowe says.

I roll my eyes at him. "I've had a friend before."

Bowe has a glint in his eye. I know that smile, see how devilish it is. "But not many."

"What I'm asking is . . . are we close? Can we tell each other things?"

"I don't know, Soto. I just told you why I'm sober, so maybe. What is it you want to tell me?"

"I want to ask you something. From your point of view . . ." I say. "Why did I tank today?"

"Isn't that for your daddy to tell you?"

"You mean my coach, who happens to be my father?"

Bowe raises his eyebrow.

"Plenty of players are coached by their father."

"Yeah, when they are starting out. You're an adult woman."

I find it interesting that for him, it wasn't a sign of disloyalty back in '79 when I fired my father as my coach. Instead, he thinks it's *childish* to go back to my father now.

"Yeah, well, at least someone wants to coach me," I say.

Bowe's jaw shifts and he nods without saying anything. He takes a sip of his drink, the condensation of the glass dripping onto the table. It's hot outside. It will only get hotter as the tournament goes on. That is a leg up I have on a lot of the other women I'll be playing— I like this heat, this blistering sun.

"Fine. You want my opinion? You slow down in the second set,"

Bowe says. "Still. It's improving, but not much. So I know that the harder I run you around in the first set, the more likely I am to win. Today, that's exactly what I did, and by the second set you were done for."

I'm disappointed in his answer. I already know that my endurance is still my weak spot. My father and I have discussed it, and for the next week, I'll be doing sprints in the mornings to gear up for sustaining my efforts longer.

"Okay," I say. "Thanks."

"Your knee seems fine," he adds. "But you're afraid to lean on it. I can tell when I hit a wide one to your forehand—which is easy to do because you favor your forehand."

I nod again; I already know this. Though it is helpful to hear that he can sense it, which means my opponents might be able to as well.

I look out onto the street, watching people walk by the bar. I wonder how many—if any—of them have tickets to the tournament. If any of them will be in the stands watching me try to make something of all this. How many of them are calling me "the Battle Axe" but meaning "the Bitch."

"But none of that is why you tanked *today*," Bowe continues.

I look back at him. "You've got more?"

"You asked the question."

"Go ahead," I say.

"Your mental game sucks."

"Excuse me? My mental game is great. My shot selection is just as good as it's ever been. I'm still planning winners out three, four shots ahead. And you're barely keeping up with them."

Bowe nods. "Yeah, but that's not what I'm talking about."

"What are you talking about?"

"Back in the eighties, you were so unflappable. You knew you deserved that trophy. You were unafraid."

"That . . . is not true."

"Well, you faked it better. Have you read *The Inner Game of Tennis*?"

"I could write *The Inner Game of Tennis*."

"So that's a no. Because if you had read it, you'd know that you, of all people, could never write it."

"What's that supposed to mean?"

"When you're out there—I mean, I'm not in your head so maybe I'm wrong—but with each mistake you make, it looks like you're getting angrier and angrier. You've got so much on the line. If I can get you off-balance early, I can upset you for the rest of the match."

"I—" I start to disagree with him, but I can't decide which argument to make. That I *don't* do that or that *everyone* does that.

Bowe leans forward on the table and moves his drink out of the way. "This guy, the *Inner Game of Tennis* guy, he talks about two selves. Self 1 and Self 2. Self 1 says, 'C'mon, Huntley! Get it together!' Self 2 is the Huntley who's supposed to be doing the getting it together."

I say, "I get you so far."

"Self 2 is doing all the work, right? Self 2 is going to win you the game. Self 2 is the hero. Self 1 just yells and gets frustrated and gets in the way."

"I see," I say.

"Look, Soto," Bowe says. His voice softens as he leans toward me. "You're a better player, physically, than me right now. You're a phenomenal player; that has not changed."

"Thank you," I say.

"But you do have weaknesses that you haven't faced before," he says. "We are older. Our bodies are different. You can't ignore that just because it's inconvenient."

"But if we both are struggling with that, I should be able to beat you, being the better player."

"The difference is that I've made peace with my limitations and you haven't. I can feel it. I can feel the struggle. I can see it on your face. And because of that, you're easy to manipulate. If I can mess with your head, if I can get you mad at yourself for not being the Carrie Soto you think you should be—I will beat you every time," he says. "And that means Nicki will slaughter you."

I take a sip of my iced tea. But then I can't bring myself to pull the glass away from my mouth. I down the rest in one gulp. And then I glance up.

"Okay," I say. "Thank you for your advice. I appreciate it."

Bowe leans back with his hands up in surrender. "Don't ask if you don't want the answer—"

"I said thank you, didn't I? Fuck."

Bowe laughs. "Yes, you did." He slaps his hand on the table. "All right, I'll bite. Do me now."

"It doesn't have to be tit for tat," I say.

"No, I want to know. I want a win, Carrie," he says. "I want a *big* one. I want to do something this season. I want to . . ." He looks me in the eye but then immediately looks away. "I want to prove I was right to stay in the game this long. If I do something great this season, everyone will say, 'Thank God he stuck around,' instead of . . . what they say now."

"'Why hasn't he given up?'"

"Yes, thank you," Bowe says.

I think about it and then chew a piece of ice left in the bottom of my glass. "You take too long to warm up. If you play somebody like O'Hara or Garcia who comes out of the gate hot, you're gonna be down a set before you know it."

Bowe nods. "I know," he says. "You're right."

"Your serve is better now that you're using the platform stance. But you don't disguise your shots enough. I can always tell where you're going."

"How?" Bowe asks.

"Your right foot turns in or out depending on how wide you're going."

"No, it doesn't," he says, blinking and shaking his head.

"Yes, it does."

"That's insane."

"It's still true."

"Okay," he says. "That's . . . thank you."

"I'm not done. You're way too lazy out there. You should be running down more balls. I can squeak any ball past you just by going wider than you feel like running. Everyone playing you knows you're old. They know your back gives you trouble. The first thing they're gonna do is hit it wide every time. You have to conserve energy, and I get that. But if you actually want to win something, you have to be willing to die to get to the ball, Huntley. And you're not willing to do that. So you're not gonna win any match that matters."

Bowe's jaw clenches; his lips are tight. He looks like he's about to get up from the table. I feel a flash of disappointment, because like most men, he can dish it out but he can't take it.

"It's not my fault if you can't handle the criticism," I say.

Bowe looks down at the table. He stares at the water ring his drink has made on the cardboard coaster advertising a beer he can't drink.

"Thank you," he says, finally, when he looks up at me. "Sincerely. Thank you."

"Oh," I say. "Okay, well . . . yeah, you're welcome."

Bowe leans into the table and keeps his voice low. He says, "I want to fucking win, Carrie. I want the crowd screaming my name. I want to know that for one moment, I am the best in the world. One last time."

I can't help but smile. "You are taking the words right out of my mouth."

Transcript

Sports Australia
SportsLine with Stephen Mastiff

Stephen Mastiff: Pivoting to women's singles for a moment, who are we keeping an eye on here, mate?
Harrison Trawley, editor of *SportsPages Australia*: Well, Nicki Chan, obviously. Everyone is expecting her in the final. But also, I'm looking at Ingrid Cortez, I'm looking at Natasha Antonovich. I'm excited to see some quick, daring moves from her. And I think power hitters like Odette Moretti out of Italy will have a good showing.
Mastiff: I notice you're not mentioning Soto.
Trawley: [*laughs*] No, nobody's looking at Soto for this. But if we want to talk about Americans, I think perhaps Carla Perez could seize the moment.

MID-JANUARY

The night before the Australian Open

MY FATHER AND I ARE SITTING ON THE PATIO OF MY HOTEL SUITE, looking out over the city, discussing the draw, which was announced earlier today. I'm in section 7. In my first match I'll be playing a twenty-two-year-old Czech serve-and-volley player named Madlenka Dvořáková. We are playing day 1 at Rod Laver Arena, the highest-profile court.

"It is not an accident," my father says. "That they have you center court against a low-ranked player. You're unseeded, but they are behind you."

I shake my head. "They just know it will make them money. To keep me in the tournament as long as they can."

I look out over the small slice of Melbourne that we can see from my hotel, including the Yarra River as it crosses through the city. I have sat outside looking at this river so many times in my life—as a rookie, as a challenger, as a champion. Now it's as a comeback. I am both stunned to find myself here again and positively sure I've never left.

"You'll go out there tomorrow," my father says, "and you'll beat her, *no le vas a dar tiempo ni de pensar.*"

I inhale sharply—imagining the opposite of what my father is describing. What if tomorrow I lose in the first round? What if this whole thing is over before it's even begun? The idea of it is so humiliating, I feel nauseated.

The phone rings, and the clang of it startles me. I walk into the bedroom to answer it. "Hello?"

"Good luck tomorrow," Bowe says.

"You too."

"Fucking crush her. Make her bleed."

"Will do," I say. "You too."

"We can do this," Bowe says. "At least, you can. I know it."

"Thank you," I say, almost choking on the words. I am suddenly embarrassed at how transparent the emotion in my voice is. "I guess this is it. No turning back now."

"No, I suppose not," he says. "But you wouldn't turn back even if you could, Soto."

THE 1995 AUSTRALIAN OPEN

WHEN I WAKE UP IN THE MORNING, I FEEL A HUM IN MY BONES THAT I have not felt in years. It is startling, the buzz of unexpected joy.

It is still early as I get out of bed. The sun has not yet risen. I feel a sense of control that I sometimes get when I wake up before the rest of the world. I have the feeling that the day's events are mine to determine, that I hold everything in the palm of my hand.

I get up to get ready for a short run. I throw on dolphin shorts and a T-shirt, a pair of sneakers. I go down to the lobby. But before I can get out the front door of the hotel, the woman behind the check-in desk stops me.

"Ms. Soto?" she says.

"Yes?" I want to get running. "What is it?"

"A package arrived for you," she says.

She hands me a padded envelope with a return address from Gwen. I rip the end off. Inside, there is a gift box not much bigger than a book. On top is a note in Gwen's unmistakable cursive.

If anyone can do this, it is you.
Track One —G.

I open the gift box to see a Discman with a pair of headphones plugged in, a CD already in it. It is Elton John's *Caribou*. I look at the first song and laugh.

"Ms. Soto?" the woman says, clasping her hands together.

"Yes?"

"Would you mind terribly if I asked for an autograph?"

I sigh, but then I remember there are a lot of people who wish I would crawl into a hole right now. So I'll take a kind face over that. "Sure, yes, of course you can," I say.

She hands me a piece of paper and a pen. "Oh, wow, Ms. Soto, this is . . . this is just amazing," she says. "Thank you so much."

I take the pen and I scrawl *Take 'em all down, Carrie Soto* across the paper and hand it back to her.

"Thank you so much, Ms. Soto," she says. "I've been a fan of yours since I was thirteen and you won here back in '85. I was there in the stands with my father. He loves you too."

"You don't mind that I'm an arrogant, ambitious bitch?"

She laughs. "No, I do not," she says.

"I'm going to win today," I tell her.

"I have no doubt," she says.

I nod at her, take the Discman out of the box, and put the headphones on. I tap the desk and smile at her as I make my way back toward the door. I press play and start running out of the lobby.

Instantly, I hear the familiar stinging riff of "The Bitch Is Back."

I run on the sidewalk past the hotel. I breeze past people out for coffee, parents with strollers moseying down the street. When I turn the corner and Elton John gets to the chorus, I know—I can feel it in the way the blood is pumping with intention through my veins—that Madlenka Dvořáková is dead in the water.

• • •

"All eyes are going to be on your first serve, to see who you are at thirty-seven. Knock the socks off her from the jump," my father says to me just outside the locker room. "Scare her, you hear me? Scare everybody out there."

I nod, staring down at the scuffs on my Break Points. I picked out the white ones with green stripes this morning, to go with my white tank top and tennis skirt.

This moment—my father and me here in the hall, waiting to go out—feels just like it used to. I'm back at war, after years of not knowing how to live during peacetime. This is the only place where I make sense to myself.

I pick up my racket and turn it around in my hand. My whole arm begins throbbing, ready to be used.

I luxuriate, for one moment, in the quiet din of the stadium that filters through the walls. I inhabit the silence of this moment with my father, when we are still asking questions and do not yet have to live with the answers.

"*Te quiero mucho, pichona,*" he says.

I open up my eyes. "I know. I love you too."

"Go out there . . ." He looks me directly in the eye with an intensity I have not seen in years, maybe even since I was a kid. "And show them that the Bitch, the Battle Axe—whatever they want to call you—it doesn't matter. They cannot stop you. And they don't get to decide what your name is. Carrie Soto is back."

I breathe in deep and then wipe the tops of my shoes clean and start walking—one step at a time—onto the court.

SOTO VS. DVOŘÁKOVÁ

1995 Australian Open

First Round

IT IS NOT DEAFENING, BY ANY MEANS, BUT AS I STEP INTO THE ROD Laver Arena I can hear it begin. "Car-rie, Car-rie, Car-rie!"

I look up to see signs with my name on them. *Welcome back, Carrie!* and *The Bitch Is Back!* I smile at the last one, and I point to the young woman holding it.

I can only imagine what the sportscasters are saying in their booths, what delightful euphemisms they are using to describe just how "too old" or "too cocky" they think I am. It will be a pleasure to make them report my win today. I breathe in deeply, ready to make it happen.

Madlenka Dvořáková looks so tiny, so far away. Her long blond hair is pulled back into a bun. She is wearing a navy blue tank and matching tennis skirt. She looks guarded and nervous, and though her right hand grips the racket firmly, I can see the fingers quivering on her left hand.

I win the coin toss.

As I make my way to the baseline, my whole chest starts thumping, my heart beating heavy and strong. The crowd cheers, and I look up into the players' box to see my father taking his seat.

The loudspeaker erupts. "Miss Soto has won the toss and elected to serve first." I can feel the vibrations of it in my sternum and feel myself turn on, every far edge of my body tingling. I hear the next part in my head before it comes over the loudspeaker, the routine as known to me as my own name.

Linesmen, ready.

"Linesmen, ready."

Players play.

"Players play."

I stand on the baseline and hold the ball in my hand. I brush the felt with my thumb, feel the roughness of it in my palm. And then I bounce it, over and over. Until my mind is clear.

I throw the ball up in the air, pull my arm back, and even before I hit the ball I know—*I can feel*—it is a stunner.

It whistles past Dvořáková so fast she barely has time to step toward it. First point is mine.

I feel the roar of the crowd underneath my feet, ringing into my bones. I look to my father, who nods.

I hold the first game.

On the second, the crowd grows wild when I get to break point. They scream when I break Dvořáková's serve, taking the second game.

I hold the third. It is now three games to none.

In the next, Dvořáková gets some fire in her, and she holds the fourth. But she and I both know the set is mine. I win the next three.

"Set is Soto's."

The crowd cheers, some boo. I try not to pay attention. I stay focused. I cannot let up.

Halfway through the second set, Dvořáková's groundstroke is getting weaker, but I am now only getting stronger. Perhaps it is the adrenaline of the fight, or the fact that I've been training even harder since my conversation with Bowe, but I have full control of my power. I am not letting up. I come in for the kill time and again.

I start smiling during the changeovers, nearly giddy. I am delighted by all of these sounds I've missed—the crowd screaming, the ball girls scrambling on and off the court, the linesmen calling shots.

I am winning this thing.

My last serve in the second set flies right past her. I jump into the air and pump my fist as the ball lands clean inside the lines with Dvořáková nowhere near it. My first match back, and it's mine in straight sets.

As the stadium cheers, I catch a glimpse of Dvořáková's face. Her jaw is tight, her head down. She looks completely blindsided by the way I have pummeled her. A twenty-two-year-old ranked in the bottom fifty, not a Slam title to her name, and she assumed she'd take me.

"Who's next?" I call out, racket in hand. I'm not sure anybody in the stands hears me, but it feels so good to scream into the roar of the crowd.

When I walk off the court, my father is standing there in the tunnel, waiting for me.

"*¡Excelente!*" he says. "Absolute perfection. You warrior, you king."

"The first of many," I say to him.

My father smiles but says nothing. His smile grows bigger as he turns and guides me toward the locker room, and soon he's laughing.

"What?" I ask him. "What are you thinking right now?"

"Nothing," he says. "It's just that . . . this is the part I missed the most. Me and you, in the tunnel."

IN MY NEXT MATCH, I BEAT AN AMERICAN I'VE NEVER MET BEFORE, A woman named Josie Flores, in straight sets. When I cinch the match with an ace, I jump into the air and spin. I bounce on both my feet, side to side, and throw my hands up.

In the post-match press conference, I am still jumpy, still pumped. My victories, no matter how early in the tournament, are *undeniable*. And I feel a near absence of worry.

Months of preparing, months of lying awake at night scared. But now the test is here, and I am killing it.

The first few questions are the usual softballs. "How does it feel to be back on the court?" "Did you expect to win your first two matches?" "What is it like to have your father coaching you again?"

I answer honestly. "It feels great to be back out there." "I expect to win every single match I play." "My father and I are both thankful for this opportunity to work together again."

A man in a sweater-vest speaks up. "Carrie, what do you say in response to players like Ingrid Cortez?"

"I'm not sure what you mean."

"This morning in her post-match, she said that you should have stayed on the bench."

This was news to me. I'd seen Ingrid around in the locker rooms—tall and humorless, with white-blond hair and wide shoulders and a lightness in her step that only a teenager can have—but I'd not spoken much to her.

"She says that she had not heard of you, before you came out of retirement," he adds.

"That's ridiculous—everyone in tennis has heard of me. Half of the world has heard of me." I lean away from the microphone, finished speaking. But then I lean back into it. "She can trash-talk however she wants, but let me say this: I'm grateful for every single woman who stood here before me. You don't see me going around asking who the Original 9 are, do you? No, because I know what I owe them. What about Althea Gibson and Alice Marble and Helen Wills? Suzanne Lenglen? Maria Bueno? I know whose shoulders I'm standing on. If Cortez doesn't, that's on her."

"But," he follows up, "is there any truth to her statement? Some people are saying this comeback is a stunt. What's your response?"

I can hear the shuffling of papers and the readjusting of microphones. But all eyes remain on me.

"I've proven so far that my game is outstanding," I say. "So everyone can whine and moan all they want about me being here, but I've earned the right."

Everyone's hands go up. There is a woman, young and focused, standing on the edge of the press corps.

"How are you feeling about the challenge ahead?" she says. "Your return may be controversial, but there are many spectators out there thrilled to see you playing again. It is expected you'll be playing Carla Perez in the next round. She seems to be the first player who could match your power. So . . . how bullish should your fans feel about seeing this run continue? How confident do you feel?"

I smile wide, and it grows into a laugh. "I'm gonna crush Carla Perez and anyone else I play on my way to the final. I am going to hold their beating hearts in my hand."

For a fraction of a second, none of the reporters in the room know quite what to say.

God, I've missed this.

Transcript

SportsHour USA
The Mark Hadley Show

Mark Hadley: . . . and Bowe Huntley appears to be doing better than anticipated. He annihilated Greg Simmons in the first round and even held up against Wash Lomal.

Briggs Lakin: Which is no easy feat, given that coach Peter Gardner left Huntley to work with Lomal. But Huntley came out the victor.

Hadley: Turning to the women's matches, Nicki Chan is sailing through, no surprise. Though we are seeing some pressure on that ankle.

Gloria Jones: She's an intense player. Intense players are prone to injury, we know that. But Nicki seems to have a handle on it.

Hadley: Natasha Antonovich meeting no resistance yet either. Let's talk about Carrie Soto. Some surprises there. Gloria, thoughts? You played her back in the day, did you not?

Jones: I did, Mark. And look, what can be said about Carrie during this tournament except that she's blowing us all away?

Hadley: She's a former world champion. Should we be impressed that she's in the third round? Dvořáková, Flores—these are not hugely formidable opponents she's faced.

Jones: Well, when you consider how many people had written Soto off before she even set foot back on the court, I do think it's impressive, yes.

Lakin: But, Gloria, I'm curious, because I consider you an incredibly gracious player—you were always respectful and polite on the court—so I'd love your take on Soto's attitude right now.

Jones: You mean the "Who's next?" thing?

Lakin: Well, yeah, screaming out "Who's next?" after your first round seems a bit brazen, no?

Jones: Well . . .

Lakin: And then in her match against Josie Flores, she gloated when she won.

Jones: She danced on the court.

Lakin: That's not gloating?

Jones: I don't know. But—

Lakin: If she has to come back, fine, I say. You know, I was one of the people saying from the beginning that it's her right to do it.

Jones: Yes, you did say that. I remember that.

Lakin: But is it not another thing entirely to come back and then act like an animal? "I am going to hold their beating hearts in my hand"? Where is the grace? The poise? This is a sport of ladies and gentlemen.

Jones: I'm not sure I agree with that. But your point, Briggs, I understand. Carrie Soto is a loud, abrasive player. She always has been. If we thought she'd mellow out, we were wrong.

Hadley: Unfortunately, Gloria, I agree with you on that. Looking forward, she's up against Carla Perez. Perez is a tough opponent. Can Carrie hold her own?

Jones: I'm not saying no—

Lakin: I would not bet on her, I'll say that.

I AM SITTING IN MY HOTEL ROOM, WATCHING NICKI PLAY ANDRESSA Machado. She has one set behind her; it's 7–6 in the second. Machado is serving, and Nicki is running all over the court, making every shot. I don't know how running with that much speed and hitting with that much intensity doesn't deplete her.

Nicki gets Machado to match point. Machado serves it low and wide; Nicki runs and hits the backhand with full force. It flies past Machado, sealing the match for Nicki. The crowd cheers. The commentators are fawning over her. "Nicki Chan sails to the third round, as if anyone had any doubt!"

No one but me seems to notice that as Nicki walks off the court, she's favoring her left ankle.

The phone rings, and I assume it's my father. That ankle won't have gotten by him either. But it isn't my father at all, it's Bowe.

"Oh, hi," I say.

"I mopped the floor with Lomal," Bowe says. I can hear his smile through the phone.

"I heard," I say. "Congratulations."

He says, "Congrats on beating Flores."

"Thank you, thank you. She never stood a chance."

"No," he says. "She didn't. But we all knew that, didn't we?"

"Knew what?"

"That you were going to come back and it would be like you never left."

"It might be a little early to say that," I say.

"You have something, Carrie," Bowe says. "You always have."

"And so have you."

"Do you really think that?" he asks.

"Yes," I say. "I do."

Bowe is quiet for a moment—a second too long. "Are you still there?" I ask.

"Yeah, I'm here," he says, but his voice becomes low and quiet, breathy almost. "Carrie, let me come up to your room."

I freeze.

"Carrie?" he says.

"Yeah."

"Did you hear me?"

"Yeah."

"And?"

"That's not what this is," I say. "It's not like that."

"It could be like that," Bowe says. "It was like that before."

"That was more than a decade ago."

"Please do not remind me how long I've been at this."

"I'm just saying . . . things are different now."

"Can't they be different in a good way?" he asks. "Like this time you don't tell me not to call you. Or if you do, I don't listen?"

"Bowe," I say, shaking my head. My heart is racing, and I immediately resent him for making me waste this much angst on something like sex, when I need to focus on my game. "No."

"Okay," he says, his voice sharper now, back to normal. "Message received. I won't ask again."

"Good, please don't."

"Good luck against Perez. I hope I get to see you crush her."

"Who do you play next?" I ask.

"O'Hara."

I inhale a bit too sharply, and he hears me.

"My thoughts exactly," he says.

"You can take him. You can."

"Uh-huh," Bowe says, laughing. "You're starting to sound like my sister. But I want you to sound like Carrie Soto."

I think about it for a minute. "He's going to exhaust you. If he gets you to five sets, you're done for. So don't let him get to five sets. Break his serve early in the first—that's your shot for an upset."

"Yeah," Bowe says. "I was thinking that too. About me being toast if it goes to five."

"So you do it in three," I say.

"Oh, sure, just take O'Hara in straight sets?" Bowe says. "It's that easy, huh?"

"It can be. If you want it bad enough."

"That's not always true, Soto. But thank you. I appreciate the pep talk."

SOTO VS. PEREZ

1995 Australian Open

Third Round

IT IS SCORCHING HOT. I CAN FEEL THE SWEAT ACROSS MY FOREHEAD and on my upper lip. I wipe it away with the towel in my hand as I sit down on the sideline, catching my breath.

On the opposite side of the court is Carla Perez. They call her the Baltimore Baseliner—and sportscasters have long talked about her forehand power. But they've never felt it like I've felt it today. It is devastating, the ball coming at me like a bullet shot from a gun.

She caught me off guard in the first set. But I came back to take the second, meeting her power and keeping my angles sharp. So now we are 5–5 in the third.

I settle in at the baseline. I bounce the ball in place, and then I look over the court to see Carla crouched, waiting.

The sun is behind me—I can feel it on my neck. Which means it's in Carla's eyes. I serve the ball high and fast, knowing Perez will have a hard time tracking it. She loses sight of it, and the ball lands at her feet. She scrambles backward to hit it on the rise. Her return is too wide.

I hold the game, which means I am now only one away from winning the set and the match.

The crowd begins to cheer. I've won many of them over. I can see it when I look up at the stands.

And here's the thing about arena sports—it's not just about how good you are at the game. It's about how good you are at feeling the crowd when they are with you and ignoring the crowd when they aren't.

It's about how swept up you can get in the momentum when winning, but also how defiant you can be when the tide turns against you.

Back in the eighties, I was great when the crowd was with me. But I was also great when they weren't. I did not need their love or their approval. I just needed the goddamn trophy.

Sadly for Carla, she does not have that single-mindedness. Not today.

I'm at break point within six serves.

Carla tosses the ball up into the air and then slams it across the net. It comes barreling toward me. I return it down the sideline, out of her reach.

Suddenly, my father is pumping his fist in the air.

Carla drops her racket onto the ground. I fall back onto the court in relief.

I'm through to the round of sixteen.

AT BREAKFAST THE NEXT MORNING, BOWE IS SITTING OUTSIDE ON THE hotel patio, eating scrambled eggs and toast.

He has a placid look on his face that reminds me of the surface of the ocean—which is to say it looks tranquil, but you know there are sharks mauling baby seals underneath.

I toy with the idea of turning around so that Bowe can't see me.

He lost to O'Hara yesterday. It was not just a defeat but a bloodbath. I saw the recap last night on the sports channels. Briggs Lakin said, "Someone come out here and put Bowe Huntley down."

I can't afford to sit here consoling him. I have a match to focus on. My father is meeting me in the lobby at eight to practice.

"You can at least not stare," Bowe says suddenly, not even lifting his head up but clearly speaking directly to me.

"I wasn't staring," I say. "I was . . . trying to gauge whether you wanted company."

Bowe laughs without a smile. "You were trying to figure out if you could ignore me because you're afraid losing is contagious."

I look at him. He looks handsome in his regular clothes—a pair of jeans and a black pocket T-shirt, his hair combed. It's like seeing an entirely different person.

I pick up my smoothie and walk over to his table. "I'm sorry you lost."

I grab a chair and sit.

"Thank you," he says. "That's kind of you, given that I wouldn't do the same."

"Is that true?"

"One time, after McEnroe lost a match to Borg, I wouldn't even look at him for the rest of clay season, in case he was bad luck."

"And did you win a lot? That clay season?"

He cocks his head. "No."

"I don't actually think luck has much to do with any of this," I say.

Bowe rolls his eyes. "If it wasn't bad luck that got my ass handed to me yesterday, then what was it?" He puts his finger out before I say a word. "Don't answer that."

"It's you," I say. "Luck didn't lose. You lost. Because you didn't break his first service game like I told you to."

"Oh, like it was that fucking easy?"

I shrug. "Could have been. If you used the platform stance Javier told you to use. It had been working for you, and then I looked at the footage from last night and you're using pinpoint again. Like a moron."

Bowe shakes his head. "You're lucky I'm on the first flight out of here. That way I can't stick around to watch you get ripped to shreds by Cortez."

"Oh, fuck off," I say as I get up from the table. "I was just trying to help you."

"Telling me what I *should have done* helps absolutely no one. You know, Carrie, you get a bad rap—but some of it is deserved."

"Or maybe some little boys are too sensitive."

Bowe looks up at me, his eyes narrow. "You are—"

"What?" I say, daring him.

"This whole thing, it's just not worth it," he says. "At all."

"All right, fuck you kindly," I say, and I walk away.

I barely look behind me as my father comes down out of the elevator with my kit. He is scanning the crowd but doesn't spot me until I walk up to him. He has a huge smile on his face.

"Oh," he says. "I didn't see you over there. Were you celebrating?"

"Celebrating?" I ask.

His smile grows wider.

"Nicki Chan tore her ankle up against Antonovich. She's out for the rest of the tournament."

"No way," I say.

My father nods.

"I could take this," I say.

"Yes, you could."

"I am going to take the whole goddamn tournament!" I say. "While she's nursing a bum ankle from her bad form, I can set this whole thing back where it belongs."

"Yes, you can, *cariño*," he says. "But not if you keep standing here bragging about it."

I am in the entryway, just two steps from the court. I can hear the noise of the crowd. I can see, from my narrow vantage point, a sign in the far back of the arena that reads *Take it to the finals, Carrie!*

There are three people standing between Ingrid Cortez and me—the guard, my father, and her coach are acting as the buffer between us. I am glad for it.

Yesterday, she told one of the newspapers, "I expect a swift and decisive victory in my favor. But I will try not to make it too embarrassing for Soto."

I hold my racket in my hand and play with the strings, making sure they are tight. I have seven more in my kit. I bounce a few times on the balls of my feet, wearing my neon pink Break Points and a neon pink sweatband to pull my hair away from my forehead.

My father puts his hand on my shoulder. I can feel the weight of him there, the weight of his belief in me, his excitement.

When I was playing pro the first time around—that decade and a half of clawing my way to the top and staying there for as long as I could—I did not delight enough in the accomplishments. I would win and then move on to the next challenge.

But right now, as I turn back to take another look at the crowd, I know that, in at least one way, I have evolved.

My older self knows that you must stop—in the middle of the chaos—to take in the world around you. To breathe in deeply, smell the sunscreen and the rubber of the ball, let the breeze blow across your neck, feel the warmth of the sun on your skin. In this respect, I love the way the world has aged me.

I inhale and hold the breath; I let it fill my lungs and raise my chest. And then I blow it out, ready to go.

I wipe the tops of my shoes and walk out onto the court.

SOTO VS. CORTEZ

1995 Australian Open

Round of Sixteen

I CROUCH BEHIND THE SERVICE LINE, WAITING FOR INGRID CORTEZ'S first serve.

She is over six feet tall. Her incisors are long and sharp, and when she smiles, she looks like she is about to bite.

She tosses the ball into the air and serves to the far-right edge of the box. I hit a groundstroke back. We rally for the point, and I take it. *Love–15.*

Another serve, another rally. My point. *Love–30.*

I look up at my father and see a small smile on his lips.

Cortez serves again, this time shorter, tighter. I hit it to the baseline. She hits it back soft. I win the point. *Love–40.* I'm already at break point in the first game.

She underestimated me. And it is a thrill to set her straight.

The sun has begun to burn, slow and hot. The crowd mumbles. I look up in the players' box to see my father. He is nodding at me, willing me to take the game. Then I look in the next section over, and Bowe is taking a seat.

He has canceled his flight, I guess. And come here, to watch me play Cortez.

My eyes soften as I look at him. *Sorry,* he mouths. I nod.

I move my eyes back to the court. Cortez serves high, with a top-spin and force that make it hard to predict. Still, I manage to get to the ball on the rise and return it deep to the baseline, a full two feet past her backhand.

The announcer says, "Game is Soto's." Bowe gives me a fist pump.

Over the next nine games, I take the set.

During the changeover, I look over at Cortez. She has talked such a big game of not being afraid of me, and I've pummeled her in the first set. I expect to see some anxiety or concern, a sign that she understands what she's up against now.

Instead, when she catches my eye, she smiles. As if none of this has worried her in the slightest.

During the second set, Cortez's groundstrokes become harder and faster. Her serves sting in my arm as I return them. I adjust quickly, reducing my shots just like I did back in the eighties up against Stepanova. I'm pulling out the Soto Slice.

It works, but she keeps pressing. She won't even take her winners where she can. She lobs the ball back over. Our rallies go sometimes as many as fifteen, sixteen shots.

I overshoot a couple groundstrokes, send a few cross-court backhands a hair too wide. *Fuck.*

The heat bears down on me. I can feel it on my neck and shoulders.

Out of the first five games in the second set, Cortez takes four.

At the changeover, I do not look into the players' box at my father or at Bowe. I bury my head in my towel and think. The momentum has shifted.

Grab control of the court. Don't slow down now.

I go back out there. Cortez gets more intense by the second. I'm trying to hit them back with as much fire as she has. I'm throwing my entire weight into my shoulder, my elbow heavy with the strain of it all. When I return one of her forehands, my racquet cracks in half.

The crowd screams.

As I get a new racket, I breathe out. *If she takes the set, she can take the match back. Don't let her take the match back. Don't do it. Don't do it.*

Cortez takes the second set.

I am breathless, drenched in sweat. My elbow is killing me. My knee has started to twinge. I pour half of the bottle of water over my towel and then put my towel over my head, cooling myself off and blocking the world out.

I have to win the next set. If I don't, the whole thing is over. And the whole thing cannot be over. Not yet.

This is what you've always been good at.

I put the towel down and stand up. I shake my head vigorously, shake the tension out of my arms and shoulders. I focus in. Get back on the court.

I serve the ball with the spin and precision that I am known for. It flies right past Cortez. An ace. The crowd cheers. And I pump my fist. I am clawing my way back.

It's 5–5 in the last set. I wipe the sweat from my face and try to stretch out my legs without telegraphing to Cortez how much my knee is aching. She isn't even sitting down during the changeover. She's bouncing on her toes, as if eager to get right back out there. My gut drops as I watch her—it's all coming into focus now. She ran me around in the second set, let me wear myself out. And now I'm slowing down when she is just getting started.

I squeeze the ball in my hand. How could I have played this so wrong? How could I have been so stupid? So green! *You did exactly what she wanted! And now you're just as tired as everyone expected you to be!*

I get myself back on the court, and Cortez's shots start coming at me again, no sign of slowing, running me left to right, playing each one she can to my backhand, knowing I don't have the energy to run around the ball to play the forehand.

I run, I hit hard. I get points off her. But it doesn't matter. I can't break her serve.

We're now at 5–6. If she wins this game, she wins the match.

CARRIE, DO NOT LOSE THIS.

I take the next point. *15–love.*

Her point. *15-all.*

Her point.

Her point.

Match point.

I serve it low. She returns it down the line. *Don't let them all be right about you.*

I hit a drop shot. I can bring this back from the brink.

She returns it short. It bounces once. I run, but before I can reach it, it bounces again.

I'm overwhelmed by a downpour of dread—as if the sky has opened up and rained shame.

Cortez wins. I am done at the 1995 Australian Open.

"YOU GOT TO THE ROUND OF SIXTEEN YOUR FIRST TOURNAMENT BACK, *hija*," my father says. I'm lying in the trainers' room with an ice pack on my knee. "That is something to be proud of!"

"Since when was losing something to be proud of?"

In a moment, I'll have to shower and head to the press room for an interview. Cortez is already in there—gloating, I'm sure. Which is her right. She won, after all.

I'm the fucking loser who has to go out there and face all of them, knowing I've been both outsmarted *and* outplayed. And what makes it worse is that I know, *I know,* that she is not a better tennis player than me. That is the full weight of my failure.

"You have no patience," my father says, shaking his head. "And I know it is not my fault, because I tried to instill it in you. But you still don't understand that you can't have everything the second you want it."

"I'm going to ignore you right now," I say, sitting up and taking the ice pack off. "And go talk to the press about throwing away my chance at a title. But feel free to remember that lecture word for word and give it to me later."

"Carolina—" my father says.

"I'll meet you back at the hotel."

My father keeps talking, but I'm not listening. I walk away, into the locker room—past all the other players—and straight into the shower.

At the post-match press conference, the cameras and reporters are all over me.

"Cortez is a strong opponent, but one who probably could not have beaten you at your height," a female reporter says before I've even sat down. "How does that feel?"

"I did not play my best today. And I have to live with that."

"After three successful matches marking your return," a man says, "does this loss today take you by surprise? What are you feeling in this moment?"

"I am feeling like I played poorly and a bunch of reporters are asking me questions about how it feels to suck. I'm not happy right now. Obviously. I will use it as fuel to play better in the future, as I always have."

"But at some point," another man says, "everyone's game declines. Is that what we are seeing here?"

"Why don't you go ask Dvořáková, Flores, and Perez if they think my game is declining?"

"What will you do now?" a woman asks.

"I will go home and get back to work, ready to win in Paris."

"Yes, but, clay is historically your toughest surface," this woman says. "You've only won the French once, in 1983."

"Yeah, well," I say. "Watch me win it again in '95."

They continue to ask questions, but I get up from the table and walk out the door.

. . .

Back at the hotel, I get in the elevator and head to my room. But as I round the corner, I see Bowe standing in the hallway with his suitcase.

I stop right in my tracks.

"I wasn't sure if you're a 'wants company when they lose' sort of person or an 'everyone get away from me' sort of person," he says.

I say, "I'm an 'everyone get away from me' person."

Bowe nods. "Roger that," he says as he grabs his suitcase. "I'll be going."

I walk toward him. "You didn't have to move your flight," I say.

Bowe looks at his suitcase and then back up at me. "I did, actually," he says. "I . . . I didn't stand a chance against O'Hara. But I wouldn't have stood a chance against any of the players I've beaten in this tournament if it hadn't been for you."

"Practicing together?" I say.

"Yeah," he says. "But also . . . the fact that you're doing this. That you've shown up and said, 'I still have more to do.' Randall's retired, Stepanova's gone. McEnroe. Borg looked like a fool out there, coming back after so many years with his wooden racket. But not you. You look like a mercenary. And it . . . it makes me feel less stupid, I guess. That I'm trying too."

I lean against the wall. He steps closer.

"Don't try to kiss me," I say.

Bowe smiles and shakes his head. "You already told me that. You don't have to keep rejecting me."

"Well," I say. "I'm just saying . . . don't do it."

Bowe nods. "I'm sorry I yelled at you this morning. You were right, about my stance. And my game."

"I . . . could have said it nicer."

"I Could Have Said It Nicer: The Carrie Soto Story."

I laugh. "Where are you headed next?"

Bowe shrugs. "Well, I'm not playing in the Davis Cup, obviously," he says. "But I'm headed to Marseille and San Jose. Then Memphis. And on it goes."

"I miss it a little," I say. "The whole tour. The constant movement and focus. You can't dwell on a loss if you're already on to the next match."

"You could have rejoined the full tour, you know."

I nod, picking at my fingernails, not looking at him. "I'm not good enough yet to dominate the way I'd want to."

"You played well today," he says. "And I'm glad I saw it. I know you didn't get what you wanted, but I'm still blown away by what you accomplished here. So many people are."

"Thanks," I say. And then I stop playing with my fingernails and look up at him, meet his eye. "Thank you."

"So I'll see you at the French, it sounds like," Bowe says, his hand on his suitcase again.

I nod. "I'll be back home trying to get myself in fighting shape until then."

"And I'll be out on the courts trying to pull a rabbit out of a hat."

Bowe puts his hand out for me to shake, and I grab it. I am surprised by how warm it is.

He turns to go.

"Do you even have a room?" I ask. "You were supposed to leave this morning."

"I'll get another one," he says. "Don't worry about it."

There's a pullout sofa in the living area of my suite. But I know that at some point in the night, he would knock on the bedroom door. Or worse yet, I'd slip into his bed on the couch.

When I play out the scenario in fast-forward, I can barely stand to watch it. He'll say something wonderful at some point, and I'll start to believe he means it, despite all evidence to the contrary. And then I'll start to like him or love him or feel something that I swear I've never felt before. And then one day, when I'm in too deep, he'll stop liking me or loving me, for one reason or another. And I'll be left with a hole in my heart.

"All right, then," I say. "Good luck. See you in Paris."

Transcript

SportsHour USA
The Mark Hadley Show

Mark Hadley: And Carrie Soto out before the quarter-finals? What do we make of that?

Gloria Jones: I think it was an excellent showing.

Briggs Lakin: It was what we all knew it would be, which was a failed attempt at a comeback.

Jones: I mean, yes. Ultimately, if she's going to be a contender to win a Slam this year, you'd want to see her get past the round of sixteen.

Lakin: If she can't make it to the final in Melbourne when Nicki Chan's gone home with a bum ankle, she has no shot at a Slam title this year. Especially once the Beast comes back. And you all know I'm no big fan of Chan. I can't get over the grunting. But she is the best player in the world right now. So this was Soto's chance to take a title, and it's over.

Jones: Yes, that last part, I agree with.

Hadley: Look at that! For once, we all agree.

Lakin: Turning to the quarterfinals, I think Cortez can take this thing to the end.

Jones: Absolutely not. Antonovich is going to stop her.

Hadley: Well, Chan's no spring chicken. Who takes the reins after the Beast is done? This could be Cortez's or Antonovich's moment. To take a Slam while she's out. To show us what the future of tennis looks like.

ON THE FLIGHT HOME TO LOS ANGELES, MY FATHER WANTS TO GO OVER what went wrong, how I can do better next time.

"*Sí, pero,* I played poorly, Dad," I say. "I got cocky. I assumed I was back to my old level of playing, and I wasn't. Cortez got the best of me. And now, anyone who saw that match knows that they can run me down."

"*Sí y . . .* " my father says, gesturing his hand toward me to encourage me to keep talking.

"So . . . I need to work on it."

My father smiles. "*We* need to work on it. We need to think through multiple strategies with each player and react more quickly once we understand what they are up to. And we need to get your volley game to the best it's ever been, so you don't have to rely on the groundstrokes, if you feel yourself starting to lose your power." There is a buoyancy to his voice—an excitement—that irritates me.

"Yes, but please stop smiling about it."

"I cannot!" he says, throwing his hands up in the air. "This is an exciting time. It is phase two. We have learned where we can improve, and now we will. The sun is shining, the birds are singing, the world is ours."

We are however many thousand miles up in the air. It is night and there are no birds up here. Only defeat and jet lag in a pressurized cabin.

"Yeah, *está bien*," I say. "*Está bien*."

We land and make our way home, where I sleep for twelve hours. I had planned to spend the next day alone in my room with the curtains drawn, ordering expensive pizza. But when I open my eyes, I make myself get up and turn on the television. I want to confirm what I already suspect.

Ingrid Cortez is on my television screen, holding up the Daphne Akhurst Memorial Cup. She's won the goddamn final against Antonovich.

She looks so happy, standing there. Like the young kid she is—so full of joy and life and eagerness. Her face is beaming; her skin is flushed.

When did I lose that? The delight of success? When did winning become something I *needed* in order to survive? Something I did not enjoy having, so much as panic without?

Before I know what I am doing, I am in shorts and a T-shirt, knocking on my father's door at eight-thirty in the morning on a rest day.

He opens the door in his robe and slippers, wiping the crust out of his eyes. But when he sees me, he perks right up.

I say, "Let's play."

"All right," he says. "Let me gather my notes on what we need to work on."

I shake my head. "No. Just me and you. Playing a match. For fun. No drills."

My father smiles and claps his hands in delight. "*¡Me encanta el plan!*"

He puts his hand up, ready for a high five. I laugh and slap it.

"*Dame cinco minutos,*" my dad says. "*Y después jugamos.*"

When he comes out, there is a bounce to his step and a grin on his face. He takes the first serve, and I kick his ass.

FEBRUARY 1995

Three and a half months until Paris

THE SUN IS BARELY IN THE SKY, AND YET I AM STANDING ON THE COURT in front of my father, already warmed up.

"This is," he says, "the beginning of clay season. We put the past behind us. We look forward to Paris. *¿Estamos de acuerdo?*"

"*Sí, está bien,*" I say. The loss in Melbourne still burns. The only thing that will cure it is a win at Roland-Garros.

As the reporters so kindly reminded me, I have only won the French Open once. Twelve years ago. The other nineteen of my Slams have been on hard courts or grass. But Roland-Garros is red clay.

Clay surfaces are softer; they absorb more of the power of the ball. Which means everything about them is slower. Players run slower, the ball bounces slower, and the ball bounces *higher*, too, which gives my opponents more time to react to my shots. Clay cuts into my advantage at almost every juncture. It neutralizes my speed, dulls my accuracy; even my angles don't have quite the same effect.

Clay is not for quick players. It favors the heavy hitters. It is a game of muscle.

Clay is Nicki's surface. And I sincerely hope her ankle's too fucked to play it.

"Are you ready to work?" my father says, holding a tennis ball in his hand.

"Obvio que sí."

He throws the ball at me. I catch it. Then he begins to walk away, toward the driveway.

"What are you doing?" I ask him.

He turns back to me, summoning me with his hand. "Today, *hija*, is an adventure."

I sigh as I begin to follow.

"You can leave your racket and the tennis balls," he says.

I look at him sideways. "Do I need my running shoes?"

He bobs his head from side to side. "No, I do not think so."

"Where are we going?" I ask as he opens the driver's-side door of the green Range Rover I bought him two years ago.

He says, "There are three and a half months until the French Open."

I open the passenger-side door and get in. "Yes, I'm aware."

He turns the ignition. "It's a clay surface . . ."

He puts the car in reverse and turns to look behind him. *Oh no.*

I say, "No. Dad, no. *De ninguna manera.*"

"Carrie, *sí*," he says.

"No, ni lo sueñes, papá."

"Lo siento, pero ya lo estás haciendo."

"What am I? Twelve again? *No necesito hacer esto.*"

"Yes, you do," he says. "It's exactly what you need to do."

I can see a tiny smile erupt on his face as he turns left out of the driveway. To the beach.

I stand there, looking out onto the ocean in Santa Monica, the soft, hot sand under my feet.

"You start here," my dad says. "I'll drive up the coast exactly five miles and meet you there."

I am once again about to run in the fucking sand.

And not wet sand either. Dry, coarse sand that breaks apart under your weight, your feet sinking with each step.

It hurts. Your calves, your hamstrings, your quads, your glutes. All of it.

They make it look way too easy on *Baywatch.*

I look around and sigh. Behind me, teenagers in oversized T-shirts and ripped jeans are walking on the paved path that follows the beach. A few women in neon bike shorts and sports bras glide by on Rollerblades, listening to Walkmans.

What I wouldn't give to run on that track instead of the sand beside it.

I turn my head north, focused on the miles of beach before me.

"¿Y bien?" my father says.

Muscle fatigue leads to a lack of agility. You can't hit your marks as accurately. Your shots don't have the same sharpness. You can't get high enough to hit your angles.

He is right. I need to do this.

"Está bien," I say. "Five miles. I'll see you soon."

My father gives me a captain's salute and then gets back in his car. I watch as he makes his way onto PCH and then drives away from me.

I look down at the sand. I take in a deep breath and start jogging.

It is effortless at first; it always is. And then suddenly, my breath is thicker, my legs feel heavier.

Forty minutes in, I am convinced I must have run the whole five miles already. My father is messing with me; he must have driven ten miles out.

My thighs are killing me. I'm panting. But I can't slow down— I have to keep the pace my father gave me. I have to be *able* to do this. This run is something I can control.

The sand is growing hotter, burning the bottoms of my feet. The glare of the sun is blinding. Sweat drenches my forehead, getting in my eyes, soaking my T-shirt.

I clear my mind; I listen to my breath. And for a moment, I stop thinking about the misery of what I'm doing. I think, only, of Nicki Chan.

She is the daughter of Chinese parents, born in London, who picked up a racket at the age of six. A left-handed player, she had an advantage from the beginning. And she was good, maybe even great, at various points throughout her junior career. She turned pro and did fine. I remember playing her. I remember beating her. But then, in 1989, she took half a year off from the tour and completely revamped her game with a coach named Tim Brooks.

Nicki's groundstrokes became brutal, her serve deadly. She no longer played what we call percentage tennis—always hitting the safe shot. Instead, she opted for the wild, risky shots, each one a cannonball, her stamina unparalleled.

In her new incarnation, she's a player who dives for the ball, jumps high into the air. She goes into splits on clay, slides like a baseball player into first base.

Her form isn't always perfect; her shots are sometimes ugly. But she does the one thing we are all out there to do: win.

Unfortunately for her, it's a bitch on her body. She injures herself more often than most players—a twisted ankle, a sprained elbow, a weak knee, a back problem. She is thirty-one now, and it's hard to say how much longer she's got. But there is immense beauty in her game too, the wild desperation of it, the brutality. She is not a dancer. She is a gladiator.

I wonder what she's doing at this exact moment. I wonder if her ankle is healing. Will she be ready for Paris? Or is this the injury that takes her down for good?

Does she know yet which it is? Is she scared? Is she as anxious as I am to see what this year holds? Or is she thrilled by it all?

I hope at least a part of her is thrilled. It is all so thrilling.

"That was abysmal," my father says as I finally approach where he is standing on the beach. "It should have been *at least* ten minutes faster. We come back again *mañana*."

I can barely breathe. "*Bueno*," I gasp. "*Mañana*."

My life becomes:

Five miles in the sand every other morning.

Forty-yard sprints on the days off.

Hitting against a machine spitting balls at me that are as fast as 80 miles per hour.

Playing against hitters for hours on end.

My father clocking my serves with a radar gun and shaking his head until I hit at least 120 miles per hour.

And then, when the sun begins to set and evening takes hold, watching tape.

My father and I watch my matches in Melbourne to figure out what I could have done better. We watch Cortez, Perez, Odette Moretti, Natasha Antonovich, Suze Carter, Celine Nystrom, Petra Zetov, and Andressa Machado at the IGA Classic in Oklahoma City.

My father's jaw tenses as we watch Natasha Antonovich dominate in the final against Moretti. He doesn't have to say anything— I already know his concern.

Antonovich plays like I used to. She's fast, with a full arsenal of shots. It will not be easy for me to go up against her in Paris, if I have to.

"I think we should go to Indian Wells," my father says as we turn off the TV one night. "See these players up close again, look for their weak spots. Train to defeat them."

"All right," I say. "Sure."

My father stands up to go to his house. "Did you see Bowe got to the quarters in Milan?" he says.

"Yeah," I say, nodding.

"We gotta get you two back on the court. The better he gets, the better you'll play. Until one day, you will play the greatest tennis you've ever played in your life, *pichona*."

"*No lo sé, papá*," I say.

"I'm telling you, *hija*, the greatest match of your career is ahead of you."

It is such a kind thing for him to say—exactly the sort of thing a father like him would tell a daughter like me. Full of heart and love and belief, and maybe a little bit untrue.

MARCH 1995

Three months until Paris

MY FATHER, GWEN, AND I PACK OUR SUITCASES INTO GWEN'S SUV AND head west for Indian Wells.

Gwen is driving, and I am in the passenger seat. TLC is playing on the radio, and Gwen's stereo system makes me feel like they are right here in the car.

My father is in the back seat and falls asleep five minutes after we get onto the 10.

Gwen turns the radio down. "Look," she says, her voice low. "I need to talk to you about something."

"Okay . . ." I say as we drive through downtown L.A.

"Elite Gold wants to pause on the photo shoot and commercials, for now."

I turn to Gwen. "But I made it to the round of sixteen."

She checks her mirrors and moves into the fast lane—which is almost at a standstill. "They were impressed with your showing in

Melbourne. But they said clay is your worst surface and they don't want to run a bunch of commercials about what a legend you are off of two . . ."

"Failures."

"They used the word *defeats*."

"I haven't lost the French Open yet, and they are already counting me out?"

"I told them they were making a mistake. I said, 'You have a contract with the most talked-about athlete of the year. You want to shoot her *now* so that when she wins this summer you have the campaign of the decade.'"

"But they didn't buy it."

"They would rather wait and see."

I kick her car door, and Gwen glares at me. "What the fuck are you doing?"

"Sorry."

"Look, you and I both know Melbourne was the beginning. You will win one by the end of the year."

"Do you really believe that?" I ask her.

"I believe in you. I think if you say something can be done, it will be done."

I close my eyes for a moment and wonder how to tell her how much I needed to hear that. But I cannot find the words.

"So, Bowe," Gwen says, looking at me for a split second before looking back at the road. "How did that all go? He said he got a lot out of it. Was it good? Did it help?"

"It was great, actually," I say. "It was really helpful to have a sparring partner at that level."

Gwen raises her eyebrow. "And that's all?"

I look at her. "I don't know what you're getting at."

"I saw a photo of you two out to dinner in Melbourne. And people are saying he came to your matches. I was wondering if . . ."

I shake my head. "Mind your own business."

"Oh, c'mon!" she says. "I could tell that Bowe maybe still had a thing for you. I could *tell*."

I turn to face the passenger-side window and watch us crawl through traffic. We are passing through the industrial side of Los Angeles at a snail's pace. "You're creating a soap opera in your head."

"I really think you two would be good together. He's rough around the edges, but he's such a good person—just like someone else I know."

"Gwen, give it up."

"I just think it would be nice if you, you know, had someone in your life."

My hand is on the door of the car, and I find myself tightening my fist. "Are you dissatisfied in your own relationship?" I ask. "Is that why you're prying into my mine?"

"I'm not prying. I just want to see you happy. Is that wrong? To think it would do you good to be with someone for a change?"

I want to open the door and jump out on the side of the freeway. "You don't get laid enough, Gwen," I say, keeping my voice low, not wanting to wake up my father. "I'm going to tell Michael he needs to step it up so you get out of my business."

Gwen rolls her eyes and waves me off. "Well, excuse me for wanting you to be loved."

"I'll just call him and tell him now," I say. "That he needs to learn how to satisfy you so you're not trying to live vicariously through me." I pick up her car phone and hit the speed dial, assuming it will be her husband. It starts to ring.

Gwen snatches the phone out of my hand as Michael picks up.

"Hi," she says. "Just letting you know we're off and running, headed out to the . . ."

I stop listening as traffic opens up and we start actually moving on the freeway. I glance at Gwen when she hangs up the phone. "You take shit too far sometimes," Gwen says.

I turn and look out my window as Gwen puts her foot on the gas and speeds us farther down the 10, headed to the desert.

My father is wearing sunglasses and a hat, like he's going to be unrecognizable sitting ten rows back on the ground floor of the venue. We are watching Ingrid Cortez play Madlenka Dvořáková. My father watches every stroke, making notes on both players in a black leather book he bought the other day. He hasn't used a notebook since I was a teenager. I wonder if he's using one now because he's old and doesn't trust his memory—or because I'm old and we can't take any chances.

Dvořáková holds the first set, which is a shock. I clap and cheer.

My father turns to me.

"What?" I say.

"You're cheering," he says. "For the worse player."

"I don't like Cortez."

"But she's a phenomenal player. Certainly you respect her game? Her talent?"

"Sure," I say. "I mean, yes. But Dvořáková is working so hard. It's gonna take everything in her to give Cortez a run for her money. So I'm clapping for her, all right?"

He smiles and shakes his head. "You're getting soft in your old age."

I ignore him and look down at the schedule. "Once we watch Cortez for a bit more, we should stop by Perez versus Zetov too," I say. "Gwen is there now, I think."

I am lucky that Gwen is not one to hold a grudge. She was cold to me for the rest of the drive out here, but the next morning, it was as if nothing had happened. I had formulated a few different apologies in my head, but the words never made their way out of my mouth.

My father nods. "And we need to see Antonovich and Moretti tonight."

"Yes, agreed."

"This is fun!" he says. He bumps my shoulder with his. "God, I love this sport."

I bump his shoulder back. I wonder how it feels to be able to love tennis without it threatening to forget you with every passing match.

A COUPLE OF DAYS LATER, I WAKE UP EARLY IN THE RENTAL HOUSE, unable to quiet my mind.

I look at the clock and see that it is just before five. I decide to go for a run.

In the early desert morning, my body is hotter than the crisp air. I run in the center of the road, through the empty neighborhood streets, slow but steady, pounding my feet over the pavement.

If I don't make it far enough in the French Open, I may lose sponsorships.

I do not care about the money. Ever since I paid off the mortgage on my compound, most of my money goes to funding youth centers across the United States and in Argentina through my foundation. I've invested well, so I will still be able to afford to donate without a single other sponsorship.

It's not about profit.

It's about the look on Gwen's face if she has to tell me they're officially pulling out. It's walking onto the court at Wimbledon while the news of my being dropped is hitting the papers. It's about sitting at a table in a restaurant and everyone around me knowing the result of my hubris.

It is about being cut down to size, just as some people have long wanted me to be.

I'd hate to give them the satisfaction.

I run with no attention to where I am going—finding myself standing outside the rental house again before I even realize I've run in a circle.

I take a shower. With my hair still wet, I throw on a pair of jeans and a T-shirt, and I get in the car. I don't know where I'm going— only that I need to move. I drive through the desert—pale red mountains and beige plains, palm trees and strip malls.

What if I've fucked this all up?

I can't let that happen. I have to practice, and I have to plan. I have to work.

My ambition has long felt oppressive. It is not a joy—it is a master that I must answer to, a smoke that descends into my life, making it hard to breathe. It is only my discipline, my willingness to push myself harder, that has been my way through.

But right now, I can feel that my intuition is lacking. I need to be able to improvise, to think faster than I did back in Melbourne, to understand my opponents instinctively.

Before I know what I'm doing, I drive to the arena.

There, I take a seat in the middle of the stands, and I watch.

I watch Nystrom vs. Antonovich. I notice the way Antonovich's serve is accurate to the inch. I watch Moretti vs. Machado. I see the sheer power behind Moretti's groundstrokes. Her forehand is stunning, but her two-handed backhand leaves her open.

When the match is over, I look down at the schedule and let my eye wander to the men's tournaments. Bowe is playing O'Hara again. Now. And so, instead of checking in on Perez vs. Cortez, I head over to another court.

Bowe is wearing navy blue shorts and a white polo. His hair looks a bit shaggy under his navy baseball cap. He is tied two sets to two against O'Hara and up in the fifth. I am surprised, but perhaps I shouldn't be. I can't help but feel some pride in him.

O'Hara is so blond that his hair is almost white, with eyebrows the same. He is a frustrating and uninteresting player, often a moonballer. He plays percentage tennis to an absurd degree. It's well known that there are big rifts between O'Hara and his coach, Henry Bouchard, for that exact reason. There's no passion in O'Hara's game, no personality.

That's what made Bowe such a compelling player his whole career—whether he won or lost. Back in the eighties, even when he was yelling at the umpire—maybe especially when he was—you knew you were watching a man throw his heart onto the court, a human being with flaws that threatened to do him in. You knew you were watching someone fighting, willing to risk everything.

I have always admired that about him.

Bowe holds the current game. He's up 6–5 in the fifth set. If he breaks O'Hara's serve, he's got the match.

I want it for him—the whole arena wants it for him. You can hear it in the way the crowd quiets. All eyes glued to the court.

For a moment, I smile at the idea that Bowe has no idea I am watching him. It feels vaguely sneaky, oddly intimate.

O'Hara scores. *15–love.*

Then, *15–all.*

30–15.

30–all.

Bowe wipes his brow with his shirtsleeve, fiddles a lot with his hat, bounces a little too fast as he crouches, waiting for the serve. He's wired up and nervous. But I suspect no one else is noticing those things right now. Because Bowe is returning beautifully. I cannot help but beam.

40–30.

Then deuce.

Bowe scores again; it's ad-out. This is break point—it's *match point*. Bowe *has this*. It is *so close*. One more and he wins the match.

O'Hara serves the ball wide and high. Bowe returns it swiftly, hitting the sideline. It's in! I stand up as people begin to cheer all around me.

Then the umpire calls it out.

O'Hara looks shocked. I turn to look at Bowe, who has already ripped his hat off his head. He slams it down on the ground. "ARE YOU KIDDING ME?!" Bowe screams as he marches toward the umpire. "YOU CROOK!"

I can't make out what the umpire is saying.

"YOU'RE A COMPLETE LIAR! YOU DON'T GIVE A SHIT ABOUT THE ART OF THIS GAME."

Multiple officials come onto the court as Bowe starts walking back to the baseline. "YOU DON'T NEED TO CONTROL ME," Bowe yells. "CONTROL THAT ASSHOLE."

O'Hara is laughing at him.

Bowe is throwing his hands up in the air.

I scan the crowd for a moment, unable to look at Bowe as he's being reprimanded by the official. He's going to get a point penalty for the swearing alone. *Oh, Bowe. C'mon.* He'll be that much further from winning now.

There are some young teenage fans in the row in front of me, watching Bowe with rapt attention. I can't decide if I think Bowe is a good influence, standing up against an umpire biased for the opposition, or a terrible influence, a grown man throwing a temper tantrum when things don't go his way. But of course there are no absolute morals or lessons. Only perspectives. One man's bitch is another woman's hero.

As I look through the stands, my eyes land on a woman in a pair of sunglasses and a baseball cap, four rows ahead of me. My heart leaps into my throat.

It's Nicki Chan.

I look at her, trying to convince myself that I'm crazy. But it's clearly her.

Her long, broad body is unmistakable. Her strong, muscular arms. Her wide shoulders. Her long black hair. Nobody ever talks about it much—which is telling—but Nicki Chan is gorgeous. Show-stoppingly gorgeous. A round face with high cheekbones, full lips.

Other women in tennis—blond women with big boobs and long legs—often get modeling contracts at age seventeen. They show up on the cover of men's magazines within a year or so of hitting the court for the first time.

But not thicker women, like me. Or dark-skinned women like Carla Perez or Suze Carter. Not women who are British Chinese, like Nicki, or downright scary in their intensity like her either. Not the women who aren't skinny and white and smiling.

And yet, no matter what type of woman you are, we all still have one thing in common: Once we are deemed too old, it doesn't matter who we used to be.

I watch Nicki for a second too long, wondering why she's here. But the thought pops out of my head the moment she turns her gaze and meets my eye. She looks just as surprised to see me as I am to see her. But she smiles, just a bit. And waves.

There's something sweet about it, unnervingly pure. I try to smile as I wave back.

Then both of us turn to watch what I know, in my gut, is about to happen.

Bowe has lost his point and then some. It's now ad-in. O'Hara only needs one more point to hold the game and destroy Bowe's lead.

He serves the ball—it flies past Bowe at a clip. An ace.

It is now 6–6.

I can't stand to watch him lose this match, so I get up and make my way home.

I am already in the car and turning the ignition on when I realize Nicki is probably at Indian Wells for the same reason I am. Scouting the competition to prepare for the French Open. She could beat my record before I've even taken it back.

I put my head down on the car horn and let it sing through the parking garage.

Motherfucker.

When I get back to the rental house, my father is sitting out by the pool, drinking what appears to be a classic daiquiri. He's making notes in his notebook but looks up when he sees me.

"Where the hell have you been?" he asks.

I throw the car keys on the table and sit next to him, keeping my sunglasses on, slumping into the chair.

"I don't know," I say.

I do not want to tell him I watched Bowe throw a tantrum on the court. And I cannot bring myself to tell him about Nicki.

I cannot bear to tell him just how impossible the task ahead of us feels right now.

Gwen comes out to the pool in a tailored blue dress and heels.

"Wow," I say. "You look great."

"Thank you," she says. "I have an early dinner with the execs from American Express. To see if maybe they want to pick up your contract with Elite Gold, among other things."

"Good God," I say. "Are we already there?"

"No," she says, grabbing her purse. "We're not there at all. But I told you I'm going to make this comeback work. And I'm not taking any chances." She looks me in the eye. "You will be in a credit card commercial this year, come hell or high water."

My father looks at me, raises his eyebrows. And then I look at Gwen.

I'm embarrassed that I'm about to cry because it is so silly. It's just the stupidest goddamn thing under the sun.

"Okay," I say, trying to hold it all in. I turn back around to the pool. "Have fun."

APRIL 1995

Two months before Paris

BY APRIL, AFTER TRAINING A COUPLE MORE MONTHS, MY SERVE IS NOW regularly clocking in at 122 miles per hour.

My feet feel light on the court. My knee feels all right. I feel nimble but mighty, exactly what I need to be for Paris.

"Unbelievable!" "*¡Increíble!*" "*¡Brillante!*" my father says at the end of each session lately, with a brightness in his eyes.

There are entire weeks of the spring when it seems like the craziest thing in the world that I could have doubted myself. I can do this. *This* is what I do.

One evening in early April, my father and I are eating dinner in my kitchen. We have spent the day working on my second serve. It is one of the first days in a long time when I am not exhausted, when hitting at the very best of my abilities did not take everything out of me. I remember this feeling from my twenties—this sense of sheer accomplishment without the weight of the cost. It has eluded me all year, but I finally have it back.

My father and I are eating his grilled chicken.

"It's bone dry," I say. "Why didn't you make chimichurri? Or a white wine sauce? Something?"

"I'd like to see you make dinner," he says.

"I don't cook," I say. "I order takeout. Because if I made chicken, it would taste like this."

The phone rings in the kitchen, and my father gets up.

"It's my phone, Dad," I say. "I'll answer it if I want it answered."

He swats me away with a dish towel.

"Hello?" he says. And then he smiles and turns to me. "It's Bowe."

I bolt up and take the phone from him.

"Hey," I say. "How are you? Nice job in Johannesburg."

"Thank you," Bowe says, but his voice is flat. He got to the third round and went down against Wash Lomal. But I saw the game, and he played beautifully. "Listen, I'm pulling out of Barcelona and Tokyo."

"Oh," I say, resting against the countertop. "Why?"

"My back is starting to hurt, and I want to save my energy. I need to regroup. Need to get ready for Roland-Garros."

"Are you going to play Nice or Monte Carlo?" I ask.

"No," he says. "I'm going to go to Paris now. Set up there, practice on clay."

"Oh," I say. "That's a great idea. Javier and I were thinking of doing the same at Saddlebrook."

"Well," Bowe says. "That's my question. What if you and Javier come to Paris instead and we train together?"

"You want us to come to Paris to train with you?" I ask.

My father hears this and immediately leaps out of his chair and starts nodding. "Tell him yes," my father says. "You need it. You both do. Tell him I have ideas for him. Two words: *Eastern grip*."

I laugh. "Did you get all that?" I say into the phone.

Bowe laughs too. "Every word, sadly. But . . ."

"What?"

"I don't want to know if your dad wants you to come. I want to know if *you* want to come."

I want to win the goddamn French Open with my whole gut. I want to shock every commentator out there who thinks I can't do it. I want to make Elite Gold vomit regret. And then I want them all to sit at my feet and sob, begging for forgiveness.

"Yeah," I say. "Let's do this. Let's train and let's win the French Open together."

Bowe laughs. "It's oddly sweet that you think I can win the French Open. But okay, yeah."

"I guess if we're being honest, I did mean me more than you."

Bowe laughs again, this time wild and delighted. And I can't help but smile.

"There you go. That's the Carrie Soto we all know and love."

My father and I are sitting in first class across the aisle from each other on our flight to Paris. Despite the fact that I am fully reclined and trying to watch the in-flight movie, my father is leaning over the space between us and quizzing me about strategy.

"The plan for Cortez is . . ." he says, after I've answered him about Perez, Moretti, and Antonovich.

"Enough for now," I say. "People could be listening."

My father lowers his voice to a whisper. "The plan for Cortez is . . ." he says again. I notice the older woman sitting next to him. She seems to recognize me but isn't making a fuss about it, which I appreciate.

"The plan for Cortez is *don't be an asshole like last time and spin out*," I whisper. "Now let me watch the movie."

My father sits back in his seat. "It wasn't exactly the answer I was looking for," he says. "*Pero bueno.*"

He turns back to his tray, looking over his notebook. And then he looks back at me, nagging me again. "Bowe needs to work on his toss," he says. "You agree with me, don't you?"

"Yes," I say, ready to put on my in-flight headphones. They are playing a movie that has Sharon Stone in it and I love her. My dad continues to stare at me, not yet satisfied by my answer.

I sigh. "He's hitting the ball too late on the toss. If he hits it sooner, his angle will be better. On all surfaces, honestly."

My dad snaps his fingers. "Yes!" he says. "¡Exacto! ¡Gracias!"

The woman next to him smiles, as if charmed.

"You're welcome. But be smart about how you tell him that."

"A player needs to be open to anything that can make them better," my dad says.

"Obviously, but each player needs to be coached differently."

My father nods, considering. "You think I am coaching him?" he asks.

"Aren't you?"

My father nods again. "Does he think of me as a coach?"

"I don't know, Dad, you need to ask him."

I move to put the headphones on, but he doesn't stop looking at me. "Are the two of you dating?" he says.

I suddenly have the burning desire to eject myself from the plane. "We're not doing this, Dad," I say. "We've never done it. Let's not start now."

"But you are dating him?"

I shake my head and close my eyes. "I'm not dating anyone. You can pretty much always assume that."

"Don't be that way, *pichona*. Please keep your heart open. Please don't close it. Please."

"Dad," I say, holding my breath, losing patience. "Let me watch my movie now." That boy from *What's Eating Gilbert Grape* is in it too, and he is so good. I really want to watch this. The only thing that saves me is the woman next to my father, who finally speaks up.

"Excuse me," she says to him. She looks to be in her sixties, and she is gorgeous. She has big brown eyes and long eyelashes. "Are you Javier Soto?"

I turn away from them, but I'm too nosy not to eavesdrop.

"I am," my father says, putting on his showstopper smile. He would get recognized a lot on the circuit in the seventies. He'd be the center of attention, other coaches and tennis parents and players trying to corner him for advice. When he did his book tour, he was the man of the hour. Everyone wanted to get a little bit of whatever gold dust he had to spread around. It doesn't happen as often anymore.

He sits a bit straighter, pulls back his shoulders, and puts his hand out to her. "Nice to meet you."

"I'm Coral," she says. "I'm a big fan."

"Of my daughter's?" he asks.

"Well, yes, but of you too."

"Of me?" he says.

"Yeah, the Jaguar."

My father blushes. He *blushes*.

"I'm a tennis player," she continues. "I have been all my life. I've always loved what you said about a classic, well-executed game. I loved your book, *Beautiful Fundamentals*."

"Well, thank you," my dad says. "I appreciate it."

I finally put my headphones on and watch the movie, though I've missed a good twenty minutes of the beginning. A few times, I look over to see my dad and Coral laughing together. Or talking back and forth, Coral even touching his forearm.

When the flight attendants serve the meals, I see them trade salt and butter. He gives her his dessert. She smiles sweetly; there is something girlish about the way she accepts it.

At some point after my movie ends, they start playing something called *3 Ninjas Knuckle Up,* and I doze off to sleep. But I wake up a few hours later, when we are about to land, and I see that my father and Coral are still talking.

She asks him something that I cannot make out for the life of me, and my dad puts his hand on her hand for the briefest of seconds and gives a very slight shake of the head.

As we all stand up to get off the plane, Coral nods at my father and says, "Goodbye, Javier, it's been a pleasure," and then walks away.

Soon, my father is walking faster than me off the concourse and into the airport. I catch up with him quickly, though. "What's the deal?" I say.

He looks at me. "What deal?"

"Did you ask Coral out or what?"

My father scoffs. "No, I did not *ask her out.*"

"Well, why not? Weren't you just telling me to open my heart?"

"I was talking about you, not me," he says as we get onto the escalator. "I have had my love."

When we get to the hotel, the concierge gives me a message from Gwen, telling me to call her, no matter the time. I look at my watch. It's almost midnight in Paris but only afternoon in L.A.

My father and I walk up to my room. I find the phone and call.

"Hi," Ali says. "One second."

I put it on speaker as Gwen picks up the line.

"So," Gwen says.

It's either that Elite Gold is pulling out or Nicki Chan is back in. And I'm not sure which I dread more.

"Chan," Gwen says. "She's playing the French Open."

Ah, fuck. That's the one I hate more. I look at my father, who looks back at me.

"You've got this," Gwen says. "Clay is her surface, but you can take her down."

"Yeah," I say. "Yeah. All right, talk soon."

I hang up the phone and say, "If she takes the French Open . . . before I've been able to win one . . ."

My father nods. "It's not good."

I stand up. "But she's not going to win the French Open."

"No, she's not. You're going to win the French Open."

"Because I am the greatest tennis player of all time."

My dad walks up to me and puts a hand on each of my shoulders. "You are the greatest warrior the world has ever seen."

Transcript

SportsHour USA
The Mark Hadley Show

Mark Hadley: And now that Nicki Chan has announced she will be playing in the French Open—how does that change everyone's prospects?

Gloria Jones: Well, we don't know what sort of player we are going to see. A lot of people are saying she's coming back too soon after her injury. There are rumors she's intent on taking another Slam title to break the tie between her and Soto and she's rushed her return in order to do it.

Briggs Lakin: I have to say, Gloria, I'm hearing the opposite. I'm hearing the Beast is playing the best she's ever played. Meanwhile, Soto's only chance at a Slam was one where she wouldn't have to face Nicki. That was Melbourne. I think it's safe to say, for the Battle Axe, it's all over.

END OF APRIL

One month until the French Open

WE MEET BOWE ON THE PRACTICE COURT AT EIGHT A.M. THERE'S NOT another soul around. He is wearing gym shorts and a white T-shirt, tapping his racket against his shoes. Bright white, they stand out in stark contrast to the burnt orange clay.

"Even with your back bothering you, you've been kicking ass," I say as I make my way onto the court. My father walks just two steps behind me.

"Thank you," Bowe says. "Though I suspect you're fighting at peak level right now. I'm a little scared."

"You should be," I say.

"All right, kids, shall we?" my father says.

Bowe shakes my hand. "May the best player win," he says.

"Don't worry, I will."

"Best of three or five?" my father asks.

I really want to earn it. I really want to run myself into the ground and see what I'm made of. "Five," I say.

He nods. "Here we go."

I serve first, and it's a stunner. Sharp, fast, with a high bounce. "Fuck," Bowe says after he misses it.

"Get used to it."

"Don't worry, I'm sure I will," Bowe says, and I can't help but laugh.

I keep it up but then find myself pulling back, going for the safe shots, worried that I'll run out of steam too quickly. Bowe gets the edge on me and wins the first set, 7–5.

I need to find balance in my game, some ability to go hard and keep going, some power to draw on that will not deplete me. I look over at my father for guidance, but he's making notes in his notebook.

I already know the answer, though. I need better shot selection. I need to go bigger on some shots—really take some risks. And I need to put more of the pressure on Bowe's side of the court. I start lobbing more frequently, constructing longer points.

I take the second set, 6–3. "Uh-oh," I say. "She's coming for ya."

"I'm not worried."

I take the next.

"Ohhhh," I say, teasing him as we stand by the net. "Now it's starting to sting, right? Starting to feel a little pinch?"

"It's out of five, Soto," he says. "I know you're used to two sets giving you the match, but you're playing a man's game now."

"Kindly fuck off."

My father shakes his head.

Bowe takes the fourth. I'm getting tired. My serve is softening.

"Oh shit," Bowe says. "It's anybody's game now, Battle Axe."

"You're both terrible in the fifth set of any match," my father calls out. "So let's not trash-talk until one of you gets *results*."

Our fifth set goes to a tiebreak. Match point is on Bowe's serve, which lands right on the T. I return it with a backhand down the line. It bounces high, and he can't reach it.

"Yes!" I say, pumping my fist. "How do you like that?"

Bowe shakes his head, visibly pissed at himself for handing me that serve.

"You win," he says. "You win this one."

My father nods at me. "I'm going inside for a drink," he says. "See you in ten to talk about what we can do better. I have a lot of notes. For both of you."

Bowe grabs the ball on his side of the net and then meets me over by the bench. I take a long sip of water just as he takes one himself. But we catch each other's gaze.

"How are you?" Bowe says.

"What do you mean?" I ask.

"Chan."

I sit down on the bench. "I feel like I set out to prove that I'm a better player than her. And I got a bit of a break with her ankle in Melbourne, but you know, I did plan on facing her eventually. I want the challenge." This is what I'm telling myself, anyway.

"So it's good, then, her coming back."

I laugh. "Yes," I say. "No. I don't know. Yes, it's good, if I'm as great as I say I am."

"You are," he says. "You'll do it. I'm the one who needs a miracle," he says.

"Maybe," I say, smiling.

"I literally just told you you're doing great. And you can't return the favor?"

"What do you want me to do? Lie? Don't fish for compliments," I say.

"Christ, Carrie," Bowe says. But he's laughing. And I am too. And then suddenly my father is there, his head still in his notebook.

"Carrie, go to the baseline. We need to work harder on your second serve. Huntley, I assume you're staying? I have notes for you, if you want them. Your game is getting better, but you still stink at the net. You could benefit from my expertise."

Bowe rolls his eyes. "The two of you, man," he says to my father and me. "Bulls in a china shop."

"Let's not pretend you're such a prize," my dad says, his eyebrows raised.

"Fine," Bowe says. "I want your notes. I'm here to win, so . . . anything you got, I'm listening."

My father's face lights up. And I'm happy for him, to be back here doing this job that he does so well, this job that has defined him for as long as I can remember.

This is not just *my* comeback.

Soto vs. Huntley, Love?

Sub Rosa Magazine

The word out of Paris is that iconoclast Carrie Soto and former wild child Bowe Huntley might be dating again.

Those who were around for the whirlwind of Soto's and Huntley's respective dominance in the eighties will remember that the two were seen canoodling in Spain back in the day.

Now, almost fifteen years later, it appears they are cuddling up close once again.

Multiple sources say they've seen "the Battle Axe" and "Howlin' Huntley" sparring on the court in preparation for the upcoming French Open.

But we have to think this isn't all business. . . .

MID-MAY

Two weeks until the French Open

IT'S LATE, ALMOST TEN P.M. BOWE AND I ARE ABOUT TWO HOURS INTO A practice match on a court just outside Paris. The court lights are bright. The clay is dense under our feet.

It's just Bowe and me. My father went to bed.

Bowe and I decided to play tonight because, earlier in the day, people had started gathering by the court we were on, trying to catch a glimpse of us. I felt myself getting more and more tight, with all of their eyes on me.

"I need privacy," I told my father in between games. "Clay is my worst surface. I need to get everything ready and in control first, and *then* people can watch me."

Bowe started walking toward us. I gathered he heard the last part of my complaint because he raised his eyebrows at me.

"You're in your head too much," Bowe said, pointing at his temple. "Didn't I tell you that?"

My father frowned at Bowe. "Hi, I missed the meeting where I hired you as assistant coach."

"The two of you comment on my game constantly!" Bowe said.

My father's face did not soften. Bowe put his hands up, giving in. "Fine, you both say whatever thoughts come into your head and I'll be as quiet as a church mouse."

My father nodded. "That'd be best."

Bowe rolled his eyes. "Are we playing or what?"

My father looked at me. "*Practicá sola,*" he said, "*dos días más. Después, tenés que estar lista para jugar con todos los ojos clavados en vos. ¿Entendido?*"

"*Bueno,*" I said. "*Está bien.*"

"*Esta noche, practicá sin mí.*"

My father then grabbed his water and his hat. "*Nos vemos después,*" he said, and headed off, I was sure, to the nearest bistro.

Bowe looked at me. "What was that?"

"You really should learn Spanish," I said.

"So I can understand your father?"

"So you can understand a lot of people. Including me sometimes."

Bowe smirked. "Are we playing now or what?"

I started packing up my kit. "We are not. He said let's do two more days with no one watching me. And then I need to be ready. So, I'm asking you, please, can we pick this match up later today when no one is here? You name the time."

Bowe nodded. "Fine, how about eight? I'll talk to Jean-Marc. I'll make sure no one is here."

"Thank you," I said. "Truly."

As I started to walk away, Bowe called out to me. "Take a moment to consider that I'm right about your mental game."

I turned back to him. "And you, take a moment to shut the fuck up."

Now, in the cool night air with no one around, my game is much better.

"Dammit!" Bowe yells as I win the current game. If I win one more, I'll take the tiebreak set and win the match.

I laugh. "Whose mental game are you worried about now?" I ask. Bowe rolls his eyes.

"Oh, poor baby is losing!" I say.

As I move across the court tonight, I'm feeling confident that I will last longer in Paris against heavy hitters like Cortez than I did back in Melbourne. I am doing *well*.

I serve the ball, and Bowe returns it wide. I get there in time and send a cross-court forehand to the deep corner. He hits a backhand groundstroke. And then I have my two-shot strategy in place. First, an approach shot, an easy return. And then a drop shot.

"It's almost too easy," I say. "Too damn easy."

"Dammit, Carrie," Bowe says, his voice low and flat. "Have a little humility."

"Humility?" I say. I have the ball in my hand, about to serve, but I put it in my pocket.

"You called off the match this afternoon when I was winning," he says. "And now, when you're winning, you're gloating."

"Oh no, here comes the Huntley tantrum."

"I don't throw tantrums," he says. "C'mon. You're playing into that sportscaster crap. And I don't do that with you."

"I mean—"

"I don't yell anymore."

"Oh, come on . . ." I say.

"What?"

"I saw you at Indian Wells. Screaming at the umpire. You called him a crook."

Bowe's face falls. He closes his eyes. "I'm really trying, Carrie. I'm trying so hard to not do the shit I used to do. You think I want to be the guy that screams on the court because he's not winning?" Bowe says. "Of course not. I know I fucked up at Indian Wells with that bad call. But I'm trying. And I wish you didn't have to be *right there* to remind me when I slip up."

I look down at my shoes. They are covered in clay. "I get—"

"And by the way, what right do you have to come to Indian Wells and not tell me?" he says.

"What?"

"You're just sitting there in the stands and you don't tell me you're watching my game? And you didn't even bother to say hi? To wish me luck?"

"What are you, twelve? You need me to wish you luck?" I say.

Bowe shakes his head. "Forget it. I don't know why I bother. Just serve the ball, Carrie. Or are you too nervous now and need to postpone until tomorrow?"

"I'm trying to get myself ready for Roland-Garros, all right? I'm sorry it's not on your exact schedule."

"You're ready now!" he says. "You're playing like it's ten years ago. And somehow you're still acting like 'Oh jeez, am I good enough? I'd hate for anyone to see me unless I'm the greatest in the world.'"

"What do you care?" I ask.

"Because. You're so afraid of losing that you fucked up my whole session today to avoid it."

"No, I didn't."

"Yes!" he says. "You did! I don't have much longer on this tour, Carrie. I don't even know if I can finish the year. I pulled out of other tournaments to protect my back, and to be here, trying to play you in the hardest conditions possible. I want to give myself a real chance of doing something great."

"Of course you're going to finish the year."

Bowe rolls his eyes. "Just serve the ball and let's get this over with."

"You have no chance of winning if that's your attitude," I say.

"I'm begging you to shut up, Soto."

"See? This is your problem. One tiny little thing doesn't go your way and you explode."

"Yeah, well, at least I don't walk away."

"What's that supposed to mean?"

"It means you're a quitter, Carrie. Now serve the ball."

I watch him as he walks back to the baseline. When he gets there, he turns, expecting to see me ready to serve, but instead I am staring at him from the net.

"If you have something to say to me," I say, "then say it."

"I just said it," he says.

I stare at him still.

He deflates. "I just want you to serve the ball," he says.

I start walking backward, still glaring at him as I make my way to the baseline. "Call me a quitter again, asshole. I dare you."

"Serve the ball, Carrie."

With lightning speed, I toss it up in the air and slam it across the court. It flies from my racket straight across the net and into the ground. It bounces out of reach before Bowe gets to it.

"Break point," I say.

"Goddammit," Bowe says as he throws his racket.

I shake my head and start heading toward the bench to drink some water.

Bowe picks up his racket and walks to the bench too. When he gets to me, he has calmed slightly. But the racket in his hand is broken—half the frame hanging by the strings.

I nod toward it. "That's what happens when you don't know how to *control your emotions.*"

"Yeah, maybe I should just quit every time I think I'm losing."

"One time!" I say. "One time! I asked you to reschedule a match because I didn't want people looking at me. One time! And you're so bent out of shape about it that you're gonna wreck your racket? C'mon. You're an adult man. Get ahold of yourself."

"I truly cannot stand," he says as he packs up his other rackets, "to be lectured by you."

"Why not? Who else *should* lecture you? You and I are the same, Bowe. Old and out to prove something. And I'm at least handling it with some dignity."

"You left!" he says, his voice rising. And then he shakes his head and laughs to himself. "You hurt your knee, you lost a couple matches, and you gave up. That's what you did. You're saying we're the same, but we're not. I stuck around. I had the guts to try. I have the guts to lose. You, you just run. Well, guess what, Carrie? People who are actually playing the game *lose*. We all lose. We lose *all the time*. That is life. So we are not the same, Soto. I have courage. You're just good at tennis."

He zips up his kit as I try to get control of my breathing.

"You're mad at me because I retired?" I ask. "Are you serious? What should I have done instead? Hung around and become a joke? Let everyone see me limping to the finish line?"

Bowe looks at me and closes his eyes slowly. He takes a breath. "You act like you've dedicated your life to tennis. But you came back to win, not to play. That's why they're all pissed at you for returning. You've got no heart."

Bowe puts his bag over his shoulder and walks away.

"Who is the quitter now?" I call out. "You're forfeiting this match, you know!"

But Bowe just shakes his head and leaves.

The next morning, Bowe doesn't show up. So it's just my father and me hitting.

"He just decides not to come? Not to practice?" my father asks as we rally a bit to warm up.

I send a soft shot back to him. "*No lo sé.*"

My father frowns. "So you got into a fight, then."

"He doesn't like it when he's told the truth. What do you want me to do?"

My father shakes his head and smiles. "The both of you . . ."

"Hey, I'm here, aren't I?"

My father nods. "I will check up on him later."

"Do whatever you want."

We run drills. My father pulls in a hitter last minute. It's not a vigorous practice. But it keeps me warm. And given how many people are lining up to watch, I realize that if Bowe had come this morning, he'd have gotten the showdown he wanted.

Regardless, I'm putting the ball where I want it. I find myself more and more unbothered by the crowd watching me. They begin growing louder, more engaged, shouting, "Carrie!" and "*Nous t'aimons!*"

With each perfectly executed groundstroke, I try to let their presence bolster me instead of scare me.

I am good. On any surface you put me on, I am good. This is a level of performance that I can allow everyone to see.

But then I notice my father's attention turn toward one of the other courts, as fans all over the complex begin to hum. I look over in their direction. Nicki Chan is signing autographs as she walks onto the court with a hitter.

My father turns and looks at me. When he catches my gaze, there is nothing we need to say. I continue to hit for another few minutes.

"*Vámonos,*" my father says. "That's enough for today."

I nod and start to gather my things. My hitter packs up. The crowd groans, disappointed I'm leaving. I think of Bowe for a moment—how he would react. He would call out something witty to them, walk to the crowd lining up at the fence and sign their tennis balls and make them laugh. There's a woman here with a toddler, and I know that Bowe would give the kid a high five.

But I can't think of how to do it without seeming disingenuous. I don't feel grateful for their attention, and I don't know how to be full of shit. I don't have the foggiest clue what to say to a toddler.

I wave briefly and head out. We have to pass Nicki's court in order to leave the facility. And as we do, I stop and watch her.

She is serving balls straight to her hitter, one screamer after the next. My father whistles low.

Her form is untraditional. Because she is left-handed, a lot of players aren't used to her angles. But she also serves the ball in a stance that breaks most of the rules and in a form that breaks even more. She grunts so loud you can hear her in Brussels. Yet as the ball goes soaring off her racket into the service court, it looks deadly.

And that's not just a turn of phrase. It seriously looks as if it is heading toward the clay so fast, with so much heat on it, that if it got you in the chest it might kill you.

"*Vamos*," my father says.

I nod but I don't move. I can't seem to take my eyes off her. I've seen her play in person before, but standing right next to her, watching her from maybe fifteen feet away, is . . . It's beautiful to see.

When she finishes with the balls she has next to her, her hitter begins collecting them all, and she looks up and spots us. She waves.

"Hi," she says as she walks toward my father and me. "I tried to catch your eye when you were practicing earlier, but I don't think you saw me." I have to actively resist rolling my eyes. I didn't want a conversation. I just wanted to be a fly on the wall.

"Hi," I say.

When she finally gets to us, she looks at my father. "You're Javier."

"Yes," my father says. "Indeed I am."

"Can I tell you what a pleasure it is to meet you? When I was a child, I used to . . . Well, Carrie, I watched every single one of your matches. I used to have one of your *SportsPages* covers on my wall. Surely I told you this, back on the tour when we met. But . . . well, Javier, I was so jealous that Carrie had you as a father. My own dad barely knows a thing about tennis. He tries, but it's futile. As a kid, I had to find my own coaches. And . . ." Nicki shakes her head, remembering. "I just thought you were the coolest."

My father smiles.

"We should let you practice," I say. "We will see each other soon, I'm sure."

"Oh, most definitely. We absolutely will. But listen," Nicki says as she leans farther toward me. I take a step closer to her, bridging the gap, the fence the only thing between us now. "I want to thank you."

"Thank me?" I ask.

"I don't think I would have worked so hard on my recovery without knowing I had you to compete against. Knowing I'd have to defend my titles."

I don't like how joyful her face looks, how sincere it all seems.

"All right, well," I say. "You know why I'm here. You know what I'm out to do. I'd imagine your intent is the same. So . . . may the best woman win."

Nicki nods. "Until then, Carrie."

Transcript

SportsHour USA
The Mark Hadley Show

Mark Hadley: The French Open starts tomorrow. Gloria, walk us through the women's singles.

Gloria Jones: Well, obviously, we are looking to Nicki Chan—clay is a good surface for her. I think Natasha Antonovich has also shown herself to be very adroit at adapting to a clay surface.

Hadley: The ads for the tournament feature a lot of old clips of Carrie Soto, but let's call it now: Carrie doesn't really have a chance.

Jones: Clay is not where Carrie Soto shines, no. The Battle Axe—which, by the way, is what I have long called her and I believe we *all should* call her unless we call her by her name—is a grass surface player. Not a clay surface player.

Briggs Lakin: Gloria, I think you're alluding to the fact that people are referring to Carrie Soto as "the B word." You and I were talking earlier—or maybe I should be honest and say *disagreeing*—about whether that's appropriate.

Jones: Yes, that's right. I find it offensive.

Lakin: But to play devil's advocate here . . .

Jones: [inaudible]

Lakin: I don't think it's much different than calling her "the Battle Axe." Remember, we all started calling her "the

Battle Axe" because she went after Paulina Stepanova's ankle in the match we still call "the Coldest War" at the US Open in '76. It was ugly and cruel. And there are countless other examples. So I'm sorry, but Carrie Soto *is* a "B word."

And you're saying that when you call her "the Battle Axe" too. You're just using a euphemism.

Jones: I think there's a difference.

Lakin: I know you do. But an athlete's job is not just to win—it's also to be someone we can cheer for. Soto puts no effort into courting public opinion at all. I guess I want to know why we all have to walk on eggshells to pretend Carrie Soto isn't the exact thing she clearly enjoys being?

Hadley: And with that, we'll be right back.

THE 1995
FRENCH
OPEN

THE AIR OF ROLAND-GARROS IS LIKE NO OTHER COURT IN THE WORLD. It is earthy and humid, heavy with the unyielding scent of tobacco. The smoke from the spectators' pipes has accumulated over the years and lives in the very molecules of this place.

As I walk toward the locker room this morning, preparing for my first match, I am struck by how intense the memories are. Each time I've played here comes back to me all at once.

The midseventies, the early eighties. Great wins and crushing losses.

I spent the first five or so years here desperate and frustrated, pushing myself to rise up the ranks. I lost to Stepanova in the semis in '78. I defeated her in the semis in '79, only to lose to Gabriella Fornaci. Lost to Mariana Clayton in '80. Renee Mona in '81. Bonnie Hayes in '82. And then in '83, I finally won the whole thing.

Was I the greatest then—at that very moment? Even though I'd also failed here many times before? Which matters more? The wins or the losses?

Despite how hard I am seeking some unimpeachable label of "greatness," it doesn't really exist. I do know that, on some level.

But then I walk into the locker room, full of players—Antonovich and Cortez talking in the corner, Brenda Johns pulling on her shoes, Carla Perez opening a locker—and suddenly, I am pulled out of my head back into the world I know best.

The world of winners and losers.

SOTO VS. ZETOV

1995 French Open

First Round

I WALK OUT ONTO THE COURT AND HEAR THE CROWD BEGIN TO CHEER.

I look over at Petra Zetov. She's warming up her shoulder, stretching her legs as men in the crowd holler. She's currently ranked the highest of her career, number eighty-nine. But she has a rabid fan base out of proportion to her ranking.

She's stunningly beautiful—tall and thin, blond hair, blue eyes. She's a model for Calvin Klein, does commercials for Diet Coke, and was in a Soul Asylum video.

And she has a burden I have never had. In order to keep getting paid, she has to keep looking beautiful on the court.

I wonder, briefly, if it weighs on her. Or, if, conversely, it frees her from the pressure I live with, the pressure to win.

Either way, it's a prison. Both her beauty and my ability—they've both got an expiration date.

"It is an honor to play you," she says.

I nod.

This will not be hard. I fully admit that I do not have what she has. But it is equally true that she doesn't have what I have.

The coin is tossed; Zetov wins. She elects to serve first, her face bright and hopeful, as if she thinks this bodes well for her, as if she has a real chance.

I take the match in straight sets.

I TAKE OUT CELINE NYSTROM IN THE SECOND ROUND. NICKI DEFEATS Avril Martin.

In the third, Nicki takes down Josie Flores. I beat Andressa Machado.

When I get back to the hotel after the match, I take a shower and open up a book.

I try to calm myself. The round of sixteen is tomorrow afternoon. Tomorrow morning, I will practice with my father. So tonight, this quiet, is my respite.

The book I brought is an unauthorized biography of Daisy Jones and the Six. I'm only reading to see who slept with who, but I can't focus.

The phone rings and I wonder for a moment if it's Bowe.

"*Hola, hija.*"

"*Hola, papá.*"

"Tomorrow morning, eight A.M."

"Yes, *ya lo sé*."

"Just reminding you. And, I . . . Did you see Bowe's match?"

"Yeah," I say. "He played beautifully." He defeated Nate Waterhouse in the round of sixteen.

"Maybe the best I've seen him all year." Bowe's now headed to the quarterfinals for the first time in a Slam since 1991.

I haven't spoken to Bowe since our fight. When I hang up with my dad, I keep the phone in my hand. I consider calling Bowe's hotel. My fingers hover over the buttons. But instead, I put down the receiver and go to bed.

"You've beaten Perez before," my father says in the tunnel, right before I set out onto the court. "Just do it again."

I turn back to him. "What?"

"You've beaten her once already," he says. "You can do it again."

"You said Perez," I say.

"Right. So you play to her backhand, keep the pressure on her, hit hard to compensate for the clay. You got this."

"I'm playing Odette Moretti," I say.

"Oh," he says, closing his eyes for a second and then opening them right back up. "Right, right. Sorry. Sorry. Nicki's playing Perez. Right, okay, Moretti. She's got a light arm, keep her at the baseline, she doesn't have the power to keep them bouncing on clay."

I look at my dad for a moment.

"It's time, *hija*. ¡*Vos podés!*" he says.

I bend down and wipe my shoes clean.

SOTO VS. MORETTI

1995 French Open

Round of Sixteen

MORETTI STRIDES ONTO THE COURT IN A WHITE-AND-NAVY-BLUE TENNIS dress, waving to the crowd. She blows kisses to the stands. She is sponsored by Nike, so it's no surprise that she is covered in Swooshes from head to toe. When she turns to look at me, she gives me a big smile.

I nod at her.

She starts strong after winning the toss. But I'm stronger.

15–love becomes 15–all. 30–15 becomes 30–all. Deuces become ad-ins and then back to deuces and ad-outs.

Three hours in, we are now in the third set. 6–6.

The crowd is cheering. I look up at my father, who is sitting elegantly behind a flower box.

It's now my serve. I need to hold this one and break hers. And then I'm on to the quarterfinals.

I close my eyes. *I can do this.*

When I open my eyes again, I am looking directly at Moretti. She hovers over the court, her hips swaying side to side as she waits for my serve.

I breathe in and then serve it straight down the middle. She returns it with a groundstroke to the center. I hit it back, deep and to the far-right corner. She runs for it, fast and hard. There's no way she's gonna make it.

But then she does. And I can't return it.

It's fine. It's fine. I can feel my knee twinging, but I have plenty more to go.

I look up at my father again in the players' box. He catches my eye.

I can feel the hum in my bones, the lightness in my belly. I serve it again, this time just at the line. She dives and misses it.

I hold my game and then begin my assault on her serve. I chip away at her, love–15, love–30. By the time I get to match point, she's exactly where I want her. I set her up so she's on the far side of the court. I return it to her backhand and that's it. She's done.

The crowd roars. I jump up into the air and pump my fist.

Nobody thought I'd last past the round of sixteen, but for the first time in seven years, I have earned my way to the quarterfinals. And as it begins to sink in, I feel myself tearing up.

I keep thinking, *I don't cry on the court. I don't cry on the court.*

But then I think, *Maybe it's a lie that you have to keep doing what you have always done. That you have to be able to draw a straight line from how you acted yesterday to how you'll act tomorrow. You don't have to be consistent.*

You can change, I think. *Just because you want to.*

And so, for the first time in decades, I stand in front of a roaring crowd and cry.

I AM IN THE MEDIC ROOM AFTER THE MATCH, HAVING MY KNEE ICED and my calves massaged. My father is making notes and flipping through the channels, to see if I'll play Cortez or Antonovich in the semis.

But then Bowe appears on the screen. He's live in the press room, sitting slightly hunched over, a baseball cap over his barely dry hair. He has on a blue T-shirt. And the second I catch sight of him, I know he is in physical pain.

"Can you walk us through what happened?" a male reporter asks. "Out on the court today?"

Bowe leans into the microphone. "I tore the cartilage between my ribs during the second set. It was hurting this morning before the match even started, but I ignored it, and now here we are." He winces as he sits back.

"How does it feel to lose today, because of an injury, when you were doing so well?" a woman asks him.

"It feels really great, Patty," Bowe says. "Best day of my life."

My father laughs and I look at him, surprised. "He's grown on me," he says. "He's funny."

"What if he's really hurt?" I say.

My father nods. "Maybe it's a small tear. With a little bit of time . . . he can get back in fighting shape."

"For Wimbledon?"

"No," my dad says. "But maybe by the US Open. If he's still in this thing."

"He won't give up," I say. The trainer comes around and starts massaging my other calf. "He'd rather lose than give up."

My father looks at me and raises his eyebrows. "Yeah, he does have that sense of honor about him."

"So, will you be going home?" a reporter asks Bowe. "You are still currently scheduled to play Queen's Club next month. Will you pull out?"

"I'm pulling out of all my events next month. Focusing on recovery. But . . . I'm not going home. I'm going to stick around and watch Carrie Soto," he says. "I think what she's doing here is remarkable. And I want to be able to say I saw it happen."

That night, after I go back to my hotel room, I lie down on the sofa and try to read the French gossip magazines that Gwen sent over to my hotel. They have some good tidbits about Pam and Tommy Lee, but other than that, it's too difficult trying to piece together, in another language, who all the French celebrities are. I throw the magazine back down onto the coffee table and stare up at the ceiling.

Then I stand up, grab my room key, and walk to the elevator.

Bowe's hotel is two blocks over and soon enough, I'm standing in the lobby asking the concierge to tell him I'm here.

I sit in the lobby, in an overstuffed velvet chair, taking in the shine of the marble floors and the gold fixtures. And then Bowe is in front of me in chinos and a T-shirt, his baseball cap on. He's holding his ribs.

"Hi," I say.

"Hi."

"I was really mean," I say. "The other day."

Bowe nods and bites his lip. "I wasn't great either."

"Are you okay?"

Bowe looks down at his torso. "I honestly do not know."

"What happened?" I saw the replay—the way he twisted and then fell to the ground.

Bowe nods at the elevators, and we head toward them. A young teenage boy and his father sneak into the elevator just as we are about to head up, and I watch their faces as they realize who we are.

"You're—" the teenager says as he begins to point at us. His father immediately pushes his hand down.

"Jeremy, don't point at people," he says, and then turns to us. "I'm sorry."

Bowe waves them off. "Not a problem."

"Congrats," the dad says to me. "Great match today against Moretti."

I say, "Thank you."

"Sorry about Alderton," the dad says to Bowe. "Rough break."

"Thank you, sir."

The doors open, and the boy and his father get off. Bowe and I are now left in the elevator together.

"It's not always so easy," Bowe says. "Standing next to you."

"I'm not going to apologize for it," I say.

"No," Bowe says, shaking his head. "Nor would I want you to."

The elevator opens on his floor. He gestures for me to go first, and we walk into his room.

It is smaller than I expected. He does not have a suite but instead a single bed, not much of a view.

When he closes the door behind us, I turn to look at him. "What is your plan?" I say, pointing to his ribs.

Bowe sits on the edge of his bed, softly. He shakes his head. "I don't know."

I sit next to him. "Are you in a lot of pain?" I ask.

Bowe nods. "It hurts like hell. I can barely breathe without feeling like my chest is ripping open."

"Are you taking anything?"

Bowe shakes his head. "No, and I'm not going to. I didn't kick alcohol just to take up worse stuff. I'll deal with it."

"What did the doctor say?"

Bowe frowns. "I'm out for weeks, at least. Wimbledon's fucked." He shakes his head. "The season is going to be winding down before I'm back on the court."

"I'm sorry," I say. I grab his hand and hold it. He looks down at our hands together, and I pull mine back. "You will be ready for the US Open. I know it. And Wimbledon isn't even your best surface. You're shit at anticipating the ball on grass."

"Yes, thank you," Bowe says. "I'm so glad you're here."

"What I'm saying is that the US Open is your best chance. And you will be better by then."

Bowe nods.

"Plenty of time to fuck shit up."

Bowe laughs.

"I am sorry," I say. "About saying you were embarrassing yourself."

"I shouldn't have lost my cool about any of it," Bowe says. "You play how you want to play—that's your business."

"Sometimes I think you're the only person who's harder to deal with than me," I say.

Bowe rolls his eyes. "Not even close."

I laugh. "You're going to be okay."

"I know, I know," he says. "It's not the end of the world."

I stand up.

"Are you really sticking around?" I ask.

"Yep," he says. "I meant what I told the reporters. I think you can win it, Carrie. I really do."

"I hate," I say, "how much that means to me."

Bowe laughs. "Yeah, look, I get it," he says. "I hate that I care so much what all of you Sotos think of me."

We are quiet for a moment, and then Bowe begins to speak. But before he can get a word out, I say, "I should go."

He looks thrown but quickly nods. "Good night, Soto. Rest up."

My father and I are at the practice courts after a sweltering session against a hitter. I'm drenched in sweat, and my father is sitting on the bench beside me, running through his plan for defeating Natasha Antonovich.

I've never played her before—only seen the devastation of her speed from the seats.

"She's quick," my father says. "The clay barely slows her down. It doesn't present the challenge for her that it does for others."

"So I have to be faster," I say.

My father shakes his head. "No. That is not what I'm saying."

"What do you mean?"

"Do not lose your temper," he says, "when I say this."

"I'm not going to lose my temper."

My father raises his eyebrow at me.

"I won't," I say, shifting my tone. "I promise."

"You are not as quick as she is," he says. "Maybe once you were. At your height, perhaps. But not now. Certainly not on clay."

I can feel my heart start to beat in my chest, my pulse rising.

"You have to be okay with that information, *hija*."

My vision narrows; my mouth tightens.

"You are not the same person you were when you played six years ago, in ways both good and bad. Your body is not the same. Your mind is not the same. You have to acknowledge the areas where you are not as strong," he says. "Even back then, clay was harder for you. We have to accept that. So that we can find another way."

"Go on . . ." I say. I thump my racket against my thigh.

"I don't want you trying to match her speed. What would be a better strategy?"

"I don't know. Just tell me."

"What do you have that she doesn't?"

"Crow's feet?" I say.

My father frowns. "*Dale, hija.*"

"Time on the court," I say. "I have at least a decade of playing professional tennis over her."

My father nods. "Exactly."

"Just get to the point," I say. "I don't need the Socratic method."

My father frowns again. "You have always excelled at shot selection and anticipation. You understand where the ball is going, how it will bounce. And you know how to construct a point—three, four, even five returns down the line. You have years of learning this. So let your body—which has done this a thousand times more than she has—guide you. You have instincts she doesn't have yet. Use them."

I sit down next to him. "You're saying play smarter."

"I'm saying control the court. When it's your serve, don't try to prove you can hit as fast. Set up the shots to benefit a slower game, not a quicker one. Because you know you're not the quicker player this time. And be economical in your movements, anticipate where the ball is going. Conserve your energy and let her tire herself out. Antonovich is the rare bird that if this goes three sets, you will probably beat her. Just stay still and slow her down. At every juncture. Even at the changeovers, stretch the time limit. Make her frustrated, make her wait. Don't play for speed. It's not how you win this one."

I am not sure he's right. I'm not sure muscle memory and shot selection is going to bridge the gap between Antonovich's speed and mine. Only me running as fast as possible can do that.

"I . . . I don't know, Dad."

"Carrie, listen to me. I have gone over this in my head a thousand times."

"Dad, I need to get through Antonovich to get to Chan. I *have* to. I can't fail this time."

"I know you feel that way," he says. "Trust me, I know that. That's why I've been up the past two nights, going over old tape in my hotel room. I'm desperate for you. You have to know how much . . ."

I wait for him to finish his sentence, but he seems to have given up on finding the words.

"How much what?"

He sighs. "How much I worry," he says, resting his back against the bench. "I worry about how you will feel if you do not win this match, or the semifinals. Or the final."

I nod.

"I do not want to see the look on your face if it were to come to pass that Chan wins. If she takes your record. I do not think I could bear to see it."

"I know, me neither."

"No, I'm saying I don't think I could bear to see what it would do to *you*," he says. "My feelings won't change one way or another if you win, *hija*. But . . ."

He looks down and then back up at me. "Sometimes I think you don't understand the heartache I feel when I see you lose," he says, catching my eye and not letting go. "Knowing how badly you want it, knowing how much your soul needs it. Sometimes I think it is enough to break me."

"Dad . . ." I say, putting my hand on his shoulder. "I will be okay."

"Is that true?" he asks.

I close my eyes and let my shoulders fall.

There have been so many times in my life when I've lost and it was not okay. Times when I paced in my hotel room for more than twenty-four hours straight; times I didn't sleep or eat for days. After I lost at Wimbledon in '88, I flew home and shut myself in my bedroom and didn't come out for two and a half weeks.

"It is my responsibility to take care of myself," I tell him. "Whether I win or lose. That's on me."

My father shakes his head with a smile. "It will never matter," he says, "whose responsibility is what. My heart hurts when you hurt because *you* are my heart."

I inhale sharply.

"So please, listen to me, and let's work on your first serve, let's work on your shot selection, let's construct some points here, hypothetically, against her."

I nod. I get what he's saying, and he is right about some of it. "Yeah, okay," I say. But I also do need to meet her speed. And if I'm not there yet, I need to spend as much of today as I can getting there. "I'll do your thing, but also, I do need to work on my speed. So let's do both."

My father frowns slightly. "All right."

"Can we get a second ball machine? Having them both coming at me? I'm gonna rise to the occasion. Watch me."

My father nods, and within twenty minutes, I'm hitting balls hurtling at me from both machines. I spend a couple hours at it. Forehand to backhand, up to the net, back at the baseline. I meet the ball time and again.

At the end of the day, as I'm coming off the court, my father raises his eyebrows at me and I shine. I can tell he's impressed, maybe even a little surprised.

"I don't think Antonovich's speed is going to be a problem," I say.

"*Bien, pichona,*" he says.

"It's so close, Dad."

My father pulls me into him, putting his arm around my shoulders and kissing the top of my head. "Go out there tomorrow and take it," he says.

SOTO VS. ANTONOVICH

1995 French Open

Quarterfinals

NATASHA ANTONOVICH IS FIVE ELEVEN AND EXTREMELY THIN. HER visor, shirt, and tennis skirt are all bright white. She elects to serve first without a hint of emotion, her face an arid desert where no smile can grow. *Like I should talk.*

I look up at the stands. My father is staring straight ahead. But next to him is Bowe. He smiles at me.

I look back and crouch down, waiting. Antonovich tosses the ball up into the air.

Her first serve is flat and angry, but it hits just outside the line and I relax. Then the linesman calls it in. I walk up to the line of the service box, ready to fight it. But the dent in the clay shows that it has indeed hit the line, by just a hair.

She's got an ace.

Fuck.

I realign.

She serves another just like it, but right on the T this time, instead of cross-court. I am stunned as I watch the ball get past me again.

The crowd begins cheering. The hairs on the back of my neck start to rise. I roll my shoulders, trying to calm myself down.

Get it together.

I get my head straight. She runs me all over the court, but I meet her there, and then I run her all over too. There are some games when I'm outpacing her. But still, she takes the first set, 6–4.

During the changeover, I wipe my face and my racket. I tap the clay off my shoes. I look up at the players' box to see Bowe and my father talking. Bowe nods as my father gesticulates gently, speaking no doubt in a whisper.

I do not know what they are saying, but I know what I need to do.

I need to get more on Antonovich's level. I need to run as fast as her, take the ball out of the air even quicker.

I close my eyes and breathe in deeply. Antonovich stands in front of me, waiting for my serve. I toss the ball in the air and spin it toward her as fast as I can. I can feel the force of it reverberating up my arm, from the elbow to my shoulder. It sneaks past her.

I pump my fist. *Here we fucking go.*

I do it again, and this time she returns it, but it lands a foot past the baseline. I have got this. I hold the first game in the set.

As the set goes on, both of us are playing at our top levels, and neither one of us can break the other's serve. It's 3–3 and then 3–4 and then 4–4. I serve another game, I hold it. We're at 5–4.

Now it's her serve.

I do not look at my father. I do not want to see the worry in his eyes. I tell myself: *Do not let her win this set. You are either a champion or a fuckup. There is no in-between.*

Antonovich sends a screamer right down the T, and I meet it

with an inside-out forehand. But it hits the tape at the top of the net. *Goddammit.*

If she holds this game and then breaks mine, it's all over. I cannot have all these eyes on me, watching me fail. I cannot be the pathetic bitch they think I am.

But Antonovich just keeps coming. It doesn't matter if I run her around the court—she just glides into position, nicks the ball with the edge of her racket, puts it where she wants it.

We're at 5–5. Then 5–6.

Now she's serving for the match. If I don't break her serve on this game, it's over.

I crouch down low. I move the weight back and forth from one foot to the other. She tosses the ball. This is my moment. My moment to take it all back.

She serves one deep into the corner. I run like hell, even though my knee is starting to ache. I return it into the net.

15–love.

30–love.

40–love.

CARRIE! For fuck's sake, pull it together!

Her serve. Match point.

She sends the ball screaming over. I return it, fast and clean. She hits a groundstroke. I return to her backhand. I can feel the hum in my bones. I can feel this match coming to me—later than I want, but it's here.

Antonovich takes the ball out of the air early. I reach it, return it cross-court. Before I complete my follow-through, she's under it, chipping it over the net. I dive, my chest hitting the ground, sliding with my racket outstretched.

The ball hits the clay and I'm still feet away. It's over.

The crowd erupts for Antonovich. I lie frozen, staring at the dent in the clay where the ball landed.

When I finally get up and dust myself off, I am covered in red clay—my shoes, my knees, my skirt, and tank top are all rust. It is in my hair and in my mouth. It feels like it is in my lungs.

My eye lands on a woman in the crowd a few rows back. She is in her twenties or so, and she's holding a sign that says *Oui, oui, Carrie!*

I cannot bear the sight of her.

"I DIDN'T PLAY MY BEST! SO IF THAT'S WHAT YOU'RE ABOUT TO SAY, Dad . . . don't."

I am standing in the tunnel about to head to the showers. My knee is screaming. I need a massage and ice. I need a lot of things.

Antonovich comes up behind me and passes by. I can feel her trying to catch my eye as she walks into the locker room, but I continue to stare at my father instead.

He is standing against the wall, his eyes closed.

"Carolina," he says. His voice is calm and slow. "Now is the time for perspective. We talked about this."

"Dad!" I say. "Don't pretend that what I did out there was good enough! It wasn't!"

"I understand that you didn't win the match as you'd hoped. . . ."

"Didn't win the match as I'd hoped?" I yell. I can hear the other coaches and players coming down the tunnel, so I pull him into an open room off the corridor. "I just lost my second shot at a title," I say. "I only have four chances!"

"I understand that."

"I think we should all be pretty *fucking* worried that I am not going to be able to do what I set out to do!"

"Do not swear at me. I told you yesterday I was concerned about this possibility."

"I went out there and told everyone that I am the greatest living tennis player, and now I'm proving myself wrong! In front of the entire world!"

My father nods but says nothing.

"You're just going to stand there? Say something!" I shout.

"What do you want me to say?" he asks, throwing his hands in the air.

"Tell me that you can see the colossal fuckup I've just committed! That you know I'm a better player than I was today! That I am as good as I think I am! Or I'm not! If that's what you think! But say something. I've lost my shot at the goddamn French Open, and we both know Nicki's gonna take it! Say something!"

He looks at me and frowns. He begins to pace, shaking his head. There's a folding chair next to a card table, and just when I think he's approaching the chair to sit down, he pulls back and kicks it into the wall. "What do you want from me?" he yells.

"I—"

"You may *not* be the greatest living tennis player anymore!" he says. "I don't know. We don't know! You want me to keep telling you that, but I don't know, Carolina."

"I—"

"I'm not allowed to have any doubts! I'm not allowed to see you as my daughter, as a human being. I'm not allowed to say that years after retirement there *might* be better players now, to express *any uncertainty whatsoever.* So I tell you what you want to hear! So that you have what you need to feel okay. So that you're in my life. Those were the terms you set up! And I live by them! What do you want me to say?"

"I want you to be honest!"

My father shakes his head. "No, you want my honest opinion to be the exact thing you need to hear."

I can feel an ache in my teeth from clenching my jaw. I try to loosen it, but it tightens right back up.

My father looks at me. "Carrie, I do not know how to have an honest conversation with you about your tennis game. Because as good as you are, you have never been able to make peace with failure."

My chest tightens. My eyes feel dry. "And why *the fuck* do you think that is?"

"I think it's because—"

"It's because of you!"

My father shakes his head and looks down at the floor. It's as if he's not disagreeing with me so much as he's disappointed that this was the turn the conversation took so quickly.

But I feel the exact opposite. I feel like it's taken decades to get here.

"You told me I was supposed to be the greatest player in the history of tennis. You said it since the day I was born! You told me it was all I was ever meant to be! And then one day I wasn't anymore. You weren't even sure that I could beat her!" I say.

"Are we talking about Stepanova?" he says.

"I asked you if you thought I could get the number one ranking over her, and you said, 'I don't know.'"

"And you've never forgiven me for it," he says. "I'm paying that price even today."

"You should pay it for the rest of your life!" I say. "For making me believe in myself like that and then pulling the rug out from under me. For giving up on me when things were at their hardest. I never gave up on this. Ever. And you did!"

"Carrie, you asked me if I thought you could take number one from Paulina. And I said I didn't know. Because I didn't. I don't know what the future holds. And I can't promise the world is going to always turn out the way you want it to.

"I owed you that honesty, I thought. So you could assess better—how to grow, how to widen your perspective. It felt like it was time for that. But you didn't want to do that then, and you don't want to do that now.

"I've messed up a lot as your father, and I take responsibility for that. But this one, I'm sorry, only you can solve it. You have to make peace with not being a perfect player," he said.

"That is giving up. I won't do it," I said.

My father shakes his head. "You have to find a way to be right with who you actually are, to face what life is really like. I expected you to figure that out by now. But you haven't. And if you don't, I can't see how you ever get past this . ... this moment. You have accomplished so much, but you are instead so focused on keeping it, rather than going out and finding something else in the world."

He walks toward the door. "Everything we achieve is ephemeral. We have it, and then the next second it's gone. You had that record, and you may lose that record. Or you may defend it now and lose it in two years all over again. I wish you'd accept that."

I shake my head and try to look at him. "I can't."

"Well," he says. "It kills me that I cannot fix that for you, *hija*. But I can't. Nobody else can."

And then, as if the door were the lightest thing in the world, he opens it and walks right through, leaving me there alone.

When I finally make my way back to my floor at the hotel, I come out of the elevator to see Bowe standing in front of my door, signing an autograph for a teenage girl. She walks away before she sees me approaching.

When I get to Bowe, he says, "I wasn't sure if you'd want me here or not. But I figured you wouldn't be shy about telling me to fuck off if you didn't."

I drop my things and hug him. I can feel his surprise, but he quickly puts his arms around me. He does it gently, mindful of his ribs.

"Dust yourself off. Your best surface is just around the bend," he says.

His arms are warm and sturdy. His body is strong. I feel like I could go slack against him and he'd hold me up, that he could bear my weight—the weight of my body, the weight of my failure.

"I was worried people would stop respecting my record if Nicki beat it. But now . . . I'm . . . I'm just ruining my record myself."

I am sitting with my feet on the coffee table, my head resting against the back of the sofa. Bowe is in the chair opposite me, trying to find a position that doesn't hurt his ribs.

"I don't think that's true," he says. "I think people respect the attempt. I think they will respect the attempt even more than the achievement. Which will happen. You will achieve it."

I look at him and frown. "C'mon."

"I'm serious."

I look up at the ceiling. "My father thinks my priorities are all fucked-up."

Bowe laughs softly. "I don't think there is a dad alive who believes in their child more than he believes in you. You see that, right?"

I look at Bowe. "Yeah," I say. "I do."

Bowe leans back slowly. I can tell he is at least feeling better than before. "You're lucky," he says.

"You mean because of my dad?"

"Yeah."

"Didn't your dad play tennis?" I ask. "Isn't that how you started?"

"My uncle," Bowe says. "Yeah. And I was never good enough. Nothing I ever did was good enough. But I just kept trying to please him. And I just kept failing."

"And your parents?"

"They didn't care. My father was a mathematician. My mom is still a math teacher. They didn't understand my obsession with tennis and would have preferred, I think, that I did something a bit more . . . traditional."

"They wanted you to be a doctor or a lawyer?"

"Or a mathematician," Bowe says.

I laugh. "So you're what happens when you don't do what your dad wants, and I'm what happens when you do exactly what your dad wants."

Bowe laughs.

"And now we're both disasters," I say.

Bowe shakes his head. "You're not, Soto. I know you can't see it—because you're one of those annoying kids in school who thinks getting ninety-nine on the test only means you didn't get one hundred."

"It does mean that."

"Yeah, and there you go, ruining the curve for everybody else."

"And everyone hates me."

"I wish you could see it from the outside."

"See what?"

Bowe looks me in the eye and is quiet for a moment. And then he says, *"Eres perfecta, incluso en tu imperfección."*

I sit up, unsure I heard him right. But of course I did. His accent is terrible, but it has knocked the wind out of me just the same.

You are perfect, even in your imperfection.

"How did you put that together?"

"I mean, that's kind of embarrassing to answer."

"Still."

"I found a woman in the lobby of my hotel who spoke Spanish, and I asked her how to help me translate a few things."

"A few things? What else did she translate for you?"

"Well, no," Bowe says. "I can't tell you that."

"Why?"

"Because I just wanted to have a few options in case any of it was relevant."

I stand up and walk over to him. "What were the other options? Did you memorize them all?"

"No," he says. "I tried, but I kept getting them wrong."

"So you wrote them down."

He's still seated, and I'm standing over him. Bowe looks up at me.

"You wrote them down, and they are in your pocket," I say.

"Please don't try to get into my pockets—it's gonna kill my ribs. Seriously, I'm begging you."

There is a past version of me that would have dug into his pockets anyway—that would tell him to deal with the pain. I cringe to remember some of the things I've said to myself—and even to other people—back when I was in my prime. *Man up and play through! Stop being a baby and dominate!*

But I don't want to say any of those things now. I just want to make sure he's not hurting . . . and to see what he's written down.

"Please," I say, my voice low. "Show me."

He frowns and then lifts himself off the chair ever so slightly. He takes a piece of hotel stationery out of his pocket.

"Please don't laugh at me," he says.

I take the paper and open it. There are three Spanish phrases, all written out in his messy handwriting.

You are perfect, even in your imperfection.

You are completely insufferable, and I can't stop thinking about you.

I want the real thing this time.

"You wrote these down? So you could say them to me?"
"Yes."
"If I kiss you, will it hurt?" I ask, moving closer to him.

"What?"

"Your ribs. If I kiss you, will I hurt you?"

"No," he says. "I don't think so."

I put both of my hands on his face and kiss him. He reaches his good arm across my lower back and pulls me toward him.

I've kissed him before, years ago. But this feels both familiar and brand-new, like a good stretch, like a deep breath.

"I don't know what this is," I say. "I don't know if it's the real thing or not."

"I don't care," he says, kissing me again. He grabs at the hem of my T-shirt and the buttons on my jeans.

"I don't want to hurt you."

"I don't care about that either," he says, kissing me again.

"You have to be careful," I say. "Of your ribs."

"Carrie, please," he says, kissing my neck. "Stop worrying."

And so I do.

Later, as the sunlight begins to filter through the window of my hotel room in the early hours of the morning, I wake up to see Bowe asleep next to me.

His hair is sticking up straight in the back, a cowlick let loose at some point in the night. His face, up close, is weathered. There are fine wrinkles around his eyes. I turn away and look out the window, overcome with this awful, sinking feeling. As happy as you are when it starts, you always end up that same amount of sad when it's over.

He begins to stir, his eyes opening slowly and reluctantly. He looks at me and smiles.

He says, "Should we order breakfast?"

"You're going to stay?" I ask.

He sits up, fully awake all of a sudden. "You want me to go?"

"Do you want to go? You can go if you want."

"I don't want to go. I told you that last night. In Spanish."

"Okay," I say.

"So I'm staying?" he says.

"If you want to."

Bowe rolls his eyes and growls. He puts a pillow over his head, but I can still hear him bitching. "You are so annoying," he says. "Just say you like me, for fuck's sake!"

I pull the pillow off his head. I want to say it. I try to make myself.

"What do you want for breakfast?" I say. "I'll call down."

Bowe and I spend the next few days together, walking around Paris. My father, who I still have barely spoken to, stays in his room. Gwen's office booked us all flights home the day after the final.

Tonight, Bowe and I are at a French bistro around the corner from my hotel. The women's final is playing on the television by the bar: Chan vs. Antonovich.

I'm wearing one of Bowe's baseball caps and a pair of sunglasses. We are sitting out on the patio. Part of me wants to run back to the hotel and hide, to not be in public right now. But if people recognize us, they don't acknowledge it. And I want to be here, at this bistro, with Bowe.

We can see the TV from our table. At first, we are both pretending not to watch, but by the time Nicki has won the first set, we have given up all pretenses.

Bowe grabs my hand as the second set begins. I don't pull it away, even when our food arrives. Antonovich takes the second set while we eat our steak frites.

"Maybe Antonovich has a shot," Bowe says.

I frown at him. "I almost wish Cortez had made it past Antonovich in the semis," I say. "I think Cortez could beat Nicki here. But Antonovich . . . I don't know. I don't know."

He nods.

Forty-five minutes later, Nicki takes the third set, 6–4. She drops to the ground, victorious and tearful.

That's the match, that's the tournament, that's my record. Shattered.

Bowe looks at me, but he knows there's nothing to say. We watch as the officials hand Nicki Chan the cup.

All of the coverage is in French, so I only half understand the commentators. But it's clear enough when I hear, *"Elle a maintenant dépásse Carrie Soto . . ." She has overtaken Carrie Soto.*

Bowe catches my eye. And for a moment, I feel the nearly irresistible urge to flip the table we are sitting at.

"She deserves it," I say. "She played a brutal match."

Down the sidewalk, I see my father walking toward me. And I know that I'm supposed to be mad at him, or he's supposed to be mad at me. But I don't really care very much at the moment. Rather, I'm overwhelmed by a sense of inevitability: Of course he would come find me.

"Hi," he says as he makes his way to us on the sidewalk patio. He puts one hand on my shoulder and then the other on Bowe's. "You both did a great job here in France."

He looks me in the eye, and I don't look away. It feels as if the two of us are cycling through decades of moments together, everything that's led to this. My unparalleled achievement. Now hers.

"I have not made peace with it," I say. "If that's what you're wondering."

"*Ya lo sé, pichona,*" he says.

I look up at the television. Nicki is crying, her shoulders heaving, actual tears falling down her face.

"Come sit," I say.

My father nods and pulls a chair over to join us.

The waitress comes by, and Bowe orders my father a drink. Dad leans over and whispers in my ear, "Nothing will ever diminish what you did and have done."

I do not want to cry, so I can't really think too hard about whether I believe him. Instead, I take the moment and pin it to my heart, as if it will wait for me to come back to it later.

I smile, and I pat his hand, and then I change the subject.

Bowe, my father, and I spend the night at that table. We drink club sodas and ginger ales. Bowe laments having to drop out of Wimbledon. My dad tells Bowe that he'll coach him full-time for the US Open, if Bowe is healed by then.

Bowe reaches his hand out and they shake on it—and I notice how gently my father moves, so as not to hurt Bowe's ribs.

When it gets late, Bowe pays the check, and my father raises his eyebrows at me—as if to pose the question that I've told him a million times not to ask. I nod: the only answer he'll get. And he looks at me and grins, a simple, bright smile.

For a moment, I'm bowled over by just how old he looks. *When did this happen?* But he looks a happy old, a satisfied old. He's had a lot of heartbreak in his life, and yet there is so much he's gotten right.

Sos mi vida, pichona, my father mouths to me. He taps a finger to his chest, right over his heart.

I smile and rest my head on his shoulder for a split second.

And then we all walk back to the hotel—a walk that feels comfortable and familiar, even though there is so much about it that is new.

The Inevitability of Chan

By Rachel Berger

Op-Ed, Sports Section
California Post

Carrie Soto has made no secret of her intention to prevent Nicki Chan from overtaking her record. So it must have made the cut that much deeper when Chan won last night.

Some have been dismissive of Soto's attempt at a comeback. But I am among the growing number of those who cannot help but marvel at the attempt.

Many have been quick to forget what Carrie Soto has done for women's tennis. She set the bar for many of the things we now take for granted: incredibly fast serves, brilliant matches that broke multiple records at a time. And we have all but lost the most exquisite thing she brought to the sport: the grace of the game.

I do not care how hard Nicki Chan can hit a groundstroke or how fast her serve can be—she cannot hold a candle to the beauty with which Carrie Soto has played. Each shot executed to perfection, every dive for the ball as graceful as a ballet. So I join Carrie Soto in mourning her loss.

And yet, we cannot deny that the tide has turned.

Carrie Soto is the past. Nicki Chan is the future.

The Queen is dead, long live the Queen.

I WAKE UP TO THE HOTEL PHONE RINGING. BOWE HANDS IT TO ME, half-asleep.

It's Gwen.

"Elite Gold is officially pausing the campaign," she says. "I thought you'd want to know sooner rather than later."

I want to scream or throw the phone or bury my head under my pillow, but I don't. "Okay, I understand."

"AmEx is exploring buying them out, but they haven't committed," she says.

"It's your job to convince them," I say.

"Yes, it is. And it's your job to remember I warned you this could happen. And you told me it was worth the risk."

"Yes," I say. "Yes, I did."

"It will be okay. This will all work out in the end."

"Yeah," I say. But neither of us sounds convinced.

. . .

A few hours later, I do my best to put it behind me as we all get on the plane back to Los Angeles. I switch seats with my father, who has the one next to Bowe. He does not tease me or raise an eyebrow—which I appreciate. He takes my spot two rows ahead.

A couple of college-age girls approach us early in the flight and ask us for our autographs. We agree, but then more people start coming down the aisle.

Soon enough, Bowe starts telling people that he's a Bowe Huntley impersonator, and I stare—mouth half-open—when they actually seem to believe him. I try it on the next woman who comes up, and she just frowns at me and says, "You can't just sign one lousy piece of paper? Unbelievable."

When she storms off, Bowe rolls his eyes and then puts his head on my shoulder. I push it away.

"Everyone on this flight recognizes us," I say.

"So?"

"So when this thing between us goes tits-up, I don't want to have to answer questions about it in a post-match."

Bowe looks at me, his eyebrows high and furrowed. He pinches the bridge of his nose.

"I just mean . . ." I add.

"No, I got it," he says, shifting his weight to the window. "Enough said."

"I'm just saying we don't know what we're doing yet."

"Okay," he says. "I got it. Let's drop it."

He's quiet for an hour or two. But when the flight attendants come by offering chocolates, he wordlessly hands me his.

The plane lands a few hours later, and Bowe reaches for my dad's carry-on from the overhead compartment, despite the fact that it clearly kills his ribs.

"Here you go, Jav," he says.

"Jav?" I say. "You're on a nickname basis now?"

"Of course we are," my dad says. Though he's joking around, he seems tired. "Thanks, B."

"Bowe is already short for Bowen," I say. "You don't need to shorten it again."

My dad waves me off. "Mind your own business, Care."

Bowe laughs, and I throw up my hands.

The line begins to move, and the flight attendants gesture for us to go. The three of us exit the row and get off the plane.

"What is our next meal?" Bowe says. "Is it dinner?"

"It's eleven in the morning, so . . . no," I tell him.

"No need for the attitude," Bowe says. "Just say lunch."

I turn back to look at my father. "Are you hungry, Dad?" I ask, but before I even finish the sentence, I can see he's stopped walking. He's holding up the line of passengers behind him. He's lost all the color in his face.

"Carrie . . ." he says.

"Dad?" I take a step to where he's standing.

He collapses on the jet bridge just before I can catch him.

THE CARDIOLOGIST, DR. WHITLEY, IS A WOMAN WITH CURLY RED HAIR and what appears to be a moral opposition to good bedside manner. She looks up at my father and me. "This is an extreme case of cardio-toxicity," she says.

My father is sitting up in the hospital bed. I'm in a chair next to him. Bowe tried to stay, but we both insisted he go home.

"What does that mean?" I ask.

Dr. Whitley does not look away from my father. "It means you are in stage three heart failure, Mr. Soto. Most likely a side effect of the chemo treatment you had last year."

My father gives the slightest scoff. "What doesn't kill you . . . might still kill you."

I grab his hand and squeeze it, offering him a smile.

"Have you been experiencing light-headedness? Shortness of breath?" she asks.

I answer "No" on his behalf just as my father speaks up. "Yes. Both."

I look at him. "I've been feeling weak too," he adds. "More and more."

"Why didn't you say anything?" I ask.

He ignores me.

"Your oncologist should have told you those were symptoms to watch for," Dr. Whitley says.

"They did," I say. "They did tell us that last year."

Dr. Whitley nods. "If you had spoken up sooner, we could have put you on beta-blockers," she says. "Now the damage is done. You will need surgery to fix the tear and put in a pacemaker."

I stop breathing for a second. I stare straight ahead at the poster on the wall, an ugly still life of a vase of flowers. I try to control my breath and focus as best I can on the mauve plastic picture frame. I swallow, hard. "When do you plan on doing that?" I ask. "The surgery."

Dr. Whitley closes the chart. "Within the next few days. And, Mr. Soto, you will need to stay in the hospital until then. And some time after, as we monitor your progress."

My father shakes his head. "I do not have time for this. We play Wimbledon in three weeks."

"Dad—" I say.

Dr. Whitley's face does not move. "I urge you to listen to the medical advice you're paying for. We have reached a point of life or death."

My father quiets and then nods, and Dr. Whitley leaves the room.

I stand up and wait for the door to close, and then I look at him. "For crying out loud, why didn't you say something?"

"*Eso no es tu problema,*" he says.

"*¡Todos tus problemas son mis problemas!*"

"*Puedo cuidarme solo, Carolina. Sos mi hija, no mi madre.*"

"*¡Sí, y como tu hija, si te mueres, yo soy la que sufre, papá!*"

"*No quiero pelear con vos. Ahora no.*"

I look at him and shake my head. I already know why he didn't say anything, and the reason barely matters now anyway.

His face is pale. He's hooked up to machines. He looks so small. I feel another rush of anger. I press my lips together and close my eyes.

"*Bueno,*" I say. "So we will get ready for you to have the surgery, then."

"And I'll recover quickly and be back on the court with you in no time," he says.

"Dad, let's not get into that now."

"There's nothing to get into. This doesn't set us back at all."

"Dad . . ."

"Say they get me in tomorrow for the surgery; it goes well. What's recovery time? A week?" He takes my hand. "This is a minor setback. By July we'll be ready for London."

"*Bueno, papá,*" I say.

He picks up the remote control and turns on the television and pretends to watch it. So I sit back in the chair and let him.

Then, suddenly, he's yelling. "I am not missing Wimbledon! We may never have another Wimbledon together, and I will not miss it!"

I put my head in my hands. "*Ya lo sé, papá,*" I say.

"The last time we were there, back in '78, I didn't know it was our last. I didn't know that I might never coach you again. And I'm not letting this one slip through my goddamn fingers."

"*Está bien, lo entiendo,*" I say. "*Te amo, papá.*"

He looks at me and for the first time in this conversation, he lets a frown take hold in the corners of his mouth. "*Yo también, cariño.*"

And then, after he takes a breath, "*Perdoname, hija. Realmente lo siento.*"

That night, I ask the nurse to help me pull out a cot.

"*De ninguna manera,*" my father says to me. He turns to the nurse. "That won't be necessary."

"Dad, I'm not leaving you here alone," I say.

"Has it ever occurred to you I might *like* to be by myself?"

"Dad—"

"Sleep at home, Carrie. Please. And in the morning, please go out onto the court with a ball machine," he says. "Do not stop training. You cannot afford to right now."

"I don't know about—"

"You're playing Wimbledon, Carolina María."

The nurse excuses herself, and I sit down for a moment.

"Por favor, no te pierdas Wimbledon. Por favor."

"Dad, I'm not sure—"

My father breathes out, a long and deep breath. He shakes his head. "Even if—I'm saying *if*—I can't be there," he says.

I have to stop the corners of my mouth from pulling down.

"Pero, por favor, play it one more time. *Te encanta jugar Wimbledon. Por favor, hacelo por mí."*

I cannot imagine leaving him. But I also know, right now, I'm not going to fight him.

"Está bien," I say. *"Lo jugaré."*

"Gracias, ahora, andá. Go home."

He seems so determined. *"Bueno,"* I say, grabbing my bag. "I'll see you in the morning."

"Come see me in the afternoon," he says. "Every day, first you train. And then you can come see me after."

I shake my head as I smile at him. "Okay, I'll come tomorrow after I train." I grab his hand and squeeze it.

"Buena, niña," he says.

I walk down the hall and hit the elevator button.

As I wait, I can see out of the corner of my eye that there is a nurse at the station whose gaze lingers on me. She either knows who I am or is trying to figure out where she recognizes me from. I let her wonder as I get in the empty elevator.

When the doors finally close, I lean my back against the wall. I sink down to the floor. "Please let him leave this hospital," I say. It is barely more than a whimper, and I hate the sound of it.

That night, Bowe comes over, and as I'm falling asleep, he puts his arm around me and says, "Everything is going to be okay."

"Everyone always says that," I tell him. "And no one ever knows if it's true."

A couple of days later, my father goes in for surgery. Instead of staying home and training like he has told me to do, I spend the entire day in the waiting room so I can hear the results the moment the surgeon is done.

When Dr. Whitley comes out, she has no smile on her face. For a moment, I feel as if life as I know it is ending. My chest constricts; the room grows hot. But then she says, "He's doing fine." And suddenly I can breathe again.

"Thank you," I say.

"You should go home," she tells me. "He will probably sleep the rest of the night."

But I don't.

I wait until he's moved to recovery and then fall asleep in the chair beside him. Just hearing his breath is enough to allow me to sleep soundly.

In the morning, when he wakes up, he is groggy and confused. But Dr. Whitley says that his pacemaker is operating properly.

"So when can I go home?" he asks.

Dr. Whitley shakes her head. "You have to stay here and recover. The surgery was long, the repairs have to heal. We need you here for observation."

"For how long?"

"Dad, you need to focus on getting better," I say.

He holds my hand and ignores my words. "How long?" he asks again.

"A week at least," she says. "Maybe more."

"Okay," my dad says with a nod. "I understand."

When the doctors leave, I start to ask my dad if he wants me to bring him anything else from home. But he cuts me off.

"If we can't train together, you are wasting your time on the home court. You need to go to London and practice on grass."

"Dad—"

"No," he says. "You know that I'm right. We would have left for London by now anyway. You need to go on your own."

"I know, Dad, but I'm not leaving for London yet, not with you still in the hospital."

"Yes, you are, and don't fight me on it. I've been thinking about this for days now. This is the new plan."

There is a gentle knock at the door. I see Bowe standing in the doorway, holding a fern and a balloon that says *Get Well Soon.*

"Hey, Jav," he says. "Hope I'm not intruding. I just wanted to check on you."

"Come in, come in," my father tells Bowe, who smiles at me. "Actually, I have a great idea," my dad says. "Bowe can come check on me while you're in London. You'll do that, won't you, Bowe?"

Bowe nods. "Absolutely. As long as you need. With my ribs, I can't play tennis. I have *nothing* to do. You could even argue nothing to live for. So yes. It would be a favor to me if you let me check in on you."

I look at the two of them.

"This is a setup," I say.

"It is not a setup," my father says.

"We discussed it prior to today," Bowe says. "If that's what you're saying."

My father rolls his eyes at Bowe. "Don't give up information that hasn't been directly requested."

"Okay," Bowe says. And then he looks at me and mouths, *Sorry.*

"You agree with me that she needs to go to London to train," my father says to Bowe.

And to that, Bowe's answer is clear and appears perfectly honest. "There's no doubt about it. You know damn well you need to go to London."

I hate that they are right.

That Saturday, I'm in a black town car, headed to the hospital to visit my father one last time before my flight. There's a ticket from LAX to Heathrow in my bag. I can barely believe I'm doing this.

When we pull up to the front entrance, the driver drops me off and tells me he'll be waiting in the hospital parking garage.

None of this feels right.

"You'll practice with a hitter every day and then call me each night to talk about the strategy for the next day," my father says after I give him a hug. "We have this under control."

"Don't worry about all of that right now, Dad," I say. I take his hand. "You have one job right now and that is to get healthy."

My father nods. "*Ya lo sé, pero no es el trabajo que quería.*"

"I know."

I rub the back of my father's hand. I can see that the years have gained on him. His skin is papery, his knuckles swollen. The hair on his wrists is nearly fully gray.

"Be well," I say to him. "Do everything the doctors tell you. Be the best patient they have. I'll be home in a little more than a month."

In this moment, it feels absolutely impossible that I could leave. For a moment, I wonder if maybe I never *really* planned on getting on that plane this afternoon. I've just been going through the motions so we'd both feel better.

Of course I can't go. Of course I'm staying.

"I don't know about this, Dad."

"Go play Wimbledon, *cariño.*"

I frown.

"Please," he says. "What would make me happiest is to watch you do something you love. So please, go play tennis. Play it like you used to. Play it like you love it, please. *Hacelo por mí, por mí corazón.*"

"Bowe is coming to the hospital this evening," I say, looking at my watch. "In about an hour. So he can get you anything you need."

"Okay. You're going to be late. So go ahead."

I breathe in deeply. And I kiss him on the head.

"Try to enjoy it, *pichona*," my father says. "That's the one thing you have forgotten."

JUNE 1995

Three weeks until Wimbledon

AS I GET OFF THE PLANE AT HEATHROW, TWO TEENAGE GIRLS ARE standing with their mother and staring at me. I do not know what comes over me but instead of ignoring them, I wave. Their eyes go wide and they each wave back, their mouths agape. I laugh.

When I get into my car at the airport, I ask the driver to take me to my hotel by way of Wimbledon. He gives me a nod. And something about the way his eyes pass over me in the rearview mirror, the way he holds back a smile on his face, I can tell he is excited to do it.

I look out the window as we begin to drive. I watch the buildings and British billboards pass, until we finally reach the outskirts of the All England Lawn Tennis Club.

"Did you want to stop?" he says.

"No, thank you," I say. I just enjoy the sight of it—seeing the park and the courts fly by my window. I like gazing up at the ivy growing over the building at the front entrance. I feel the most like myself just outside that arena. As if I fully embody my own promise.

It is an unparalleled pleasure to be as good at something as I have been at playing Wimbledon.

I miss my father.

"You hold the record," my driver says as he catches my eye in the rearview mirror again. "Don't you now?"

"Which one?" I ask.

"Most Wimbledon wins. Men's or women's."

"Yes," I say. "I do."

He nods and puts his eyes back on the road. "Good on ya."

I check in to my hotel and unpack. I open the curtains and look out over the Thames and the Waterloo Bridge. The city is busy with cars and people—it is, after all—four P.M. in London. But I need to get some rest.

Ali has booked me courts to practice double sessions for the next three weeks. I requested different hitters each time. I need to be able to practice with all types of players.

I watch red double-decker buses cross the bridge, and I consider the biggest hurdle to my game: I need to get my mind right.

I take a shower. Scalding hot, so scorching it reddens the skin of my chest and legs. And then I call my father's room at the hospital.

Bowe answers.

"Hi," I say. "How is he?"

Bowe whispers his response. "He's sleeping now. But he's good. How are you?"

"I'm all right." I look at myself in the mirror of the bathroom as we talk. My hair is wet and pulled back; the white robe around me is bulky and warm. All I can focus on are the bags under my eyes—like two soft bruises. I can blame jet lag and age but also: When I'm alone, I cry.

"It feels weird being here without him," I say. "Or without you, to be honest."

"That's nice of you to say."

"I'm worried I won't find anyone to hit off of who is as good as you."

"Oh," Bowe says. And then he laughs.

"What?"

"No, nothing. Listen, your dad made these notes, and he'll be pissed if I don't relay them."

"Okay."

"He said, 'Spend tomorrow remembering the joy of grass. Do not play to win or to find perfection. Play to observe yourself and the ball.'"

"That's good advice," I say.

"He is, unfortunately, quite good at this," Bowe says.

And now I laugh. "Yes, I suppose he is."

We hang up the phone; I pull the curtains closed and put my eye mask on. I lie down on the gigantic bed.

The windows are thick, and the walls are thick too. My room is about as private and expansive as it gets in central London. And so, despite it being afternoon in a bustling city, things are eerily quiet.

I keep imagining my father coming over from the next room, knocking on my door to tell me he just had a brilliant idea. Or him bothering me to complain about a photo of him printed in the newspaper. Or some other thing that I would be annoyed by, as I tell him I want to go to sleep.

But he is not here.

I don't know when I finally doze off. But when I wake the next morning, I am rested.

I brush my teeth, put on my sweats, grab my kit. The hum is in my bones.

I head out to the courts. Alone.

My father was absolutely right. I have needed to feel the specific crispness of grass.

The hitter I'm playing this morning is named Bridget. She's fast but not terribly powerful. And yet, still, I feel a thrill as I run from sideline to sideline, up and back from the net to the baseline. It is such a joy to play on grass. I relish the snap, the speed, the low bounces, the unpredictability, the strategy. It is an entirely different game—lawn tennis.

And I fucking love it.

At the end of the session, Bridget says, "I fear I did not give you much of a run for your money." I have sweat on my forehead and upper lip. She's drenched through her tank top.

"That's all right," I say. "You did your best."

Her face tightens, and then she makes her way out. I sit down on the bench and drink some water. I begin running through what I want to work on with the ball machine—which shots I'll start with. My slice, in particular, needs some sharpening.

I take stock of my grass game. My footwork feels good. My serves are sharp. I'm putting the ball where I want it. I've come such a long way since Melbourne.

Still, even on grass, I'm probably not as fast as Antonovich. So if I do come up against her again, I will have to find another way to offset her speed. But that's what I'm here to do.

I look down at my yellow sneakers on the green turf. Maybe this whole season has been leading here. Maybe I just needed to come back to Wimbledon.

I stand up, trying to find one of the facility managers to get a ball machine. But when I scan the area, I see Nicki Chan walking past my court.

I pretend not to see her at first, but it soon becomes clear she's not the type to let me get away with that. Why are people like this? Honestly. Let's all just walk by each other all day and not stop to small-talk.

"Carrie," she says, smiling, extending her hand.

"You practice here?" I ask. "I would have thought you'd—"

Nicki shakes her head. "This place is a bit quieter. And I needed some focus. I booked a court out here for the next few weeks until we all head over to Wimbledon Park. You did too, then?"

"Yep."

Nicki laughs. "We both had the same good idea. All right, well," she says. "Maybe one of these days we can grab a drink."

"Maybe," I say. "I mean, no, I'm probably not going to do that."

Nicki laughs again. And I find it irritating, that laugh. It feels performative, like some false unflappability. "You know what somebody on the tour told me about you back in the day?" she asks.

"Oh great, here we go."

"No, no, it's not bad. Just . . . she said that you seem tough, you seem cold. But really, you're one of those players who keep to themselves because you feel conflicted when you have to kick somebody's ass."

"I just think it keeps it a lot simpler . . . to not care too much for anybody."

Nicki nods. "I understand."

"You don't feel that way?" I ask.

Nicki shakes her head. "I'd wreck my best friend in cold blood on national television."

The next morning, I'm awake at four. I can't stand to lie here, turning from one side to the other, fluffing the pillow, staring at the ceiling, thinking about Paris.

How I fucked it all up.

Handed Nicki that record.

I get out of bed and go into the living room. Ali put the matches I requested on VHS tapes and sent them over. I shuffle through the box until I find the one I need.

Soto vs. Antonovich.

My chest tightens as I put the tape in the machine and press play.

It's painful to watch. I hate how helpless I am to prevent what I know will happen onscreen. But it is my only way of ensuring that it does not happen again.

Right from the jump, I'm fast but I'm sloppy. My pace is so hurried, I'm not setting up my angles. I'm running for shots I know I can't get.

I have to will myself not to turn off the television.

The second set, I'm just plainly making bad choices. Not disguising my shots well. Hitting a groundstroke right to her. Sending a slice way too short. I'm choking. Just choking out there.

All because I'm trying to prove to Antonovich that she's not faster than me. When I can see it so clearly on the tape.

She is faster than me. That's exactly what she is.

I head down to the courts hours earlier than I'd planned. There is no one there. I've got the place to myself. And so I start hitting against the ball machine.

Part of what I love about a grass surface is how it requires such quick thinking. Other players may be able to run faster from one side of the court to the other. They might even be able to hit the ball so it moves faster across the net. But what I have always been good at, the challenge I have always taken pleasure in rising to, is thinking on my feet on a tennis court.

You have to ask and answer a series of questions in rapid succession: Where is the ball going? What way will it bounce when it hits? How do I want to hit it back? And where do I need to be standing in order to do that?

When I was a child, my father focused on the fundamentals—the stances, the form.

Look at the ball, turn, swing.

Look, turn, swing.

Look, turn, swing.

Look, turn, swing.

With a serve, it was legs bent, arms up, toss, hit, follow through.

Legs, arms, toss, hit, follow.

Legs, arms, toss, hit, follow.

Legs, arms, toss, hit, follow.

Hour after hour, day after day, the same drills. Sometimes not even hitting an actual ball but just doing the motions, feeling the routine of it. My dad would even make me do it in front of a mirror, watching each movement in my body as I flowed through the form.

I remember getting so frustrated at the repetition—the sheer boredom. My father made me practice long after I'd perfected it. And I would rail against him when I was a kid, but he would not be swayed from his plan, even one session.

"Do you think about breathing?" he asked me one afternoon on the courts when I was complaining. "You are breathing, with your lungs, every second you are alive, no?"

"Yes," I said.

"But do you think about it?"

"No, my body just does it."

"Think about how little else you could do if you had to think about how to breathe every time you did it."

"Okay . . ."

"I want your form to be like breathing. Right now, *hijita,* you are still doing it with your mind," he told me. "We will not stop until you have done it so many times, your body does it without thinking. Because then, you'll be free to think of everything else."

I don't know if I understood it then or just resolved to do as I was told. But when I joined the junior circuits and then the WTA, and I looked at the other women I was playing, I could see how slowly most other players reacted.

My father had crammed my forms, my stances, my strokes into my mind with such repetition that it made its way into my cells. It lived in my muscles and joints.

It's true, still, today.

And so, with every ball that comes at me, my mind remains free to run through every single shot I have in my arsenal, to consider the flaws in the court. I can better anticipate a bad bounce, or find a shot my opponent isn't expecting.

And then comes the moment when I make contact with the ball—and in that split second, muscle memory takes over.

Grass has always been perfect for that type of play.

As I stand here on the court, up against the ball machine, meeting each ball after the bounce, I am fluid. My body is just doing this. It is almost as if I'm not even here. This grace, this flow, this effortlessness—*this* is 1983 me.

When the machine runs out of balls for the fourth time, I stop. All hundred of them are strewn about on the other side of the court.

I am sweating and breathless. I look at my watch. I've been out here almost three hours—but I would have sworn it was twenty minutes. And for one brief moment, it feels like I am Carrie Soto.

"Hello."

I turn to find Nicki watching me through the fence, one hand gripping the grate. *Goddammit.*

"Oh. Hi."

"I came this early to avoid you," Nicki says, laughing.

"Sorry, been out here since about five A.M."

Nicki nods. "It is stunning," she says. "Watching you play."

I walk toward her. "Yeah, well, I am very good."

Nicki laughs again. "Yes, you are. The beauty of your form is . . . it's breathtaking. I remember it always being that way. You could see it even on TV back in the day. Just now, as I was spying a bit . . ." She shakes her head. "It's gorgeous tennis."

How am I supposed to respond to that? "A drink, tonight," I hear myself say. "If you still want. At the Savoy."

Nicki nods. "I'll be there."

Later that afternoon, I'm on the phone in the living room of my suite, looking out the window. "*No sé, papá, pero* . . . I just . . . I'm feeling that hum. I'm feeling like this could be it. This one could be mine."

His voice is small. "It will be, *hija*," he says. I keep pressing my ear harder into the receiver, as if by pressing hard enough, I can force myself through the line and be right next to him. "It will be."

"How are you feeling?"

"*Bien, bien. Pero* do not worry about me. Bowe is coming later this morning. I'm going to demolish him in another round of chess."

"And what does Dr. Whitley say?"

"She says everything is great. Stop worrying," he says.

"Okay," I say. "*Está bien.*"

I don't say what I'm thinking. *You are all I have.*

When I get down to the American Bar at the Savoy, Nicki is already there. She's talking to the bartender, who slides over a cocktail glass.

There's something so casually confident about Nicki, so unbothered. We're in an elegant bar and she's wearing a pair of black jeans and a T-shirt with a pair of Doc Martens. Her long hair hangs down her back.

Nicki waves to me, and I make my way over to the bar. She's drinking what seems to be gin with a twist.

"Absolut and soda, please," I say to the bartender, who nods but then looks back up at me. "Are you Carrie Soto?" she says.

I look at Nicki, who smiles as she takes a sip of her gin.

"Yeah," I say.

"Wow, big fan of yours," she says. "I mean, I don't know much about tennis, but I love your sneakers."

I laugh. "Well, good, I'm glad to hear it."

She heads down the bar, and Nicki laughs, shaking her head. "I've been sitting here talking to that beautiful woman for at least ten minutes, and somehow she doesn't recognize me. Even though my tennis shoes are better than yours, by the way."

Her line is with Nike. They are called 130s—a reference to the fact that she once hit a serve that clocked in at 130 miles per hour. They are the *second* bestselling women's tennis shoe in the UK.

"It appears she disagrees," I say.

"It's not that I *want* to be recognized, mind you," she says. "But if she's going to recognize you and not me . . . well, c'mon."

"You know," I say, sitting down, "I once showed up to cut a ribbon at a tennis center named after me in Arizona, and the woman at the front door wouldn't let me in because I wasn't on the list."

Nicki laughs and takes another sip of her drink. "It's a weird life."

"Yes, it is."

"I'm not always sure I like it."

My drink arrives, and I take a sip of it. "Not always much to like."

"Isn't it strange? How you get into this because you like to hit a ball around a court . . . ? And then, suddenly, you don't belong to yourself anymore? As if it's okay for people to call you 'the Beast' just because you're strong? And they can comment on your clothes and your hair? And make racist comments and pretend they are just joking? Just wait until they find out I'm a lesbian."

Nicki looks at me out of the corner of her eye, as if expecting me to spit out my cocktail. But I have long suspected she is gay, and I couldn't care less. Romantic relationships are so goddamn impossible, I'm honestly impressed with anyone who can keep one going at all.

Though, it's occurring to me now, that probably doesn't account for how hard it is for her to deal with the world's hang-ups about it. Or how hard it must be to decide who to confide in.

And she confided in me. And fuck if it doesn't make me like her more. *Goddamn her.*

"You don't have to tell me how shitty the press are. You're talking to a woman referred to as 'the Bitch,'" I remind her.

Nicki laughs. "I just wanted to play the game. And now, instead, I'm shooting TV commercials and telling twelve-year-old girls to believe in their dreams and agreeing to be a guest host on breakfast television. It just feels like . . . so many things get in the way of the actual point."

I look at her, and then I look down. I turn the glass. "Once you retire, then it's *only* about the TV commercials. And the charity functions and playing to the crowd for exhibition games. And the real tennis just sort of goes. Poof. Gone."

Nicki frowns. "No, I don't believe that."

I shrug. "Believe whatever you want."

"When I retire, I want to take up at my place in the Cotswolds and quit all the rest. Just spend my days playing on my court in the countryside."

"But against who?" I say. "There's no one to play except maybe other retirees. You're not gonna play the neighborhood girl—that's not fun. And you're not going to play anyone in the WTA, because they are busy on tour. And they certainly don't want to be beaten by you. The exhibition games are all right, but they are just for show— there's no real intensity. There's no one to play in any serious way. I swear there were days I'd wake up and my right hand would be jit- tery, wondering where the racket was."

Nicki nods. "So that's why you're back, then? Your right hand is jittery?"

"No," I say, shaking my head. "I came back to destroy you."

Nicki cackles so loud that people turn and stare. When she qui- ets, she leans in toward me. "I don't buy it for a second," she says, smiling. "It's about more than that."

"No, I'm dead serious. I want my fucking record back."

"Of course," Nicki says. "Of course you do. Who wouldn't?"

"And you took it."

"I didn't *take* it," Nicki says. "I earned it. The same way you did. But just one more Slam than you." She winks at me and then takes a drink.

"You haven't had to go up against anyone great," I say. "In the past six years, there's been almost nobody who can hold a candle to you."

"Exactly."

"Give me a break. It's easier to win when you don't have a Stepa- nova. Or somebody like Mary-Louise Bryant, who started out so stunning. Or me, even. The field has been leveled for you. It's not the same as the way I set the record."

Nicki shakes her head. "You sound like every pundit on ESPN."

"What?" I say. "Are you kidding me? Every sportscaster in the world is tripping over themself to crown you the best!"

"That's how it may seem to you. But what I hear—over and again—is that even when I beat your record, it's not good enough. I will never be Carrie Soto. I'll never be as graceful as you. I've never had a truly formidable opponent. Yes, I'm good on clay and hard court, but 'Carrie Soto reigns in London.' This is my hometown, but somehow it still belongs to you."

She takes another sip of her gin. "And then," she adds, "just when it looks like I'm finally going to silence them all, it becomes 'Wow! Carrie Soto is back!' And they all do cartwheels over you."

"I mean this from the bottom of my heart: Are you fucking high?" I say.

Nicki laughs.

"Try being told—over and over and over again—that if you do manage to win anything this year, you will set a record for being the oldest bitch to ever do it."

Nicki laughs. "Yes, I'm sure it's terribly awful to know that if you win Wimbledon, you will set two records and match mine."

My fists clench. It takes everything I have not to slam my hand on the bar and remind her who had that record first, who *made* that record. *There is no you without me.*

But I have no leg to stand on anymore. I lost it back in Paris.

"Do you have any idea," I say, "how hard it is to work your entire life toward one goal—*one goal*—and then to have someone else come in and try to take it away?"

Nicki looks at me, incredulous. "Yes!" she says. "In fact, I do."

I look at her and realize what I've just said. I cannot help but laugh, and neither can Nicki.

"God, you must hate me," I say. "I would. I would hate me."

Nicki downs the rest of her glass. "I don't hate you. I told you before. I'm thankful."

"Yeah. I'm sure."

"I'm serious," Nicki says. "I can't fight unless I have something to fight against. And I like fighting. I like it even more than winning."

"I . . ." I say. "Okay."

"Without you, I wouldn't have much left to fight against. It would be like trying to knock out a deflated punching bag. And without me, you'd be back home, shooting a commercial for Gatorade, would you not?"

I huff, knowing she's right. "Yeah, maybe. Yes."

"But instead, we're here, training, living for something bigger than the two of us."

I take a sip of my vodka soda. And consider her. "I'm not sure I ever thought of it that way with Paulina," I say.

"Stepanova?" Nicki says, rolling her eyes. "Who would? She faked injuries every time she was down, and then the one time she actually messes up her ankle, she doesn't have the courage to either retire or play through."

"Thank you!" I say.

"Crocodile tears, the whole lot of them."

"Yes!"

"She was not a worthy opponent for you."

"That's what I said from the beginning!"

"But I am," Nicki says, her eyes focusing in on me.

I look at her. "I guess that's what remains to be seen, doesn't it?" I say.

"Yes, I believe it does."

Nicki throws down thirty pounds and stands up. She pats me on the shoulder. "What time are you practicing tomorrow?"

"I don't know," I say. "Depends on whether I can sleep."

"All right. Well, work hard. I want to know, when I beat you, that you were playing at your best. I want to know that I can beat the greatest tennis player of all time. I need it. And I need the world to see it."

"Feel free to fuck right off with that bullshit," I say.

Nicki laughs. "It is only by playing you at your best that I can get better," she says. "Just like you up against Stepanova with that slice all those years ago. I'm the best player in the WTA. I need someone else—someone great—to push me up against the ropes. And here you come back, just in time. Just for me."

"Not for you," I say.

"Right, for you," she says. "I'm just the excuse you needed."

She's right, despite how it irritates me. I was never really done before. I was always going to do this: show up and fight one last time.

"Either way, one of us is the catalyst for the other reaching their greatest height yet."

"All right," I say. "Good night, Nicki."

"Good night, mate."

"I'm not your mate," I say, shaking my head. "I may have had a drink with you, but we are not mates."

"We *are* mates," Nicki says. "And that's good—do you know why?"

"Why?"

"Because if you'd made a few mates during your time in the WTA the first go-round, I don't think you would have had such a jittery right hand these past few years."

I look up at her and it's clear she meant to cut, but I can't tell whether she knows how deep the knife just went in.

"All right," I say. "That's my cue to leave."

The bartender pops her head up. Her eyes go wide, looking at the two of us. "Wait, are you Nicki Chan?"

Nicki smiles wide and lopsided, a dimple forming. "Why, yes, I am," she says. "Number one in the world. Record holder for the most Grand Slam singles ever."

"And yet she's only won Wimbledon twice," I say to the bartender. "Isn't that funny?"

Two days before the start of Wimbledon, I find out that my father is being released from the hospital, and I breathe out so completely that I wonder how long I've been holding that breath. When the draft comes in, I call him at home to discuss.

"Read it to me," my father says over the phone.

"I play Cami Dryer in the first round," I say, looking at the pages that had been faxed to my hotel earlier today. I throw myself down on the sofa.

"Piece of cake, she can't anticipate," my dad says. "Hit your marks, you'll be fine. Who is after that?"

I gauge who is likely to win the other match. "Probably Lucy Cameron."

"She's easy to ruffle," my dad says.

I look up at the ceiling. "Yeah, I was thinking the same thing. Break her early and I'm probably good. Then after that it's . . ." I pull the chart up to my eyeline for a second. "Martin or Nystrom."

"It will be Nystrom, most likely," my dad says.

"No way," I say. I'm up now, pacing. "Martin is the better player."

"Martin has had a lot of trouble in the past adjusting her game to grass. She plays too far back on the court. It will be Nystrom, unless Martin has gotten a better coach."

"Well, Nystrom I can take. Her volley game is good, but her serve is shit—I can break her in the first game."

"Exactly. Next?"

"Could be Johns."

"Slow as an ox," my dad says. "She can't keep up. If she gets to you, just keep the ball moving quick. If you set the pace from the jump and don't let up, she's out."

"Yeah, you're right."

"Who's next?"

"Don't you think you should be relaxing?" I say.

"No, I don't," my father says. "Not while my daughter prepares for Wimbledon. Now, who is next?"

"Probably Moretti," I say. "By the looks of it."

"Who else could it be?" he says.

"Maybe Machado."

"I'd put money on Machado," he says.

"Why?"

"She's an underestimated player, but she adjusts very quickly. Moretti only has one mode of play: power. Machado has more shots. I think it's Machado."

"So then what do I do?" I say.

"If it does end up Moretti, she's not strong on the run, so keep her there and her game will fall apart. If it's Machado . . . I think you stay economical at the beginning, play percentage tennis. If you win the first set, you're well on your way. If you don't, you have to win the next two sets, but you're not as tired as she is."

"Okay," I say. "Sure."

"Who's next?"

I look at the chart. "Uh, hard to say," I tell him. I look out the window at the river. "Could be Antonovich, though."

My father is quiet for a moment.

I turn my attention back to the phone. "But I have a plan for Antonovich."

"What's your plan?"

"She's faster than me, and she's good on grass," I say.

He pauses and then says, "Okay."

"So I follow your advice from Paris. I don't try to match her speed. I won't win that game. If anything, I slow the game down."

"*Sí, es un buen plan . . .*"

"But I've played on Wimbledon grass my whole life, so I know better than anyone where that ball is going."

"That's right."

"So I disguise my shots, don't let her figure out where I'm going. I aim for brown spots in the grass, I watch for bad bounces. If I can get her to three sets, I will win. Because by that point, I'll have run far less than her."

My father takes a deep breath and then lets it out. "Yes, I like it."

"Is it what you would have said?"

"I'd add this: She's going to anticipate that you have something to prove after last time. She'll be expecting that you're coming in hot. So hold back, and make it seem like you're giving it your best, until she realizes you're only getting started."

"Okay," I say. "Yes. That will work."

It is what Cortez did to me in Melbourne.

"And then?" my dad asks. "Who's next?"

"Chan."

"No Cortez?"

"Chan will defeat Cortez in the semis when I'm up against Antonovich."

"All right, so assuming I've called these correctly—which is absolutely impossible . . ."

I laugh.

"In two weeks, you're standing there holding a tenth silver plate."

"That easy, huh?"

"Not easy at all, *pichona,*" he says. "But if anyone can do it, you can. And I'll be watching it all from right here."

"*Gracias, papá.*"

"Bowe wants to talk to you," he says. "He's taking the phone from me—he's literally taking it out of my hands."

"Hi," Bowe says. His voice is warm, and I wish he were here with me instead of thousands of miles away.

"Hi," I say. "How are your ribs?"

"Fine," Bowe says. "Better. Your father and I are a real pair over here."

"Thank you for what you're doing. I don't think I could stand to be *here* if you weren't *there.*"

"Don't mention it, honestly," he says. "But, hey, listen, I wanted to ask you something."

"Okay . . ." I'm worried he's going to ask me if I want him to visit or how things will be between us when I get back. And I don't want to have to think about that right now.

"Have you given any thought to the Self 1, Self 2 thing?" he asks.

"What?"

"All that strategy you and your dad were talking about . . ."

"Yeah?"

"Look, you're a better player than almost anyone on the court. And I don't just mean over the course of your career. I mean right now."

"I hope that's true. I don't know. I need it to be true—let's say that."

I stand at the window and watch a Thames riverboat tour float by. My father and I did that tour once, when I was barely a teenager and we were here for my first Junior Wimbledon. I fell asleep, and later he told me all the history about the Tower of London that I'd missed. "Next time, stay awake," my dad said. "You are getting to see the world, *pichona*. It's an opportunity so few people have." Even then, I didn't know how to tell him that I was too tired, that sightseeing was a luxury that I didn't have, never wanted. What we were doing took all of me; there wasn't anything left over.

"It is true—you're the best out there. But that's the problem," Bowe says. "You need to *know it* instead of needing to *prove it*. You need to quiet Self 1 and let Self 2 do its thing."

"Okay," I say. "Okay."

"I know you don't want to take advice from me—" Bowe begins. But I stop him.

"Yes, I do," I say. "I do want to take advice from you." I sit down at the window and grab a piece of hotel stationery and a pen to make notes for myself. He is right. I do need to calm down, to listen to my instincts. I need to get the voice in my head to shut up. "Go ahead," I say. "Tell me more. I'm listening."

It is the morning of my first match, facing Cami Dryer. I've gone for a run and I'm just getting out of the shower when there is a knock at my door.

I wrap myself in my robe and answer. I'm expecting room service with my breakfast, but when I open the door, it's Gwen. I take it all in—her in front of me in a green velvet suit and a big, bright smile on her face.

"Hi," she says.

The sight of her makes my shoulders relax. Before I know what I'm doing, I throw myself into her arms.

She squeezes me tight and then lets go. "All right. That's enough of that, until you get dressed."

I pull her into my suite.

"You're here," I say. "I had no idea you were coming."

"Ali and I both flew in to surprise you. She's back at the hotel."

"Wow," I say.

"You know I love London. And I love you. And so here I am."

I suddenly feel my voice quivering, and I get control of myself. "That's kind of you."

"Yeah, well, you know I need my yearly strawberries and cream."

When I come back out after getting dressed, she's set herself up in my living room, and she's already on her cellphone, scolding someone. She finishes her call and looks at me. The intensity of her gaze makes me sit straighter.

"How are you?" she says, frowning.

"Well . . . I feel better than I've felt in years."

Gwen nods. "Great. Good. I love that."

"But . . . playing without my dad here . . . I don't know."

Gwen nods.

"It feels like the late eighties all over again. Playing without my dad, when the whole point was to do this *with* my dad. For us to have one last season together."

Gwen grabs my hand and squeezes it. "So go win it and bring him back the trophy."

WIMBLEDON
1995

IN THE ENTRANCE HALL AT CENTRE COURT AT WIMBLEDON, THERE IS an inscription just above the double doors that lead out to the grass. It is from the poem "If—" by Rudyard Kipling.

IF YOU CAN MEET WITH TRIUMPH AND DISASTER

AND TREAT THOSE TWO IMPOSTORS JUST THE SAME

It has never resonated with me. Every time I have walked onto the courts at Wimbledon, I have considered triumph to be paramount. And when I have held it in my hands, it has not felt like an impostor at all.

But as Gwen and I walk into the hall this morning, she says, "I've always loved that quote."

"You know," I say as we head to the clubhouse, "I read the whole poem years ago, to try to understand the inscription better. But it didn't help. I do remember thinking the first line of the poem made more sense to me than that line. But now I can't even remember what it is."

Gwen smiles. "'If you can keep your head when all about you / Are losing theirs and blaming it on you.'"

I look at her. "Yeah, that's it. What, were you an English major or something?"

Gwen pulls her head back. "Yes."

"Wait, really?"

"Yes. I got my BA from Stanford before going to UCLA for my MBA."

"Oh," I say. "I didn't know that. That's cool." I never officially finished high school, never set foot on a college campus. And I am convinced sometimes that, despite all my accomplishments, this lack of sophistication shows in ways I'm unaware of.

"Not sure how cool it is. It doesn't often come in handy that I know the entirety of 'If—' by Rudyard Kipling."

"Well, I still think it's impressive," I say as I head toward the dressing room.

"All right," Gwen says, "I'm going to make some calls, and I'll see you in the players' box."

"Okay," I say.

"Good luck, Carolina," she says.

I cannot help but smile. "Thank you."

I start to walk away, but then I turn back.

"Hey," I say, calling to her. "Thank you for being here. And for supporting me in this, from the beginning. The whole year. Even though it's crazy."

Gwen smiles. "Do you know what part of 'If—' is actually relevant right now? To this moment? 'If you can make one heap of all your winnings / And risk it on one turn of pitch-and-toss, / And lose, and start again at your beginnings / And never breathe a word about your loss.'"

She must be messing with me. Surely she knows she's just described my greatest fear. But no, I can tell from the look on her face that she sincerely thinks that I'm that brave, that I am doing this because I am okay with losing big. Not because I am terrified of losing at all.

And it stuns me silent, for a moment: just how vast the gap is between who I am and how people see me.

I am so much smaller than the Carrie Soto in Gwen's head.

SOTO VS. DRYER

Wimbledon 1995

First Round

AS I STEP OUT ONTO THE COURT, I FEEL THE SUN BLAZING DOWN. I hear the commotion of the crowds. I look up to see stands full of well-dressed Brits with large hats and fascinators. I am flooded with the comfort of the scent of Wimbledon—fresh-cut grass and Pimm's and lemon.

I am home.

I bounce on my toes, feeling the grass and dirt beneath my white Break Points.

I look across the court at Cami Dryer. She is young, not even eighteen.

I smile and shake her hand as we come together at the net.

She is adorable—all perky and eager. She shakes my hand with an excitement that reminds me of myself when I was younger. And I feel this sudden contentment deep within my gut.

You could not pay me enough money to go back to being seventeen. When I was seventeen, my talent was all potential and no proof. The world was a giant set of unknowns, barely any past to pull from.

I am so grateful, right now, for every match and every win and every loss and every lesson that I have behind me. It feels so good, right now, to be thirty-seven years old. To have figured at least *some* things out.

To know the ground underneath my feet.

Poor Cami Dryer doesn't know what is about to hit her. She wins the coin toss and calls first serve. I get into position and take her in two sets.

Transcript

BBC Sports Radio London
SportsWorld with Brian Cress

And in women's tennis it's been nearly a fortnight of stunning wins and crushing losses.

London's own Nicki Chan has sailed through each of her matches. As have favorites such as Ingrid Cortez and Natasha Antonovich. Meanwhile, it's been a hair-raiser for firebrand Carrie Soto. She has clawed her way through the five rounds—beating Brits Cami Dryer and Lucy Cameron in the first and second, Swede Celine Nystrom in the third, and the Baltimore Baseliner Carla Perez in the round of sixteen.

She's now defeated Italian Odette Moretti in the quarterfinals.

Bringing her to the semifinals, where she and Russian phenom Natasha Antonovich will go head-to-head.

Transcript

SportsHour USA
The Mark Hadley Show

Mark Hadley: And wow, Carrie Soto.

Gloria Jones: Carrie is headed to the semifinals! At this point, the fact that she is still a force of nature is undeniable. Briggs, call her whatever you want, but you have to admit this is fun to watch. This is a player giving audiences a rip-roaring good show as she fights her way to the finish.

Briggs Lakin: Look, I am the first to admit when I'm wrong. I said earlier this year that Carrie wouldn't make it to Wimbledon, and I stand corrected. But in hindsight, it seems obvious, doesn't it? Of course this was Soto's move. Of course Wimbledon would be her only real shot at a title this year.

Hadley: And can she do it? Gloria?

Jones: I think it's going to be hard. She now has the three best players in the game ahead of her. She will go up against Antonovich next. This is Carrie's best surface, but this is also Antonovich's.

Lakin: In some ways, it's an interesting match, these two. Natasha Antonovich, her style of play—the quick pace, the great volleys—owes a lot to Carrie Soto. We saw that back in Paris. I said, "Natasha is the new Carrie." It's almost as if this is Carrie's chance to play her old self on her best surface.

Jones: If Carrie wants to prove there is only one Carrie Soto, well, this is the chance.

I AM SITTING IN THE LOCKER ROOM WITH MY EYES CLOSED, LISTENING to the waves of my breath. I pick up my cellphone and dial my dad.

He doesn't miss a beat.

"Don't think about strategy now," he says. "The time for that is over. This is the time for instinct."

"I know," I say, taking in a deep breath. "I know."

"You are prepared. Trust your preparation."

"I know."

"Don't listen to Self 1," he says.

I laugh without opening my eyes. "You've been listening to Bowe."

"Be Self 2."

"Don't think," I say. "Just act."

"Don't think," my father says. "Just *play*."

SOTO VS. ANTONOVICH

Wimbledon 1995

Semifinals

NATASHA ANTONOVICH HOVERS ON THE OTHER SIDE OF THE COURT, adjusting her visor. She's steady now, both feet firmly on the baseline. But we both know the second she wants to, she'll go flying across this court.

She hits a kick serve. It bounces high, and I hit it back over the net. I watch her dive, but it bounces too low for her to get it.

Love–15.

I smile up at Gwen and Ali in the players' box as I walk back to the baseline.

I know my father is watching. I know Bowe is with him. I know they are cheering for me, even if I can't hear them.

Less than an hour later, I'm at break point on the first set. I'm up six games to five. It's her serve.

She sends a fast flat one my way, and I race to it. I notice she hasn't moved toward the center of the court. She's anticipating a cross-court forehand.

I take the ball out of the air quick, sending it right down the line. She dives hard for it, slides across the grass. She can't return it.

The first set is mine.

I see Gwen applauding, Ali hollering. I wonder if Bowe is cheering in front of the television.

But I do not need to imagine my father's reaction. I know he is clapping and smiling ear to ear, for once unworried that the cameras will get an unflattering picture of him.

Antonovich catches up faster than I'd like. She's starting to read my serve. I need to do a better job of disguising my ball toss.

And I need to do it quick, because I'm not getting any more aces off her. I can see her gaining confidence as she starts returning more and more of my junk shots too.

We are now tied 6–6 in the second set.

She's serving for the set. She sends three kick serves in a row, and each one bounces differently. It knocks me out of my flow.

The second set is hers.

It's the final set, 4–4.

I'm sweating down my back, across my forehead, on the backs of my knees. There's a flutter—an unrest—in my stomach. I can barely hear the crowd. The dominating sound is the propulsive and angry *whoosh* of my pulse in my own ears.

My knee is burning.

My strategy is shot. I had hoped to run Antonovich down, but the games are happening too fast. We have such short rallies that I can't wear her out.

During the changeover, I sit down to drink my water. I breathe in deeply and close my eyes. I have to rethink my strategy here.

Antonovich has settled into the game. She is anticipating better. She is moving smarter.

I need a way to get her on the run again, to unnerve her.

When I stand up, I find myself looking into the players' box to meet my father's eye. But of course he isn't there. Instead, Gwen and Ali are smiling at me.

What would he say? I give myself the briefest of seconds before I walk back onto the court.

Slow the game down.

I walk out onto the court and get into position, my own voice churning through my head. *Do not let this slip through your fingers, Soto. You're so goddamn close. And if you fuck this one up, you'll be zero and three.*

My hand tenses around the racket.

I am afraid.

I am afraid of losing. I am afraid of how it will look to the world. I'm afraid of this match being the last match my father ever sees me play. I am afraid of ending this all on a loss. I am afraid of so much.

I loosen my grip on the racket. I clear my mind. I let go. I have to.

Instead of racing to serve the next one, I take a moment on the baseline. I imagine myself serving the ball. I imagine how it will feel in my calves to get up high on my toes, I imagine the swing of my arm, the way my ribs will follow the line of my shoulder.

My body knows what to do. Now I just have to let it do it.

When I open my eyes, I see her crouched in place, waiting. My eye goes right to her feet. I'm going to piss her off. I toss the ball in the air and serve the first shot of the game so that it will bounce straight to her toes. She has to jump out of the way, and she misses it.

Ace. *15–love.*

She walks back to position, shaking her head.

It's working. This time, I wait as long as I can to serve the next one. I bounce the ball over and over, not indicating when I might finally toss it. Then I hit the exact same serve again. She gets in position better, but she still can't return it.

30–love.

She bites her bottom lip, clenches her fist, crouches down. I wait again, hold off on serving until the last second. I serve it short, so that it bounces just over the net. She dives for it and misses. *40–love.*

On the next serve, I hit the net. As I set up for the second serve, I see her visibly relax, assuming my second serve will be safer.

Instead, I angle it to the corner. She returns it, but then I hit it back down the opposite line and it goes whistling right past her.

Game is mine. Now we're 5–4. If I break her serve on this one, I win the match.

I watch her crack her knuckles as she goes back to the baseline. Maybe up against another player she'd be less nervous. It is her serve, after all.

But I am Carrie Soto. Break points are my moment. The evidence of it is branded all over my feet.

I can tell Antonovich's muscles are tight. She did not think she would be here—the match this close, a loss to me threatening her 1995 season.

Her first serve is fast and hot. It has more fire on it than anything she's hit so far. Still, I take the point. *Love–15.*

She stomps back to the baseline. And then hits her racket against the ground before catching herself.

I smile. She's mad. She's so mad.

On the next serve, she footfaults. Then nets it. *Love–30.*

I wink at her. Her face grows tighter.

On the next one, we rally and then she lobs it too high and the ball lands behind the baseline.

Match point.

I can do this. I am doing this. I just have to trust myself.

She hits a high kick serve. I get it on the rise. She returns it fast, exactly like I hoped. Here it is. I take it out of the air early and quick—a drop shot, right over the net.

It lands with such a beautiful, sweet, delicious thud.

Antonovich cannot get to it. She falls to the ground.

I leap into the air and shout. Gwen and Ali stand in their seats. The crowd roars.

I look right at the TV cameras for a brief second, knowing my father is looking right back at me.

Finally, over the loudspeaker come the words I have waited to hear.

"Carrie Soto advances to the championship final."

MY FATHER IS SHOUTING AT ME THROUGH THE PHONE. "YOU WERE incomparable! You were dynamic. You were *interesting* today, *hija.* Interesting! You played in a way that kept us all glued to the TV."

I laugh as I sit down on the couch. The phone was ringing the moment I got in the door. I've barely had time to put my things down. "Thanks, Dad."

"I am not exaggerating! Let me tell you something. . . . At the end of the third set, you two were neck and neck. I watched you at the changeover. I saw you thinking it through. And I *knew.* I said to Bowe, I said, 'She's got it.' And you did. Oh, he was so proud of you. He was beaming."

"Where is he?" I ask.

"He waited around for you to call, but there's only so long the man wants to spend in an old guy's house. Don't worry. He and I talked at length about your brilliance today. I told him, I said, 'She goes after what she wants on the court but not in real life. In real life, you have to be patient.'"

"What are you even talking about? And stop, you don't need to be discussing me with him."

"Oh, Carrie, that ship has sailed. He comes every day, and after we are done playing chess and discussing his strategy for the US Open, what do you think we are going to do? Talk about the weather? This is Los Angeles. It's sunny."

"He's coming every day?" I ask. I look over the room service menu as if I don't know already that I'm going to order grilled chicken.

"Yeah, every day. He brings me breakfast and stays until after lunch. Or he brings me lunch and stays until after dinner. Honestly, it makes sense to me why he's here all the time. Did you know his own father was embarrassed he was a tennis player instead of a professor or something?"

"I know a little."

"Imagine! Imagine having your head that far up your own ass that you're embarrassed your son is a champion."

"All right, all right," I say.

"I like him, Carrie. Even with all those tantrums."

"I can tell."

"No, I like him for you. I think this thing is *verrrry* interesting, you two."

"Dad, cut it out."

"And he thinks so too."

"STOP IT OR I WILL GET OFF THE PHONE," I say.

"*Bueno, pero tengo razón,*" he says. "When does Chan play?"

"Tonight. Soon." I look at my watch. "Any second now, actually."

"*Ay,*" he says. I hear him start to wrestle around for the remote. I can hear the TV turning on. So I sit down and turn on mine. I flip through the channels until I see that the match is just beginning.

Nicki stands tall and sturdy on the court. Her tennis whites are crisp and bright, a tennis skirt and tank top. Her shoes are her own 130s, bright white.

I watch her, bouncing on the balls of her feet, stretching out her shoulder, standing at the baseline. She has a huge smile on her face, like she's living for this moment.

Ingrid Cortez's face is all business.

"This is it," my dad says. "Chan wins this, and then you beat her. And suddenly, it's a whole different story."

"I know," I say, watching her first serve. "I had a drink with her the other night. I . . . liked her."

Nicki hits her first serve. My shoulder starts to sting just watching Cortez return it.

"You didn't talk strategy, did you?" my father says.

"Dad, give me a little credit."

"You know what I say about making friends out of your opponents."

"Honestly," I say, sighing, "no, I don't. Because you just told me to never do it."

"Well, yeah," he says. "*Exacto, hija.* But if you do—don't talk strategy, don't tell them how you felt about your last game, don't tell them your fears, don't tell them your strengths either. And you sure as hell never tell them how much it hurts you to lose."

"Oh, is that all?" I say. Nicki and Ingrid are still rallying for the point.

"Don't tell them what you had for breakfast either," he says. "They could use it against you."

"You sound insane."

"Every genius sounds insane."

Nicki hits a groundstroke to Cortez's backhand, and Cortez misses it. First point Nicki.

"Oh wow," my dad says. "These two."

"They are well matched," I say.

"Two of the greatest in the world," my dad says. "Duking it out for who gets to play you."

I laugh and then sit back on the couch and put my feet up.

My father and I stay on the phone throughout the entire match. Multiple times he worries about the long-distance charges, but I refuse to let him get off the call. We watch and we analyze. Sometimes we are stunned silent at the tension between Nicki and Cortez. It is a close one. Cortez is up, then Nicki is up. Both of them are breaking each other's serves. Cortez slides across the court at one point and skins her knee. Then Nicki steps wrong on her ankle.

"Ouch," I say.

"What is she doing?" my dad says. "Landing like that on her bad ankle? She can't keep playing like this and stay in the game many more years."

"I know."

It's the third set. 5–5. Anybody's match.

On Cortez's serve, Nicki is limping on her way back to the baseline after each point. Cortez holds the game.

"She plays through it, which is impressive," my dad says. "It's not stopping her. But I wish I could just reach through the TV and tell her she's shortening her career."

When it's Nicki's turn to serve, she can't get the height she needs. I gasp when Cortez gets to 30–40. Match point.

"Oh no," my dad says.

On the next serve, Cortez returns it right on the sideline. Nicki can't run fast enough.

"Oh no," my dad says again.

It's over.

I can feel my heart drop as Nicki falls to her knees onto the grass.

"No, that can't be," my father says.

I close my eyes in disbelief.

I am not playing Nicki in the final. I'm playing Ingrid Cortez.

"Actually," my father says, "this is fabulous."

I can barely hold back my tone. "Why is it fabulous? It's not fabulous! I wanted to play Nicki. *Now.* I wanted to put this whole thing to rest."

"Nonsense," my father says. "You will beat Cortez—she is the more predictable player. You already played her in Melbourne."

"And lost."

"But now you know what to do. And she will go down just like Antonovich did the second time. This is great news," my father says. "This is it. This is your next Slam."

The night before the final, I toss and turn.

I lie awake, staring at the shadows on the ceiling, thinking about what tomorrow holds.

The more I think about how important it is that I go to sleep, the more impossible it becomes. The harder I chase it, the more it eludes me.

I get up and check the time. It's early evening in L.A. I think about calling my father. But, instead, I dial Bowe.

"Hi," I say.

"Oh," he says. "Hello."

I say, "I can't sleep," just as he says, "You should be sleeping."

Bowe doesn't say anything else for a moment, but the silence between us feels easy.

"Do you often find it hard to sleep before a big match?" Bowe asks.

"No," I say. "Almost never."

"Not even against Stepanova in '83?"

"No, I slept like a baby that night. I'd worn my body down with so much training, I could barely stay awake."

Bowe is quiet again. "So which self is keeping you awake?" he asks, finally.

It clicks right into place. "Okay," I say. "I get it."

"Let your thoughts go," he says.

"All right, I'll try."

"What did Coach say?"

I laugh. "I didn't call him."

Bowe whistles like a cowboy. "Wow, you called me instead?"

"Yeah," I say. "I think maybe I needed you to tell me that. I knew that you would."

"Or," he says, "and I'm just taking a stab here, maybe you also have a thing for me."

"Would you cut it out?" I say.

"Oh, for fuck's sake," he says. "All right, go to bed. Glad I could help."

"Thank you," I say.

"Yeah, yeah."

"No, Bowe, I'm serious. Thank you."

"Sleep well, Carrie. You have this."

When I get back in bed, I watch the moon as it hangs over the river. I stare at the gentle sway of the curtains. I do my best not to think about Cortez in Melbourne. Not to think of the moment I lost the match. The drop in my stomach. The sheer shame of it.

Instead, I close my eyes and think of the sound of a tennis ball. The *thunk* of a good bounce. The *pop* of a drive volley. The *tap* of a drop shot. The honest-to-God exquisite soundtrack of a great rally. *Pop, thunk, pop.*

All I can do, I understand for one startlingly clear second, is play my grass game and be okay with the outcome.

Impossible.

Transcript

BBC Sports Radio London
SportsWorld with Brian Cress

All eyes are watching as Carrie Soto and Ingrid Cortez go head-to-head in the championship final at Wimbledon today. Both players have shown incredible resolve here in London. Carrie Soto, thirty-seven, has shocked everyone by making it to the final. And Ingrid Cortez, at the age of eighteen, defeated powerhouse Nicki Chan in the semis this week in order to earn her spot up against the Battle Axe.

Soto lost to Cortez in Melbourne earlier this season. But she has been gaining momentum all year and has won Wimbledon nine times previously. Still, betting odds are putting Cortez ahead by 3 to 2.

It will be, no doubt, a rousing event—the Rookie vs. the Comeback.

When asked, Carrie Soto said, quote, "I am eager to get on the court and show Ingrid Cortez why I've long dominated at Wimbledon," unquote. Ingrid Cortez said this morning, quote, "I beat her in Melbourne. I'll beat her again today," unquote. Oof. Harsh words for such ladies. Watch out, gents.

In just a few hours, we will know the victor.

SOTO VS. CORTEZ

Wimbledon 1995

Final

I AM STANDING AT CENTRE COURT. THE GRASS, WHICH JUST TWO SHORT weeks ago was a lively green, is now pale and bone dry. I inhale and take in the distinct and glorious sight of the Wimbledon final court. I hold back the smile on my face.

Ingrid Cortez is standing on the opposite side of the net, fixing her sweatband. Her golden hair shines in the sun; her long limbs hover delicately at the baseline.

She smiles at me. It's not so much a friendly gesture as a baring of teeth.

I adjust my visor. I close my eyes.

Then I toss the ball into the air and open up the court with a flat first serve that fires right over the net, wide to her backhand.

We rally for the point until I hit a slice that she can't return.

First point mine.

I look up to the stands at Gwen and Ali. And then, in the royal box, I see Princess Diana.

Once my eye lands on her, it is hard to look away. She is wearing a pale yellow dress and blazer, and she is, as always, the most elegant woman I've ever seen.

I know that so many people across the world feel a kinship with her. But right now, mine feels especially sharp. I want to win, today, with her here. I want to say to her, *They can't make us go away just because they are done with us.*

I refocus as I set for my next serve.

I take a breath. Before I even know what I am doing, my left arm tosses the ball as my right arm comes up to meet it. The ball goes screaming past Cortez's racket and bounces just inside the sideline. An ace.

I don't bother to smile at Cortez, to even give her the satisfaction of my satisfaction. I show nothing, as if this is nothing. Beating her is nothing to me.

But the truth is, I can feel the hum beginning in my bones.

I take the set.

At the end of the second set, we go to a tiebreaker.

The championship and the record are in the palm of my hand.

But I can feel myself tightening up as victory gets closer; the hum starts to fade into the background.

Cortez takes the tiebreaker.

Third set, 5–4. I'm up, but it's Cortez's serve next.

For a moment, as Cortez begins her toss, I have this flash of wanting it all to be over, wanting to see how it all ends.

Will I do it?

If I win, do I feel at peace knowing Nicki and I are tied again? Does elation run through me as I look around and understand that at age thirty-seven, I am now the oldest woman to ever win Wimbledon? That I have set a new record for the most titles here? Does it fill some sort of hole in my heart? Does it make it all worth it?

Or.

Or do I lose my shot at taking my record back this year?

Is this match the one in which Ingrid Cortez cements her own type of domination in women's tennis, winning in Melbourne and London in the same year—just as I did for the first time back in '81?

Is this Cortez's day or is it mine? I just want to know.

But as she starts to serve, I remember that if I want to win, I have to *hit the fucking ball.*

It comes speeding across the court. I close my eyes for the briefest of seconds and let my body take over. I can't help but let a smile break out on my face as I feel the sheer, undying, intoxicating thrill of pulling my arm back and then smashing my racket into the ball.

It hits the sideline just where I placed it and bounces off the court.

"Point is Soto's."

Cortez is smart and she is agile. She can put herself in position to make whatever shot she wants. But the ball surprised her on that point. And that is because she has not played Wimbledon as often as I have. She may know intellectually that the grass changes over the course of the match, but she doesn't understand it like I do.

She has to *think* about it. I don't.

I *know* this court. I know the bad bounces. I know the wind. I know the stickiness under my feet in this humidity.

After all, this is my grass.

And it is time for Ingrid Cortez to get off my lawn.

She serves it, I return, she hits it into the net. Love–30.

I aim straight for a pale spot where the grass is worn away, just beyond the net. It bounces fast and straight sideways. Cortez dives to return it, but her angle is desperate. It doesn't make it over the net.

And here we are. *Championship point.*

My father is watching. Bowe is with him. Gwen and Ali are here. And I wonder, for a brief second, if my mom is seeing this. Wherever she is. If she's proud of me.

I *know* Nicki Chan is watching. It's probably killing her.

I shake them all out of my head and breathe.

Cortez serves the ball, and it flashes, yellow, as it barrels across the court. I watch it curve—the seams spinning so fast they blur— over the net and into the service box. I pull my arm back, ready to strike.

And now, I do not want to fast-forward through the next moment at all. I want to experience every second of this.

I hit the ball cross-court; she returns it down the line. I take it right out of the air with a backhand drive volley, and I move up to the net.

The ball bounces just at her feet. She chips it over. I hit a drop shot, aiming for a spot of dirt. It lands flat, bouncing low and to the side.

Cortez dives for it, but it's too late. The ball bounces again.

Cortez gasps. Her mouth goes wide; her hands go up to her face in disbelief.

For one stunning moment, I can *see* the crowd screaming for me before I can hear them. And then the thunderous roar kicks in and overtakes me. I fall onto my butt and then onto my back as I drop my racket and look up at the sky. I lie there and I can feel the ground vibrating underneath me.

My tenth Wimbledon.

My twenty-first Slam.

The crowd continues to scream. I stand up as the announcers declare me the winner of the 109th annual Wimbledon Championships. I feel as if I can hear my father cheering. I can hear Bowe clapping. The whole stadium is going wild.

But I cannot hear anything as clearly as the sound of my own voice, begging me: *Let this be enough.*

Transcript

SportsHour USA
The Mark Hadley Show

Mark Hadley: And what do we make of this? A shocking upset, a stunning victory for our American, Carrie Soto.

Briggs Lakin: I'm here eating my words, Mark. She pulled out a scorcher of a win.

Gloria Jones: This is what we have seen with Carrie Soto from the beginning of her career. She is relentless. She does not stop. She will not be counted out.

Hadley: And what a match she gave us.

Jones: What a tournament, I say. Not just a match. Look, as tennis fans—certainly as a player who had to play Carrie a few times back in my day—I can tell you that what we all show up for is the beauty of the game. The sheer joy of a great match. And Cortez and Soto gave us that today.

Lakin: Soto, in particular, stunned with that last game. She's the oldest player to ever win Wimbledon, and it was hours into the match. She had to be tired. And yet, now, you understand why she's known as the break point champion.

Hadley: She's given us quite a show this season.

Lakin: If you told me this time last year that Carrie Soto would be winning Wimbledon and Nicki Chan wouldn't even make the final, I'd have thought you'd lost your mind. But here we are.

Jones: Never underestimate Carrie Soto. And to any other women out there, wondering if they are too old to play tennis, let the Battle Axe be all the evidence you need to get in the game.

Hadley: Uh-oh, Gloria, are you considering a return to the sport?

Jones: [*laughs*] Absolutely not. You couldn't pay me to train again, Mark. But that's what's all the more impressive, if you ask me. We had a saying back when I was on the tour. "Carrie Soto is human. But she's superhuman." And I'd say she's proven that tonight.

ALONE IN MY HOTEL SUITE, I PUT MY GOWN ON. IT'S BLACK SATIN AND sleeveless, floor length, though there is a slit cut high to my thigh.

Gwen picked it out for me when we went shopping this afternoon. I can see she made a good choice.

I leave my room and make my way down to the lobby. I'm meeting Gwen here so we can head out to the Wimbledon Champions Ball, at a hotel near Buckingham Palace.

It's almost midnight, and the party is only just about to begin. We all have been waiting—*I have been waiting*—for the men's final to end. The party can't start until then.

The finalists were Andrew Thomas and Jadran Petrovich, neither one of whom would set a record by winning. We live in a world where exceptional women have to sit around waiting for mediocre men.

Petrovich finally takes the fifth set just after eleven P.M., and apparently *now* we are all allowed to celebrate.

In the lobby, I see Gwen arrive in a bright red strapless dress, her hair pulled back, her lips crimson red.

"Wow," I say. "You look good."

"To you as well," she says. And then she grabs my arm and escorts me to the ball.

Just as in years past, there is a horde of people here. They are all coming in and out, trying to find me, trying to shake my hand, trying to tell me that all along, they knew I would succeed.

Board members of the ITF are asking me if I will consider continuing on in the sport after the US Open. One of the directors of the WTA asks if I will join the full tour. A head of the All England Club tells me that he knew from the moment I announced my return that I would win Wimbledon.

"Isn't this nice?" I say to Gwen through gritted teeth. "A whole room full of fair-weather friends."

Gwen laughs. "That is one thing I have always loved about you," she says. "You are the rare star who doesn't like the smell of bullshit."

Not long after we arrive, I get stuck talking to a woman who is some sort of duchess.

"A rather exceptional win you've accomplished," she says to me, taking a restrained sip of her drink.

"Thank you," I say. "I'm quite proud."

"Yes," she says. "And at such an age. It's impressive. I quite admire your fighting spirit. You have that American virtue, don't you? That dogged obstinance—even in the face of indignity."

Gwen can see my face and nods at me slowly, encouraging me not to tell this woman to go fuck herself. "Ah, yes," I say, keeping my tone light. "Well, it was oh-so tempting to roll over and die once I turned thirty, but somehow my *American obstinance* persists."

Suddenly, Gwen's hand is on my arm, and I'm being dragged away.

"Just smile and nod," Gwen says. "How hard is that?"

"Very," I say. "I hate half these people. I hate half of all people."

Gwen leads me through the room. "You love Wimbledon," she says.

"I love London and I love winning," I say. "But I don't care about any of these idiots who thought I was crazy for trying this in the first place."

Gwen keeps us moving, and I can see now that she's ushering me toward Jadran Petrovich—with whom I am going to have to take a photo. I pull her to a stop, ever so briefly.

"The only people who thought I could come back were my father and Bowe," I say. "That's whose opinion I care about. And yours, because you have stood by me every single moment."

Gwen smiles. "Well, I have always admired your American obstinance."

"Thank you for supporting me. And for being here," I say. "When my father couldn't."

Gwen nods.

"And . . . I'm sorry about Indian Wells. I was . . . rude."

"You mean when I gently asked you about your dating life and you acted like a brat?"

"Yes," I say. "I know you were just trying to . . . care about me. And I'm not an easy person to care for."

Gwen shakes her head. "Yes, you are. You think you're so tough, but you're not, Carrie. I can see right through you. To all the raw, scared bits you think you're hiding."

I look at her. "I hate you," I say.

"Anyway," she says, waving me off. "You were wrong, but you weren't *wrong*. Back in Indian Wells."

I'm not sure what she means.

"Michael and I are getting divorced," she says finally. Before I can ask her how she is or what happened, she says, "We will talk about it later, but, you know, maybe I *was* living vicariously through you for a moment there."

I put my arm on her shoulder. "I'm sorry."

She waves me away.

"Well, I did sleep with Bowe," I say. "So there ya go: There's the gossip you wanted."

Gwen laughs abruptly, tossing her head back and delighting in it all with such force and freedom that multiple people turn their heads to look at us.

"Can we leave?" I say.

Gwen nods. "I'm going to go connect with a few sponsors. You go take the photo with Jadran, and then yeah, let's go."

Ten minutes later, I'm posing with a smile across my face as Jadran Petrovich and I have our photos taken. Once the flashes stop, I congratulate him on winning.

"Thank you, it is exciting. My first," he says.

"It's thrilling," I say. "I remember my first one."

"You have won before," he says.

"Ten times," I say. "Yes."

"Hm," he says. "But it is three sets."

"Excuse me?"

"The match is best of three in the women's. We play best of five. The men's tournament."

"Right."

"So it's not comparable, is it?"

I see Gwen coming to meet me. I look Jadran right in the eye. "I assure you," I say, all smile—fake or not—gone from my face, "if I played you two out of three or three out of five, I would drag you across the court and murder your—"

"All right, that's it," Gwen says as she hooks her arm into mine and hauls me away.

Sometime around three in the morning, Gwen and I are in my hotel suite, opening a second bottle of champagne. Gwen's thrown her heels off and is sitting in the club chair, pouring. I am lying, still in my fancy dress, across the sofa. She hands me my refilled glass.

"You should have let me tell that fucker off," I say.

Gwen shakes her head. "If I let you say all the things you wanted to say in public, your career would be over in about two hours."

"Why do I have to be nice when most of the men aren't? Last year, Jeff Kerr called an umpire a 'dogshit salad,' and he's hawking underwear for Fruit of the Loom."

Gwen shakes her head. "You know damn well there's another set of rules for you. Just like there's even *another* set of rules for me."

I look at her, understanding that as much as I know what it's like to be a woman in this world, I have no idea what it's like to be a Black woman.

"Yeah," I say. "And it's not right."

Gwen shrugs. "Most shit isn't."

I nod. "Good point."

"And look, I know you might not care about all the money you stand to make, because you've already got your villa and your foundation, but I want that money! And what you've done this week will catapult you to the top of everyone's list. The figures people are throwing around now—I could retire off this."

"Oh please, you're not gonna retire," I say as I look up at the ceiling.

"I don't know," she says.

I sit up and stare at her.

"The twins are going to college next year. Michael is leaving. He met someone else, apparently. Her name is Naomi. Which is such a pretty name. And that irritates the shit out of me. And, anyway, I don't know. I'd like to do . . . something. Something big. Something unexpected."

"Like what?" I ask, putting my drink down.

"I don't know yet. But where's my midlife crisis? Aren't I allowed one?"

I nod, considering. "Absolutely you are!"

"Yeah, I am."

"Maybe I'll have one too," I say. "Or maybe this is mine."

"You're still a bit young for it, I'm afraid. You have another crisis in front of you in about ten years."

"Oh, good," I say, laying my head back down. I rest my hands across my chest.

"You should do it," I say. "Retire. And do something crazy. Travel the world or take up deep-sea fishing. Or be one of those people who walk across the country. But you do what calls to you."

"Yeah?" Gwen says. "I really am thinking about it, Carrie. It's not just a joke. I wouldn't be your agent anymore."

"I get that, but . . ." I look away from her, at the lipstick on the empty champagne glass in front of me. "I mean . . . you're not . . . Listen, I don't have a ton of people that I trust. But you . . . you mean something to me. So I don't care if you're not the one who brokers my deals. You're not just that. In my life."

Gwen doesn't say anything. She's turned away and is dabbing a tissue against the underside of her eye.

"Was it okay I said that?" I ask.

"Yeah," Gwen says. "I love that you said that. You're almost a sister to me. My irritating, cocky, pain-in-the-ass little sister." She leans over and grabs my hand and squeezes it. And then she bursts into tears. "Ignore me. I'm just drunk and going through a divorce. It's like being pregnant. You're always one good or bad second away from crying."

"I'm sorry you're getting a divorce," I say. "You always seemed so happy."

"We were and we weren't. But when one person wants to end it, it's over."

"Yeah," I say. "I know."

"I will meet someone else," Gwen says. "That's what I keep remembering. All the good stuff at the beginning. The butterflies and the swooning. I'll get to have that again. And that's a gift."

I think about what she's saying. I think about Bowe and his Spanish phrases, the way he inches toward me, the way he spends each day with my father. So many butterflies, so many things to swoon for.

And I keep them crammed down inside a tiny box in my chest and I forbid them from coming out.

"I think that's brave," I say.

"You came out of retirement, announced a nearly impossible intention, and then achieved it on an international stage," Gwen says. "You're brave."

"No," I say. "Not about what you're talking about. Not about love. I've never felt brave about that."

"Oh, for fuck's sake, Carrie," she says, shaking her head. "You just won Wimbledon at the age of thirty-seven—when no one thought you could do it. And now you're going to sell yourself short on the easy stuff?"

"It doesn't seem easy to me at all," I say.

Gwen stands up and puts her hand on my shoulder. "Falling in love is really quite simple," she says. "You want to know the secret? It's the same thing we are all doing about life every single day."

I look to her.

"Forget there's an ending."

I wake up hungover, my makeup smeared all over my face. I've slept in my dress.

My flight is scheduled for midmorning, so I get up and pack my things. I take a shower. I inhale three ibuprofen. I check the time and try to convert it to Pacific Daylight Time but give up. And then, just as I am about to dry my hair, there's a knock on the door.

"One second!" I call out, putting my robe back on.

I open the door to find a bellman holding a bizarre-looking bouquet of flowers. Most of them are bright pink and spiky, but between them all are tiny gold blooms that look like buttons. It is an unusual and interesting bouquet. Every aspect of it unexpected.

I suspect they aren't from my father; he would have sent roses. And I let myself imagine, briefly, that they are from Bowe. But the idea seems too indulgent, too embarrassing.

"Thank you," I say, and I tip the bellman. After he leaves, I put the vase on the coffee table and search for the card. Maybe Gwen got up early and sent them.

Brava, Soto! Take a breath and fill your lungs with your victory, friend. I promise there will not be another one. See you in New York. XO, Chan

P.S. The pink flowers are amaranth, which represent immortality—what we're fighting for, after all. And the yellow are tansy. They are said to represent a declaration of war. Fun, right?

Ugh. I hate that I like Nicki Chan.

MY FATHER IS WAITING FOR ME IN THE DRIVEWAY WHEN MY CAR PULLS in. His color is back, and he looks healthy and strong.

The moment he sees me, he beams. It's a smile so big that it takes over his face. I'm not sure I've seen him smile like this in decades. The sight is enough to knock me over. I drop my things and run to him.

He holds me so close I think he might snap my bones. My dad has always had this same smell—a smell I've been fond of my entire life. I always assumed it was his natural scent. Until one day, as a teenager, I wandered into the fragrance section of the pharmacy and smelled English Leather.

I'm embarrassed to say that, for a second, it mystified me—how could a drugstore bottle what my father smelled of? And then I realized the answer was much more mundane. My father wore drugstore cologne.

But right now, in this moment, I love this drugstore cologne more than I love the smell of Wimbledon grass or California oranges or the rubber of a freshly popped can of tennis balls. This drugstore cologne is my home.

"I have never, never been prouder, *cielo*," he says when he finally lets me go.

"I know," I say. "I'm the oldest woman to ever win a singles Slam. And I've tied Nicki. If I beat her at the US Open, I'll have done everything I set out to do."

My father shakes his head. "That's not what I'm talking about."

"What do you mean?"

"Have you rewatched the match?" he asks me.

"No," I say. "Should I?"

"It was a beautiful game, *pichona*. Every shot was loose but perfect. You were there. You were present. It was tennis at its finest and it was *your* tennis at its finest and I have never been more proud of the player you are."

"Thanks, Dad," is about all I can croak out.

"And do you know what else?" he says. "The whole third set, you were smiling. Smiling!"

"I like winning."

My father shakes his head. "No, you were happy," he says. "Just playing like when you were a kid. I saw it with my own eyes. It was joy."

Later that night, after I have unpacked, my father and I go over everything the doctors said when he was released from the hospital. He implores me not to worry anymore and then heads back to his own house.

I take a shower and put on a T-shirt and a pair of sweatpants. I comb my hair. But I don't feel settled. I pick up the phone and dial.

"Hey, it's me," I say. And then I wonder why I think I can do that—act like I am the most important person who could possibly call him.

"How are you, champion?" Bowe says. His voice has changed. It sounds different, even from when we spoke so often in London. It is quieter, heavier, breathier.

"I'm good," I say. "I'm really good. How are you feeling? How are your ribs?"

"Much better, actually," he says. "I think Javier and I are going to start training again. I've been doing a little bit on my own. But I would be lying if I said I wasn't looking forward to having my hitter back."

I laugh. "Is that me?" I say. "Am I your hitter?"

"I don't know what you are," he says.

"Yeah, me neither. I *am* a little lonely, though," I say.

"Yeah?" Bowe's voice picks up a lightness again, that bounce. I like both versions of him.

"Yeah, a little."

"Well, that I can do something about," he says.

The second half of the summer is a train heading full speed toward Flushing Meadows.

There is not much time between Wimbledon and the US Open. My father has his work cut out for him, training both Bowe and me, day in and day out.

He sits on the bench for my morning training sessions, barking drills at me. After the first day, I buy him a megaphone so he won't strain so hard to yell.

After I go in for lunch and to take a shower and rest, Bowe usually shows up and trains with my father for a few hours. Sometimes, as I'm getting dressed, I watch the two of them in the backyard. Bowe and my father are always either passionately agreeing or disagreeing about what Bowe should work on next. The two of them bicker at full volume—Bowe yelling to be heard over my father's megaphone.

As the days pass by, I can see Bowe's first serve growing more and more bold, his second serve more consistent, all from my window.

Then, every day around three, I get back on the court. And Bowe and I play a match.

Bowe always starts off trash-talking. And then I often trounce him—and my father gives us both a series of pointers for the next day.

At which point, Bowe says he'll see us tomorrow. My father and I have dinner. And then I say I'm going to bed.

But instead, I wait until nine-thirty, when I open my door, and Bowe is always standing on my doorstep.

"Hi."

"Hi."

Every night, I grab his hand and pull him inside and bring him to my bedroom. And every night, he presses himself against me and kisses my neck and makes me wonder if anyone has ever survived jumping off the edge of a cliff.

A month before the US Open, Bowe is lying in my bed in the middle of the night. His arm is cradled perfectly under my neck; his right hand is tracing shapes on my upper arm, and I'm almost asleep.

"Your dad knows what's going on," he says.

"He just thinks you're into me."

"No," Bowe says. "He knows that I'm parking across the street and sleeping here until the morning, when I go home for four hours and then come right back, pretending I've been gone the whole time."

"He doesn't know any of that."

Bowe laughs. "He does. Today after he was done barking orders at me about my backhand, he calmly asked me if I had any idea of my plans after I retire. And when I said I wasn't sure, he said, 'Well, do you think settling down is in your future?'"

I cringe so hard I nearly spasm. "No, he didn't," I say, sitting up. I'm now fully awake. "You must have misunderstood him."

"I assure you, I did not."

"Yes, you did."

"We could tell him the truth," Bowe says, turning onto his side, toward me in bed. He's been sleeping here so consistently that I've started wondering if I should get another nightstand. But I have always had one nightstand, and I can't conceive of being the sort of idiot who would buy a second.

"No, c'mon," I say. "Let's not make anything weird, all right? I want him to train you for the US Open. I want you to win the damn thing. And I want to win it too."

"Of course."

"So we know that we're going to be training together for the next month . . ."

Bowe looks at me, his eyebrows furrowed, as if he cannot tell where my train of thought is headed.

"But who knows if we'll even be sleeping together tomorrow."

Bowe pulls his arm away from me. "You're fucking impossible," he says, rolling onto his back. "Absolutely impossible."

"What are we doing, Bowe?" I say.

"I don't know," he says. "You won't tell me."

"*You* tell *me*."

"I don't know!" he says.

"See? You don't have a plan. You don't know what you want."

"I do know what I want," he says. "I'm here, aren't I? You fucking rejected me back in '82 and took up with Randall, of all people. You rejected me back in Melbourne. You all but rejected me back in Paris. And still, I'm here, every night, any second that you want me. I know exactly what I want, Carrie. I've made it clear."

I watch him throw his head back on the bed. And I let myself believe for a moment that maybe he means it. Maybe this time, maybe this man, means it.

"Just forget it," he says. And then he turns his back to me and fluffs his pillow angrily. And I smile to myself because you don't fluff a pillow you're not planning to sleep on.

. . .

Bowe and I both take Sundays off from training. We need one day to recuperate. And sometimes, in the morning, I'll watch tapes with my dad. But in the afternoons, even I need a break from tennis, and I can tell that my dad does not know what to do with himself.

Bowe starts coming over in the afternoons to play chess with my father on Sundays. Then it evolves into the two of them going to Blockbuster together and renting war movies.

They pop popcorn and watch the movies in our home theater, pausing every few minutes to talk about historical references to World War I or II or Vietnam. And I normally sit in the lounger in the same room, only half paying attention.

I've never realized until now that my dad is into war movies. But in hindsight, it's painfully obvious that he would be drawn to them.

One Sunday, the two of them catch me tearing up at the very end of the movie, when the sergeant salutes his captain.

AUGUST 1995

Two weeks before the US Open

I AM RUNNING SPRINTS ACROSS THE COURT, TRAINING HARDER THAN ever.

"*¡De nuevo!*" my father says as I stop short at his feet.

"*Sí, papá.*"

Bowe has a wild card for the US Open. But I do not need a wild card or to qualify, because I am now ranked twelfth in the world.

Twelfth. A delicious, enticing number, with the capacity to carry a boatload of fuck-yous.

When I am done with another sprint, I look at my father for what to do next. But instead of sending me to the baseline, he pats the spot on the bench beside him.

"*¿Qué pasa?*" I say, sitting down.

"I see a change in you that I can't quite describe, since Wimbledon. You're . . . freer."

"I'm less afraid," I say. "Of losing."

"Because you've made your peace with it?" he asks.

"Because it's unlikely."

My father laughs. "Well, then you need to keep that with you, heading into New York. Especially up against Chan. New York is her best court."

I nod.

"And I think we both know that I can't go with you."

We've spoken *around* it for weeks—that he is not yet healthy enough to travel. "I know."

"I will be watching," he says. "I can't wait to see you take that record back. Probably right out of her hands."

I breathe in deeply, trying to push down the grief that is blooming in my chest.

"I'll just be doing it from here," he says. "Instead of in the stands."

"Yeah," I say. "Of course."

"You will go and win the US Open, and then you can retire again and come home, and we can throw a party," he says.

"You make it sound so easy."

"It is not easy," he says. "But you will do it."

"And if I don't?"

My father looks at me and narrows his eyes, trying to gauge my reaction.

"I don't need you to guess what I want to hear," I say. "I just want the truth. If I don't win, then what?"

"Well, if you don't win the US Open, I don't care. That's the truth."

I erupt in laughter. "Unreal."

"You said you wanted the truth. It will be no different to me if you win or you lose. It won't affect me at all."

"I mean, it matters a little," I say.

"To you, maybe. But to me? It was never the point."

I put my head on his shoulder and absorb what he's saying. I look up at the bright, unending L.A. sky, palm trees swaying in the breeze.

"He's in love with you," my father finally says.

I don't pull away. I don't even flinch.

"And he knows you're a better player than he is," my dad says. "I was always worried about that with you. Because the only person who could ever understand you would be another player. But how many players would be okay knowing they were second place? He takes to it well, though. Which is about the highest compliment I can think of. I'm not sure there is a greater strength."

"Playing second to a woman?" I ask.

My father winks at me. "Feeling secure, even knowing you are not the best."

I feel both sides of that sword, the compliment and the sharp edge meant for me.

"He is a good guy," I say.

My father nods. "Even if he is sneaking into your house every night like some sort of *pirata*."

I laugh. "Well, that's on me," I say. "I'm not . . . I don't know if there's any future there, and I don't want to make it too much of a thing."

"So you push it away, because it's easier to pretend you don't want it," my dad says.

I look at him.

"Please," he says, pulling me under his shoulder. "Open your heart the tiniest bit, *pichona*. Being married to your mother changed my life. She made me feel joy. She gave me purpose. We became a family. Tennis is nothing compared to that."

"But then she was gone. And you were left with such . . . heartache. And I don't . . . I don't know how to do that . . . to live that way," I say.

"If you did not know how to do something on the court, it would not stop you from figuring it out." He grabs my hand. "I was so broken when your mother died that I buried my heart in the earth. And I taught you to as well. I thought I was showing you how to move on, but I was showing you how to never open up to anybody. I taught you the wrong thing. But I've told you that now, and it's on you to fix it. Okay?"

"Yeah, Dad," I say. "I already knew it. But thank you."

"I know you did. Sometimes, you're much smarter than me. So much stronger too. You're like a bright diamond, one shiny, tough . . ."

"Bitch," I offer.

My dad laughs. "Okay, sure. One shiny, tough bitch."

I laugh, and he pulls me back to him. "*Te amo, cielo.* Being your father is the best thing that has ever happened to me. My Achilles. Greatest of the Greeks."

"Dad . . ." I say.

"No," he says. "Just accept it. Let me feel it and say it. You're the meaning of my life."

That afternoon, Bowe comes over and we play a set with my father barking at us from the sidelines through his megaphone.

"Bowe, get higher up on your toes when you make contact," he says. "And Carrie, don't get lazy on that follow-through!"

Bowe squeaks out a win against me—he's getting better and better, almost by the hour, lately. And it stings to fall just short of him.

At the end of the session, my father gives me a few pointers, but it is Bowe he's focused on. "I think you need a more open stance," he says as Bowe zips his racket into its case. "So your weight is on the right foot as you prepare to move for the return."

"I told you I'm not messing with my footwork now," Bowe says. "Not when it feels right and feels intuitive. I just beat one of the greatest players in the world with my stance. C'mon."

"Good is the enemy of great," my father says.

Bowe looks at me and then my father. "Spoken like a Soto."

Bowe puts his kit over his shoulder, and my father starts discussing dinner.

"See you all tomorrow," Bowe says, waving goodbye as he heads toward his car. I watch him go, so casually, with no expectations.

I look at my father, who looks back at me, incredulous.

Oh, fine.

"Bowe!" I call out.

He turns around.

"Stay for dinner," I say.

Bowe looks at both my father and me. "Really?"

"Yeah," I say. "Yes."

I walk toward him and take his kit off his shoulder. "Stay. Please."

He watches me take his racket bag and put it down on the bench. When I catch his eye, I can tell that he wants to ask me many different questions. But I have just one simple, precarious answer. "I want you to stay."

He smiles. "Okay," he says.

He claps his hands together and says, "All right, let's do this. What are we having? Javier, don't even try me with the steak or the salty food right now. You know what? Why don't I fire up the grill and make chicken?"

My dad laughs. And then he begins walking to my house with Bowe and me. Bowe walks up ahead of us, ever so briefly. And my father puts his arm around me.

"Siempre supe que no hay montaña que no puedas escalar, paso a paso."

I have always known there is no mountain you cannot climb, one step at a time.

Bowe makes dinner, and we eat outside. They play a game of chess while I look up at the stars. My dad hugs me good night. And nobody pretends Bowe is going home tonight.

Bowe and I go inside. I start doing the dishes, and Bowe comes up behind me. He kisses me and I laugh. He says he loves my laugh, and then he says, "Can I say that? Can I say I love your laugh?"

And I say, "I don't know. I mean, I guess yes. Sure."

I can see my father's living room window from my kitchen. I watch as his light goes off.

Bowe grabs my waist and spins me toward him.

And I wonder for a moment why I have spent all my time worried about losing things, when there is so much here.

. . .

When Bowe and I wake up in the morning, instead of sneaking out, he goes downstairs in his underwear and makes me a blueberry smoothie. I drink it while he makes himself a black coffee. When we're done, he picks up the paper and goes into the den. I go out onto the court.

I stretch my legs. As I start on my shoulders, I look at my watch. It's three past eight.

Where is my dad?

My heart drops through my belly.

I run toward my father's front door. I put my hand on the door-knob and I turn it.

There he is. Lying on one of his sofas, with the TV on ESPN.

Here but gone.

And all that escapes from my mouth is a hushed yelp. *"Papá."*

FROM THEN ON, EVERYTHING FEELS LIKE THOSE MOMENTS JUST BEFORE you wake in the morning. I am not asleep but somehow still dreaming, the world an ambiguous combination of reality and hallucination.

At some point, I am standing on my father's front stoop, staring at my sneakers when somebody—I can't tell if he's an EMT or someone from the coroner's office—comes to find me. I look over and realize Bowe is at my side, holding my hand.

"Your father had another heart attack last night and passed away, most likely sometime between eleven and one A.M.," the man says.

"Yeah, no shit, genius!" I hear myself shout.

Bowe pulls me into his arms.

I think someone gives me a sedative.

. . .

Gwen comes over with dinner. Bowe tries to make me eat something. When I look at him, I can't figure out why Bowe Huntley is in my house, why he is the one beside me.

Gwen tells me this is going to make the news soon. "I'll do my best to hold it all off until you're ready."

I tell her I don't care who knows. Hiding it won't fix it.

Bowe feeds me lunch and dinner and breakfast the next morning. I know that because I can see the dishes piled up around me in my bed.

I see my own face on the television and see Greg Phillips reporting that "Javier Soto, father and coach of Carrie Soto, has died unexpectedly. He was not with his daughter at Wimbledon this past July, and some speculated it was due to health concerns. But he was expected to be with Carrie in New York next week for the US Open."

Bowe tells me later that I threw the remote at the TV and cracked the screen.

In the paper, they print a picture of him from the early seventies at the French Open. He looks young and handsome in his polo shirt and panama hat. He would have loved it. I try to tear it out of the paper to save it, but I accidentally rip it.

At some point, Bowe gets in bed and holds me. He makes me smoothies every morning. He always gives me the wrong type of straw, but I don't know how to tell him without screaming at him and I don't want to scream at him.

I walk into the bathroom, thinking Bowe is in the shower. But instead, I find him sitting on the edge of the tub, with the shower running. When he sees me, he looks up and his eyes are bloodshot. He stands up and asks me if I am okay.

I wonder when he is going to leave. I'd have left by now.

"I'm not going anywhere," he says, even though I can't tell if I said any of that out loud.

After my father's funeral and the reception, Gwen is packing up all the food as I stand there in the kitchen, not moving. She's telling me about all the times my dad made her laugh.

"Can you please, for the love of God, shut up?" I say.

She stops putting cheese slices into Tupperware and looks at me.

I say, "I'm sorry."

She takes my hand, but hers is cold and I want her to let go of me. But I also know that even if I ask her to, she won't.

Bowe goes out onto the court every day. Sometimes I watch him from my window.

He comes inside after a particularly grueling session with a hitter. "How are you?" he says, breathless.

"How the fuck do you think I'm doing?" I say.

I look down and see I'm wearing my father's slippers. And I don't remember when I put them on.

Later, I ask Bowe if I should drop out of the US Open, and he tells me I already know the answer. But he's wrong. I do not.

I am in a T-shirt and pair of Bowe's boxers when Bowe comes into the room and tells me he's scheduled to play Franco Gustavo. I'm scheduled to play Madlenka Dvořáková in the first round in New York.

I hear my father's voice. "*Ah, será fácil.* You can whoop her ass." I turn to see him, but he's not there.

I am standing in the middle of my living room, looking at all the flowers people sent. The house is overflowing with blooms that are starting to die.

So many people have *sent* something but not come by. Which is more than I would have done for any of them.

The phone rings as I am lying in bed, and I don't answer it. But I can tell by the way the ringing stops that Bowe has picked it up.

He comes in a few moments later.

"It's Nicki," he says. "Chan."

"I don't want to talk to her," I say. But then I take the phone from his hand anyway.

"Hi."

"I'm so sorry, Carrie," Nicki says.

"Thank you."

"Listen, I want to tell you something. . . . If you don't play the US Open, I will consider bowing out as well."

I can't quite process the rest of what she's saying until she adds, "Just let me know what you're thinking. I want it to be a clean win. I want a fair fight."

"Honestly, Nicki," I say, "it just doesn't matter very much."

Nicki laughs, like I am making a joke.

My first moment of clarity is the following day—when I finally get up the guts to go into my father's house.

I stand in the same spot where I stood when I found him. I look at his things: his remote controls and the half-filled water glasses, his magazines and his books lined up on the shelf, his movies stacked to the side, his leather chairs, his panama hats.

I pick up one of his hats. It smells like English Leather and shampoo, earthy and human.

I wonder if this is how he felt when my mother died: flattened by the impossibility and yet inevitability of tomorrow. I am suddenly so tired, no match for the heaviness of gravity. I look at the floor and it calls to me, as strong as a magnet.

I lie down on the carpet of the home I bought for my father. The gift I gave him. And I do not get up for what feels like hours.

I am so angry at myself for thinking he'd be okay.

Don't I know better? Didn't I learn this lesson earlier than most? That the world doesn't care about you? That it will take the one thing you need, rip it right from your arms?

Grief is like a deep, dark hole. It calls like a siren: *Come to me, lose yourself here.* And you fight it and you fight it and you fight it, but when you finally do succumb and jump down into it, you can't quite believe how deep it is. It feels as if this is how you will live for the rest of your life, falling. Terrified and devastated, until you yourself die.

But that is the mirage.

That is grief's dizzying spell.

The fall isn't never-ending. It does have a ground floor.

Today, I cry for so long that I finally feel the floor under my feet. I find the bottom. And while I know the hole will be there forever, at least for now, I feel as if I can live inside it. I have learned its boundaries and its edges.

I stand up and feel ready to leave my father's house. But as I walk toward the door, I notice a notebook on the kitchen counter. It's the one he started keeping this year, full of all his coaching notes.

I walk into the kitchen, and I pick it up. It is a black leather book, as unassuming as can be. The front says *Carrie*.

I flip through it and see that every page is devoted to a player in the WTA with stats and plays, strategies—for how to beat them.

Players like Dvořáková and Flores and Martin and Carter and Zetov, they take up maybe half a page. Perez and Moretti and Nystrom and Machado each get more. And then there are multiple pages on Antonovich and Cortez.

Nicki Chan takes up the entire back half of the book.

He's clearly rewatched some of her games, made notes on how she performed against every other player. He's compared our serves and groundstrokes. Our shots. Our stances. Our forms.

And at the top of the last page, he's written in all capital letters *CARRIE CAN BEAT HER.*

His handwriting is a mess, and there are whole sentences I can't read. He has shown no concern for legibility, or whether any of it would make sense to anyone but him. Which is how I know this isn't a book he wrote *to me.* He wrote it for himself. This was his plan for New York.

I hold the book to my chest. I inhale sharply. When my mother died, there was almost nothing of her left. And as hard as I tried, I couldn't summon her. I couldn't hold on.

But there is still a huge piece of my father here. There is still work for him to do. This is one last tournament with my dad. I am holding it in my hands.

And I am going to fucking win it.

"Gwen," I say into the phone. I am in my kitchen, getting blueberries out of the refrigerator. "I'm going. Confirm with the USTA."

"You're sure about this?" she asks.

"Yeah," I say. "I'll fly out with Bowe."

"All right, I'll call you back."

I hang up the phone and walk upstairs, where Bowe is reading the same book I've seen him carrying around for days. I finally register the title. *How to Go on Living When Someone You Love Dies.*

"Hi," I say.

He puts the book down and sits up. "Hi."

I stare at Bowe as he waits for me to say more. He is in a heather gray Henley T-shirt and a pair of jeans. His hair is a mess. His stubble has grown in quite a bit.

He is here. He has not left.

"I'm going to New York with you," I say. "I'm playing the US Open."

"Okay," Bowe says, nodding. "Yes, great."

"My dad would like that," I say. "If I did that."

"I completely agree."

I walk toward him and put my arms around his torso, lean my head against his chest. Here is someone else who knew my father, someone else who knows what I have lost, someone who lost something too.

"I'm gonna go and I'm going to win the whole goddamn thing," I say, pulling back.

"I love it," Bowe says, nodding and smiling. "Yes, I'm gonna do that too."

Both of us laugh, and I don't have a shred of guilt for feeling joyful without my father on this earth. This is the tiniest beginning of a terrible, beautiful whole new life.

THE MORNING OF MY MATCH AGAINST DVOŘÁKOVÁ, THERE IS A KNOCK at the door of my hotel suite, and Bowe answers it. Gwen comes in holding a blueberry smoothie.

"I didn't know you were coming," I say.

Gwen smiles softly. "Yes, you did, honey," she says. "It's okay. I'm here." She hands me the smoothie.

Bowe is gathering my kit and my clothes. But when I watch him do it, I realize I didn't do any of the packing. He did it all back in L.A. And now he is doing it all here.

So far this morning, as well as asking Gwen to get the smoothie, he's woken me up, called down for almonds, run the shower, put me in it, and then when I just stood there, he got in with me and washed my hair.

"You're playing Dvořáková?" Gwen says.

"Yeah."

Gwen looks at Bowe. "And you're playing Gustavo?"

Bowe nods. "If I win, I'll play Ortega, probably. And then maybe Griffin or Bracher. But, you know, when I lose, that's it for me."

"You're retiring," Gwen says.

"Yeah. I'm done. I'm ready to be done."

Gwen nods. "And are you retiring?" she says, looking at me. "After this?"

I don't have an answer. I can barely consider this afternoon.

"Okay," Gwen says. "We'll prepare for all scenarios."

Bowe returns to whatever he's doing and then pops his head back up a second later. "Oh, don't forget your notebook."

He hands it to me, and I breathe in. I've read every line of it over and over again since I first found it. I fell asleep reading it last night. I read the page on Dvořáková three times this morning alone. I look at my watch. I'm playing her in a matter of hours.

"What is that?" Gwen says.

I open my mouth to explain, but I can't. I can't get the words out.

"Jav put it together," Bowe says. "His coaching plan. So Carrie's gonna follow it and win."

Gwen nods. "I love it."

"Do you want to see it?" I say.

"Your coaching plan that your father gave you?" Gwen says. "You don't have to share that with me. Or with anyone if you don't want to."

"I want to," I say. "Check it out."

I crack the book open, and I take her through each page. When we get to Dvořáková, Gwen and I read through it together.

Since Carrie beat her back in Melbourne, she's gotten stronger. Her baseline work is better. But she wants to be a power baseliner so bad, even though she's better at serve and volley. Keep her playing at the baseline. It will thrill her, but she won't be able to keep up.

I start to feel that hum in my bones. It feels small, right now, like a nascent flame. But I know it will grow. I know soon it will roar.

Gwen looks up at me. "You've got this," she says.

"Yeah," I say. "Plus, my dad didn't write it down, but Dvořáková is intimidated by me. I've beaten her every time I've played her so far. So if I don't let her get a foothold at the beginning, I think she'll go down like a house of cards."

Gwen nods. "You're a smart one," she says.

"Thanks. Taught by the best."

Gwen holds my hand and gives it a squeeze. "Yes, you were. And you've absorbed it all."

"Thank you."

I get up as she keeps flipping through the pages.

"There's a lot on Chan," she says.

"Yeah, I have to study that section."

"Well," she says, "I'll be in the players' box for each and every match, all right?"

I nod. And then Gwen kisses me on the cheek and hugs Bowe goodbye and leaves.

I turn to Bowe. He is holding up a navy tank top and a white tennis skirt. He has put my yellow Break Points on the bed.

"I fucked up. I forgot socks," he says. "When I was packing your things."

"We will get some on the way," I say. "It's gonna be fine."

THE 1995
US OPEN

I STAND IN THE LOCKER ROOM, SURROUNDED BY OTHER PLAYERS—
Martin and Carter are laughing in the corner. Zetov and Perez are
ignoring each other. Antonovich comes in and smiles and greets
everyone. When Perez sees me, she gives me a pat on the shoulder.
Flores tells me she's sorry for my loss. I say thank you.

When Madlenka Dvořáková walks in, we catch each other's eye.
She looks so childlike in her white dress, her hair pulled back in two
braids. We give each other a nod, and then I shut my locker and
make my way to the training room.

It's oddly quiet in here, just me and a few trainers. I take in the
delicious solitude as I have my knees and elbows taped. But then,
when I'm having my calves massaged, Nicki Chan walks in.

She's smiling sweetly, greeting the trainers she recognizes with a
levity I find puzzling. It is as if it is any other day to her—and not the
first day of a two-week tournament in which she might just break
another record or lose it altogether.

When she sits down next to me, I speak up. "Always so chipper."

"Yes," she says as she sits down on the bench next to mine. "It's rather annoying, isn't it? People tell me that all the time." She laughs as the trainer begins taping her foot. I make a mental note to run her around the court, if I get the chance. Her ankle has to be hurting. She has to stop going so hard on it.

"Thank you for calling," I say, my voice low. "The other day."

Nicki nods. "Of course."

"It was . . . kind of you."

"Like I said," she says, waving me off, "I want to skin you alive and eat your heart for breakfast." She smiles at me and winks. "But I want to know I did it when you were at your strongest."

I nod. "I get it," I say. "And you will get your chance. And you will fail. And everything will go back to the way it should be." I switch positions as one of the trainers starts massaging my forearms.

Nicki keeps her eyes focused entirely on watching the trainer wrap her foot. But her next words are aimed squarely at me. "I don't think you've ever understood what I can do. What I am doing."

"I do," I say. "I see it."

"I am better than you," she says.

"Give me a break, Nicki."

"You think that if this was 1982, I wouldn't stand a chance against you," Nicki continues.

"I *know* that if this was 1982, you wouldn't stand a chance against me," I say. "Because it's 1995, and you don't stand a chance against me."

Nicki scoffs. "You just can't see it."

"How good you are?" I say. "I see how good you are."

"You don't respect what I've done for tennis the way I respect what you've done."

"What have you done that I haven't done?"

Nicki turns and looks at me. Her gaze is heavy. "I'm the first Asian woman to ever win Wimbledon. The first woman like me to do *almost any of the things* I've done in tennis—hitting these records. Because we both know tennis doesn't make it easy for those of us who aren't blond and blue-eyed."

"Yes," I say, nodding. "Absolutely."

"I've increased the fastest serve recorded in tennis. Tennis is a quicker game now, since I served at 132 miles per hour. Now almost every player on the WTA is serving faster than we all were even ten years ago. My forehand *averages* 81 miles per hour. You can't come close to me on that either. So pay me a little respect, Soto. I've won the US Open more than any woman in tennis history, including you. My forehand and backhand groundstrokes have more spin than any other female player ever—last year I topped two thousand revolutions per minute. I am currently the highest-paid female athlete in the world. For someone like me, do you understand what that means? And I've spent the most weeks at number one—which is currently three hundred and seventeen. You only have three hundred and—"

"Nine," I say.

"Right."

"So you just go around memorizing your stats?" I say, even though I know I'm being a hypocrite.

Nicki laughs. "This matters to me, Carrie. Putting my whole soul into this game matters to me. These tournaments matter. I've dedicated my life to this."

"Well, so have I," I say.

"And you had your chance to shine—you were given that opportunity."

"I *took* it," I say. "It wasn't given to me. Nobody wanted *me* to be the face of women's tennis. They still don't. I had to demand it. Just like I am doing now. So if you want it, you're going to have to take it from me."

"No," Nicki says. "That's what you don't seem to get. I *have* taken it from you. *I* have the record. And if *you* want it, you're going to have to take it from *me*."

I stare at her, and she continues.

"I am the best player women's tennis has seen," she says. "And I deserve to be recognized for it."

"You are recognized for it," I say. "Constantly."

Nicki shakes her head. "No, by *you*. By the person I've respected my entire life. The woman I've looked up to."

There is no smile on her face anymore. Not even the hint of one. I look over at the TV. It's playing sports commentary with the sound off. The closed captioning says they are talking about Nicki and me right now.

"I see it," I say, finally looking at her. "Me hating it is me seeing it."

Nicki sighs. "Okay, Soto. I guess I can't squeeze blood from a stone."

"Look, what do you want from me?"

Nicki looks me in the eye.

"Don't worry about what I say," I tell her. "Pay attention to what I *do*. I'm back, aren't I? I'm playing here today. That's how good you are."

The trainer is done. I stand up. I walk past Nicki and put my hand on her shoulder.

"Good luck," I say. "I'm rooting for you up until the last second when I play you."

Nicki smiles. "You should be so lucky."

I put my hand out for her to shake. And she takes it.

Transcript

SportsNews Network
Wild Sports with Bill Evans

Bill Evans: It is the first day of this year's US Open, and Nicki Chan started it off by absolutely *crushing* journey-man Suze Carter this morning. Natasha Antonovich, Ingrid Cortez, Carla Perez, Odette Moretti, Josie Flores, Whitney Belgrade, Erica Staunton, and more are all heading into the second round. And now in the afternoon, Wimbledon champion and all-out sensation Carrie Soto goes up against rookie Madlenka Dvořáková here in the first round at Flushing Meadows. It is just two weeks since her father and coach, Javier Soto, died. Carrie has said she is playing in his honor.

There's a lot of talk about who will come out the victor over the next couple weeks. But we know one thing for sure: There may be one hundred twenty-eight players competing for that trophy, but all eyes are focused on just two of them.

Nicki Chan and Carrie Soto have made no secret of their rivalry. Each of these incomparable women wants that title and the record that comes with it.

Who will it be? The Beast or the B-I-T-C-You-Know-What?

It is sure to be a nail-biter. Stay with us over the next two weeks as we find out who makes it to the final.

SOTO VS. DVOŘÁKOVÁ

1995 US Open

First Round

I AM STANDING IN THE TUNNEL. I LEAN DOWN AND WIPE THE DIRT OFF my yellow Break Points. I remember the words my father wrote down. *Keep her playing at the baseline. It will thrill her, but she won't be able to keep up.*

I breathe in deeply. Here we go.

The second my feet hit the court, the crowd cheers. They cheer so loudly I can barely hear myself think.

I know what the sportscasters are saying. They are telling all the people at home that I've just lost Dad, that I am out here playing my first match without him.

I expect the roar to die down, but it doesn't. The crowd keeps cheering as I set up my things. It is almost eerie—the way their voices ring through the air, the way the howl of it echoes throughout the arena. Their sound is a deep rumble, shaking the net.

I look up all around me—thousands of people stomping and

calling. I wave in a wide circle through each section, and I watch as people in the crowd start standing up.

Bowe and Gwen are in the players' box. Gwen is clapping. Bowe catches my eye, and we look at each other as each section stands, rising like a tide.

They are clapping for my father. For this one moment of time, it feels as if everyone in the arena misses Javier Soto as much as I do.

A tear leaves my eye. I wipe it away.

Poor Dvořáková. She stands no chance. It's over in fifty-one minutes.

Transcript

SportsRadio Nation with Grant Trumbull

Grant Trumbull: We are here with the editor of *SportsSunday*, Jimmy Wallace, to talk about what's going on at the US Open. Jimmy, give us the lay of the land here. Start with the men's game.

Jimmy Wallace: Well, there's no story coming out of men's tennis quite like that of Bowe Huntley.

Trumbull: He's soaring.

Wallace: There was nobody—and I mean *nobody*—favoring Bowe Huntley as we came into this tournament.

Trumbull: This is his last, is it not?

Wallace: All of us were saying, "The guy's retiring, he's the oldest one on the court, his salad days are long behind him."

Trumbull: And he had to pull out of Wimbledon with an injury.

Wallace: He tore the cartilage in his ribs back in May at the French. This was not a player anyone was betting on.

Trumbull: And yet.

Wallace: [*laughs*] And yet! Huntley comes out onto the court in the first round and just pummels Franco Gustavo. Takes him in straight sets. Still, we're all thinking, "Okay, but it won't happen again."

Trumbull: And we were wrong.

Wallace: Dead wrong. He takes Ortega in the second round, again in straight sets. Then Bracher. Then Mailer.

Trumbull: And now he's in the quarterfinals.

Wallace: He's in the quarterfinals. At the age of forty! And let me tell you, the crowd is with him in these matches. I haven't seen a crowd this energized in years. You know I'm a skeptic, Grant.

Trumbull: [*laughs*] You're a believe-it-when-you-see-it kind of guy.

Wallace: But Huntley's got me on the edge of my seat. He's got me rooting for him. I don't know how this ends, but I'll tell you it's a hell of a show.

Transcript

SportsHour USA
The Mark Hadley Show

Mark Hadley: I'm cleaning my glasses over here, disbelieving what I'm seeing. Bowe Huntley just beat Wimbledon champion Jadran Petrovich in the quarterfinals of the US Open?

Briggs Lakin: I wouldn't just say he beat him. Huntley demolished him. It was *embarrassing* for Petrovich. He's ranked two in the world, and Huntley took him down hard.

Gloria Jones: That last serve was simply stunning.

Hadley: Let's get into Huntley's serve—I want to talk about that. It wasn't official, but there's been talk over this past year that Bowe Huntley was being coached by the late Javier Soto. Have either of you heard anything about this?

Jones: I have, yes. We've been seeing Carrie Soto and Bowe Huntley together a lot these past few months. There's an assumption that they are dating. Obviously, we don't know.

Lakin: I mean, we know.

Jones: No one has confirmed anything.

Lakin: I don't need anyone to confirm for me that two plus two equals four.

Jones: [*laughs*] There are many people who say Bowe Huntley and Javier Soto were working together before the French Open. So it stands to reason they may have still been working together when Javier Soto passed away just a few short weeks ago.

Hadley: So maybe Javier Soto is behind this turn in Bowe Huntley.

Jones: Maybe he was.

Hadley: He certainly did beautiful work with Carrie Soto, didn't he?

Jones: That he did. And let's take a moment, if we can. We all expect greatness from Carrie, but she's just lost her father, she's lost her coach. And now we are on the eve of the semifinals and she's handily defeated *every single opponent in front of her.* That includes Odette Moretti, who she beat in the quarterfinals just a few hours ago today.

Lakin: She's shown a lot of heart this tournament.

Jones: Javier Soto was a great coach, a coach for the ages. And I think we're seeing that in this tournament. I think we are seeing, in Bowe Huntley and Carrie Soto, what Javier Soto was best at. The "beautiful fundamentals," as he would say.

Lakin: Well said, Gloria. Absolutely.

HUNTLEY VS. MATSUDA

1995 US Open

Semifinals

GWEN AND I ARE SITTING IN THE PLAYERS' BOX. I AM CHECKING MY watch because I need to leave soon for my own match. But I can't quite tear myself away just yet.

It's the fifth set, 3–5. Bowe is behind, but he can still get back in it if he holds this game and breaks Matsuda's serve on the next one.

He looks at me and smiles.

This morning at breakfast, I was reading *NowThis* in an attempt to clear my mind. The front cover was about this pop star who left this rock star, and I wanted to know if it was true she'd been sleeping with this actor. But when I opened up the magazine, it was my face that was staring back at me.

There was a photo of Bowe and me on the court from the week before. They had caught us kissing.

I closed the magazine, almost reflexively. And then I opened it back up.

In the photo, we are both in shorts and T-shirts. He is wearing his navy blue hat. He has his arm around my lower back, pulling me toward him, and I have to look up to meet his lips.

I didn't know the paparazzi were there. I wouldn't have kissed him if I had. But instead of feeling horrified to have it printed in the magazine for all the world, all I could see was just how grotesquely happy I look in it.

Bowe walked by and glanced over my shoulder. From the look on his face, I could tell he'd already seen it.

"What do you think?" he asked.

I stared at the photo a moment longer. "We look happy," I said, finally.

And Bowe smiled. "Yeah," he said. "I think so too."

Bowe holds the game; it's now 4–5. During the changeover, he comes up to the players' box and winks at me. I smile at him and wink back. I am once again a fool.

Bowe gets back to the baseline. The pressure is on him now. If he does not win this game, it is the last professional match of his career. But you wouldn't know it looking at him. He's waving to the crowd, laughing as they cheer for him, lifting his hands up to encourage them all.

Last night, he told me he would like to make it to the final. "This is all I've ever wanted out of this year. To do something great like this. I never thought I'd get this far, and now I have," he said in the quiet of the night. "So why not dream further?"

But today, right before he went into the locker room, he told me the opposite. "I never thought I'd get this far, and now I have," he said. "So the rest is all icing on the cake."

Matsuda serves a fast one. It lands at Bowe's feet, and Bowe jumps backward to return it. It lands just over the net. Matsuda scrambles for it and misses.

Love–15.

Bowe smiles. The crowd cheers. It's clear that all the cheering annoys Matsuda. And so in between serves, Bowe looks at the crowd, pumping them up to cheer louder. Matsuda shakes his head, sends off another blistering serve.

Bowe lunges for it but hits it into the net.

15–all.

I check my watch again. I have to go.

15–30.

30–all.

30–40.

Deuce.

Advantage Matsuda.

Deuce.

I have to go.

Advantage Bowe.

Deuce.

Advantage Matsuda.

Deuce.

I'm late to warm up.

Advantage Matsuda.

Deuce.

Advantage Matsuda.

Bowe's tired. I don't know if Matsuda can tell, if the crowd can tell, but I can. He's not up as high on his serve. I will him some strength, a burst of energy. Just two points in a row can save this game and maybe take him to the final.

Deuce.

Advantage Matsuda.

Matsuda sends another serve to Bowe's feet. This time, Bowe runs back as fast as he can. He gets into position, gets his racket on the ball. But then it hits the net.

My heart falls. It's over.

Bowe stands still on the court and closes his eyes. I watch his chest rise and fall. He nods and opens his eyes.

The crowd is oddly quiet for the end of a match. They wanted it for him. But it is Matsuda who is going to the final.

Bowe Huntley has retired.

I watch his face for signs of distress or grief—though I'm smart enough to know that grief will take various shapes over the next few months, maybe years. Still, his face now shows only a smile and wet eyes. Not a tantrum in sight.

I wish my father were here to see this. To witness what Bowe has done here at the US Open. He would have cheered the loudest.

Bowe waves to the crowd.

Suddenly, the whole stadium is on their feet, including me. They are screaming so loud for him that it pierces my ears. He waves to each section, nodding as he does.

Matsuda shakes his hand and then hangs back. He gives Bowe the moment.

Bowe looks at me and smiles. I smile back. Bowe turns to the crowd and lifts both of his fists above his head. And then waves goodbye.

He comes right to me, and I lean over from the players' box to talk to him.

"Beautiful run," I say. "A beautiful end to a stunning career."

"I love you," he says.

My eyes go wide.

"Sorry if that makes you cringe," he adds, taking my hand.

I thought if this moment ever came I wouldn't be able to look at him, but it's easy. It's terrifying how easy it is. "It's okay," I say. "I already knew. My dad told me."

He laughs. "It's that obvious, huh?"

"No," I say. "Or maybe. I don't know. Do you need me to say it back?"

"No," he says. "I know who you are. And you're late to warm up."

"Are you okay?" I ask, hugging him. "You're sure?"

"Yeah, I'm sure."

"Okay, I'm going. But I do too, you know. What you said."

"I know," he says.

"That obvious, huh?" I joke.

"Not really, Carrie," he says, laughing. "But you have your tells."

SOTO VS. CORTEZ

1995 US Open

Semifinals

IT'S THE THIRD SET. I'M TWO GAMES AWAY FROM CLINCHING THIS thing.

I'm not tired yet. But Cortez is angry. I can feel it when she starts smacking the tuft off the ball.

She wants to get to the final. She's probably got a chip on her shoulder about London. She's used it to push her forward, and I respect that.

I keep thinking about my father's notebook.

Cortez is irritable and cocky. She does not like losing. She does not like believing someone has bested her. Piss her off and she will start messing up. Very familiar.

I knew he meant me. But as I stand across the net from her now, I can see that Cortez and I are perhaps even more alike than I'd realized. Cutting and relentless, bloodthirsty. Cold but passionate. Needing to win because we cannot bear to lose.

Knock Cortez off her game, make her upset. She's a confident player; undermine her confidence and you will cut her down.

If my father is right and Cortez's mental game is like mine, then I know what I need to do.

I need to hit as many aces as possible. I need to not even give her the chance to fight for the point. If I shut her out of my service games completely, she'll get exasperated and desperate. She'll start making mistakes.

Yes, I think I know Ingrid Cortez very well. The downside of perfectionism is that you are so used to getting it right, you completely collapse when you get it wrong.

And it will not be me who collapses today.

To serve aces, you have to be bold. You have to risk hitting the net or going wide. You have to play like you're not afraid. I can do that.

I toss the ball and whip it right into the far corner of the service box. Cortez can't touch it. *15–love.*

I keep at it. Soon, I've held the game.

Cortez's shoulders tense and her hands turn to fists with every point I chip off her. Each time she walks back to the baseline, she shakes her head at herself and looks at her coach.

I hold steady. And soon I'm at match point.

Cortez bounces the ball at her feet, gearing herself up for the toss.

I feel a wash of affection for her. She is so young. She still has so much time to do all the things she wants to do. But going to the final of the '95 US Open will not be one of them.

She serves a screamer—hard and fast with a quick drop. I run backward, ready for it. I take it on the rise, a forehand cross-court. She returns it with a groundstroke wide to my backhand.

The ball comes at me. I pull my racket back and take it out of the air before the bounce, send it back wide to her forehand.

She runs for it, but it bounces hard and then spins farther off court. She dives, hitting the ground at the same time the ball lands softly out of her reach.

The crowd erupts. Bowe shoots up out of his seat. I see that Gwen is hollering. I fall to my knees, the hard court scraping my skin. I am not proud, as much as I am grateful.

Ahí vamos, papá, I think. *A la final.*

THAT EVENING, BOWE, GWEN, AND I SIT IN MY HOTEL SUITE, IN FRONT of the television. I'm acting calm, but I can feel the stress gathering in my knees. I'm trying to stretch them out.

Bowe's back is killing him, so he's watching TV from the floor with his legs up the wall. Gwen's the only one of us able to sit properly.

Nicki is playing Antonovich in the semis. She's now serving for the match.

"We want Chan to win," Gwen says. "Right? I'm just confirming I'm rooting for the right thing here. It's not an easy one."

I nod, reaching for my toes. I can feel my hamstrings and the backs of my knees sing. "Yeah, we want Chan."

Nicki serves a kick serve. Antonovich returns. Nicki hits a groundstroke, bouncing just at the baseline and then into the stands. Nicki can anticipate the ball better than almost anyone I know.

"Fuck, she's good," I say.

Bowe nods. "She is."

"And she's got no coach," I say. "She doesn't have that magic in her back pocket, like I've had all these years. She's doing this all herself."

Nicki serves another, fast and ugly, like she's dropping a bomb.

"Nicki's gonna take it," I say.

Nicki serves, jumping big and landing hard on the court as she follows it through. I'm not sure Antonovich can reach it. But then somehow Antonovich gets high up and manages to smash it back before she falls onto the court.

Bowe sits up. Gwen is leaning toward the TV. I get to my feet.

Nicki's head looks up as the ball arches across the net. She's running backward watching it. Antonovich, still on the court, is staring at it.

The ball soars through the air and careens down as Nicki rushes for it. It hits *inches* past the sideline. It's out.

Natasha Antonovich pounds her arms on the court.

Nicki jumps into the air.

So here it is. Soto vs. Chan.

I WAKE UP THE NEXT MORNING. THE SUN IS SHINING; THE AIR IS COOL. It is a perfect day to win the US Open.

Bowe is already up, despite the early hour. And when I come out into the living area, he is reading the paper. Beside him is a blueberry smoothie and a jar of unsalted almonds.

"Good morning, record breaker," he says.

"You know better than to say shit like that before I've actually broken a record."

Bowe shakes his head. "No, look," he says. He shows me the paper he's reading. The headline says SOTO VS. CHAN GUARANTEED TO BREAK MULTIPLE RECORDS.

I pick up the paper and read through the article. Among other facts of tonight's match, I learn that between Nicki and me, *one* of us will be the oldest to win the US Open in the Open Era. Nicki, at almost thirty-two, will beat out Margaret Court by nine months. If I take it, I'll beat Margaret Court by almost seven years.

I am officially the oldest player to make the women's singles final of the US Open. I also stand to break the record for most aces in a tournament, and it is looking like Soto vs. Chan will create a new record for viewership numbers.

One record they don't know about yet: Gwen called me last night to tell me AmEx has offered to buy out my contract with Elite Gold. And since Elite Gold now wants to *keep* my contract, AmEx is offering me the largest endorsement fee for any tennis player—male or female—in history.

I told her I'm directing every dollar to my youth center funds. Gwen said she'd donate too.

"I mean, I can do that and still retire off this check," Gwen told me.

I laughed and told her to go for it.

"I'm going to do it, Carrie," she said, her voice now serious. "I'm going to tell my partners I'm retiring next year. Officially."

"Good for you," I told her.

Now I hand the article back to Bowe.

"So many statistics," I say. "Good God. It is exactly what my dad said all those years ago. You just pick one randomly and decide that's the one you're committed to. But when you take a step back, how can you say one means more than another?"

Bowe sips his coffee and nods. "Still," he says. "'Most Slams' means something to a lot of us, let's not kid ourselves. You are defending the one that means the most to you."

I take a breath. "Yeah," I say. "But it didn't ever mean as much to my dad. My dad just wanted me to play beautiful tennis."

Bowe smiles. "And look at that," he says. "You do."

Walking through the tunnel, I can just see the edges of the court. The crowd is already loud. The lights are on, barely brighter than the evening air. When I get to the opening, I pull my shoulders down. I roll my neck. I wipe my shoes.

I inhale sharply. I let the air leave my body like a deflating balloon. I am loose. I am ready.

There is a guard standing behind me. And then I hear footsteps. "Nicki," I say.

She's wearing a white shirt and a navy blue skirt. Her Nike 130s are white with a blue Swoosh. "Carrie."

"You feeling all right?" I say. "How's your ankle? How's your back? Any injuries I should exploit?"

Nicki laughs. "Unfortunately for you, I'm feeling one hundred percent."

"Good," I say. "The win will be sweeter."

Nicki shakes her head. "I read an interview with you years ago, when I was still a kid," she says. "Where you said your father called you 'Achilles.'"

"Yeah," I say. "The greatest of the Greeks."

"I was always jealous of that. That sense of destiny you seemed to have. Do you remember what Achilles said to Hector after Hector killed Patroclus?"

It has been a long time since I've actually read *The Iliad*. I shake my head.

She smiles. "He says, 'There can be no pacts between men and lions. I will make you pay in full for the grief you have caused me.'"

SOTO VS. CHAN

1995 US Open

Final

Too many people, possibly even Nicki, believe that Nicki is new tennis. That my Carrie is old tennis. They don't realize I taught Carrie to play any tennis. So Carrie should start wild and powerful, start with a splash. Make it clear, from the beginning, that whatever version of Carrie Nicki prepared for, she didn't prepare for this.

I win the toss and elect to serve first.

Nicki's forehand is brutal, so everyone serves to her backhand. Not me. My first serve is low, short, fast, and wide to her forehand. She has to scramble to meet the ball. She returns it just past the net. I chip it back. She doesn't get under it in time. *15–love.*

Nicki looks at me and nods calmly.

I hold the first game.

. . .

Her first serve comes at me like it was shot from a gun—exactly as I knew it would. I return it right to her backhand. She returns it deep. I send it back with a drive volley, pulling her up closer to the net.

Nicki succeeds by getting people to play her type of tennis. Carrie can meet her at that level, but Nicki cannot meet Carrie at hers. Carrie should lure Nicki into Carrie's kind of tennis—the kind of tennis where a centimeter matters. I believe the best Carrie will beat the best Nicki. And that means GET HER TO THE NET.

Nicki runs up to meet my shot and makes it just in time. But her return is too long. The first point in her service game is mine. *Love–15.*

Still, she holds the game.

We each hold our games—neither able to break the other. 1–1 becomes 2–2. 2–2 becomes 3–3, 4–4, 5–5.

At 6–6, we move to a tiebreaker.

Nicki clobbers me with her serves. On my serves, she hammers her returns. The tiebreak quickly gets to 0–4, Nicki's favor. I have to adjust.

I try cutting off the pace of the ball, hitting slices, stopping her short. It works quickly, and I am unyielding until she gets the hang of it.

Now we're 4–4.

5–5.

6–6 in the tiebreaker.

The crowd is beginning to rumble.

Nicki hits a winner past me, bringing her to 6–7. But she's got to win by two.

It's my serve, and I send a fast shot right at her heels. She misses it. 7–7.

Minutes later, Nicki is up 12–11. It's her serve.

I stare at her, watching her toss, trying to guess where it's going. By now I can see that she does have a small tell. She holds her shoulder ever so slightly lower when she's going cross-court.

I watch her, see her shoulder high. I know she's sending it down the line, to my forehand.

It whistles through the air so fast it's gone by the time I hear it. I reach wide, but I can't snag it. *Fuck.* The crowd screams.

At 13–11 in the tiebreak, the first set is hers.

I haven't been looking at anyone during the changeovers. Not Gwen, not Bowe, not Ali. Not the crowd. I keep my head down. I focus on drinking water, drying my face, keeping my father in my head. I only want to hear his voice right now.

If Nicki wins the first set, Carrie has a better chance of winning the second. We can use Nicki's confidence—her arrogance???—against her here. And we should. Stay the course. Keep at it. Don't change it up. If we don't take the first set, we can win the second.

The second set begins. I move her up to the net. I hit the balls low and soft so she can't get as much power off them.

We trade games. 1–1. 2–2. 3–3.

But soon, Nicki starts getting the hang of it. She is staying closer to the net, hitting with more control. Our rallies go ten, twelve, sometimes fifteen times back and forth.

Nobody breaking anyone's serve.

It begins to feel like a perfect rhythm—the ball back and forth, the two of us meeting it. No unforced errors, no mistakes. Perfect execution. Just a dance.

There are times I am looking at the ball and other times I am watching her. I can feel her watching me. I know, as I'm swinging, that she can see the skill in what I'm doing. I can barely take my eyes off the gorgeous brutality of her power. She swings with such concentrated force, screaming as she does it.

I zero in on the yellow dot as it barrels toward me time and again. I feel the ease of my arm pulling back, over and over, my racket gliding on in the follow-through.

I'm playing the best goddamn game I can, moment by moment, shot by shot.

When it's 5–6, her serve, it's time to knock her out. I volley it back to her; she runs up to the net. And just when it seems as if she has settled into this fast, volleying tennis, I hit a flat crushing groundstroke past her.

And then I do it again, and again. Just when she hangs back, I send a drop shot. Just when she thinks I'm pulling up short, I hit it long. It's her serve but she's on the run, one step behind me, trying to catch up. *30–40.*

And now here I am. The moment in which I know I can take the set. Break point.

If Carrie gets to break point, she will convert it to a win. She is great at turning momentum into points. Nicki is a good defensive player—players rarely get to break point against her anymore. And she's a fan of Carrie, she knows Carrie. She knows Carrie lives at break point. We just need to get Carrie to break point once every set. And the rest will fall into place.

Nicki serves the ball. It goes right up against the line but lands inside, bounces high. I jump and hit a smash overhead.

She takes it out of the air early. And I can tell she's expecting a groundstroke return; the ball has too much fire on it for me to try a softer shot. But rather than send it cross-court, I go for the winner. I send it right down the line, along the sideline. She has to rush across the court to get her hands on it. I watch her running, and I can see her ankle roll a bit as she slides.

And she's too late. The ball bounces once, and she can't save it. When she stands up, I can tell her ankle hurts. And thank God, because both my knees, especially my bad one, are starting to ache.

"Set is Soto's," I hear over the loudspeaker as the crowd jumps out of their seats. Everyone begins to scream.

I smile at Nicki, expecting a smile back. But she looks pissed, on the verge of throwing her racket. I don't blame her. I've been there. She thought the match would be hers by now.

But I'm stealing it out of her hands.

This is fun, I think. *How did I forget this is so fucking fun?*

I sit down on the chair and wipe my face dry. I take a drink of water. I look over at Nicki, who will not look at me, her jaw clenched. She unscrews the top of a Gatorade and takes a big swig. If I had to guess, her ankle is swelling. Clouds have started to settle in over the arena. It cools the air, and I am grateful.

Gwen catches my eye. She points at me, right at my chest.

I tap my flat palm to my heart and point back at her.

The deciding set. Nicki's serves get faster, harder. They come at me with a whistle. It is startling. But I don't worry myself with trying to outdo her. My serves are accurate down to the inch. They are sniper shots.

Nicki's playing at full capacity right now. She's fast and watching my tosses. I have to keep my serves unpredictable and sharp.

1–1 to 2–2, 2–2 to 3–3. When I take the ball low, she gets under it. When she goes deep, I get there. When I go short, she pulls up.

She is breathing heavily. I am sweating.

The crowd is going wild with every rally, screaming at every winner.

4–4. 5–5.

My dad was right. The third set is when Nicki plays her hardest.

When she slams another groundstroke past me, I return it just in time, only to see her setting up for another. I am in awe of the firepower of her arm. The way it crushes the ball when it makes contact. I've never seen power like this. Certainly not with this much intuition about where the ball is going, what the ball will do.

My left knee is twinging, my right knee not far behind. I'm breathing harder than when I was running on sand all those months ago. Sweat is pouring off my face. The sky is getting darker. But I'm not letting up. And neither is she. I can tell by the way her eyes have lost their brightness, her shoulders have tightened. Even her gait seems angry as she limps away from the net after every point.

Nicki Chan is a great player. But not great enough to destroy me as quickly as she wanted.

On her next service game, Nicki starts serving so fast it feels like a blitz.

I can feel the fatigue in my legs. They are starting to give out, my thighs quivering when I squat. My knees are screaming. She shuts me out of the game.

I can barely hold her off on my service game. But I do.

It's now 6–6 in the third set. We're going to another tiebreak.

And then lightning cracks, and the sky roars. I look up at the clouds, and rain starts falling.

Gwen, Bowe, and Ali all rush into the locker room during the delay.

"Guys," I say. "I'm fine. I've got this."

"You are dominating!" Gwen says. It is the most intense I've ever seen her. "Raining sheer motherfucking terror!"

I laugh. "Thank you."

Bowe smiles. "She's right."

I lock eyes with him and smile. "I have to stay focused on winning the tiebreak. Do we know how long the delay will be?"

Ali speaks up. "The storm is passing already. They don't think more than twenty minutes."

"In that case, everyone get out of here," I say. And then I add, "Please."

Bowe grabs my shoulder and squeezes it, then escorts the two of them out. He turns back to me at the last second.

"This is a beautiful match," he says. "An absolutely *beautiful* match."

He doesn't wait for my response. He just taps the doorframe and leaves.

Suddenly, it is so quiet around me that I can hear the churn of the pipes in the walls.

I try to think of what my father would say to me right now. I open my locker and look through the notebook. I read his notes again. He says nothing about a tiebreak for the third set. I flip through the pages, searching for something—anything—but there's nothing I haven't already read.

What would he say if he were here? What would he have written in this book if he'd had more time? There are still things I need to know; there is still advice I need to get from him. There is more to do together.

I run through strategies—start slow, let her get tired; come out fast, don't let her get a foothold; go for the big serves; now's not the time for big serves—desperately trying to assess which one sounds the most like him.

But . . . I don't know. I don't know what he would say.

I feel as if the wind has been knocked out of me. From this moment forward, I do not have him with me. I do not know what he would be thinking. I do not know any more of his strategy, his plan. His logic. His advice. Because he is gone. And he will never be back. I have come to the end.

Suddenly, I feel as if the pain is enough to level me.

I pick up the notebook and put it back in the locker. If I win this tiebreak, it will be because I know how to beat her on my own. And if I don't, it will be because she is the better player. This is the test I asked for.

The door opens, and Nicki comes in.

"I was waiting in the training room," she says. "I didn't want to see you."

"Oh."

"But now it's gonna be at least another ten."

"Okay."

She sits down next to me on the bench. She doesn't say anything for a long time. And neither do I. I just sit next to her with my eyes closed, trying to control my breathing, trying to ignore the pain in my knees.

"This should be mine already," Nicki says, finally.

I open my eyes and look at her. "Well, it's not, sunshine."

Nicki shakes her head. "You are the best player I have ever played, then and now," she says. "You bitch."

I laugh.

"I'm trying to be funny to hide how much I hate you with every atom in my body," she says. I check her face, and she's not smiling.

"Don't hate me," I say. "It is a waste of your time."

Nicki huffs.

"You're playing some of the best tennis I've ever seen you play," I tell her. "Thanks to me."

She rolls her eyes. "Okay, Soto."

I add, "You deserve every single place you claim in history."

Nicki looks me in the eye. "I am going to beat you."

"No," I tell her. "You are not."

Nicki laughs, despite herself. A coordinator comes in and tells us they are preparing for us to head back out. We both stand up, and Nicki puts her hand on my shoulder.

"Playing you this year . . . beating these records—with Carrie Soto, against Carrie Soto—it's been a dream come true."

I look her in the eye and nod, unsure quite how to tell her that this match has meant the same for me.

"And now I'm going to shoot an arrow right into your heel so I can say I was the one who finally took down Achilles."

And *that* I instantly have the words for: "I'd like to see you fucking try."

The tiebreaker begins.

A point for Nicki, a point for me.

For Nicki. For Nicki.

For me. For me. For Nicki.

Around and around in circles. It is the most fun I've had in years.

This will be the last tournament that I will ever play. And I can't help but enjoy it.

I did not pick up a racket to grow tense and weary and afraid of failing. I picked it up to feel the joy of smashing a ball as hard as I can. I picked it up to spend time with my dad.

This is it. My last moment of what he and I started together. This match. This tiebreaker. I could live in it forever.

Me. Then Nicki.

Then me. Then Nicki.

Then me. Then Nicki. Then me.

I serve my sharpest, most deadly serve, trying to get an ace off her. But she returns it just as fast. And I can't match her power now. Her point.

Nicki serves maybe the fastest serve I've ever seen in my life. But I gear up and return it. She hits a smash so high I have to leap into the air despite my knees. But I jump higher than I think I've ever jumped before, and I manage to graze the ball with my racket, somehow landing it where she can't reach. My knee is killing me now, but it's my point.

I serve it, and she returns with a groundstroke. I hit a cross-court backhand and watch as it bounces in. But she's too far from it. No one can get across the court in the time she has, certainly not with her ankle. I watch as the ball flies over the net. Nicki is running too fast. I can tell. She's going to overshoot. But the ball bounces lower than I think it's going to.

It shouldn't have bounced that low. It's a fresh ball, and I sent it over hard. But sometimes you get a bad bounce, and the ball doesn't do what it's supposed to. And usually, in those moments, the returner misses the shot.

But not Nicki. Not now. Somehow she saw it happening before it happened. She meets the ball outside the line and skids across the court as she drops low to her knees. She leans back, overextended, and gets under the ball just as it's flying past her, her shin already bleeding from the skid.

She turns ever so slightly and returns it with a shot I can't touch.

Her point. It's now 16–15.

And for the first time, I know something as terrifying as it is freeing.

Nicki Chan might just understand the ball better than I do.

She serves the ball again, whipping it at me. I return it so deep it hits at the baseline and then bounces high off the court. Nicki jumps into the air and returns it with a lob.

It glides, slowly, above us. I watch it as gravity brings it back toward the ground. I move two steps to the right, one step back. I hedge my footing, staying on my toes, ready to run whenever it lands. My left knee feels like steel grinding against steel. The pain rings through me, reverberating, absorbing into every part of my body.

I do not care.

The ball descends toward the court. I have to decide whether to hit it before the bounce or get it on the rise. I cycle through my options, all my shots. And then, instead of choosing, I just let my arms fly.

I take it out of the air, quick—send it careening back. Nicki starts running.

I might beat her today. If that ball is in and she misses it, I can beat her today.

But that will not change the fact that she is *incomparable*. And she will win another Slam in '96. And then probably another, if she goes easier on her ankle.

And what am I going to do? Keep coming back to try to take it from her? Keep holding on for dear life to what I should have let go of long ago? Is that what I want my life to be? Trying to deny what Nicki Chan is?

Where is the beauty in that?

My shot arches toward her, over the net. Nicki's running deep. The ball goes past her. She's not going to get it.

I can feel myself winning this thing and then letting go of it all. Letting her take the rest from here on out. I am ready for that. I am ready to give it to her. To let her have it. Finally.

But as I watch, the ball lands one centimeter past the baseline. The linesman calls it out.

I can't quite believe what I'm seeing. Nicki screams into the sky, both arms outstretched. The crowd is up on their feet, cheering.

I just lost the tiebreak. I just lost the match.

I can barely catch my breath.

I don't slam down my racket. I don't scream. I don't bury my face in my hands. I just look at Bowe.

Nicki Chan has won the US Open.

I lost. The match and my record, twice in one year.

I wait for the skies to open up and shame to rain down on me. I wait for my belly to split in half. For the grief to overtake me. But . . . it doesn't come.

Bowe is smiling. And Gwen has her arms out, waiting to give me a hug. Ali is clapping wildly, even though I lost.

And the thing I don't understand is that I still feel that hum. That hum in my bones. That sense of weightlessness and groundedness. That sense that the day is mine. That I can do anything.

Nicki Chan looks at me. And I smile at her.

I am no longer the greatest tennis player in the world.

For the first time in my life, I can be . . . something else.

CHAN VS. CORTEZ

1996 US Open

Final

IT'S 5–4 IN THE DECIDING SET. IF NICKI BREAKS CORTEZ'S SERVE ON this last game, she will set a new record.

I am sitting in the players' box. Bowe is next to me. Nicki's parents are on the other side of us. Her new girlfriend, who *cannot stand me,* is sitting with a tight smile on her face in the corner.

I watch as Nicki returns Cortez's heavy forehand with a slice. I nod. The Soto Slice was the first thing I taught her.

"You need to improve your volleys, your short game. That's how I almost beat you back in New York," I said, on our first day on the courts together.

"I don't need a volley game when my baseline game is as good as it is," she said.

"You will never win Wimbledon again with just your baseline game, and you know it. You're gonna give up one-fourth of all Slams a year because you don't want to perfect your volley?" I said. "Now, come on, *de nuevo!*"

Nicki frowned but then did what I told her to. Just like she did when I made her start going easier on her ankle—so she could extend her career a few years. She gets pissed and mouths off, but I can tell she's always listening to me, even if she doesn't act like it.

It makes me laugh—how often my father must have seen my own frown, knowing I'd still do what he said.

And now, here we are—coach and player—at the 1996 US Open, me sitting here in the stands, helpless to do anything but hope she can harness all the new skills we've worked on.

My God, how hard it must have been for my father to do this. To sit here, a ball of nerves, knowing that all of the control was in my hands. He could not think for me on the court, he could not hit the ball for me. He just had to have faith that I could play the way he'd taught me.

What a gift it is, to be able to guide someone to a point and then let them finish it themself. To give someone all the knowledge you have and then pray they use it right. It's a skill I am learning, one I am determined to perfect.

Nicki's now at break point. Which means she is at championship point.

She looks up at me. I nod at her. She nods back, a small smile erupting across her face.

If she takes the next point, she'll win the US Open and hit a record-breaking twenty-three Slams—a feat that, just a few short years ago, was unheard of. But that's Nicki for you. Unstoppable. Raising the bar for absolutely everyone.

Cortez tosses the ball into the air and sends it screaming over the net. Nicki starts backing up, stepping into position.

"She's got it," Bowe says, quietly under his breath. I stare straight ahead, bouncing my knees. He grabs my hand to calm me.

I sit forward, praying with all my might, as Nicki pulls back and swings—

ACKNOWLEDGMENTS

I loved creating Carrie Soto with all of my heart and I only got to do it because of readers. So thank you, to every single person who picked up *Malibu,* or *Daisy,* or *Evelyn,* or *One True Loves* and any of the books that came before it. Thank you for showing up for these characters.

This is a story of a woman who often acts like she does it all on her own but, in fact, benefits greatly from the talented people around her. And because of that, I've dedicated this book to my manager, Brad Mendelsohn, who was the first member of the incredible team I have now—and directly and indirectly led me to the wildly talented people mentioned here whom I am incredibly fortunate to work with.

Thank you to my editor, Jennifer Hershey. You understood Carrie and pushed me to bring her fully to life with all of her flaws. I'm so thankful to you for your commitment to her. And to my agent, Theresa Park, thank you for seeing the joy and fun in this book and feeling it alongside me.

To the team at Ballantine—Kara Welsh, Kim Hovey, Susan Corcoran, Jennifer Garza, Allyson Lord, Quinne Rogers, Taylor Noel, Maya Franson, Paolo Pepe, Elena Giavaldi, Erin Kane, and Sydney Shiffman. I cannot believe I got so lucky as to be published by such a talented and powerful publishing house. Thank you for your passion and all of the effort that goes into getting these books into people's hands. It doesn't happen without you.

To the PFLM team—Emily Sweet, Andrea Mai, Abigail Koons, Anna Petkovich, Kathryn Toolan, Jen Mecum, and Charlotte Gillies. I would not be able to do any of this without your insights. You all are invaluable, and I consider your expertise paramount to my success.

Carisa Hays and Hayley Shear, thank you for always having my back. Each and every time.

Julian Alexander, you are always such a bright spot on every Zoom! Thank you for your faith in me. And to Ailah Ahmed and the entire team at Hutchinson, I cannot tell you what it means to have such a phenomenal, robust team behind my work in the UK.

Leo Teti, you have saved me! This book needed you, and I am so grateful to have had you in my corner.

Stuart Rosenthal and Sylvie Rabineau, thank you for being there—calm, cool, and collected—for every curveball that gets thrown our way.

Kari Erickson, I don't think I would have gotten through 2021 without you. And I certainly wouldn't have been able to get this book ready in time. Your insights, thoughtfulness, and conscientiousness have become indispensable. Thank you.

I wrote this book during a pandemic. And I could not have done that without the people closest to me stepping up to help with child-care. I have said it before but I don't think I can ever say it enough: This book does not exist without my mother-in-law, Rose, and my grandmother-in-law, Sally, stepping in to spend time with my daughter. I cannot do it alone. And I do not have to. I thank you for that. Thank you to my brother, Jake, for talking me through it all, even the parts that have no easy answers.

And thank you to my peanuts. I can't make any decisions without you all so I'm very grateful that one of you is always there, at any reasonable hour eastern time, to help me through it all.

Of course, I have never written a book without you, Alex Jenkins Reid. It's not just because you watch our daughter. Or that you help me to remember that these things are only books, after all. It is because you also help me figure out when I should listen to what other people are telling me and when to go with my gut. It is an incredible skill, to understand when you are right and when you are wrong. You have helped me to see it as clearly as I can. And in so doing, you've helped me become more myself than I have ever been before.

And lastly, to Lilah. You've heard me talk about Carrie Soto for a while now. You've patiently listened to me try to figure her out. And you had a very good idea for the title of this book, which I almost used. So, I don't know, maybe you're a writer. But let me tell you something: You are capable of so many amazing things. I hope, as you grow older, that this gives you a sense of peace. I, for so much of my life, have had something to prove. But I think you have a real chance of knowing you don't have to prove a single thing to anyone. If it should come to pass that you feel the need to go do something big, to go be the greatest there ever was, I will stand by you for that journey. I will be there, cheering you on, for anything you go out there and do. But just know that, to me, you showed up perfect. You don't have to prove a single thing.

ABOUT THE AUTHOR

Taylor Jenkins Reid is the *New York Times* bestselling author of eight novels, including *Malibu Rising, Daisy Jones & The Six,* and *The Seven Husbands of Evelyn Hugo.* She lives in Los Angeles with her husband and their daughter.

taylorjenkinsreid.com
Instagram: @tjenkinsreid

ABOUT THE TYPE

This book was set in Fairfield, the first typeface from the hand of the distinguished American artist and engraver Rudolph Ruzicka (1883–1978). Ruzicka was born in Bohemia (in the present-day Czech Republic) and came to America in 1894. He set up his own shop, devoted to wood engraving and printing, in New York in 1913 after a varied career working as a wood engraver, in photoengraving and banknote printing plants, and as an art director and freelance artist. He designed and illustrated many books, and was the creator of a considerable list of individual prints—wood engravings, line engravings on copper, and aquatints.